Street Magic

Edited by Lyn Worthen

Camden Park Press

Street Magic

Copyright © 2021 by Camden Park Press
Distributed by Bundle Rabbit
www.bundlerabbit.com
Cover and layout copyright © 2021 by Camden Park Press
Cover design by Lyn Worthen
Layout by Lyn Worthen
Abandoned Hallway © unkreatives | DepositPhotos
Urban Fantasy characters © Ravven | DepositPhotos
Magic Effects © NeoStock
Sea Lion Watercolor © Yuliya Derbisheva | Dreamstime
Siren © Microstockmilan | Dreamstime
Black Cat © Ilya Shalkov | Dreamstime
Chains © Olga Novoseletska | Dreamstime
Dragon Egg © Shepherd302 | Dreamstime
Graveyard © Benchart | Dreamstime
Punk Music © Linnea Eriksson | Dreamstime
Magic Wand © Tetiana Chaban | Dreamstime
ISBN: 979-8513702092

"Cicada Song Ringing Through" © 2021 by Meyari McFarland
"Clarence Hemlock, Computer Wizard" © 2021 by Mike Jack Stoumbos
"Out of the Light" © 2007 by Douglas Smith, Originally published in *Dark Wisdom* magazine (July 2007, issue #11). Used by permission of the author.
"Siren's Call" © 2019 by J.L. Madore, Originally published in *Love Among the Thorns*, Camden Park Press (2019). Used by permission of the author.
"Heart Magic and Cardboard People" © 2021 by Travis Heermann
"Betwixt and Between" © 2021 by Jessica Guernsey
"Touched by Faelight" © 2021 by Taylen Carver
"See You Later, Alligator" © 2021 by Jena Rey
"Not Their Kind of Not Suitable" © 2021 by Tina Back
"Spirit of the Law" © 2021 by Leigh Saunders
"Gone Fishing" © 2021 by Sam Robb
"One Final Request" © 2021 by Danielle Harward
"Necromancy for Dummies" © 2021 by Tami Veldura
"The Working Stiff" © 2021 by C.E. Barnes
"The Veils with Johnny Nyx" © 2021 by Joseph Borrelli

This book is licensed for your personal enjoyment only. All rights reserved.
This is a work of fiction. All characters and events portrayed in this book are fictional, and any resemblance to real people or incidents is purely coincidental.
This book, or parts thereof, may not be reproduced in any form without permission.

If you enjoy this book, please leave a review!

Table of Contents

Introduction: The Magic of the Streets
Lyn Worthen 1

Cicada Song Ringing Through
Meyari McFarland 5

Clarence Hemlock, Computer Wizard
Mike Jack Stoumbos 25

Out of the Light
Douglas Smith 49

Siren's Call
J.L. Madore 67

Heart Magic and Cardboard People
Travis Heermann 93

Betwixt and Between
Jessica Guernsey 119

See You Later, Alligator
Jena Rey 143

Touched by Faelight
Taylen Carver 167

Not Their Kind of Not Suitable
Tina Back 187

The Working Stiff
C.E. Barnes 209

Spirit of the Law
Leigh Saunders 231

Gone Fishing
Sam Robb 249

One Final Request
Danielle Harward 279

Necromancy for Dummies
Tami Veldura 303

The Veils with Johnny Nyx: Dead and In Concert
Joseph Borrelli 319

About the Editor... 335

About BundleRabbit 336

Other Anthologies from Camden Park Press........................... 337

Introduction: The Magic of the Streets
Lyn Worthen

Magic. Hiding right under our unsuspecting noses, or swirling all around us. When we're talking about *Street Magic*, it's probably closer than you think.

I fell into urban fantasy gradually – role-playing in the *Shadowrun* universe in the late 1980s and reading Emma Bull's *War for the Oaks* in the 1990s, followed by bingeing on Jim Butcher's *Dresden Files*, which I've consumed in both print and audiobook versions. And the addiction has only continued to grow. I'm grateful to authors like those in this volume for keeping the genre alive and well.

There's a sense of possibility in urban fantasy that other flavors of fantasy don't provide – at least not in the same way. While it's great fun to be carried off to the castles and quests of high fantasy, the idea of a dragon curled up on a pile of gold beneath a distant mountain isn't as immediately relevant as the dragon – it must be a dragon, right? – whose smoke wafts up from the grates in the sidewalk, a reminder that the fee for crossing over its domain is far greater than the mere risk of a broken high-heel.

For *Street Magic*, I asked the authors to create characters grappling with contemporary-style issues in a world where magic might be either a resource or an obstacle. I asked for a sense of wonder and a sense of power. I asked them to create settings and cultures that were mysterious, arcane, and plausible. Most of all, I asked them to make our readers want to live in their worlds – and reluctant to leave when the stories were over.

And they delivered. From the back alleys of Tokyo to the Louisiana bayou, from brokers making deals with shadows to necromancers communing with a deceased rockstar, the stories in *Street Magic* offer diversity in people (both human and non), locations, and magic. In some stories the magic is out in the open, while in others it is a closely guarded secret. But whether they're solving huge problems or dealing with intensely personal stakes, the characters in these pages are folks I wouldn't be surprised to see at the local pub — though there are several I might prefer to watch from afar, just to be on the safe side.

Join us then, as we walk down the city streets, one foot in the mundane world and one in *another* world. Listen to the siren's song, do a double-take at the slow blink of an inner eyelid or flick of a forked tongue, and catch a glimpse of a mysterious form in the alley just beyond flickering neon lights.

If what you see seems a little out of the ordinary, it's probably magic.

Welcome to the street!

– Lyn Worthen
Sandy, Utah
May 21, 2021

STREET MAGIC

Meyari McFarland has been telling stories since she was a small child. Whether writing in her space opera/romance Drath series or her Mages of Tindiere epic fantasy world, her stories always feature strong characters who do what they think is right no matter what gets in their way. Her other series include Matriarchies of Muirin, the Clockwork Rift steampunk mysteries, and the Tales of Unification urban fantasy stories. You can find all of her work at the MDR Publishing website, www.MDR-Publishing.com

About this story, Meyari says: "I love Japan, and have been there many, many times. Japan has a magic of its own – the culture, buildings, history, and food all fascinate and delight me. But no matter how many times I visit, I will always be an outsider. That awareness of my essential alienness combined with the idea of urban magic to give me this story. I've walked down those streets. I've eaten at those restaurants. The mix of alien and familiar, modern and fantasy, perfectly matches the Japan of my mind and heart."

What better way to lead off a collection of other-worldly tales than with a visit to a place many of us have never been? Meyari McFarland deftly intertwines the elements of Japanese culture and magic together, bringing Tokyo's sweltering back alleys to life. And if you leave the story craving a bit of dragon-grilled salmon, there's a selkie who can point you to the right place. You'll just need to get there ahead of her...

Cicada Song Ringing Through
Meyari McFarland

Cicada shrilled from the trees, an endless echoing call that mixed with the sweat dripping down Harlow's spine as she slowly strolled the street next to the Imperial Palace gardens. She'd expected the heat to ease somewhat after the sun set, as it did outside of Tokyo each night. No such luck. The sun had baked its heat into Tokyo's concrete sidewalks, the stone buttresses around the garden's moat, and the softening asphalt of its streets.

Her coworkers had long since gone off toward home, leaving Harlow alone to wander the streets in the darkness. Fine for them. They had families and responsibilities to attend to over the weekend. Harlow was free to do whatever she wanted.

Not that she wanted to do much when it was this hot and humid. Harlow huffed before pulling her long black hair away from her neckline, twisting it up into an awkward knot on the back of her head that she secured with a pencil from her bag and a touch of magic.

Didn't help a lot, but it was better than having the weight of her hair baking her back and making her as wet as if she'd been swimming in the Puget Sound back home. Harlow shut her eyes and sighed. The thought of shifting forms, throwing off her clothes, dropping her purse, and kicking her flats off before diving into the murky green of the moat's quiet waters was tempting.

Not a good idea, of course. The patrolling water dragon would take it as a threat instead of a selkie getting a bit of relief from Tokyo's summer heat. Harlow opened her eyes and watched the drifting orbs of dim gold light that danced over the moat like fireflies.

Heh. *With* the fireflies. They darted in and out of the orbs, hunting the smaller insects drawn to the dragon's lights.

She could always go back to her little apartment's single room. Take a long shower, soak in the wonderfully deep – if plastic – tub. That appealed, too, but it never got shock-your-breath-from-your-lungs cold the way the Puget Sound's water did even in the depths of summer.

No point to it.

Food then.

Harlow sniffed the air and hummed before heading across the wide, softened asphalt street, down the sidewalk with its raised braille bumps for blind people and into the back allies between Tokyo's book district, Jimbocho, and the Kanda River wending its way through Tokyo's urban precincts towards the ocean.

This late in the evening, the businessmen and students that hustled through the streets while the sun was up were long-gone. The students were in karaoke parties, drinking and laughing with their friends. Most of the businessmen were drinking in bars and complaining about their bosses.

Midnight in August in Tokyo was the time for being inside, for talking and eating, for laughing and complaining.

Felt rather strange to walk through the dark alleys and wide streets with only a car or two every minute rather than a constant flow. Harlow sniffed the air again. There was something good, something delicious, tempting her nose but she wasn't sure where it was. Not enough air movement for her to get a proper direction on it, so she listened over the shrill cry of the cicada for the sound of grilling meat.

She passed a ramen shop with steam-shrouded doors. Men hunched over wide bowls filled the shop, slurping their noodles and grunting appreciatively. Chicken, pork, the over-cooked smell of shrimp filleted and breaded and fried… definitely not the smell teasing Harlow and drawing her onward.

Besides, all the men in the ramen shop were human, other than the one kapa carefully sipping his bowl of broth so that he didn't spill the water from his bowl-like head.

Red lantern light spilled out of a narrow alley with bamboo in huge tubs marking the entrance. Harlow had learned to pick out some kanji since her arrival in Japan six months ago, but she was less than fluent in the written language. *Udon*, one lantern offered, swaying invitingly outside one tiny izakaya, the Japanese version of a hole-in-the-wall restaurant. *Teriyaki* was the label on the yellowish lantern across the ally from the Udon shop.

Sprays of bamboo with shrilling cicada hung over the alley, covering the narrow, two-foot opening between the shop's traditional-looking overhangs. Masses of wires tangled above the overhangs, weaving a web that a spider would loathe. Or maybe adore, if it had been fed acid. Harlow shrugged, sniffed the air and then shuddered with pleasure.

There was that smell again, rich and fatty. Salmon, so fresh that it was still wet with sea salt, grilled over charcoal. She breathed it in, then set down the alley of izakaya.

"Hungry, honored lady?" a bucket-spirit called outside the udon shop. It bounced and waved little wooden arms for her to come in. "We have good food, very good food."

"No," Harlow said, sniffing the air again. "Thank you."

The bucket spirit sighed and settled back down on its base, waiting for the next passer-by. Harlow spotted an umbrella spirit waiting outside a steak izakaya further up the alley, a stool that had lived long enough to gain sentience and a fan that slowly moved in the humid, bath-water warm air.

And a spider-like Jorogumo shifting her spider legs inside of a lovely blue and white kimono as she came down from the rooftops on a strand of silver that gleamed in the light of the lanterns.

Harlow froze, along with the fan spirit who clattered back against the red-painted wall of the izakaya she guarded. The Jorogumo was huge, with legs easily eight foot across and black, glittering fangs as long as Harlow's hand. As Harlow watched, the Jorogumo curled inwards, black hairy spider limbs curling up under a kimono that billowed and fluttered until a woman stood there, looking at Harlow with interest, rather than a spider that could bite Harlow's head off in an instant.

"Interested in company for a bite to eat?" the Jorogumo asked with an enticing smile and glittering eyes that betrayed who she really was. Her hair was as black and smooth as Harlow's, hanging loose and lovely around her angular face.

"Only of salmon," Harlow said with a grin that showed off her seal's teeth.

Go away, her teeth said. *I bite back,* they implied, not that Harlow's bite was anywhere near as deadly as the Jorogumo's.

The Jorogumo snorted and waved a languid hand up the alley with an amused little smile. "That will be Calhoun's. They've fresh salmon, shipped in on ice."

"Thank you," Harlow said earnestly. "I could smell it from the Imperial Gardens. Been driving me crazy all evening."

The Jorogumo laughed and minced away towards the entrance to the alley, hips swaying in a hypnotic figure eight that had everything to do with magic because that motion was anything but enticing-looking. All the household object spirits shivered and settled into their original forms as she passed. Harlow slowly nodded her agreement with them and waited until the Jorogumo left the alley.

Never turn your back on a hungry predator. The Jorogumo was clearly still hunting for her dinner. Harlow hurried up the street so that she wouldn't become the spider-woman's choice.

Besides, the smell of the salmon grew as Harlow hurried up the alley. The further she went, the more household spirits she saw. Then three kapa strolled by, chatting grumpily with a round-bellied tanuki whose raccoon-masked cheeks were decorated with bits of rice and the gleam of sauce. Harlow nodded to them, sniffed the air, and then hurried onward.

Calhoun's sat at the intersection between two narrow alleys. A typical British pub, or the Japanese version of one at any rate, it had a round door worthy of a hobbit hole that had been flung open and propped there by a huge wooden bucket full of tiny glowing goldfish. Its bulbous lantern was white, decorated in English on one side by the word "Calhoun's" and on the other side with the word "teriyaki".

Where the other izakaya had wooden fronts that recalled the days of the Edo period, all wooden slats and frosted glass to mimic paper screens,

Calhoun's bricks and beveled glass façade shocked. Enticed. Though that was mostly the smell of grilling salmon, honestly.

"Is she gone?"

Harlow started and whirled, looking around wildly until she realized that there was a fox staring up at her from behind the bucket of glowing goldfish.

"So? Is she?" the fox asked, black-tipped ears flipping back irritably at Harlow.

"The Jorogumo?" Harlow asked.

"Yeah, the spider bitch, of course," the fox asked.

"I believe so," Harlow replied. "At the least, she put on her human shape and headed out of the alley."

"Oh, thank fuck," the fox said, flopping on Calhoun's stone step. "I've been hiding back here for an hour. I'm dying."

The fox wiggled out of the too-small space, shook violently enough to spray red fur everywhere, and then wagged her tail at Harlow. She tipped her head to the side, ears tipping back and then forward until her whole body radiated mischief.

Harlow grinned, showing her seal teeth.

"Ah, damn," the fox groaned. "I was hoping for an easy mark."

She bounced and turned into a young woman with red hair pulled back in a pouf of a ponytail, wide brown eyes, and a nose so long and pointed that Harlow chuckled despite herself. A nose like that had to have a talent for finding trouble.

The kitsune grinned as she shoved her hands into her cargo shorts pockets. She dressed like a teenager, in tan shorts with a neon green and gold T-shirt emblazoned with a coiled snake over the words *"Why Care? Not me."*

"Not gonna get a free meal, am I?" the kitsune asked, wagging her eyebrows and her bush of a fox's tail.

"Not likely," Harlow said. "But then, I fully intend to eat all the salmon they've got, so there might not be much left to eat anyway."

The shrill call of the cicada faded away as the kitsune widened her eyes and pouted out her bottom lip. For a moment it felt like they'd drifted down under the water so that all sounds from the surface disappeared. But Harlow couldn't feel whale song on her skin and the air was still hot and muggy against her cheeks.

She blew air and snapped at the Kitsune who yipped and darted a few yards away.

"I'm hungry, too," Harlow said as the cicada song roared back into her ears and the sweat on her spine went cold from the effort of breaking free from the Kitsune's allure.

"Ah, yeah," the kitsune said, fidgeting. She danced in place for a moment and then her shoulders slumped as her tail sagged so much that it brushed against the scrupulously clean asphalt. "Sorry. I'm bored. It's so hot that no one's doing anything. I just want something interesting to happen. You know, that doesn't involve a spider-bitch trying to bite off my tail. Or head. Or anything else."

Harlow snorted a laugh. "Well, you can always come watch me eat all the salmon. Other than that, I don't care. I'm far too hungry to worry about you being bored. Or anyone being bored, actually."

She shrugged the kitsune's laugh off and headed into Calhoun's.

Where the izakaya Harlow had passed were tiny little things with six or eight seats at most, Calhoun's was huge. Stairs by the entrance led upward toward a second-floor seating area. Harlow ignored that in favor of diving into the narrow depths of the first floor and its long bar. Something like thirty stools filled with various oni – Japanese demons – sat shoulder to shoulder with round bellied tanuki who tucked their plumed tails close to their bodies as Harlow passed.

The wall behind the chest-high bar was covered in bottles of sake, rice wine, and miniature kegs of Japanese beer. Glasses stood in ranks on the counter behind the bar, all of them frosted and cold, waiting for whatever drinks the patrons asked for.

Between the drinks and the bar, there was a long, narrow grill filled with charcoal that glowed red. Dozens of skewers sizzled and popped over the coals, filling the air with the scent of meat, sauce, and burning fat.

How very perfect.

Harlow hummed as she made her way to the very back of the bar, looking for an open seat. The oni turned their long Pinocchio noses at her until she snarled at them. Then they grinned back, nodded, and turned back to their drinks and tiny skewers filled with grilled meat. Few of the supernatural folk of Japan would pick a fight without reason. There was enough food in Calhoun's to make that pointless.

Chicken, beef tongue sliced thin, and pork belly dripped fat onto the charcoal, making the fire flare up and pop.

Three chefs worked behind the bar. One was a human with burly arms and a bushy beard, grinning as he chatted quietly with the tanuki closest to the door. The second one was a kitsune who glowered not at Harlow but at the kitsune she'd met in the street.

"You eating?" the third chef asked in a rumble that felt like an earthquake and smelled like lightning.

A dragon, an oriental dragon with just one juvenile point on his horns, hovered behind the bar, turning skewers with all four paws and the tip of his tail. He was black over his back, pale grey over the belly. His scales gleamed in the low light of the izakaya. His mane looked reddish from the glow of the coals, but it was probably a mixture of greys.

"You got salmon?" Harlow asked as she slid into the very last seat.

"She's hungry," the kitsune explained as she slipped up onto the stool next to Harlow. "Snappish even."

"You eating, Asuka?" the dragon asked, with a stern glower that made his catfish-like mustache quiver. "I can see that she's hungry. It radiates off her like steam coming off a mud puddle at dawn."

Asuka, the kitsune, sighed and slapped a five-hundred-yen coin on the counter. "Fine. Two chicken and a sake, Shuji. Bully. Can't just let me watch."

"Salmon," Harlow said. She met Shuji's eyes, held them. "All the salmon."

Shuji's ears went back as his mane bristled in surprise. "*All* of it? We got six salmon in."

"What sort?" Harlow asked. "If you've got Chinook, I'll take one. If they're Pink, it'll be more. Probably all of them, honestly."

Shuji laughed, electricity rippling over his body. "Pink. They're two kilos each."

Harlow snorted. "Start cooking. I'll probably end up eating at least four of them, if not all of them."

No one ever believed Harlow when she said she ate a lot. The humans she dealt with always doubted that her belly could hold an eighth what she normally ordered, and that was when she ordered fractions of what she really wanted. There were reasons Harlow wandered the streets at night after her coworkers went off to bars. Getting enough to eat was just one of those reasons.

Not dealing with their nonsense was definitely a bigger one.

Asuka, on the other hand, leaned on the counter with a grin and an eagerly wagging tail, while Shuji hummed and set to work with Harlow's salmon.

They were lovely fish, silver and gleaming as Shuji pulled out knives. Lovely knives with long thin blades and a long slender handle that reminded Harlow of bamboo. The blades themselves were rather like samurai swords with a thicker spine and a narrow edge that had been polished until it gleamed. Shuji's knives even had the wavy pattern along the edge that came from careful hand-forging.

"Cooked?" Shuji asked.

"One of them, yes," Harlow said. "First one, no. Just give it to me."

Shuji snorted.

A laugh.

Huh, that was a laugh.

Shuji dunked two chicken skewers from the grill into sweet, sticky sauce, then plopped them onto a little plate. His magic swirled over the shelves behind him. One of the big sake bottles floated down as a tiny vase and a little pottery shot glass danced forward. The big sake bottle filled the vase, then returned to its spot as the vase and cup floated over to Asuka who scooped them up with a huff and a snap at Shuji.

Who ignored Asuka entirely.

So did Harlow. There was salmon to eat.

There was a sort of art to Shuji's presentation of the first pink salmon. It wasn't as big as she expected, lacking the distinctive hump on its back, but it smelled like salt and fat and the kelp in the waters back home in the Puget Sound.

A long way from home, that salmon was. It must've been flown in. This dinner was going to wipe out her budget for the month, not that Harlow cared.

Shuji peeled a fillet off with beautiful precision. His long, slender knife peeled the ruby flesh away from the pink's bones as if they'd been pre-separated and this was only a trick of sleight of hand. He flipped one ear when Harlow huffed at him for even thinking of taking the skin off. The second fillet went as easily as the first, letting Shuji pull away spine and tail.

He left the head, the frilly edges of its gills emerging from behind its cheek, then cut the fillets into perfect, bite-sized pieces laid out exactly as they had been when they'd been attached to the living fish.

"That was way more effort than you really needed to go to," Harlow commented once she had the salmon in front of her. "Beautiful, but much more work than necessary."

It smelled so good.

So *incredibly* good. Harlow's mouth watered as she broke a pair of cheap chopsticks apart and scooped up the first slice. Rich and red, smelling still of the ocean it'd swam through this morning, the salmon hit her tongue like heaven in her mouth.

She groaned.

"Told you she was hungry," Asuka said with a laugh into her sake cup.

The oni on Asuka's other side rumbled something to his neighbor, accent and language slipping beyond Harlow's control when there was salmon to eat. Pink salmon, salmon like the ones she'd grown up eating. It was home, delivered on a lovely plank, sliced and salted and perfect.

Harlow swallowed the bite down and then demolished the rest of the fish, shoving the pieces into her mouth with her hands, because chopsticks were way too slow.

Vaguely, off in the distance where there was something other than delicious salmon that tasted like heaven, she heard Asuka yip and skitter backwards. There was a vague sense of Shuji waving to the oni, warning them not to interfere.

None of that mattered compared to getting the salmon into her belly.

"Did you not eat at all today?" Asuka asked when Harlow came up for air after she'd eaten the fillets and then chomped her way through the head in four big, crunchy bites. "Or, like, for the last week?"

Harlow laughed, looking at the second salmon that popped and hissed as Shuji grilled it. "Close enough. We selkie eat a lot, you know. And this is very good salmon, just what I needed. Tuna isn't the same. Salmon are what I grew up on, what my family eats the most. This is perfect." To Shuji, she said, "I think that's grilled enough for my needs. Hand it over and get to work slicing up the third one."

Asuka giggled into her sake. "I think you might just eat all six. I should take bets."

"A thousand yen she eats only three," the oni next to Asuka said instantly.

"Ten thousand that she eats all six!" Asuka declared, ears up and tail straight out with pure delight.

Harlow snorted as the bets rolled up the bar and then back again. Well, at least Asuka was getting her excitement now, just as Harlow was getting the salmon she needed.

Fish number two was warm on the skin, crunchy and flavorful with salt crumbled over its surface. The flesh was cool still, as red and lovely as the first's had been. Fish number three went away in long slurps of fillets cut into fleshy noodles instead of small wedges. Harlow laughed at that innovation and grinned at Asuka's exclamations of awe.

Number four was where Harlow finally slowed down enough to really taste the salmon. There were subtle differences from the fish she ate back home. Not bad, really, just not the same. A wild-caught pink salmon back home, on its run to its breeding grounds in the thousands of streams and rivers of the Puget Sound, went red and fatty with a hump growing up on its back, so rich that it coated the tongue and suffused the body.

These salmon were lovely, yes, but younger. Not juveniles, but not full adults heading back to their breeding grounds either. It was the season for pinks to run, but these couldn't have been caught making the run to their breeding grounds. Wrong shape, wrong color to the scales; still delicious.

"Dyed," Harlow commented once she got the fifth salmon off the grill. "Or spelled red? This isn't natural coloration for them."

"They… were spelled," Shuji said, ears all the way back against his skull so that they hid in his mane. "The boss saw them in the market and got them despite their being out of season here. Overcatch from a different fishing trip. Special treat was his thought."

"Mmm." Harlow nodded as she demolished the salmon. This one was cooked through, slowing her down enough that she could taste the way the charcoal smoke had permeated the flesh. "It *is* a treat. A really good one. Give me the last."

A groan went up from the other end of the bar as several people cursed while Asuka laughed and gathered up her winnings so far. A couple of others had also bet on Harlow wanting all the salmon. They collected their winnings much more quietly than Asuka, who danced all down the bar between the plates and glasses, as dainty as could be even as she thrust her tail right into the chef's faces.

Half the bar turned and stared as Harlow set to work finishing off the last of the salmon. Her belly finally felt full enough that she wasn't going to go to bed grumbling. Japanese people, magical and otherwise, ate so little.

It was ridiculous, really. At least today she got something properly delicious – and enough of it, too.

"I win!" Asuka shouted as Harlow picked up the last bite of salmon and popped it in her mouth. "That's amazing!"

She got five-hundred-yen coins thrown at her, along with curses that Asuka dodged easily. Harlow chuckled as she chewed, much happier with the world now that her belly was full. Even the sweat dripping down her chest and pooling under her breasts was less of a bother. The sizzle of the meat, the chattering tanuki, the rumbling oni, and Asuka dancing her victory over the bar blended into something very like joy.

"So," Shuji said as he took the empty planks of wood back and sent them flying off to be washed in their spelled sink behind the counter, "how much more could you eat?"

Harlow shrugged, sipping the little glass of water she'd been given for the first time since she sat down. She patted her wide hips fondly. "Probably one more. Selkie eat a lot. Got to maintain that figure, you know."

A tanuki up the bar shouted a laugh, shaking his wide, round belly at Harlow. She raised the glass of water back at him.

"Banzai!" Asuka shouted as she danced up near the ceiling.

"Banzai!" Everyone else shouted, drinking up and laughing as they saluted Harlow with their glasses, mugs, and tankards.

She still had her little vase of sake and the tiny shot glass. Harlow suspected magical shenanigans because Asuka poured her sake in every glass but Harlow's and it never went empty. Shuji rolled his dark eyes when Harlow raised an eyebrow at him.

Several stacks of Asuka's winnings disappeared.

Well, then.

Not Harlow's problem to deal with.

The clock behind Shuji read ten after one when Harlow settled up her bill and stood. She'd spent more on the pink salmon tonight than she normally did in a month's worth of dinners, but Harlow couldn't find it in herself to be unhappy about that.

A full belly and the taste of home on her tongue made it worth it.

"Night, all," Harlow said before heading back out into the alley.

Cicada shrilled in the night.

Harlow breathed deep, letting the bath-warm air fill her lungs as she stood at the crossroads of izakaya. The cicada's song shimmered underneath the rumbling oni voices from Calhoun's. All around her, the air hung still and stagnant, heat from the day trapped along with the humidity that roiled up off the Imperial moat and the Kanda River.

With the rich fat of the salmon on her lips and tongue, Harlow found the smell of hot asphalt and tar mixed with the urine of a passing drunk far more bearable than normal. She smiled and rubbed her broad belly, patting her wide hips and checking on the bag slung over her shoulder. Yep, still there.

Full and happy; she really ought to go home.

Instead Harlow tipped her head back to stare at the sky. The intersecting clusters of wires overhead screened the sky as surely as a roof would have. Against the black-coated wires, the sky was navy velvet, stained with hints of gold, red, and blue from distant neon signs. This little intersection had no cars. The ally was too narrow for them when the izakaya had their signboards and lanterns out. She could hear cars purring along further away, off towards the palace and the heart of Tokyo's business district.

Not here, though. Tokyo never slept, not really, so stars never got to twinkle overhead, and silence was a thing you had to pay for, not a thing that happened naturally. Harlow hummed and rubbed her belly while contemplating a slow walk home or taking a quick, and certainly empty, subway back to her apartment.

"So," Asuka said as she sailed out of Calhoun's and bounced to the ground next to Harlow like the teenager she looked to be, "what now? No drinking for you? Dancing? Go wander the streets and look for someone to mug?"

Harlow snorted a laugh. "You can do that if you want. I'm not going to. No, I was considering walking home versus a subway ride. It's Friday…, Saturday now. I don't need to be up anytime in particular tomorrow. A nice long walk seems like a soothing thing to do."

Asuka groaned and wilted like spinach in a hot frying pan. "Why are you so exciting one moment and so boring the next?"

"Exciting happens around me," Harlow said, unreasonably amused by Asuka's dramatics, "not to me. Besides, I would've thought all the bars would be shutting down soon."

"Nah," Asuka said, bouncing back to her bright cheerfulness. She rocked on her toes; hands clasped behind her back right above her slowly wagging tail. "Just depends on which ones you go to. Lots of izakaya are open midnight to seven, eight in the morning. Someone's got to serve the needs of the night folk, you know."

A skitter echoed up the alley.

Harlow froze.

So did Asuka.

A moment later, the skitter repeated loudly enough that the cicada's shrill dipped as survival dented the insects' drive to breed. They resumed screaming a couple of seconds later. Harlow didn't relax.

She could see the Jorogumo slowly mincing her way up the cross-alleyway towards them.

Harlow probably should've been surprised when Asuka hid behind her, quivering against Harlow's broad back, but she wasn't. As cheerful as Asuka was, she was not brave. After all, she'd spent an hour hiding behind a bucket full of glowing goldfish rather than risk attracting the Jorogumo's attention.

"Eat well?" Harlow asked as the Jorogumo glittered a smile in her direction.

"Quite," the Jorogumo said with a brittle little smile that was as smug as could be. She tossed her gleaming black hair over her shoulder. "Oh, stop that, kitsune. I've no interest in your fluffy tail."

Asuka peeked over Harlow's shoulder. "...Did you really eat or are you just trying to lure me out?"

The Jorogumo shook her head and glared at Asuka. "I ate. He was delicious. You're not."

"I could be delicious!" Asuka protested so automatically as she darted around Harlow at the Jorogumo that Harlow groaned and grabbed her by the scruff of the neck. "Hey! Leggo!"

"You actually are a teenager, aren't you?" Harlow said.

She gave Asuka a little shake that didn't do a thing to stop the kitsune from pouting. It did make the Jorogumo laugh with the back of her hand pressed against her mouth to hide the fangs that Harlow knew hid behind that lovely façade.

"One tail," the Jorogumo said with a snide little jerk of her chin towards Asuka. "Obviously. She won't settle until she grows her second tail. If she survives that long."

Asuka pouted, arms crossed over her chest, tail thrashing. She weighed almost nothing in Harlow's hand, but Harlow still put her down. Now that

Asuka wasn't charging at a spider-demon-woman like an idiot, it was safe enough.

Probably.

"I'd say that you ate well, too," the Jorogumo commented to Harlow, glittering black eyes sweeping Harlow from head to toe and back again. "You smell... satiated."

"Close enough," Harlow agreed with a little nod. "Close enough. Though I think I need some ice cream. Not sure where to get it at this time of night. All the parfait shops I know are closed already."

To her surprise, both the Jorogumo and Asuka cocked their heads consideringly. Asuka bounced up into the air, floating six inches or so off the asphalt, frowning as she slowly rotated in a three-sixty-barrel roll. When Asuka pointed off to the left, in the direction the Jorogumo had been going, the Jorogumo huffed and shook her head.

"I doubt that she wants to deal with prostitutes and gangsters while getting her parfait," the Jorogumo said, so scathingly that Asuka bristled.

"They've got really damn good parfaits, though!" Asuka said. "I mean, you gotta be careful not to spend too much, but they're super-good."

"No yakuza, please," Harlow said. She laughed at Asuka's drooping tail. "I don't want ice cream that much. Besides, I'm getting the feeling that both of you want ice cream, too."

"It's tempting," the Jorogumo admitted with a little nod and then a glare at Asuka who gaped at her in shock. "Dessert is always nice after a big dinner."

"Wow," Asuka breathed. Her ears perked up and her tails started wagging with delight. "Wait. Wait, wait, wait! That means that whatever shop you go to, the clerks are gonna have to deal with a foreign selkie built like a brick wall *and* a Jorogumo. At the same time."

"And you," Harlow said, laughter bubbling under her words as if she was swimming in the kelp forests back home, chasing her sisters' tails. "Yes."

"I'm in!" Asuka exclaimed. "That's sure to be exciting!"

Harlow laughed.

It was so very familiar. Despite the Jorogumo being nothing at all like any of the fae creatures back home and Asuka being a completely different sort of creature entirely, it felt like making plans with one of her aunties, the strict ones, and one of her nieces, the hyperactive ones, at the same time.

Asuka laughed along with Harlow, changing to her fox shape and running up the wall of the neighboring izakaya and onto the wires overhead. Once there, she pranced along as happy as could be, her tail held up high like a flag in the night's darkness. The red and white and blue and gold lights of the various signs for the izakaya colored her fur, changing it as she bounced along.

"I'm not sure I am," the Jorogumo commented to Harlow. "The shop she's headed to is... well, less than impressive."

"They have fresh mochi ice cream," Asuka called, bouncing from power pole to power pole and back again. "Strawberry and green tea and mint. And they've got a chocolate parfait that's got brownie chunks with chocolate sauce and chocolate shavings, topped with nuts and whipped cream. All for only fourteen-hundred yen!"

"Now, that's tempting," Harlow said. She looked at the Jorogumo who just gave a chittering little laugh while shaking her head. "Admit it. You're tempted, too."

"If you were a quarter again as small as you are, I'd be tempted for other things," the Jorogumo said as if that was compliment. "But yes, the mochi ice cream does sound good. Fine. I've nothing better to do until dawn. Why not?"

Which led to Harlow introducing herself to the Jorogumo, whose name turned out to be Natsumi – which meant "beautiful summer" according to Asuka. The cross-alley wound along between taller buildings, silent and still. None of the household spirits moved or spoke as they passed. None of them dared risk gaining Natsumi's attention. Harlow couldn't really blame them for that, but she didn't feel threatened. At all.

It wasn't like Asuka's attempt at a glamour earlier.

That had been as obvious as the smell of salmon or the give of the still-hot asphalt under her shoes. No, Natsumi didn't feel threatening because she wasn't *being* threatening. She was dangerous, yes. Deadly, even.

But she didn't seem to see either Asuka or Harlow as a threat.

Or maybe, possibly, they were equal threats in their own ways and Natsumi had decided that discretion was the better part of valor. Spiders were very sensible creatures, after all. They'd rarely take risk against a foe or prey that they weren't certain they could defeat.

Nice to be considered a threat, then.

The parfait shop sat at the very end of the cross-alley where it spilled out onto a major street, complete with overhead walkways to keep pedestrians from crossing through traffic and dividers between the four lanes of traffic made of concrete berms that had been planted with shrubs, grass, and spindly young trees. Harlow smelled the shop long before they reached it, the scent of sugar and baking waffle cones filling the slowly cooling air. Its façade was pink and white, with an awning striped and bedecked with lacy scallops that Harlow couldn't believe weren't already stained by exhaust and weather. Some magic definitely went into maintaining that fabric.

"This is it!" Asuka exclaimed as she bounced on the awning, tail going a mile a minute. "I can't wait to see how they react to the two of you!"

Natsumi shook her head, chittering another laugh. "Child, you are ridiculous."

"I'm not a child," Asuka snapped, shifting form to perch on the awning with her ankles crossed and her tail sweeping against the pink and white striped fabric.

"No, but you are ridiculous in a fun way," Harlow said.

Asuka opened her mouth to snap something, then paused as she registered what Harlow had actually said. Her head tilted slowly to the right as she blinked repeatedly. Then she shook her head sharply and jumped back down to the sidewalk in front of Harlow.

She was tiny, barely up to Harlow's breastbone, and for a moment, Harlow felt about eight feet tall. But only a moment. The only place she'd ever been above barely average height was here in Japan where everyone else was shorter than she was. Then Asuka grew about eight inches, leaving her as tall as Natsumi and about half a head shorter than Harlow.

"You have very strange tastes," Natsumi commented.

Harlow shrugged. "Not my fault. Asuka reminds me of my nieces, the pot-stirring ones that always look for trouble and find it regularly. You remind me of my aunties, the ones that put a stop to the trouble, but not until after they've had a good laugh over it and gotten whatever they can from it. Told Asuka this already, but trouble doesn't happen *to* me. It happens *around* me."

Natsumi tilted her head back too far to look even vaguely human but she didn't sweep off her human disguise. Instead she peered at Harlow with her other eyes, the ones hidden under her severe bangs. At the same time, Asuka frowned at Harlow with her hands on her hips like she was getting just a little bit offended.

"Around you," Natsumi said slowly.

"Mmhm," Harlow hummed, amusement welling up again. "Trouble finds me and then goes around me. It's a gift."

A patrol car purred by lights washing over the three of them. As the light hit them, Natsumi's lovely kimono shifted into a fashionable blue and white dress. Asuka's tail and ears disappeared, leaving them looking like nothing other than a couple of lovely young women talking to a third outside of a parfait shop.

Harlow stayed stout and wide and flat-faced, with a mess of straight black hair looped up in a messy bun on the top of her head. Her flats were boring and black, her trousers a simple tan. She saw the way the police in the petite little patrol car eyed Asuka and Natsumi. Their eyes slid right over Harlow as too tall, too fat, too ugly to be interested in.

Then they visibly dismissed all three of them, because why be interested in a group that included someone like Harlow?

Harlow grinned as the patrol car rolled onward, the three women forgotten entirely as soon as the patrol car rolled around the corner and headed south.

"That... was amazing," Asuka whispered. She clutched Harlow's arm, starting to giggle and wag her returned tail.

"That was," Natsumi agreed with a fascinated look on her narrow face. "Hm. I may need to alter my disguise."

"After ice cream," Harlow declared. "Who knows? More trouble might come find us and then Asuka gets her excitement and you might get another meal."

"And you?" Natsumi asked, amusement curling her thin lips in a smirk.

"I might get to punch someone and then drag them off to drown them in the river," Harlow said. "Been a while since I got a good swim, though I'd have to have someone reliable around to guard my skin for me."

That was... probably going too far. Asuka was as far from reliable as you could get. Flighty, excitable, prone to causing trouble just to see what happens; she was the opposite of reliable. Natsumi might, if you desperately stretched the definition, qualify as a reliable guard of her skin, but only when she wasn't hungry. Or cranky. Or, possibly, irritated at the world.

But they were women.

And they acted like Harlow's pod back home. Younger and older, snippy and violent and hungry and dangerous. Harlow spent so much time around regular humans; too much time. It was important to the pod, to her family, but she *missed* being around women who weren't safe and mild and meek around men.

Damn, Harlow hadn't realized until Asuka bounced her way into her night just how much she missed dangerous women, powerful women, women with magic and teeth.

Natsumi snorted, smoothing her kimono over her smoothly arched belly. "You're a fool."

"A lonely one, yes," Harlow agreed. "Who wants some ice cream with women who aren't harmless?"

"Uuuugghhh!" Asuka groaned, rolling her eyes so hard that Harlow was mildly surprised that they didn't spin all the way backwards in her sockets. "I know! I mean, the shop I work at is all humans during the day, and the stupid boss keeps putting me on day shift because I'm 'cute'. I'm not cute! I'm fierce!"

Natsumi laughed, another laugh with the back of her hand pressed to her mouth, but her eyes wrinkled with real amusement. "Oh, child, you're adorable. Don't try to fool yourself."

"Yup," Harlow agreed with a nod that made Asuka whine at them. "Cute. Don't fuss over it. Use it to your benefit. No one expects the cute ones to be dangerous. Just like no one expects me to be smart."

"Or me to… bite," Natsumi said with a glittering little smile that hinted at the fangs hidden behind her mask.

Asuka shook her head. "What*ever*. I was promised ice cream. We should get some."

"Absolutely," Harlow said.

She opened the door, letting out a blast of wonderfully cold air that felt like a breath of home, and held it for both Asuka and Natsumi. The sweat dripping down Harlow's back and sides chilled, cooled, dried, for the first time in ages. The clerks looked up, two young girls who looked like they were barely eighteen and seemed even younger than that in their pink and white striped uniforms. Both of them went bone white.

"Time for an ice cream break," Harlow announced as she sauntered up to the counter and looked at the laminated picture menu all of these parfait places had. "The big chocolate brownie parfait for me."

"Green tea mochi, please," Natsumi said with a little nod to the shivering girls.

"Strawberry milkshake!" Asuka exclaimed, bouncing on her toes and clapping her hands.

"We *need* dessert," Harlow said when the girls didn't move. "Sometimes you just need something sweet after a good, rich meal."

"Ah, yes," the stouter of the two girls finally gasped.

They scrambled to put together the order, leaving Harlow, Natsumi, and Asuka to settle around one of the little ironwork tables with their nerve-wrackingly wobbly ironwork chairs. They held Natsumi perfectly, and of course Asuka only weighed as much as she wanted at any given moment. Harlow's chair creaked alarmingly when she sat on it, but it held, much to Harlow's surprise.

The girls brought out their ice cream remarkably quickly, but then they were the only customers. Harlow nodded her thanks, snorting as Asuka giggled and clapped her hands. 'Cute' really was the proper word for the kitsune, even if the shop girls found her terrifying.

"Ahh, this is almost sweet enough," Harlow said as she dug through the whipped cream and nuts to the chocolate ice cream drenched with chocolate sauce.

Natsumi chuckled as she carefully cut off tiny wedges of mochi-wrapped green tea ice cream and nibbled at it as delicately as a crab slowly shredding a fish it'd caught. "Perfect. This was a splendid idea."

"Yeah," Asuka agreed. She slurped her milkshake, smirking around the straw. "So when's the trouble start?"

Harlow shrugged. Then stopped as the door opened, letting in the cicada song along with two drunk young yakuza toughs who were very much in the wrong place at the wrong time. Not that they realized it.

Yet.

Harlow raised an eyebrow as Natsumi set her spoon down, and Asuka slurped her milkshake with extra force. Behind the counter, the girls were shaking twice as hard as they had been when the three of them walked in. Natsumi lifted her head in just the right way to make her hair sway and spill over her shoulder like black silk. Asuka's tail and ears had disappeared, but the promise of mischief in her eyes was a thousand times more obvious.

As the girls behind the counter stammered apologies that they didn't have the Godiva ice cream the drunk yakuza boys demanded, despite it not being on the menu, Harlow took a big bite of her parfait, then leaned back enough to make her fragile little chair scream against the tiled floor.

Both yakuza toughs turned, frowning, at the three of them. Sneers appeared on their faces.

"Leave," Harlow told them, setting her spoon down and standing up. "Now."

"Huh," the stupider of the two yakuza drunks grunted. "Or what?"

Harlow turned to the girls and smiled. "Duck."

She strode over to push the girls into the freezer-chilled back room, shielding their eyes from what Natsumi and Asuka were about to do. No reason for them to be traumatized, after all. Harlow would keep them safe while Natsumi and Asuka… did what came naturally.

And once they were done, well, there would still be ice cream to eat with her new friends, wouldn't there? It wasn't home. But it wasn't half-bad.

Harlow would take it, gladly.

Mike Jack Stoumbos, an emerging fiction author disguised as a believably normal high school teacher, lives in Seattle with his wife and their parrot. He won 1st place in the first quarter of the 2021 Writers of the Future contest, and his stories have appeared in several science fiction and fantasy anthologies, including Galactic Stew *and* Hold Your Fire. *When not writing fiction, Mike Jack publishes stageplays, academic/informational articles, and lovably geeky parody lyrics. You can find him online at MikeJackStoumbos.com, @MJStoumbos on Twitter, and on several karaoke stages in the Seattle area.*

About this story, Mike Jack says: "So many stories show magic mucking up the works of complex technology, but haven't you ever wanted to wave your hand at your computer and fix a technical glitch with a spell? A part of me believes that every tech expert out there is actually hocus-pocusing our devices back to life, and then calmly saying, 'Yeah, I just restarted the system.' Naturally, they inspired Clarence Hemlock: a literal computer wizard, with tech-based adventures in the tradition of urban-fantasy detectives like Harry Dresden and the Iron Druid."

I've worked in the tech industry for far too long not to believe in technical wizardry – and am fairly certain computer code is a form of magic...

CLARENCE HEMLOCK, COMPUTER WIZARD
Mike Jack Stoumbos

The electronic chime sounded as the door opened, and a sweaty, nervous man filled the customer space of my little strip-mall kiosk. Even in a half-zipped jacket, he exuded the aroma of pickled stress and the waxy stripes of ineffective deodorant, neither of which was a red flag for sorcery.

"I Ii," he said, then cleared his throat to add, "Pick up for Jared."

Flashing a genuine smile to overshine his forced one, I said, "Jared! Welcome back. I'll just grab it for you."

As a slim-hipped gent, accustomed to cramped spaces, I lithely navigated through the shelves of mismatched inventory, stepping over interwoven power cords en route to Jared's laptop. From his perspective, he could not see the warding amulet resting on top of it, which I removed and pocketed as I retrieved the laptop. The amulet's worn ceramic grooves had already cooled down considerably.

I set his machine on the counter, then spun it to face him with a practiced flourish of the wrist. "Why don't you go ahead and sign in before you go? You'll find that all traces of the virus have been removed."

"Oh, really? That's… that's excellent," he stammered, cautiously hopeful. Even after giving me full access to probe around on his personal computer, the poor man was still embarrassed to log in in front of someone else. Perhaps a part of him suspected I hadn't done my job as well as I claimed, or maybe he was just conditioned to worry.

Misgivings aside, the pleasant tones piping through tinny speakers assured my client of some success. His shoulders must have dropped half a foot, now that some of their tension was released. He clacked away at his keys, confirming a clean computer with every new turn, while I calmly produced the invoice.

"This is… I mean, wow," he concluded.

Some people had the gift of eloquence.

Jared laughed in relief, as his cheeks finished the transition from scarlet to pale and finally to splotchy. "Incredible. How did you do it?"

The phrase *a-magician-never-reveals* itched the back of my throat. Instead, I shrugged and pointed to the framed IT certificate on the wall – which only proved my graphic design savvy and that people trusted paper. "I've learned a lot of tricks of the trade, Jared."

"I thought *I* had, too, but, man—" He blew out a hollow whistle with an odor like fried onions. "I figured I was cursed."

I shook my head with confidence. "Not this time. Some things do come down to probability and choices."

He was too distracted by the blue-light of his functioning screen to catch my hint. But I let him putter and self-check for another minute or two. "So it's all clean?"

"Should be." I tried the more direct approach this time. "Although I'll caution you about downloading cheat packages for fantasy games in the future. You don't know where they've been." Or what kinds of bugs liked to piggy-back on them.

"Yeah. Man, you're a life-saver. If my wife found out I was ransomwared out of my computer for a… a…"

"A couple of pixel pixies?"

"Yeah. I mean, you know how it is," he said, suggesting a man-to-man assumption that was missing some information.

"Sure," I agreed, tactfully. "Let's get you settled up."

He was surprised to see that I'd stayed within my original quote and wasn't creating a new form of ransom. It made me seem quite agreeable, so it wasn't a hard sell when I tossed out, "But hey, if you want, you can sign up for my personal protection plan. That way if anything else goes wrong, you can drop it off here, and I'll run a quick diagnostic and scrub on the house."

"Yes. Absolutely."

So I let him fill out the paperwork and add the extra charge himself, with as much enthusiasm as he'd downloaded shady software.

This particular trick kept my five-by-nine parking-lot building lucrative, bucking even Seattle prices. I didn't even feel guilty about it anymore. I knew that with my wards, nothing short of a lightning bolt – or lightning-equivalent spell – would taint that laptop for at least the next six months to a year. I also knew that, with the glint in his eye, this fellow would rack up a thousand more viruses if he employed any other tech geek without my unique skillset, so he really was getting what he paid for.

Jared barely read the membership eDoc before signing with his finger and authorizing the credit card.

I maintained a professional smile. However, to be honest, his brand of tech problem bored me to tears. It was mindless, mundane. There was no ghost in his machine, let me tell you. Just because *he* couldn't rout out the software bug didn't mean it presented a challenge to me after so many years.

I had gotten into this business to chase dangerous hexes that made their way into computers, but hadn't seen more than a basic charm in months. Like anyone who has ever been told "be careful what you wish for," I longed for an exciting, challenging case again.

Not that I minded a bit of ego stroking or the cash the simple viruses brought in.

"Excellent," I said, when the purchase finished processing. I printed and placed the updated record of transaction on top of the laptop. Along with a small stack of business cards, each of which proudly proclaimed my purple logo and name in stylish caps:

Clarence Hemlock
Computer Wiz

I figured a guy like Jared would be good for word-of-mouth business.

"You're all set," I told him, one eye now on the next client, waiting patiently outside the caged-glass door.

"You, Sir, really are a tech wizard." He grabbed his laptop in both hands, then tucked it into his faded spring jacket, which was more of a windbreaker than an anti-rain layer.

Judging by the woman outside, whose black coat was a hood-up, thunder-storm number, he might not have been prepared enough to protect his laptop. I guess if everyone were smart about electronics, they wouldn't need me.

Jared pushed, then held, the door open for the woman. There really was only room for one person, or maybe a close couple, to stand comfortably in my receiving area at any given time, but this woman appeared uncomfortable even sharing the side-walk of an open-air parking lot.

She recoiled from Jared's boisterous recommendation: "This guy's great; you're gonna love him."

One hand drew up the collar of her coat, and the other clutched a high-quality computer case closer to her body. Jared, well-meaning but oblivious, continued on his merry way as soon as she had crossed the threshold.

Once inside, she eagerly pulled the door shut behind her and shuddered.

"Good evening," I said, making a point of softening my tone, not wanting to come across as a Jared-type. "Welcome to *Computer Wiz*. I'm Clarence. What can I do for you?"

"Um…" was her first response. She pushed back the hood, revealing a round face with cheeks that still had dimple marks even though she wasn't smiling. Her hair was tied back simply, but it was naturally wavy enough that it announced its unwashed state. And her brown eyes remained eerily unblinking, with eyelids that were a little puffy but not yet red.

She was in need of a good cry, but too shocked to do so.

I swallowed, pressing any shared discomfort into the pit of my stomach, to deal with later. I could imagine my husband telling me that I had too long of a neck to swallow subtly – which was accurate – and now brought a pinkness to my cheeks.

She paid no attention to me, however. She glanced around at the various chargers and mini-USBs on display, as if she was the one who had something to hide.

"Um…" Again. "I'm wondering if you can help me get into a laptop."

She placed the whole briefcase on the counter, handles up, then stepped back without unzipping it. Her eyes had continued to work their way furtively around the room, and finally settled on mine—*un*settled mine, if I'm being honest.

The style of the leather, the bulky zippers, and the grooved vinyl handles were definitely high-end enough, but not consistent with the woman's style. Her coat was much more chic and trendy; despite the unkempt hair, her nail polish was well-maintained and matched her nose-stud – all of which clashed with the obvious *dude* briefcase.

"Look, I'm not in the business of stripping parts," I said, taking a small step back and getting ready to press the button for security. "If it's not your computer—"

"Oh no, um…" She faltered in the explanation, but it was discomfort, not guilt. "This belongs – *belonged* to my brother."

And there it was. "I'm so sorry for your loss."

"Thank you." The response was automatic and a bit numb. "I was hoping you could get into the computer. Rather, help my family get into the computer. So we could recover data, close accounts. That sort of thing."

"I see." And I did, but I maintained whatever distance the small space would afford while my mind went on unproductive tangents. The germaphobe in me was not a constant voice, but presently, it seized the microphone and told me I didn't want to touch the computer either. "If you don't mind my asking, how did he…"

"He killed himself. Two days ago. Was battling depression for a long time." She hugged her elbows and blinked away the lack of tears. Definite shock. "I brought some paperwork if you need to see." This, she could touch, and was much more comfortable handling. She laid out a death certificate for one Wallace Brown, and her own driver's license to match a *Next of Kin* cell.

I didn't exactly doubt her. She looked like she'd seen at least one ghost, and I know what I'm talking about there. I might not have been able to read minds or auras, but I accepted the story as presented.

And I accepted the job.

"I'll do what I can. It might take a bit, depending on how thorough he was with his security. You just looking for passwords?" Even though the deceased hadn't been diseased, I opted to put on gloves before opening.

"Yeah. Just to log on."

I lifted the laptop, pretty standard 17-inch, only a couple years old. "Any sensitive information that I should be on the lookout for."

"Sort of." She tilted her head noncommittally.

I made a show of waiting for her.

I wasn't trying to be insensitive, but I wasn't about to open anything incriminating because a client was tongue-tied. I had a lot more techniques for self-protection than your average geek, but I still paid attention to modern law.

"He was a writer," she said, eventually, then added, "Aspiring. And so all of his stories are on there. The novel he was working on, it was making him really happy and seemed to be pulling him out of a dark place. Anyway, we thought so… The family wants to have them."

"Ah." Examining the computer from the outside, I could tell it was well maintained. The corners had the tell-tale smoothness of a device that had traveled; the absence of dust and hand oils said the owner regularly wiped it down. "Have you tried logging in?"

"No. I can't."

I eyed at her, hoping for more clarity.

"I just get this feeling. Like I'm not supposed to. Does that sound crazy?"

I shook my head. "Not at all. It sounds pretty normal to me." I had just meant the emotional impact, but when I lifted the screen, I encountered a whole new sensation. A jolt, sort of like static discharge, but much more green and smelling of funky cheese.

A ward. A crude mystical guard on a piece of modern day hardware. No wonder she felt resistance.

Tingling with rapid-fire sensory signals, I shut the laptop, with enough speed to startle the client.

I played a hunch. "You don't really want to be here for this, do you?" My tone was calm, even somewhat natural, but my heart was thudding. It might sound completely inappropriate, but I could hardly contain my excitement.

"Sure," she said. Then, after a few more nods, she sniffed in something that seemed like the start of a much-needed cry. "So, do I just leave it here with you? Can I pick it up tomorrow?"

It worked. "Yes. Just input your contact info, and I'll be in touch as soon as I've figured out the logins."

She did so with pained gusto, entering her cell-number and email as quickly as she could without making an error. The wind outside hissed at the seal in my door, and shook the loosest pane of glass. I made no comment on the darkening evening sky; my client was picking up enough ominous vibes without me pointing them out to her.

Clearly, she wanted to be away from the laptop as soon as possible, and I didn't blame her. Even without my level of experience, she could sense that something was wrong, in a manner far less natural than a death in the family.

The difference between her and me was that I couldn't wait to dive into the root of the problem. And I could solve it.

"Okay." She clutched the lapels of her coat in both hands "That's everything?"

"Yeah," I said, but as she turned away, I thought of one more thing. "Do you know the title of the book he was working on?"

She opened the door with a chime, and this time, the wind whipped in a noticeable chill. "Um… It's a witch story. He called it *Gretel's Grimoire*."

◆

Shortly after the client left, I, too, was hustling through the parking lot, with the supernatural laptop in its bag under my arm. Storm clouds amassed overhead and rain beat down prematurely. I was also alone and grinning unabashedly.

By the time I'd reached my car, my body was speckled with water, but my mind was forming theories and mini-narratives. My favorite was that this would-be novelist had downloaded, read, or typed an incantation for his book, which triggered an actual spell. Something powerful or twisted enough to be self-warding, with an aura more pungent than Roquefort.

Good thing the laptop had come to me, someone who could recognize and deal with tech-magic. If I weren't a digimancer, I could end up just like poor Wallace Brown.

I stepped into my Subaru and set the volatile cargo in the passenger seat. My car was similarly warded to both prevent theft and detect malicious magic, and the sudden interference announced itself. The vehicle's frame buzzed in annoyance at the intruding tech, but it gave me no further trouble as I headed home.

The weather, on the other hand, decided to get worse.

It was a full-on dark and stormy early evening when I took the ramp onto I-5. Could I pretend I didn't think anything was spooky or eerie? Sure.

But it didn't help that the underpass flashing board told me to tune into the AM station for a *severe weather warning.*

"What the hell are you?" I asked the laptop, or more accurately, whatever the ward was guarding.

Despite being inanimate, the laptop seemed to respond with a literal flash of lightning in the darkening sky.

I knew that some things were legitimately a matter of probability and choices—like the choice to live in a region affectionately known as the Pacific North-wet. This was not one of those things. For one, the sound of thunder is not supposed to smell like gorgonzola, even to experienced casters. I was dealing with a doozie, and I was thrilled to get my hands dirty again.

On the dash mount, my phone lit to display a text from my husband:

Saw crazy storm warning. You driving? Stay safe.

I looked guiltily at the computer case after reading *safe.*

Pressing for the voice-to-text feature, I dictated my reply, "Hey Kelly. Almost home. The weather is nuts. Maybe you should stay at the office 'til it clears. Love you. Talk soon." And *send.*

Don't judge me, but there was something exhilarating – like sneaking out of your parents' house to go skinny dipping kind of thrilling – about having some alone time to wrestle with dark magic and not telling my loving (worrying) Kelly.

I thanked my lucky stars I was married to someone who worked later hours with a longer commute. And I prayed to the goddess my home's electricity wouldn't go out before I got there.

♦

"Damn, that's cold!"

I continued to shudder long after I'd slammed the front door behind me. Every inch of my clothes and skin glistened with ice or recently melted ice. My shoes dripped solid prints on our *Home-Sweet-Home* mat. One white-knuckled hand still clutched the laptop case by its now uncomfortable vinyl handles. I was pretty sure the surface had to be below 32 for the rain to have frozen to it, but I'm not a meteorologist.

Intrigued though I still was, I couldn't help but acknowledge a certain amount of shaking when I went to unzip the threatening case. And I couldn't blame it all on the cold.

Instead of dwelling on it too long, I poured a circle of salt around the briefcase and lit some incense. Reasonable precautions.

I stripped out of my wet clothes, layered myself with dryer-fresh flannel, and poured myself a scotch. Also reasonable.

Next, I switched on literally every light in our cozy townhouse and cranked up the heat. And I caught sight of my paranoid face in the living room mirror.

"You're scared to open it, aren't you?"

The question was addressed to me, but I didn't feel like answering myself just yet. So I settled onto the love seat, with a second scotch, and glared down the briefcase.

I scowled. It sat.

I scratched my head. It continued to sit.

I decided against having a staring contest with it.

Eventually I said, "The thunderstorm was a tad dramatic, don't you think?"

There was no answer. In fact, the sound of the rain pelting against the window had slowed to a trickle.

"Maybe it would be best to just destroy you. Smash, scramble, incinerate. That way if there's a curse on the laptop…"

But I knew better than to do that. If a legitimate spell or curse had worked its way into the system, it could get a lot worse if I smashed its container. Also, I had my reputation to think of. I'd probably catch some flak and lose some business if I blew up someone's dead brother's computer. Of course, my client would never know that I might have just saved her life by risking my own.

On the other hand, it might have been nothing more than a simple misdownloaded charm which only appeared scary. Nine out of ten viruses were entirely non-magical, and most mystical ones were more frustrating than dangerous.

Given the fate of Wallace Brown, I readily assumed the spell had mucked with his mind. Like the kind of mal-charms that might compel to impulse-buy shoes, or to become hypnotized by a social media ad, or to convince you of one right way to pronounce *gif*. A close-proximity suicide was more damning, but I didn't have enough information yet. Wallace Brown, aspiring occult author, could have been either responsible for – or victim of – whatever was in that laptop. I'd already Googled him before closing up shop, and discovered literally zero online presence for an author by that name. If his first novel really was what killed him, I had to feel sorry for the guy – unless it turned out he was a truly terrible person who'd turned his computer into a magic bomb for someone else to find.

I sipped some more liquid courage, idly musing that the average pleb didn't take that phrase literally. Of all the strong spirits, scotch was the strongest for bucking fear. I had no talent for potion-making, but – despite my swimmer's build – I could hold my liquor well. And I understood what to put into my body to guard against volatile magic.

"Let's keep the mood positive," I told myself, while I set up a playlist. Minor digimancy, a positive-energy counterspell woven into the harmonies of a few songs I knew well enough to background. It was second-nature to me, but 'all Greek' to plenty of experienced wizards out there – most of whom can actually speak Greek. Old magicians rarely bother to learn new tricks to contend with the information era, or so I told myself. But it was true, believe it or not, a cheap pair of earbuds and a simple weave could render most mind-affecting spells completely useless. This was especially true against magic computer viruses, which were often laughably uninspired.

With my music on, the feeling of foreboding left, the ward unable to dissuade my intent.

Finally, I put on rubber gloves, to reduce the risk of shock. That part was just practical.

I unzipped the case and took out the laptop. Nothing strange happened.

So I opened the screen, hit the spacebar a couple of times, clicked the mouse. The screen lit up, but there was no jolt, and no synesthetic clues like the smell of cheese.

Rubber gloves, happy music, the residual taste of Macallan 12-year. Possibly none needed. I should have programmed a *crickets* sound effect for the occasion.

"Huh." Maybe whatever the charm was had used up all its juice already, and maybe the storm really was a coincidence – not likely, but worth considering. I closed my eyes, did what I could to sense… anything.

The screen only showed non-magical programming. The keys and touch-pad were shiny from frequent use. There was a prompt for a password, which I didn't know, but could backdoor with only a touch of magic.

"Alrighty," I said, slipping off one of the rubber gloves, significantly less worried about electrocution from an unplugged machine with forty percent battery life.

Still, when I touched the keyboard with my bare hand, there was a sudden, warm flood of green, and a heavily accented woman's voice calling, "Help me!"

"Yow!" I wrenched my hand away and regarded my fingers. They were all still there. It hadn't been an assault, or anything painful, really. The sensation had been like a campfire's glow at a pleasant distance, just before it got too hot and you needed to change seats. And it had definitely been a voice, loudly piping through the computer's speakers, enough to cut through the sound-track in my ears. Jarring, but not painful, and totally different from the foul cheese smell earlier. In fact, the smell was floral, or maybe that was the incense.

Someone had asked for help.

I didn't hear anything now, but if anyone was crying out from within the laptop, I shouldn't let anything distract me.

Closing my eyes, I tried to read the energy from the keys, opening myself up just enough, but with a corner of my mind hanging on to the protective concert coming through tiny rubber speakers.

The author had preferred to strike the period and *Enter* keys, but would kiss the spacebar. So many letters had formed so many combinations, but I sought a common pattern. I let their residual force guide my fingers, and typed eight letters that must have been repeated a million times.

I opened my eyes to find *"I love you"* staring back at me.

I tried again, and sure enough, I again typed, "I love you." This system's most frequently-used phrase.

I had to shift my impression of the occult author, or at least leave it open for interpretation. Dear Wally might have been a lovesick puppy, who typed those three little words ad nauseum; or he might have been a creepy loner who had somehow, through misguided will, trapped someone's spirit on his hard drive.

Urgency overshot curiosity, and I still hadn't detected any deadly traps behind the ward.

Rubbing my hands together, I told the laptop, "Okay, let's do this."

I drew heat from my surroundings into my palms, which began to hiss with steam and tremor like the strings of a cello. My *command* voice always sounded much deeper, more imposing, and – if I'm honest —a little more robotic. "Show me your password!"

I planted my hands on the keyboard and felt the spirit move my fingers, knuckles awkwardly hyperextending then contracting. It came to me as gibberish, a computer-genned password, far too many characters long. And the longer my hands produced it, the more my fingers burned and pressed into the keys.

Conflicting sensory details sprang out at me, like a bad wine and fish pairing, not enough to drive someone mad, but hardly healthy. The musty, sour, bitter blue-cheese scent enveloped my smell receptors, despite the total lack of real dairy products or mold. Fighting against it, trying to cut through, was the freshness of lilac.

Hard to care when your hands are burning…, when you've come this far…, and when you're as stubborn as I am.

Channeling the user, I slammed that *Enter* key.

The ward snapped, and the laptop let me in. The green shade of cheese vanished, dissipating entirely without any lingering trace. Even the rain, which had slowed to a periodic trickle, now ceased.

As the laptop populated to life, it all seemed perfectly normal. A desktop background of a mountain, and a reasonable assortment of icons lay gridded on the edges.

I felt no immediate magic – at least none on the surface.

I also scratched my head over the nature of the ward that had tried to steer me away in the first place. Wards usually smelled kind of like burning hair and ozone and had little to no color association. "Weird," I observed, and, coming from a digimancer, that's saying something.

"Hello," said a soft voice, as if in response.

That was weirder. I blinked twice.

"Who is there?" she asked again, in an accent that was some bizarre mix of central European. Then, in fear, she stammered, "W-Wally? Is that you?"

I leaned forward. "Can you hear me?"

The voice hesitated. "You are not Wally…"

Of course she could hear me. There was a built-in microphone, right next to the camera eye.

"No, my name is Clarence," I said. "Who are you?"

"I am trapped!" she said. Her voice rang out in a tinny echo, as if one speaker was delayed. "Please, you must help. I have been imprisoned in this text."

The way she said it, I immediately thought of old, hand-written pages rather than a computer. "How did you get in there?" Secretly, I wondered, *How do I get you out?* – but one thing at a time.

"I was awakened in the dark, without my body, amongst a sea of tiny flashes. Had I been asleep for days or centuries, I do not know, but the writer was there. He spoke with me, wrote to me, told my story, and helped me understand where I was."

Her formal, literary language had me glancing at the icon with *Gretel's Grimoire* on the desktop.

"He said he would help me be whole again." Her voice became more animated, the discrepancies between left and right speakers increasing as she expressed her frustration and heartache. "But he misled me! He kept me shut in here, where I could be his and his alone, and would never let me out!"

The static and crackle of the speakers wound up to a feedback whine. I winced away from it, even with my indirect ear protection.

Well, crap… It sounded like Wallace was both a love-sick puppy *and* someone who imprisoned women's spirits in computers. Maybe he knew far more about the occult than his sister was aware; maybe it was just part of his hidden life. I'd spent a lot of time lurking in various forums of amateur magic enthusiasts – most of whom were into stage magic or the woowoo-wicca label – without leaving comment, but I didn't imprison people.

The idea of Wallace sitting at his computer, trying to convince this poor creature (and himself) of his genuine love was kind of sickening. The picture painted itself: an emotionally unstable man who thought he'd found the perfect woman, one incapable of leaving him, and who took advantage of an old spell cast on her, and learned a little bit about magic himself. Then, when she wanted to leave, he'd trapped her. Probably disabled the internet connection, changed his password to that 32-key monstrosity, created a ward of will, and took his own life. It was the final act of *I can't have you, no one else will.*

The speaker hiss was like a sharp exhalation, as the captive tried to purge her own disgust. "I am growing weaker," she admitted. "Even now, I am drifting farther away. Fading. If I do not find some way to escape…"

"Right," I whispered to myself. "Right." It didn't matter anymore what kind of pig Wallace Brown had been. I had a job to do.

Without knowing more about what kind of spell had imprisoned her in the first place, I wouldn't even be able to counter it in my own element. "Hey, I'm gonna switch on a chat," I said, opening a videocall app. "I want you to keep talking. I'm going to see if I can find where you're written into the source code. Maybe I can shore up your—"

"I see you!" she exclaimed.

I looked at my own slightly fuzzy face, captured by a camera that would have been mid-range years before. My narrow nose and high cheekbones were always apparent, but in this rendition, I still had a little bit of the *drowned rat* left over from my time in the rain.

"You have kind eyes," she said, a nicer statement than I would have given myself.

"Thank you." I began typing in command prompts, starting general and working my way into systems currently using processing power. To keep her talking, I observed. "You found this quickly."

"Yes, Wallace used the same tool. It was how he saw me, as well."

Fingers poised between clacks, I glanced up at the screen, and what I saw in the video chat window would have been perfect for a horror movie. Someone else's shadow, slightly offset from my own silhouette, was fading into view.

I swallowed and watched my long neck bob. "He wanted to picture you, huh?"

The shadow nodded. "I was his muse. He called me his inspiration. He said he wanted to see, hear, touch, and taste all of me."

"Uh-huh." I minimized the video chat, needing screen space and eschewing the distraction. Two black frames ran my system commands. I tried to up my odds, leaning into the machine and pouring some more *will* into the process. "Who were you before you were trapped?"

A sigh. "It is so long ago. I cannot remember. But he called me Gretel."

"Like Hansel and Gretel, right?"

"He said that too. You are findin—" She fritzed. Or, rather, her voice cut out, and several of the computer's inner workings protested with screeches and flashes.

"Damn it!" One of my fingers had sparked and was now sporting a charred mark on its tip. That hurt, not gonna lie.

I could keep running tests, continue to try to sort out what, who, how, and why – but I was pretty sure her code wasn't in just one place. It was everywhere. She had filtered into every active part of the computer, but not as copies. No, she was distributing, dispersing. It was like scattering a pebble to each square foot of a beach, then hoping to find them after wind, waves, and pedestrians trundled through.

She also hadn't spoken for several seconds. "Hey, are you still there?" I asked. Not knowing what to call her, I tried, "Gretel!"

Electronic tones responded, more like a *Star-Wars* server droid than a real voice, but coalescing into, "Clarence? Where are you? I cannot see—"

The screen blipped to blue, then returned. I pulled up the chat window and jumped in shock, though not fear. I was no longer in the camera. Instead, there was a frozen image of a woman. She had piercing green eyes, strawberry-blonde hair, a partially open mouth whose scream went unheard. The image had captured someone terrified for her life.

I wasn't doing any good out here. And if she was fading fast, maybe it was my fault, for trying to do too much at once, overtaxing the delicate balance of the system.

I had to get in there.

I ripped out my earbuds and donned my command voice again. Had computers been invented an era ago, there might have been fancy Latin incantations. Instead, I called, "Compress and upload!"

I've never had a chance to see myself when I do this. Apparently, it's one of those times when I black out all cameras attempting to record. According to Kelly, it's also horrendously freaky. My eyes roll back, my jaw drops, my ribs press forward like they're going to break, and a ghost of me jumps into the computer.

Goddess help me.

◆

Neither *The Matrix* nor *Tron* got it totally right, but then again, they're popular SciFi and only know so much. The actual human experience in a computer does not involve a body.

You're not standing in a 3-D holodeck grid or running around on the motherboard. You are two-dimensional, if that, and fragmented beyond belief.

It takes a willingness to literally abandon all five senses in exchange for flat analogs, but it also requires an extreme sense of self-preservation to keep yourself coherent. I'd only ever been under for a handful of minutes at a time, close to an hour once, because I was too afraid to dissipate.

This woman – whom I now knew as Gretel – was on another level entirely, if she had managed to stay in here this long.

I called out to her. If I'm being technical, my program-self emitted a stream of data addressing her, while I ran a subroutine trying to find the most concentrated parts of her. I knew her voice and could translate it to a voiceprint, like a mental waveform. I had only seen her face once, in that one worried freeze-frame, but I had a sense of color and shape and features which even I would call striking. I put out parameters for whatever bits of her I knew, and I should not have been surprised by what I found.

GretelsGrimoire.docx

Thousands of hits and traces, all peppered into the book. *That's* where she would be. So I maneuvered into the words and world of the writer, calling out to the person trapped inside.

I half-expected to find endless lines of *All work and no play makes Wally a sadistic maiden-capturing perv*. But what I discovered instead was surprisingly normal. No, normal wasn't exactly correct, but it began as a narrative. It represented longing and hope, even though, from the first page, it seemed to be about a girl straight out of a German folktale trapped in a witch's book of spells.

"Gretel?" I called, using an analog of voice, and sending bits of text and search commands through the document. Naturally, I found thousands of results, few of which were actually what I wanted to find.

But there was a light at the end of that tunnel. A spark of consciousness, and the type of life magic that didn't belong in a digital environment. It called, "Help me!" in a distorted non-voice, and I followed.

"Hang on, I'm coming."

"Please, I can feel myself slipping…" The word echoed and trailed around me, spontaneously changing random letters throughout the document to spell out *slipping*. The deeper I dove, the more paragraphs were cut off by haphazard insertions of *love*.

To look at her, it hardly seemed that she was slipping at all. In fact, when I found her, I was amazed by how much she had rendered and held onto a human form. Perhaps that was the thing she most remembered and would be the last part of her to fade away.

I sent out a signal to reach her, in some way she could perceive.

"Clarence?" she wondered.

"Yes, I've got you." I pulled on pixels and created a fast mock-up of myself, wire frame and face, for her to see. "Are you okay? You look okay."

"I am wonderful now!" She threw her arms around me, or rather, she tried. She may have imagined herself in a full body, but I saw myself as a code, tunneling through the system. Her hands sloughed off of me, creating a small sense of spark, but no actual interaction. "I can hardly hold onto you…" To say *she pouted* would feel more than a little judgmental, and yet, the lady appeared to be pouting.

"No, I need to figure out the spell that trapped you," I said. Realizing that that wasn't much of an explanation, I switched gears and rephrased, "I'm not going to be here long, and it's easier to move around if I'm more digital."

"Please stay with me," she said. "Just for a little while. It has been so long since I could touch someone. Or been touched." She made a swooning sigh, eyes closed, bosom heaving, the sort of thing you'd find on the covers of overtly straight romance novels.

A part of me wanted to call her on her priorities, but who was I to judge someone who's been out of body for centuries and has spent at least a chunk of that time in a sterile laptop with a nutty writer?

Instead, I said, "Right. Hopefully soon. For now, if I can find the spell that trapped you in the first place, I might be able to reverse it. Or if it wasn't a spell…" I sort of shrugged, sending out confused what-ifs from my digital shoulders and fingertips.

Then, the damnedest thing, I *felt* her. She actually reached up and placed a hand on my cheek, her thumb at my ear, her fingers wrapping around the back of my neck. "You seem tired. You should rest with me here. It won't be too long."

I could see how otherwise wired men could be drawn into those big, green doe eyes. Even I'll admit, I had half a mind to snuggle up, eat chocolate, and watch an episode of *Outlander* with her. But I also had a mission.

"No, this is serious, Gretel. And I can't stay here too long," I said. "I need to get back to my body before I get lost in here, too. So, please, tell me, what do you remember? What trapped you here?"

She drew back, a little stunned, maybe even hurt, by my brusqueness. Maybe she had gotten used to the tender affections of her captor, and now *I* was weird by comparison.

"It is…" she gestured around us, to the edges of the document in which her code resided, "…in the book. He said the spell was *down-loaded*, then *pasted-in*," she recited, her accent making the tech lingo sound even more foreign.

"Okay," I said, happy for more direction. "That's something. I can look for a quote or an incantation. Oh! Was it in German?"

She shook her head. "I am not sure."

"Okay. You stay here. Hold on however you need to. I'm going to find it, and I'll be right back."

I zoomed away, splitting myself in several directions, scanning document histories, downloads, and other temporary files. Even as a student, I'd been a lightning-fast researcher – neither the teacher nor my peers knew I'd employed magic. I did so now, as naturally as an entropist could make fire. And I *did* find German – which I do not speak – in a downloaded page, a PDF scan of some ancient-looking text, but that was hardly important.

I cross-referenced the date of download with that date's version of the novel, then opened it as a separate doc. The whole process was going so smoothly that I was hardly worried about my own consciousness fading. The translation popped up in front of me in fragments. I knew enough about real-world magic to know that there must have been some pretty powerful energy to transfer someone into a book, but the how and why were unclear.

So I scrolled forward through more edits, earlier versions of the document, with more than an inkling of my quarry, growing more aware of magical sensations.

I was smelling lilacs, seeing glances of darker purples. I picked up the abrasiveness of potato sacks. When in digital, I only ever registered scent when there was definite evidence of magic. Now, the scents increased as the document aged, as I jumped to each newer version.

Then – suddenly, jarringly, overwhelmingly – more flashes came into view with a list of *I love you*s and other, more elegant, declarations. The woman trapped in the laptop had been recorded, represented on the pages, as snapshots in time. I was reminded of geological samples, with evidence of previous forest fires along each line, and this was the brightest and hottest flame to date.

She had… sketched herself, producing face first, careful to color in her eyes. Then she had drawn her body, conveniently leaving off any clothes. She had also spoken to the author, in text on the page that was clearly hers

– purple and floral but scratchy. To me, the love letters and overtures were hair-raisingly creepy, possibly because I was now the voyeur, intruding on a strange affair between author and character. I had looked in on other people's computers many times before, but nothing had made me blush like these descriptions.

Did I lose track of time in my fascination? I must have. Was I numb to what should have been an obvious reality? Even in retrospect, the factors were strange enough that I want to give myself the benefit of the doubt.

She was seeming less and less the frail captive, shut tight in a spell-book with magic of her own. Now, decanted into a computer, she was bold, assertive, seductive like only a pixelated fantasy could be. Hints became requests, and soon thereafter demands, which might have seemed subtle if I was watching them as they had come in, over days rather than seconds.

Then, after one more promise of the woman's *love*, I found the directive that chilled my digital blood:

Bring her to me, so I may live in her body and we can be together as flesh.

Did I know who *her body* belonged to? Maybe not consciously or immediately. But the suspicion creeping through my code was unignorable. The horrifying reveal from which I could not look away. I had to discover, with certainty, who it was, and in doing so, I learned the rest of the story, a fractured block of text created by two people trying to type at once, battling for control.

She, the purple, wanting to seem velvety but rough and unforgiving, the delicate flower scent belying her nature. She needed a body, a female body, that would trust this reclusive author enough to enter his house and lie down at his computer.

He tried to refuse. As he did, he'd wrapped his will around the computer – an unattractive shade of green, smelling of moldy cheese that needed to be let out. A funk of despair from too much time depressed and alone, turned resolute. He'd been losing his mind to her, losing the battle, but trying to hold his ground. He told her no, told the woman in the computer who said she loved him that he would not sacrifice his sister. No, he would die before he gave this witch a new body.

A dying wish.

That created a ward…

"Oh… shit." It was then that I realized what should have been obvious.

I leapt out of the document, accessing several locations at once. I needed the speakers, the microphone, the camera. I didn't bother to look for her – I knew where she was going.

She got there first.

Through the camera, I saw myself. Rather, I saw my face, wearing an expression of minor disorientation. The eyelids were fluttering, and then they opened, looking at me with a very different shade of green – the eyes of the witch who had jumped into my waiting vessel.

She didn't waste time; she closed the screen of the laptop, using *my* hand and wearing *my* insufferable smile.

The speakers cut out, silencing my shout. The camera shut off. I was by myself, in the dark, surrounded by data.

But I was in a computer!

Claustrophobia and despair be damned. True, I didn't know every inner working of this specific system. But I was in my element and could use the power at my disposal.

I accessed the wifi – more importantly, wifi calling.

◆

I could feel myself ringing in Kelly's phone, and didn't even wait for him to pick up. A little creepy if you think about – called as a signal, hacked his phone into answering – and yet, there I was.

"Don't freak out," said my stacticky, distorted voice. Even as a digimancer, I was far less accustomed to this than the wicked-witch-of-the-Pacific-Northwest.

"Clarence? Is that you?" Fortunately, Kelly was more confused than panicked, for he recognized me instantly. If I could feel my heart, it would have warmed. "Where are you calling from?"

"Yeah, that's the thing. I may have done something foolish."

"How bad?" He took on a kind of tone which said he would be helpful but was also judging me.

I could not disagree. "I… tangled with an ancient evil stuck in a laptop. She tricked me into trying to help her, and I got myself trapped in the laptop when she… took my body."

"What?"

"Yeah." My code cringed with embarrassment. "I didn't even manage to leave a trail of breadcrumbs."

"Jesus Christ," he said, a remnant of his family's upbringing, albeit back-burnered when he, like me, discovered the power of magic.

The microphone picked up the quiet hum of his environmentally-friendly hybrid, and I asked, "How close?"

"Almost home." The engine got louder; he was accelerating.

Thank the goddess. "You have to stop her before she gets too far with my body. I'll handle the rest."

◆

The practical mechanics of a laptop are difficult to explain from within the casing. Most of the moving parts don't self-motivate. You need a hand to lift the screen.

But I was a computer wizard, and I would figure out how to get mechanical leverage. If there were a known spell, I'd name it, but I was making this up as I went. With the proper focus, I was fairly certain I could render some of the circuits into repelling magnets, and with even more directed force, I should be able to push up the lid.

It was a risk. If I did the wrong thing and destroyed the system, I might blip out with it. But that was a chance I had to take, because I had to have the laptop open by the time Kelly got home.

I flitted through the system, creating strategic little sparks. Different sections of the computer triangulated in my mind, even pieces that shouldn't have had any programmable material.

It was like taking a big gulp of air, compressing into a little ball, then pushing as hard as I could with every muscle from the nose down. And, even with no muscles to strain, it was the toughest thing I'd ever done.

When the screen gave, it opened fast, jarring the laptop, so the image bounced while I watched myself – or my body – now visible through the camera. My own computerized voice came out strained, like I was trying to give birth, and interrupting the concentration of the witch inhabiting my body.

She whipped my head around to face the computer, demanding, "What is the meaning of this?" The Clarence vocal cords and her accent combined to resemble Sesame Street's Count more than sounding seductive or sinister.

Before she could close the distance of a few steps to attack the laptop, the front door burst open, and my husband came in.

Kelly had a thick neck, a beard that was greying in places, and more of a balding pattern than he was comfortable admitting. He was also quite a bit bigger and beefier than I. "Clarence!"

"I'm here!" I squawked through the speakers. "Stop her."

The witch snarled. She raised my hands, pointed my fingers, and rattled off something that sounded incredibly malicious. If I spoke more German, I might have known how deadly.

Kelly turned away, tried to shield his face. I cringed on his behalf.

But no spell was cast. There was a wisp of purple, the smell of lilac, but not a jot of offensive magic.

She may have been a powerful witch at one time in her own skin, but she was in the body of a digimancer, who had absolutely no power of evocation.

"*Scheisser!*" she spat, recognizing the limitations of my body too late.

Kelly tackled my body to the ground, once again trapping the witch.

He pinned my body and raised one fist. "Sorry about this, Clarence!" He punched the body-snatcher the face – and I'll admit that I was incredibly thankful for this singular display of violence.

The witch's gaze shifted, and I saw my eyelids flutter. She sagged under the blow, moaning. She had not been corporeal in a very long time and clearly had trouble adjusting to the pain. She seemed to want to nurse the bruise (that I would have to bear) instead of fighting back.

But I was ready.

It might not have sounded imposing over the speakers, but I cranked up both the volume and my will when I commanded, "Compress and upload!"

My body spasmed. The eyes rolled back, the jaw dropped open in a silent scream, and the chest heaved upward. My command wrenched a purplish ghost from my skin and dragged it toward the screen.

The witch condensed into pixels all around me, writhing sparks of code jetting ire to one another. Now back in the computer and the unfinished novel, the witch was herself again. I could sense her shape, simultaneously old-world seductress and horrible hag.

"*Nein!*" she hissed.

I was in control of the laptop, so when she tried to jump right back into my body, I held on. "Don't you dare."

"Clarence!" called Kelly, holding my unconscious form. "Come back, quick."

"First thing's first," I told him, hardly straining to block her attempt. "Dealing with the witch."

"Fool," she said. "Pathetic excuse for a sorcerer. I possess tenfold the strength you will ever have."

"Maybe out there. But this is *my* territory."

She had incantations at the ready, but in this environment, they were nothing more than data. Every time she tried to string letters together, I deleted or scrambled them. I messed up the formatting, changed the character language. After I'd rendered her mute, I started stripping away her elements.

She had already been somewhat scattered throughout the system. I continued that process. I seized each bit and byte of her code and scattered them. I took away each iota of her command.

When she was too faded to fight back, I selected it all and dragged the files to the trash. She tried one last desperate burst of lilac-smelling power, but I was too fast. *Empty* was, for me, a keystroke.

A collection of nothing more than ones and zeroes, she was gone.

◆

I sat there, with Kelly's arms around me, for the next few hours. Part of it was his residual sense of worry, and part was just to warm me up again. My core temperature took its sweet time getting up to normal.

I snapped a selfie of my newly-earned shiner, but neglected to post it online. I wasn't too keen to explore even the brightest parts of the web that night.

"How are you going to explain it to the client?" wondered my husband.

"I guess *I fell* is a little cliché…"

"No, not that. And sorry. But the laptop. What are you going to say about the stories?"

I regarded the machine. It was sitting inside a constant-current chicken-wire cage, strapped shut, adorned with cleansing amulets, *and* surrounded in salt. But there was no trace of the witch left, no smell of lilac or Wallace Brown's funky cheese ward.

I sighed. "I can't imagine her handling the truth."

"What? That her brother downloaded a centuries-old succubus-witch who tried to mind-control him into delivering her as a sacrificial vessel, and he killed himself to save her? *That* truth, or some other truth."

"Maybe I tell her he wiped the system?" I looked up, hoping that Kelly had a better suggestion, but his contemplative scowl said he didn't. "Or that *I* goofed and accidentally did it."

"You've done enough for them already without taking the blame, too."

I shrugged. It was hard to be callous toward the late Wallace Brown, whom I'd so mentally maligned before discovering that he'd sacrificed himself in a way his sister would never know. "I think I'll extract the story – versions without the witch. It'll be unfinished, but maybe it'll provide some closure for the family. Then, I'll wipe the computer. Best of both worlds."

"You sure?"

"Yeah. It's probably what he would have wanted. I mean, if I know him as well as I think I do."

I had, after all, been in his unfinished novel, and had spent some time with the woman who'd driven him crazy, and assumed I was hetero enough that she could get her hooks in me, too. I had also avenged the man, in a twisted, indirect way. I wasn't okay with doing all that and leaving the job incomplete.

A little weakly, I pushed myself to standing. "Can you put some coffee on? I've gotta get to work."

It would take much longer, but no way in hell was I using any more magic on that computer tonight. I may have been exhausted, but, magic or no magic, Clarence Hemlock: Computer Wizard had a reputation to maintain.

Douglas Smith is a multi-award-winning Canadian author, described by Library Journal as "one of Canada's most original writers of speculative fiction." His fiction has been published in twenty-seven languages and thirty-five countries. His books include the novel, The Wolf at the End of the World, *the collections,* Chimerascope *and* Impossibilia, *and the writer's guide,* Playing the Short Game: How to Market & Sell Short Fiction. *Doug is a three-time winner of Canada's Aurora Award, and has been a finalist for the Astounding Award, CBC's Bookies Award, Canada's juried Sunburst Award, and France's juried Prix Masterton and Prix Bob Morane. You can read more about him and his work at smithwriter.com*

About this story, Douglas says: "I loved Jack London as a kid. Loved any stories about animals, really, which perhaps explains my fascination with shapeshifter stories. Every society around the world has had (or still has) shapeshifter legends. Were-wolves in France, were-tigers in India, were-lions in Africa. Simply put, wherever there are animals, there are legends of people who can change into them. Which led me to the question: what sort of shapeshifter would live in a modern city?"

There's a reason Douglas Smith has been published so widely and received so much acclaim – I could wax eloquent about the depth of his characters or gush about his innovative ideas, but I'd rather just let you read the story and discover his work for yourself.

Out of the Light

Douglas Smith

The morgue door swung open. Jan Mirocek hesitated at the threshold, clinging to the hallway's bright comfort. Ahead in the dark room, under a lonely cone of light, Detective Garos loomed over a shroud-covered corpse. Jan glared up at the single ceiling bulb. *Forty watts max*, he thought. He turned to a clerk slouched at a desk in the hall. "Got any more light?"

The man just shrugged. "Our guests don't do much reading."

Scowling, Jan stepped inside. The door clicked shut behind him, cutting the light even more. He cursed and pulled a small flashlight from a coat pocket, his breathing slowing as the beam brightened his path. *I can do this*, he thought. Trying not to look into the shadows, he walked to Garos.

Morgues didn't bother Jan. He knew death. And corpses.

He just wanted more light.

Garos eyed the flashlight, but the big man didn't comment. "Good to see you in action again, hunter. It's been a while since... last time." His beefy hand swallowed Jan's.

Last time. At least, old friend, you have the decency to leave it at that, Jan thought. "I'm retired, Andreas. Why'd you call me?" Ignoring the frown from Garos, he studied the contours of the white shroud. Slim, short, female.

Garos shrugged then turned to the corpse. "White female, early thirties. Found about one this morning – just twelve hours ago – on a well-lit, still-busy, Toronto street."

Stabbing his beam into dark corners, Jan pulled two extra flashlight batteries from his pocket. He shook them in his hand, calmed by the clicking noise. "So? What do you need me for?"

"You tell me." Garos pulled back the sheet.

Maybe it was the light. Or the darkness. Or perhaps seeing Garos in a professional role again had brought her back, brought it all back. He looked down, and *she* was there. Her face. The way it used to be in the mornings – peaceful – beautiful.

Then the face shifted into someone else – some*thing* else. Jan stared at the desiccated corpse of a stranger, black sunken eye sockets and cheeks, lips pulled back from rotting gums, white hair framing gray translucent skin. The shadows closed in and with them, his terror. He ran from the room.

◆

Ten years old. Lying in bed beside his brother Pyotr, in their house in the woods. His mother's voice rose and fell in her sing-song way of telling stories. But these stories were not of frog princes, or bears and honey pots, or little girls chasing rabbits down holes. These were... different.

"To begin his change, the werewolf put on a belt of wolf skin, then drank water from a wolf's paw-print," their mother whispered. Jan looked at Pyotr. The younger boy was wide-eyed. Jan smiled. *These are stories*, he thought. *Just stories.*

◆

Five minutes after leaving the morgue, Jan sat huddled at a window table of the first bar he had found. The afternoon sun of a Toronto winter did little to remove the chill he felt. A familiar face peered inside. Moments later, Garos eased his bulk into a chair beside him. "You okay?"

Jan lied with a nod. "For a second, I saw…" Her name caught in his throat and he swallowed. "I saw Stasia's face."

Garos frowned, his eyebrows forming a single bushy line. An old woman in Sicily had once told Jan such eyebrows were a sign of the *lupomanari*. She had missed the true signs in her own son. He killed nine people before Jan and Garos had brought him down.

"I shouldn't have called you," Garos said.

"I'm okay!" Jan snapped. Garos looked away. *No, you shouldn't have*, Jan thought, *you of all people*. Jan stared at his hands gripping his beer as if it were a beast about to leap at his throat. He held life that way now, a wild thing to be feared, never trusted to lie quietly at his feet. "Who was she?"

Garos said a name. It meant nothing to Jan. He looked up. "Why *did* you call me, Andreas?"

"Did that look like a fresh corpse to you?" Garos asked.

"The rotting doesn't mean it was done by a shifter."

"Come on, Jan. We saw the same rapid body decay in shifter victims back home."

"Any 'bodies' we saw were in pieces and mostly eaten." *Her* body would've been too, if he had been able to bring himself to see it. "This one was intact. That's no were-beast."

Looking around, Garos lowered his voice. "We've had other killings, similar to this. We're barely keeping a lid on it."

Jan swallowed. "What's similar about them?"

"Victims killed at night on bright, busy streets. No robbery. Victims in good health. No drugs or sign of sexual assault. No violence except some contusions around the throat, but death wasn't by strangulation, and…" Garos leaned forward. "…and the corpses rot within hours."

"Any pattern to the killings?"

"None I can see. Both genders, all ages and professions. All over downtown. The only consistency is the body decay and autopsy results, plus the time of night and type of locations."

"Anything else?"

"A witness saw a guy standing over this body. She says she chased him into a dead-end alley. No door, window, fire escape. Nowhere to hide. But also no suspect – the alley was empty."

Jan felt cold. "That still doesn't say shifter."

"Put it with the body decay, it says something weird."

"You believe her story?"

"She gave a description. We're checking it out. And her."

"I'll bet your theory went down well with the brass."

Garos snorted. "I keep my own counsel. They're not from the old country. Don't believe as we do, haven't seen what we have." He stared at Jan. "I need your help."

Jan avoided his eyes. "I came to this country, to a big city, to escape the beasts of the night, Andreas. They don't come to the cities. You don't have a shifter. Even if you did, I can't help you. And you know why."

They sat not speaking, Jan's shame burning him. "Well, I had to try," Garos said as he stood. He looked at Jan. "I know what she was to you. I know you blame yourself. But she knew the risks." He squeezed Jan's shoulder. "It's not your fault, Janoslav. Give yourself a break for God's sake."

He walked to the door, then stopped and looked back. "What if you're wrong?"

Jan stared at him, puzzled. "What do you mean?"

"What if I do have a *kallikantzari*? A beast of the night in your big safe city. What then, hunter?" Not waiting for an answer, Garos turned and left. Jan stayed until the winter sun sank too low. Walking home, he watched the shadows all the way.

◆

Fifteen years old. Returning home from friends, far too late, through winter woods oddly silent. The house dark, even the light in the front room not burning. The door open, tilted at a strange angle. His heart leapt. He ran.

He burst past the ruined entrance to stumble in the dark and fall amongst bloody bodies. His parents. Upstairs, Pyotr's bed empty, room in disarray. Outside again, father's rifle in hand, following prints in the snow. The prints of the beast.

He found it near the quarry. Half-human, yellow eyes looked up from where it fed on his brother. He raised the rifle.

His childhood died. The hunter was born.

◆

After leaving the restaurant, Jan walked home to his apartment over his book store on Queen West. His place was small, but he'd left most of his possessions behind in the old country. Too many memories tied to them. Besides, he liked this area. Lots of shops and bars that stayed open late. Plenty of neon.

Plenty of light.

Once home, he checked that every light in every room was on. He read for a while after dinner then went to bed early as usual. Two flashlights lay on a table beside the bed. He made sure they both worked, then he lay down leaving a lamp on. Maybe tonight he could sleep. Maybe he was tired enough. Closing his eyes, he prayed for escape from dreams.

He awoke screaming her name, sitting bolt upright on sweat-soaked sheets. Sobbing, he fell on his side. There, bathed in light that never touched the night world inside him, he prayed again for deliverance from his darkness.

◆

Twenty-five years old, in a Paris bistro, a stack of papers from around the world beside him. Serial killings got good play. And sometimes the signs were there that spoke to him of shifters. He sat forward. Like this one. Athens paper, one week old. He paid his bill and left, heading for the nearest travel agent.

He had hunted were-bears in Norway and were-tigers in India. He carried a ragged scar on his thigh from a leopard shifter in Kenya. Towns paid a man well to be rid of a beast, a man who knew the signs and was brave – or foolish – enough to follow them.

Jan Mirocek had become such a man.

◆

The morning sun found Jan curled shivering in an armchair in his living room, a flashlight clutched to his chest. Jan thought about the old times and about what he'd become. He realized that he didn't like himself anymore. He realized also, to his surprise, that he had known this for a long time.

Finding his phone, he punched Garos's number, taking vindictive pleasure in waking him. Garos swore, listened, then gave a phone number for the witness and directions to the dead-end alley. Jan swore back when Garos thanked him for the third time. Promising to keep in touch, Jan hung up.

Hell, just like old times. Grabbing his coat, he checked the pockets for his flashlight and batteries, then stepped out into a cold but bright February morning.

◆

Twenty-five, in an Athens bar. Listening to a young cop named Garos complain. "They won't let me talk to the press."

Jan nodded. "They always hush it up."

"Damn bureaucrats. Well, thanks for the lead."

Jan shrugged. "Thanks for backing me up. I probably wouldn't be alive otherwise. Didn't figure on two of them."

"We worked well together," the big man said.

Jan looked at him. "I'm thinking of taking on a partner."

Garos grinned.

◆

The alley was as Garos had said. Nothing but a few bits of trash. A neon sign over a bricked-up door at the end of the alley advised that "Clancy's Eatery" was now on the next street.

"You the guy who called me?" a voice said from behind him.

Jan turned, startled. She stood at the entrance to the alley. Five-six maybe, short brown hair, long black coat over a slim figure. "Kate Lockridge. You called me, right?"

Jan walked up to her. "Jan Mirocek. Thanks for coming."

"You don't look like a cop."

She had nice eyes, he decided. "Friend of one. Garos."

"Big guy from last night? He was okay." She looked Jan over. "Okay, let's talk. But not here. Gives me the creeps. I know a place nearby. Lousy food but great coffee." She started to move to the street, then stopped, scanning the alley again.

"Something wrong?"

She shrugged. "Place seemed brighter last night. Guess it's coming in here out of the sunlight. And things are always different in the dark, right?" She walked to the street.

Yeah, he thought, *things are different in the dark.*

◆

Thirty years old, in a little tavern in a little village in Poland, waiting for Garos to get to the point.

Garos coughed. "Mara and I, we're getting married."

Jan had seen this coming. He nodded. "And you want out."

Garos reddened but nodded back.

"I wish the best for you both, Andreas. You know that."

Garos smiled and shook his hand. "Thank you. These have been good years, my friend, but Mara needs a different life."

And I need a new partner, Jan thought.

◆

Late afternoon. *The Big Mistake* was almost empty. They sat at a sunny window table in the long narrow tavern. A jungle of neon signs, each a visual scream of a beer brand, colored the dark room in a random rainbow. Kate called to the bartender. "Two coffees, Harry." She turned to Jan. "So what do you want?"

"Garos asked for help on these… this killing." He watched a corner of her mouth curl up. "We worked together in Europe."

"How so?"

"I was an advisor on one of his cases." He hurried on before she could probe any further. "So tell me what you saw."

Her story was the same. "…I reach the alley and there's no one, nothing. Including no way out. Well, you saw, right?"

Jan nodded and sighed. He asked a few more questions, but it added nothing to the story. "Listen, sorry I wasted your time. Let me buy the coffees." He reached for his wallet.

"So is this body rotting like the others?" she asked. Jan stopped in mid-motion and looked at her. She smiled. "I'm a reporter for the *Toronto Star*, Mr. Mirocek. We need to talk."

Jan sat back again. A reporter, covering the killings. For a moment, despite the sunshine, he felt an old darkness close in.

◆

Thirty-one. Working alone again. He met her in a village in Poland, a reporter up from Warsaw to cover the killings in the town. Her name was Stasia. He trained her. He loved her.

A year later, she was dead.

Harry brought refills while Jan gathered his thoughts. A bluff, trying to see how he'd react? No. She might guess that the separate killings were linked but not about the body decay. "How'd you know about the corpse?" he asked when Harry had left.

"Corpses," she corrected. "Got a source in the Coroner's office who likes to supplement his income." She leaned forward. "That's why Garos called you, isn't it? You know why the bodies are rotting like that, right?" Her voice was eager.

Jan began to growl a denial but stopped. What could she do? No paper would print it. Besides, he didn't believe it himself. He shrugged. "You're right. I've seen those signs before."

She flicked on a micro-recorder. "What's it mean?"

"It's a sign of a shifter killing," he said, straight-faced.

Her brow furrowed. In a very pretty way, he thought. "Shifter killing? What's that?" she asked.

"Shape-shifters. Garos and I used to hunt them. He thinks you saw one."

Pause. "Shape-shifters?" Her eagerness melted into a dead-pan then hardened into a glare. "Like a were-wolf?"

"Shifters aren't limited to wolves."

She clicked off the recorder and stuffed it back in her purse with a near ferocity. "A were-beast. Right. Thank you for the coffee, Mr. Mirocek." She stood up and grabbed her coat.

To his surprise, he realized that he wanted her to stay. "So how do you explain the rapid decay? How did the Coroner?"

She bit her lower lip. "I can't. Neither could they."

Jan stood and faced her. "I can." He could smell her perfume, a hint of vanilla.

She stared at him then shook her head and sighed. "Twenty minutes, no more." She sat down, arms folded.

An hour later, Jan sat back, having summarized his life story. He had left out the part about Stasia. Kate looked hard at him. "Jan, I'm certain you believe every word you just said. I also know it can't possibly be true."

"Does it matter? The *Star* wouldn't print it anyway."

She groaned. "Okay, so Garos thinks we have a were-beast in Toronto. Because of this corpse decay, right?"

"Plus the time of the murders. Most shifters assume animal form only at night, to hide in the dark. Out of the light. But actually, beyond that, I don't think it fits with a shifter."

"You mean you don't believe Garos either? Why not?"

"Shifters live where their animal form is common. Then if seen, they aren't viewed as anything unusual. So were-tigers live in areas with tigers, were-wolves with real wolves."

"So?"

"So what animals are common in downtown Toronto?"

"Dogs and cats, for starters."

"Yeah, but not running free, which they'd need to be."

"How about birds? Maybe it's a were-pigeon," she said.

"Very funny. Too small. So are raccoons from the ravines."

"What's size got to do with it?"

"Mass-energy conservation. It has to be as big as us."

"Sounds like we've run out of animals," she said.

"That's what I think. No such beast."

"So what about the corpse decay?"

Jan frowned. "I don't know. I can't explain that." He looked at her. "It almost sounds as if you believe me now."

Kate shrugged. "I've heard worse. You meet all sorts of weirdoes on these streets."

"Thanks. I love being tolerated."

She grinned at him. "You want to stay for dinner?"

He looked outside. The sun had set and streetlights were winking into life. He should leave. But the area was well lit. Lots of neon. And Kate was smiling at him. "I'd like that," he said. He just wished she didn't remind him so much of Stasia.

◆

Thirty-two years old. Sunday. A small church outside Budapest. Stasia, tall and fair beside him, a hunter for a year now. At the altar in the otherwise empty church stood Father Karman. Their prey. "His parish suspects," Jan whispered.

Stasia nodded. "But simple tourists like us don't, right?"

The priest turned from the altar and noticed them. He smiled. "Are you here for Mass?" he called.

Jan hesitated. His Catholic upbringing made this hard. A priest in a church. He could at least let the man hold a last mass. They should be safe. Karman needed either time or the taste of blood to shift. Jan nodded. Stasia looked at him, puzzled. "After Mass, outside the church," he whispered.

During the Liturgy of the Word, Jan felt in his jacket for his gun. Stasia's presence at a capture still made him uneasy. As they approached the altar for Communion, Karman stared hard at Jan. He turned his back to pour the wine. The communion began.

After the ceremony, Karman took the cup from them and turned back to the altar. Only then did Jan notice another cup on the altar. The one from which the priest had drunk. Jan's eyes froze on a drop of liquid hanging red and thick on its lip.

Thick as blood.

Jan struggled to his feet, but the room swam. He fell, panic rising in him. The wine. Stasia screamed his name. A face loomed before him, cruel, already bestial, the reek of blood on its foul breath. Jan fumbled for his gun but the beast struck him hard on the temple. Darkness took him.

♦

As Harry brought Kate and Jan their dinners, Jan noticed an old man sitting in the back, out of the light. He wouldn't have seen him except that the man gestured to Jan with a jerky motion of a stiffened hand. Jan turned to Harry. "Who's that?"

Harry looked over. "Solly? Street person. Comes in sometimes. I'll give him a coffee, sandwich maybe. Don't know how he stays alive. He's usually in the shelter by now. Doesn't like the streets after dark. Last time he stayed late, I had to walk him there after we closed. Only way I could get him out."

Jan stood up. "I'm going to see what he wants."

Solly was a small round man. Round bald pate ringed by gray scraggly hair. Circle of a face under stubble and dirt. Rounded shoulders under a filthy coat, once an actual color, now unknowable. Round balls of hands, fingers twisted in, peeking surprisingly clean from tattered sleeves, guarding an empty coffee cup. Jan smiled then struggled to maintain it as he caught the smell. Solly waved at a chair across from him.

Jan sat down. "Harry says your name is Solly."

One eye was almost shut. The other pinned Jan then darted over the room. "Harry's is a good place. Stays the same, you know? S'important, you know? Some places – change. Don't like that. Can't tell if they're just different, or…" He fixed Jan with that eye again. "Heard you talking." Jan glanced back to where Kate chatted to Harry. Not a word reached Jan. Solly glared as if he read Jan's mind. "Heard you!" He pounded the table with a crippled hand. "Solly's seen things," he rasped. "Seen things." He looked around again, then lowered his head.

Jan waited, but Solly said no more. Standing, Jan started to walk away when a wheezy whisper stopped him.

"…out of the light. Gotta know the signs."

Jan turned back to the old man. "What did you say?"

Solly's head was still down. "Remember. S'important." Hunched over his empty cup, he sat muttering to himself.

Kate looked up when Jan returned. "What'd he want?"

Jan shrugged. "You've got me. Get him a coffee on my tab, will you, Harry?" Harry nodded and left.

They ate and talked. "So if you hunt shifters," Kate said, "and they don't come to the city, why do you live here?"

Jan looked out to where the gathering dark fed on a dying day. "I live here because they don't. I don't hunt them anymore. I got someone killed, Kate. Someone who trusted me."

Kate bit her lip. "I'm sorry," she said. They sat silent for a moment, then she gave a small smile. "Anybody could understand why you'd want to get away from those things."

Jan looked back to her. "I wonder if I have."

"What do you mean?"

"Every civilization has had shape-shifter legends. I've always wondered why no such myth exists for our modern cities."

"Why would such creatures live in a city? Why not stay in the wild? Less chance of being seen," she said.

"Also less food. They're predators who prefer human flesh." He shuddered, remembering. "There's more of that in a city."

"Sure, but you eliminated all the animal options."

He stared out at the night. "This is a different jungle. Maybe we've created a new niche, supporting a different predator. Convergent evolution. Its other form may not be animal at all."

"If it's not an animal, what would it be?"

"Don't know, but it's more likely to be seen in a crowded city, so its other shape would need to be downright mundane."

"But *what?*" Kate repeated.

Jan looked out to where shadows fought pale neon. He wanted to say that it would be a thing at home with concrete and glass as a wolf was with earth and forest. A thing that breathed ozone like a summer breeze and held metal in its heart and electricity in its veins. A thing that not only lived in this realm of the lonely but fed on it. But he just said, "I don't know."

Kate shook her head then checked the time. "Oops. I've got to go. There was another witness last night – a hooker. She won't talk to the cops but she's meeting me at midnight." She looked at Jan and bit her lip.

"Why don't I come with you?" he asked.

She broke into a huge smile. "Great!" She put on her coat while Jan wondered what he had just done. Solly shuffled over. "I also told Harry I'd walk Solly to the shelter," she said.

Solly peered outside. "We take Talbot?"

Talbot was little more than an alley, with no lights. Jan shivered. "Let's keep to well-lit streets. We'll use Richmond." As Solly started to argue, Harry called Jan to the phone.

It was Garos. "Janoslav? Did you meet Kate Lockridge?"

"Yeah. I think she's on the level, but she's a reporter. She, uh, knows about the corpse decay and the other victims."

Garos swore. "We checked her description of last night's suspect." He paused. "Jan, it matches a prior victim."

Jan felt a sudden coldness in his gut. "Victim? That doesn't make sense. How could it be a dead guy?"

"Jan, she was at the scene of the most recent killing and described a victim from another. Now you say she has further knowledge of these deaths. We'll be talking to her again. In the meantime, be careful around her." Garos hung up.

Jan stared at the neon signs over the bar, trying to lose himself in their colored swirls. A hand touched his shoulder. He jumped and turned to find Kate, Solly in tow. Jan's face must have betrayed something. She looked puzzled. "What's wrong?"

Jan shook his head. "Nothing," he lied. "Let's go."

Waving good-bye to Harry, they stepped out onto Richmond and turned east. The snow had stopped, and the sidewalks were slushy. "We take Talbot?" Solly asked again.

"Richmond, Solly, or you go alone," Jan said. Solly glared but fell silent, hanging by the curb and scanning the street as they walked. Jan kept thinking of Garos's call. They reached Jarvis. A young blond woman stepped from a doorway, long white coat over a short red leather skirt, black stockings and boots.

"There's Carla," Kate said and started towards the girl.

A shout made them turn. Solly was backing away, wide-eyed and pointing a shaking hand to something above their heads. "No! Solly knows the signs. You won't get Solly!" Terror on his face, he ran onto the street. Jan spun back. Above the doorway where Carla stood open-mouthed, a neon sign glared "Franny's Tavern." The first word was red, the second blue.

The blue one was moving.

In an eye-blink, the letters slid down the wall to form a glowing pool on the sidewalk. In another blink, a humanoid shape rose radiant white from the pool – female torso, face, hair, the shape of clothing, then colors, facial details.

The face of the murder victim from last night.

"Carla! Behind you!" Kate yelled.

A spear of light stabbed from the creature's hand, striking Kate full in the chest and Jan in the shoulder. Electricity flamed into him. Numbed, he collapsed to watch as the thing grabbed Carla by the throat and lifted her into the air.

Slush seeping into his clothes, choking on ozone, Jan tried to move. A violent tremor shook Carla. Jan's arms twitched. The creature held Carla higher, its glow brightening, colors cycling. Jan could feel his legs again. Carla fell limp, and the thing slapped her down like a wet towel. It turned to Kate.

Gasping, Jan heaved himself to his knees and lunged forward. Somehow he got his hands under Kate's armpits and dragged her just out of reach. "Get up!" he cried.

"Can't... move," she gasped. He pulled her to her knees. The thing's colors were fading, its features melting back into a smooth humanoid shape. It shimmered and changed again. And became Carla. The Carla-thing smiled. It stepped toward them.

Inches from its outstretched arms, Jan hauled Kate up and they lurched into the road. Stumbling but with returning strength, Jan scanned the street. From a dark alley across the road a small round figure waved, a jerky motion from a stiff arm.

Half dragging Kate, Jan struggled towards Solly. Footsteps sounded behind them. The back of his neck tingled as if an electrical charge was building at his back. He pushed Kate into the alley as something brushed his coat. Shoving a trash can behind him, he heard a thud and a sound no human throat ever made. The alley was dark, and Jan's eyes still burned from the electrical flash. Ahead, Solly's gray form disappeared to the right. Jan moved along the wall, Kate's hand in his.

"Now that thing looks like Carla!" she panted.

"It takes the form of what it kills," Jan gasped. *That* was why her description of the suspect had matched an earlier victim.

A hand grabbed Jan from the darkness and yanked them both sideways. He could see nothing but he knew the smell. Solly pulled them along. Jan could feel walls to either side. They stopped. Jan reached ahead in the dark and touched another wall.

Solly had led them into a dead end.

"No!" Jan screamed. His nightmare seized him. Trapped in the dark with a monster. And with a woman who trusted him.

◆

Thirty-two. In a church basement outside Budapest. Waiting to die. Total darkness. Lying on damp earth, bound hand and foot. Stale smell of mildew stinging his throat. As he fought to awaken, a scream sliced the black, clearing the flames of pain in his head like a bucket of ice water. Stasia.

He raged against his bonds. She screamed again. "Jan! Oh God, no! No! Help me!" Jan threw himself forward and managed to roll once. Her cries were clearer. But so was another sound.

The sound of something feeding.

Jan threw himself again but something held him fast. He could do nothing but lie in the dark, listening to the beast feed on the still-living Stasia. Praying in the dark for her screams to cease. Praying in the dark for her to die.

An eternity passed. Then only the grunts of the beast remained. The stench of rotting meat grew strong. A huge shape moved in the darkness. Moved closer. Jan screamed.

Blinding light suddenly flooded the room, and the roar of the were-wolf echoed in the roar of gunshots. Blood, thick and black and hot, struck Jan's face as Garos shouted his name.

In the dark alley, Jan shoved Solly away and turned to run back. Solly grabbed him, holding on with surprising strength. "No! Stay here. *Out of the light*. Solly knows!"

A glow began at the entrance to the dead-end, but Jan still couldn't see. Kate's hand found his. "Jan?" she said.

Hearing her fear, his panic fled, replaced by a feeling of resolve he had almost forgotten. He squeezed her hand. She would not die. "Solly, talk to me. Tell me what you know!"

Solly's voice quavered. "It don't like the dark. We're safe here. Right?" At this, Kate groaned.

Jan swore, his mind racing. Light was the key. "It must feed off electricity, hiding as part of signs. When you chased it last night, it joined with the sign in the alley."

"That's why the alley was brighter last night," Kate said.

"Sunlight must sustain it in the day, plus electricity. But when night comes..." Jan stopped. When night comes, it needed more. It needed its real food: human life force.

The light at the entrance grew and the glowing form of Carla appeared. "I thought it doesn't like the dark," Kate whispered.

Jan swore. "It must still be hungry and figures we're worth the risk. Solly, how long can it go without light?"

"Five minutes," he whined, "but a lot more if it just ate."

"Wonderful," Kate said.

Twenty paces away now, the thing lit the entire area. Its glow was dimmer but Jan doubted that would save them. At least now he could see. He looked around, and his heart leapt. The wall behind them and the walls on either side each held a door.

Jan grabbed the door handle behind them. Locked. So was the one to their right. He tried the last one. The handle turned a bit. He leaned on it and heard a click. He threw his weight against the door and it squealed open with rusty protests.

"Inside!" Kate cried, rushing forward, Solly in hand.

"No!" Jan grabbed her, an idea forming. The thing was ten paces away. Pulling out his flashlight, he stepped into the room and flashed the beam around. The stock room of a store, twenty feet square. Not much space to maneuver. Could he do it? Could he finally face his darkness? By walking into it? He turned back. The thing was five paces away. He aimed his light at it.

"No!" Solly cried. "It eats light!"

Jan ignored him. "Kate, take Solly into the corner. After I lead it inside, close the door and don't open it." Kate turned pale but nodded and pulled Solly back. Jan stepped up, playing his beam over the creature. It turned to him. Keeping his light on it, he backed into the room. Darkness closed in on him and with it his fear. What had he done?

The thing stepped inside. The door slammed shut behind it.

It stopped and looked back. Its mouth opened, and a sound like fingers tapping fine crystal filled the room. And somehow, in that sound Jan heard its hunger and its pain. A wave of empathy flooded him. They were alike. Hunters. Hiding their true shape. Fearing the night. The creature reached for him. *I'm sorry*, Jan thought. He turned off his light.

The thing trembled, and its aura dimmed. But then Carla's features and clothing faded, seeming to melt back into its body. A featureless human form remained, glowing blue-white.

It's conserving energy, Jan thought. It no longer needed to pretend to be human. He swallowed. How intelligent was it?

A deadly game of tag began – the thing pursuing with the same plodding step – Jan retreating, avoiding corners, always leaving two paths of escape. With each passing minute, the thing's aura dimmed, fading to blue, then yellow, then red.

Finally it stopped, arms drooping. Jan sighed and relaxed.

He noticed too late that the arms weren't just drooping.

They were growing.

Both arms flashed out, three times normal length, easily covering the space between the thing and Jan. Taken by surprise, Jan dove aside but a hand brushed his thigh. Electricity numbed his leg. He fell. Looming over him, the thing reached down.

And stopped. Its colors cycled the spectrum then faded to gray. A sound like breaking glass fled a suddenly grotesque mouth. Its feet melted into a pool. The arms flowed back into a shrinking torso. Soon only the pool remained, faintly glowing.

Jan walked to it. The pool bulged once toward him, then its last light died and Jan stood in the dark. He waited before flicking on his light. The pool was a dull gray. He kicked, and it shattered with a crystal cry, imploding into sparkling powder.

He opened the door, and Kate threw her arms around him. Back on the street, Solly checked every bit of neon in sight, then fixed Jan with that eye. "Gotta know the signs," he said.

Jan phoned the police about Carla's body and left a message for Garos to call.

"So what now, hunter?" Kate asked.

Solly stared up at Jan. "You gonna get the others, too?"

Jan and Kate turned to him. "Others?" Kate groaned.

Jan shrugged then looked at her. "I could use a partner." She said nothing but took his hand as they walked Solly home.

They took Talbot.

◆

Thirty-five. A midnight street. He waits in the dark, watching the signs. She waits beside him. He knows the ways of the beast; she knows these streets. A town pays well to be rid of its creatures of the night. Creatures that breathe ozone like a summer breeze, wear glass for skin, and burn electricity in their veins. Creatures that feed on this realm of the lonely.

Once, he shunned the dark where shadows hide their secrets. Now he stalks the night streets, a shadow himself slipping from alley to alley. Now he keeps to the dark.

And stays out of the light.

J.L. Madore is a multi-genre romance novelist of 14 full-length, fantasy, paranormal, and time-slip historical novels. She loves to twist alpha heroes and kick-ass heroines into chaotic, hilarious, fast-paced, magical situations and make them really work for their happy endings.

*About this story, J.L. says: "*Siren's Call *was written as a challenge to myself. I have written fifty full-length fantasy and paranormal novels under two pen names and never tried to write shorter fiction. When I saw the call for a short story, I gave it a try. It took a bit to wrap my head around how to keep the story compact and still make it engaging for readers, but I love urban fantasy. The elements and tropes are constant whether in a short story or novel-length and, of course, Max and Ellie were fun characters to write. I hope you love it."*

Is the voice that stops you in your tracks an actor or a siren? And what about the song that transports you to another place. You may want to think twice before you follow their song – as you'll soon see, not all sirens lurk in the shallow waters or rocky shores.

Siren's Call
J.L. Madore

Max Hawken scanned the half-dressed, leather and chain crowd smoking outside the busy club. Even with everyone wearing dusters, guyliner, and silver skull rings, it wasn't hard to separate the hardcore lifers from civilian wannabes and groupies. How did shirtless men flexing their muscles and women panting over cut abs justify swigging cheap booze and subjecting themselves to emo-screamo music that did nothing but offend the senses?

"You lost, fancy man?"

Max met the gaze of the nipple-pierced male with painted-on leather pants and straightened to his full six-foot-four. After being on the road for three days, his heavy stubble, bloodshot eyes, and murderous mood had him looking more Walking Dead than his usual broody stranger, but the welcoming committee got the message.

Suburban tough guy raised his bottle in salute and stepped off.

Disappointing. After identifying his cousin in the morgue an hour ago, bloodying his knuckles to release tension might be to everyone's benefit. Deprived of his first choice of venting outlet, Max selected door number two – liquid sedation, and set his sights for later in the evening on door number three – anonymous sex.

With his mind buzzing and his body numb, the weight of the door caught him by surprise. He eased back and took stock. Solid mahogany, carved with ornate detailing and a ghoulish gargoyle door knocker. It was a thing of beauty. He followed the arching lines of the entrance to the point of the gothic peak centered five feet over the double doors. With stirred curiosity, he entered the building proper.

In his fog of fury, and arriving in the dark, he'd missed the meaning of the club's name.

The Gothic Grind occupied an historic Gothic cathedral.

With his back against the doors, he studied the floorplan. The building was laid out in a standard Latin cross, the long rectangular nave rounded at the far end and two transept sections in the distance opened left and right.

The floor was paved with massive stone slabs, vaulted ceilings reached up three stories, and church pew booths ran up both the outer aisles. He wound his way deeper down the center of the space and passed two beer centers with girls in red corsets serving chilled cans straight out of ice-filled coffins.

Where is the real alcohol?

The further he strode in, the tighter the crush of people became. The conversations of the patrons focused around their excitement for the singer about to perform. The band seemed extremely popular, everyone packing into the nave of the church to get a good view.

Which left fewer people in his way as he zeroed in on the bar.

The music track of tortured cats ended at the same time he slid onto an empty leather barstool and ordered a double bourbon. A four-person band stepped onto the raised stage against the back wall, their arrival met by a round of thunderous applause.

"Ellie! Ellie! Ellie!" the crowd chanted.

An ebony-haired woman in ripped jeans and a black, silk camisole slid her guitar strap over her head and smiled to the crowd. "How's everyone tonight? Having a good time?"

The deafening response rose to the darkness far above, ancient acoustics still in prime working order. As glad as Max was to have a drink in hand, he opted to leave and come back after hours. He was in no mood for this.

He downed his tumbler and ate up the burn.

Pulling a couple of bills from his wallet he tossed them on the bar and stood to leave.

"Glad to hear it," Ellie said, smiling out at her fans. "I'm starting with a new one. Let me know if you like it… keep it to yourself if you don't."

The crowd laughed, and the drummer clacked his sticks together to count them down.

Max made it twenty feet toward the exit before the woman started to sing. Her voice rooted him to the spot. He was powerless against its effect. Haunting, mystical notes echoed all around, hanging in the air with the allure of the most exotic perfume. The eerie tune played through his body, invaded his senses, woke him in places he'd long forgotten.

He pivoted back to the show, and his body tightened. Power and strength pulsed in his veins and flowed through his tired, worn muscles. Was the woman glowing – or was that a trick of the lighting? Damn, she was tantalizing. Enticing. Sinfully sexy.

What the hell is going on?

The desire that froze him in place was wholly unnatural.

◆

Music was the breath in Ellie's lungs. She didn't think about it, didn't plan it, or need to practice. She opened her mouth, and her heart's emotion soared – the emotion of her heritage. Here, in her place of worship, before the backdrop of the church's massive stained-glass rose window, her muse flowed free. Most fans enjoyed her talent as entertainment, a rare few sensed the 'other' behind it – the truth of her disturbing ancestry.

The heat of a gaze caressed her skin like the stroke of a lover's tongue, and she searched the crowd for its source. The man by the bar was tall, dark, and devastating. A predator. Dangerous. The intensity of his expression exposed the truth.

He sensed who she was – who she truly was.

A lifetime ago, when she was young and foolish, another man had looked at her that way. Had almost destroyed her. She'd mistaken intimate gazes for rapt devotion. He saw through the veils of secrets and loneliness, and she thought he saw *her*. Pent-up regrets resurfaced in a rush.

She couldn't go through that again. She wouldn't.

Distracted as she was, Ellie almost missed Aiden's transition into the next song. The error was unnoticeable, except perhaps to her bandmates.

She fought the urge to run from the stage. Was the chaos in her mind apparent to the hundreds of prying eyes watching her so closely?

The man's stare never left her. Could he see her panic?

To avoid losing herself, she withdrew from the dark stranger and focused on the set. Working the stage, she seduced the crowd, inviting them to join the tunes they knew, and giving them the performance they came for.

The heat of his gaze remained a tangible touch, a caress over her naked curves.

Focus, Ellie! She steeled herself against his effect and kept up the act. The sooner the set was over, the sooner she'd dissolve into the shadows and pull herself together.

◆

Hawken felt the loss of Ellie's attention like the removal of a serrated blade from his chest. It hurt. It tore at him. It infuriated him. What kind of enchantress was she? He glanced back at his empty tumbler sitting on the bar. Was he drugged? That was the only thing that made sense. In all his years in the military, and private security after, he'd never been taken so off-guard, and he'd certainly never fallen victim to the wiles of a woman.

He studied the enraptured faces of the crowd. Were they *all* drugged? Why? What purpose would it serve? Maybe that's what Clay had wanted him to expose. He wished his cousin had given him more to go on than *the Gothic Grind*. What did that mean? Was his killer tied to this place? Was Clay dead because of something he uncovered here?

A vast difference separated being tight-lipped and hanging someone out to blow in the wind. Max outed his phone and read the text again, as if some new insight would appear to him

—the Gothic Grind.

Screw you, Clay.

Okay, cursing the dead guy wouldn't win him any points.

That sucked more than anything. He and Clay were the last two members of the Hawken family, and with them married to their work, there would be no others to carry on the name. A shame, really, the Hawken's line boasted a long history of brave, upstanding men.

The song cut abruptly short and broke his mental meandering.

The music clamored to a halt.

The sudden vacuum of unnatural silence brought his instincts raging to the fore.

His raven-haired temptress dropped to the stage.

A woman's scream pierced the bubble of silence, and the place erupted. He raced toward the stage, shoving people to the side in the flood of pandemonium. What happened?

The band rushed toward the singer as the crowd turned in a panicked frenzy. The floor thundered with the pounding of feet racing to the exits. He pushed closer and saw the blood covering the singer's bare arms. The drummer bent over her.

The *crack* of a shot rang out, and the drummer went down.

Shit. A shooter. Hawken followed the trajectory of the shot into the shadows of the arched ceiling. He drew his Sig and returned a couple of ineffective rounds into the darkness.

He pointed to where the attack originated and yelled, "He's up there. Get the bastard."

He didn't know the layout of the building well enough to find the access doors to the upper levels in the dark. Instead of trying, he went for the singer and hoped his bluff of backup convinced the shooter to bug out while he could.

The woman's still form sprawled on the raised platform, blood pooling on the stage. Her drummer lay on top of her, dead, his gray matter splattered across the stage. The other two, were in shock, blood-sprayed but seemingly unharmed.

"You two, off the stage. Now!"

He shoved the still-warm corpse to the side and scooped the woman into his arms. He had no time to examine her wounds, they needed cover. Following the two musicians through the stage exit, he searched for a defendable place to lockdown.

"What's in there?"

The bass player blinked blankly. "The staff room?"

Good enough. "Open the door."

The guy wasn't tracking, and he didn't have time to hold his hand. "Open the fucking door before your girl bleeds out."

That must've sunk in, because the door got opened. He pushed his way inside and lay the woman on the table in the center of the room. Lifting the blood-soaked camisole, he assessed how much shit they faced. The entrance wound was small, but the exit wound was large and messy. The bullet had torn through her body at a downward angle and had likely done serious damage to her organs.

"Call 911."

◆

Ellie rose to the surface of consciousness, dizzy and nauseous. In the swirling darkness, she followed the husky timbre of a man's voice. Something about him called to her. She shivered, the cool of the night wreaking havoc on her damp, heated skin. Her insides ached, but even now, her healing took hold. Her eyes flickered, meeting the gaze of the dangerous stranger. "No ambulance."

His brow pinched. "You'll die without medical care."

No, I won't. She needed to focus, which she couldn't do with him assessing her. "Please, leave me."

He barked a laugh. "Not gonna happen."

The wail of sirens in the distance meant someone had already called for help. She lolled her head to the side to find Axel and Bryan. "Where's Aiden? Is he all right?"

Axel shook his head.

"Don't worry about him now," the dark stranger said. "You've got troubles of your own."

"I'm fine." Ellie struggled to sit and lifted her cami to show him her uninjured side. "I fainted when the shooting started, but I'm not hurt."

His gaze narrowed. "Bullshit."

"Willowbrook Police Department," a man shouted down the hall. A moment later, two uniformed officers stepped inside. "Everyone all right?"

Ellie ran a hand over her face. "A man shot up my club. No, we're not all right."

The officer nodded, looking contrite. "We've got men combing the club. You're safe now. Are you hurt?"

She shook her head. "No, I'm fine."

"That's a lot of blood," he said, pointing.

"Her drummer collapsed on her," the stranger said. "You'll find his body on the stage."

"Did anyone see where the shots came from?"

The stranger gave her one last scrutinizing glare and nodded. "I'll walk you through it."

"And you are?" the officer said, exchanging his gun for a notepad.

"Max Hawken."

Ellie's heart tripped in her chest. "Any relation to Clay Hawken?"

"Yeah, he's my… *was* my cousin."

The officer's expression fell. "Everyone at the station is real shook up, Mr. Hawken. Our condolences. Clay was one hell of a cop and a great friend."

Ellie's breath froze in her lungs. *Was?* Clay was *dead?*

◆

Hawken ran the boys in blue through the scene and left them to their investigation. The shooter must have known the layout of the church, because the upper floors were a maze of crawl spaces and rickety stairwells. He knew his way around a gun, too. To hit Ellie from that distance wasn't a Hail Mary shot, but it took skill.

And he *had* hit Ellie. Max had no idea what the hell was going on, but that bullshit about fainting was just that — *bullshit*.

He watched the lying seductress setting out sandwiches and coffee on the bar. Okay, feeding the local PD didn't seem nefarious but obviously she was playing a long game. Maybe Clay caught on to her game and she'd killed him for it.

The image of his cousin in the morgue hit him.

He didn't see her able to inflict that kind of damage, but maybe she had men working for her. Men who fell under her thrall. "Any chance you'll level with me and tell me what actually happened tonight?"

Ellie, freshly showered and dressed in jeans and a t-shirt, gave no indication that a sniper took her down three hours earlier. Ebony hair emphasized her pallid complexion, but no evidence of her injuries remained, no signs of PTSD or shock. She just seemed sad.

"It's been a long night, Mr. Hawken. Help yourself to something to eat."

Despite the gnawing emptiness in his gut, no way would he consume anything she offered. Whatever power she'd held over him while singing had drained away. He preferred to drive his own train, thanks. "Let's stick to the mystery at hand."

If he hadn't felt the weirdly inexplicable pull earlier, he might've bought her heartbroken exhaustion act. She wouldn't ensnare him again. The woman couldn't be trusted.

With a swipe of an unsteady hand, she brushed hair from her face. No wedding ring. No visible tattoos. "What mystery, Mr. Hawken? A madman invaded my home and killed a dear friend of mine. Aiden was sweet. He had talent and plans and... ."

She broke off, staring at the forensic techs and cops working the stage. "I'm sorry about Clay," she said, tears thick in her voice. "I'll miss him, too."

"You knew him?"

Ellie swept her tears away, the private grief in her eyes stirring his insides into a rage. Was he jealous? Jealous of his dead cousin having a relationship with this woman? What was wrong with him?

"I did... we were...," she said, her voice soft.

Okay, that didn't help. He needed to stay objective. He was supposed to find out who killed Clay and why. "Do you know what he was working on that got him killed?"

For a micro-second, the grief in those eyes turned to guilt. "That's something to ask his boss at the station."

Hawken nodded. "I did. It's been a slow month in Willowbrook. Clay had nothing more than a few domestics and stolen property cases. He did, however, tell his partner he was working on something on his private time."

Ellie closed her eyes. Yep. Whatever storm Clay got caught in, this woman stood in the eye. After the night's events, her defenses were down. This was his chance to take advantage. "Did Clay get too close to your secrets? Did he threaten to expose you? You regret he ended up dead, but what, he left you no choice?"

The slap to his face hit with a blur and stung like a bitch. Wild green eyes pegged him with such venom he eased a step back.

"How *dare* you. Clay was my..." Tears welled for another round of heartfelt sorrow. "No. I don't owe you anything, Mr. Hawken. Once the police are finished with you, I want you off my property."

As her long legs put distance between them, he fought the urge to chase after her and apologize. He cursed the adrenaline pumping in his veins. No woman affected him like this. He didn't like it. Not one bit. He touched his cheek, the sting of her fingers hot on his flesh.

Maybe he was off-base about her being behind Clay's death, but he knew one thing for certain – she was hiding something. Maybe a lot of somethings.

♦

Restless and edgy, Ellie abandoned her attempt at sleep and headed to the kitchenette in her loft. For six hours she'd tumbled and tangled in her sheets and felt as refreshed as a battered sock in a dryer. Coffee. She needed coffee — not that caffeine changed anything. Aiden was dead. A fun, slightly neurotic, guy with a love of mountain biking and a bad habit of saying any thought that entered his head, would never offend anyone again. She chose her favorite mug and set it under the nozzle of the coffee machine. Was he aware? Had he suffered? He leaned over her in a moment of concern and took the shot meant to end her life.

Aiden saved her. She owed him everything.

Another man saved her, too. Axel and Bryan said Max stepped into the line of fire, shot back, and ushered them to safety. What did she owe *him*? Unbidden, her body warmed with lusty ideas of how to express her gratitude. The attraction she felt for him was insane, especially after him accusing her of Clay's murder. She didn't blame him. He saw the guilt she felt for getting him killed and misinterpreted it.

It was the way he looked at her during her performance that did her in.

So intense. So hungry.

She shook her head and squeezed her thighs together, fighting the aching depths she refused to feel. Max Hawken was off-limits.

She learned the hard way what happened when she trusted the wrong man.

Aiden was her primary focus. He deserved her full attention.

The police removed his body shortly after four a.m., but his body wasn't all Aiden left on that stage. The last thing she wanted to do was clean up his remains, but she owed him. He deserved respect for his sacrifice.

Bolstering her courage, she sipped her coffee and left the serenity of her private space. The ancient wood floors creaked with her weight, the slight smell of damp in the winding stairwell due to a section of roof needing repair. Maintaining this old place on her own was a full-time job. Going it alone was hard, especially lately.

At the bottom of the stairs, she said good morning to George, her favorite gargoyle, and made her way to the club floor. Her stomach growled. Better to do this on an empty stomach. She'd do right by Aiden and then – "What are *you* doing here?"

Max Hawken straightened from his labors on the stage and submerged her mop in the bucket. Piercing gray eyes met her fury and measured her reaction. "I'm helping."

"I told you to leave. I don't want you here."

His attention lingered too long. It was unnerving. "A crime scene isn't easy to face if you're unaccustomed. I was an ass last night. By way of an apology, I came back to clean up so you wouldn't have to."

She chuckled, though she found none of it funny. "And maybe I'd be so grateful, I'd open my heart and confess all my deep, dark secrets? Who elected you my white knight?"

One side of his mouth quirked up. Max Hawken knew how devastatingly attractive he was with his firm jaw, sculpted lips, and body of a military soldier. This little 'ask forgiveness not permission' routine probably worked on most women.

She wasn't most women.

"Confidence is a quality I hold in high esteem, Mr. Hawken, but arrogance is another story. Having you flash a smile and do a bit of domestic work won't make me swoon and forget you outright accused me of having Clay killed."

He scratched the nape of his neck. "Not my best moment. I'm sorry. In my defense, you aren't telling me the truth, and I owe it to Clay to find his killer. My only lead is a text he sent that led me here."

Ellie swallowed past the thickness at the back of her throat. "What did he say? Please, you have to tell me."

Max studied her a moment. "Let's talk over breakfast. Other than a gas station burrito I had around nine last night, I haven't eaten. I'm getting hangry."

Ellie didn't appreciate the restriction on him answering her questions, but she hadn't been forthright with him either. With the stage cleanup mercifully removed from her to-do list, breakfast sounded like a great idea. No way did she trust herself cooking with this man in her loft — the bed was only fifty feet from her kitchen. "All right, I know a place."

◆

Max let Ellie take the lead and observed her in her natural habitat. Yes, he understood she wasn't a creature in the jungles of the wild, but part of her remained untamed. While Ellie chatted with the servers, and then the cook, assuring them she wasn't hurt last night, he realized she was almost as closed off with them as she was with him. Reevaluating his usual MO, he decided to take another tack. Coming at her head-on hadn't gotten him anything but a sore cheek.

Playing a little quid pro quo might get them further.

Handing the menu back to the server, he flashed a smile. "I'll have the lumberjack breakfast with a large orange juice and an Earl Gray with cream, please."

She noted his order and turned to Ellie. "You want your usual, hon?"

"Please. Thanks, Trace."

When left to their own devices, Max leaned over the glossy tabletop. "I propose that – for Clay's sake – we try again. I'm not blessed with social graces, but I'd like to understand your relationship with him and why he sent me to your bar."

"Is that what happened?" she said, her cheeks paling. "He told you to come to me?"

Max called up the text and showed her the message. Sadness clouded those green eyes, and again it gutted him. She was lying to him – hiding facts that mattered in the death of his cousin. Why wasn't he pinning her up against the wall and forcing the truth from her?

In an instant, his libido inundated him with images of pinning her up against the wall, but it wasn't to ply her for information. His body responded, and he cursed the sudden tightness of his jeans. "I haven't slept in thirty hours, my cousin is dead, and you were shot, then mysteriously healed. Nothing makes sense in my head right now. I've been short-tempered – and will try harder – but maybe you can meet me halfway?"

She sat back in the booth and studied him. "In theory, I might be able to do that."

He chuffed and rapped his knuckles on the table. "Well, don't worry. You haven't overcommitted yourself with that answer."

That, at least, made her smile. "Sorry. Trust is a thing with me. I don't give it often, and I don't take it lightly."

Ahh, so she does know how to be honest. "Something we have in common. In my life, I've trusted three things: the men I served with, my sidearm, and my family. With Clay gone, that list is now down to two."

Her gaze drew him in, and he wondered if any man ever plummeted into the emerald pools of her eyes. She licked her lips, and he followed the tip of her tongue as she glossed her mouth. She noticed him eyeing her, and a ghost of a smile softened her expression. "Clay was your only family?"

"He was."

The server returned with two silver teapots and a bowl of cream and sugar. Ellie dumped two milks into her mug and then poured in her tea. "Were you two close?"

He picked out the creamers and did the same, *tinking* his spoon on the ceramic rim after stirring. "We were only children to our parents. We grew up together more like brothers, hunting, fishing, family picnics, and then, after high school, we took separate paths. His was the law. Mine was the military."

She blew across the surface of her tea. "Do you think he knew his life was in danger?"

"I do." Her guilt returned, but he discarded the possibility she engineered Clay's death.

"What makes you so sure?"

"If not, why send the text? I think the person who killed him might be the same man – or involved with the person who attempted to kill you last night." Max watched her reaction. Typically, a woman with a killer gunning for her looked panicked. She'd glance around the restaurant, case the exits, examine the faces of the other patrons.

Ellie did none of those things.

He leaned forward and tapped the rim of the bowl between them. "You can tell me, Ellie. Was Clay working on something for you? Do you have a stalker? A violent ex? What am I dealing with here?"

She shrugged. "Detective Lambton believes it's a stalker."

"A run of the mill stalker wouldn't have taken down Clay."

"The police will handle it."

"If you think I'll back off, you're crazy. You *will* tell me what you know."

True anger flashed in her eyes. "Despite your enormous ego, Mr. Hawken, *my* business is not *yours*. The family resemblance is striking, but you are *not* Clay. You're not my friend. I don't owe you any explanation."

Despite his irritation, Max was impressed. Ellie played things close to the vest and felt confident she could handle this on her own – even though she obviously couldn't.

◆

They ate their breakfast in silence, and Ellie tasted nothing. After Max picked up the bill, he pressed a warm hand to the small of her back and escorted her to his car. She shivered. The contact of his hand to her body, even through the cotton of her t-shirt, was too intimate. Her heart raced, blood thundering past her eardrums in a rush.

Max Hawken would be her undoing.

When he asked about Clay, his expression remained determined. He wouldn't stop asking. Until he figured out what happened, there would be no derailing him. Why did Clay send him to The Grind? Did he send Max to help her?

Max might end up dead, too. The thought churned her breakfast in a swirl of nausea. He couldn't get involved. She couldn't bear the responsibility of another death on her account.

"Jesus," Max said, pulling into the parking lot of Clay's apartment. "You're white as a ghost. What is it?"

She dropped her head into her hands and bent over her lap.

He brushed gentle circles on her back as she gasped for breath. "Ellie," he said, close to her ear. "You don't know me, and I understand you don't trust me, but I *am* one of the good guys. I don't judge, and I'm a loyal friend. There's no reason to take this all on yourself. I'm here, and I'm not going anywhere."

Him staying should terrify her, but instead – with the timbre of his voice intimately low, and his touch gentle on her back – she wanted to tell him the whole truth. He deserved to know why Clay was helping her. But how did she explain her gift, the crazed obsession it sometimes caused, how she couldn't stop singing even though it drove some men to madness?

Steeling herself, she sat up and met his gaze.

"Hey, there," he said. "You okay?" A storm brewed in his cool gray eyes, but the concern seemed genuine. His slow grin altered the natural rhythm of her heart.

The urge to confide in him was incredible.

No. She couldn't afford weakness. Keeping the particulars to herself was safer for both of them.

"I'm fine," she said, shaking herself inwardly. "It just crashed in on me, you know? Clay. Aiden. The shooting."

His smile hardened, and he shifted sideways in his seat to face her. "I was an interrogator for many years in the military. If you don't want to tell me what's going on, that's one thing, but stop the lies. I'll figure it out one way or another."

In one flowing movement, he pulled the key from the ignition and got out of the car. A cool morning wind smacked her in the face, and she welcomed it. Good.

Despite the ache of wanting that look of warmth back, angry and distant was better.

◆

Max stormed into the vestibule of Clay's apartment and pulled out the sealed envelope of personal effects he'd signed for at the morgue. Unwrapping the little red string that kept things closed, he retrieved a set of keys. Ellie was stubborn as hell. He thought she might've been ready to open up to him, but something shifted, and he was back to being the enemy.

"I don't think you're my enemy," she said, her brow pulling tight.

He cursed himself for putting the hurt in her eyes. "I didn't realize I spoke aloud." In fact, he was quite sure he hadn't. "Is mind reading another of the mysteries you don't share?"

She ducked under his arm and went through the doors. The elevators weren't directly across from the entrance. They were off to the right and around a corner, but Ellie rounded the corner and pushed the button without needing direction.

Max's jaw clenched so tight it was a wonder he didn't crack his molars. "So, you and Clay? How long were you two a thing?"

The elevator doors opened, and she stepped inside and pushed the button for the fourth floor. "Not a *thing*. We were friends."

That lie stung more than the rest.

Whatever she saw in his face had her taking a step back. Great now he was scaring her. Since when did emotion cloud his ability to do his job? He met the heated stare of the raven-haired beauty and shook his head. "I'm fucking this up." He gestured between them. "This pull between us has knocked me off my game. It's none of my business if you were sleeping with Clay. I don't know why I feel so possessive with you."

"It's *protective*, not possessive."

Wrong. Max gauged the demand his body exuded, the electricity they shared, the thrum of his pulse. He moved without thought and sealed his mouth over hers. He was momentarily shocked at how soft her lips were and how quickly she succumbed to his kiss. His tongue swept the seam of her mouth and gained full access, tasting her in long, leisurely licks.

He distantly registered the elevator slowing to a halt. The doors opened and then closed behind him. They didn't move, so he returned his full attention to Ellie. Her kiss was confident, skilled, and the perfect amount of wildly aggressive to confirm what he felt wasn't one-sided.

He gripped the silky strands of her hair as her hands splayed against his back, crushing their bodies together. The intimate contact had her pressed against every achingly hot, hard inch of him. She groaned, kissing him like she might eat him alive.

He'd gladly be devoured.

She cupped the front of his pants, and his vision fritzed like his brain misfired. His cock stood hard, thick, and happy for the attention even through too much clothing. The investigator in him wanted to know what this was between them, wanted to ask questions.

Ellie didn't answer questions, she retreated. He didn't want that. Not this time.

The elevator bumped into motion, and the two of them jumped apart.

Ellie scrambled into the corner and pressed a hand to her heaving bosom. Her hair was tussled, and her lips were pink and swollen from their kiss. "What the hell was that?"

He shoved both hands through his hair and tried to get some oxygen to his brain. It was the middle of the fucking day, and they were in a public elevator investigating his cousin's murder. Furious at what he'd done, he shook his head. He reached to flatten her hair, but she slapped his hands away. "Your hair's a mess."

As the numbered lights above the doors flipped from seven to eight, she smoothed things into place. He liked that she didn't wear makeup. It would be a crime to alter the natural allure of her beauty.

"Stop looking at me like that."

He didn't get a chance to reply before the doors opened, and an old lady with a white mop dog joined them. The woman looked from him to Ellie and back to him. "Ground, please."

Max hit the button for the ground as well as the fourth floor. This time, when the doors opened on Clay's floor, they got out.

♦

"Clay's apartment is this way," Ellie snapped, still breathless from the kiss. She stomped up the corridor, aroused, angry, and thoroughly embarrassed.

When they arrived at the apartment, she leaned against the wall and closed her eyes. "That shouldn't have happened."

He lifted her chin with a gentle finger and forced her to look at him. "Hey," he whispered. "That kiss is on me, not you. Don't beat yourself up. It was incredible but doesn't have to mean anything beyond what it was."

Was it *all* on him?

Her throat burned. Her body thrummed. There was no hiding the peaked tips of her nipples poking at the thin cotton of her shirt. "I don't do casual, Max. I believe a girl worth kissing is not easily kissed. But that—" She looked down the corridor toward the elevators and felt her cheeks flame hot.

He brushed the back of his fingers over her blush and stepped closer. "That was hands down the most incredible kiss I've ever experienced. Maybe it'll happen again, maybe it won't, but I hate the panic in your eyes. Ellie, whatever you're afraid of, whether it's stalkers or betrayal or what really got Clay killed, you never have to add me to that list."

She wanted to believe him – *soooo* badly – but just wasn't sure.

He leaned forward and pressed a kiss on her forehead. "You're dealing with a lot. I won't make things harder for you. I swear. I want to help. Whatever you need, however you need it."

Geez, Max Hawken was too much. Too sexy. Too good to be true.

Stepping back, he squeezed her upper arms and made sure she was steady. "Come on. Let's see if Clay left me anything to go on."

◆

Max unlocked the door and let them in. Clay's place was everything he expected, small table, big TV, and a soft couch to sack out on after a long shift. The tossed mess registered as he turned to close the door, but his radar went up a second too late.

The first shot zinged past his shoulder and took Ellie to the floor.

He dropped beside her as a second shot unloaded. Blood bloomed across the front of her shirt as he drew his gun. He rolled to his feet – hoping her healing wasn't a one-time fluke – and came up shooting.

Drywall and wood exploded from the doorframe. The intruder pushed through the opening, and Max launched toward the hall. A scream brought him to the gunman holding a woman as a shield. The guy backed toward the stairwell door, as a bag of groceries spilled across the carpeted hallway.

"Let her go," Max said, considering his options.

The man locked gazes. "I will, unless you force my hand."

With him only two feet from the stairs, Max tightened his grip. "Give it up. You're not going anywhere."

He felt more than saw the guy squeeze the trigger. He dove out of the line of fire, the bullet whizzing past his ear. The woman dropped, crying out as the shooter disappeared through the opening. Max rolled to his feet and threw himself at the steel door

Blocked from inside the stairwell.

He hit the button to call the elevator and watched as the numbers didn't change. *Fuck*. He rushed back in to check on the woman. "Go inside and call 9-1-1. Ask for Detective Lambton. Tell him Max Hawken needs him, and give him this address."

When she headed inside her apartment, he ran back to check on Ellie.

Pale as a ghost, she was covered in sweat, her breathing thready and labored.

"Why aren't you healing?"

She looked up at him with tears in her eyes. "Need... my church."

Shit. Okay. In five running strides, he grabbed a blanket off the couch and then what he came for from the fridge. Ellie looked bad — like end game bad. "An ambulance to the hospital would be faster."

Tears streamed down to her ears, and she shook her head.

He wrapped her in the blanket and got the keys in his hand. She cried out as he lifted her to his chest, and it hurt him nearly as much. "I'm sorry. It'll be over soon, I promise."

He regretted his choice of words immediately. Racing down the hall, the same woman had her head out, presumably waiting for the police. "Tell the officers there was an intruder in Clay's apartment. The door's open."

The elevator door opened as he arrived, and he'd never been so glad for good timing in his life. He thumbed the button for the ground, thankful Clay lived on the fourth and not the twenty-fourth floor.

"I've got you, Ellie," he said, rushing through the lobby. He avoided the puzzled and panicked glances of the few residents he passed, backed into the glass doors, and a second later eased her into the back seat of his car. "Don't you die on me."

The roads passed in a blur and though he'd been in near-death situations and car chases and warzones, his heart had never hammered this hard. His tires screeched as he slammed to a stop in the parking lot, and he raced to get his girl out of the back seat.

Her eyes were closed, her body limp.

Oxygen refused to fill his lungs, and he panted as he raced up the front steps. He didn't have keys to get inside so, he sank on the front stoop and tried the pockets of her jeans. Bingo. He got her inside and dropped onto the center of the dancefloor.

"Come on, angel. Don't you die on me."

He held her in his lap, staring at her face, her throat, anywhere that might indicate she was responding. Seconds ticked into one minute. Two. Three.

Last night, she was recovering by now.

His chest ached, knowing he'd gotten there too late.

Emotion clogged his throat, and he fought to swallow. "I never told you I loved your new song. You asked people to tell you what they thought. It was amazing. *You* are amazing."

♦

Ellie heard the panic in Max's voice, and she didn't like it. Max had a strong, sexy voice and the unsteady, breathlessness didn't belong. What was he saying?

"Wake up right now and sing it for me. Please, angel, open your eyes."

He liked her song. She fought through the fog of her unconsciousness, following the call of his voice. People said she had the voice of a Siren. Little did they know how true that was.

Max had that effect, too, on her, anyway.

And he was singing to her – *American Pie* of all things.

She drew a deep breath, and her cells absorbed the magic of her healing. It was both incredible and awful as the veil of numbness fell away and the pain of injury took hold. She followed the lyrics in her mind and tried to join in.

Her voice was weak, but she knew the moment Max heard her. Warm breath covered her neck as he hugged her close to his chest. "Thanks for not dying."

Ellie blinked up at him. "Thanks for getting me home." Tall, dark, and dangerous looked wrecked. It had been one helluva twenty-four hours for both of them. "Can you help me get upstairs?"

One thing she knew about men like Max – they did best with a task in front of them. She winced as he lifted her off the floor and carried her into the private section of the church. "There's no elevator. Let me walk."

He strode up the steps like she weighed nothing. "Tell me where to go, don't you worry how we get there."

She rested her cheek against his throat and closed her eyes. He smelled amazing. A warm flash of pleasure rushed over her, and for the first time, she didn't squelch it. "Third floor, hang a right at the top of the stairs."

The next thing she knew, he lay her on her bed and straightened. A scowl marred his face as he glanced around. "Where's your bathroom?"

Ellie pointed and closed her eyes. "Was that the guy from the club last night?"

"Maybe. Could even be the guy who killed Clay, but I can't prove those two things are linked yet." Max returned with a damp cloth, a few towels, and the same scowl.

"What's wrong now?"

"We need to take off that bloody shirt. The police won't be far behind us."

Ellie struggled to sit and tug her shirt over her head, but two gunshot wounds so close together had left her all but helpless.

Max sat on the edge of the bed. "May I help you?"

She let him ease off the sopping mess and fell back onto her pillows. He used the warm cloth to clean up her ribs and stomach, frowning at her blood-drenched jeans. "Sorry, those, too."

She lifted her hips, and he slid the denim down her thighs.

"This wasn't how I envisioned undressing you," he said, his voice low and intimate.

"But you *did* envision it?"

His smile was an erotic invitation. "Since the first moment I saw you on stage. I'm not sure if you bewitched me or the bartender drugged me, but I'm tired of fighting it."

The warm cloth brushed under her breasts and over the soft round of her belly. His touch was slow and deliberate, each gentle stroke erasing the violence from her torso to reveal tender flesh beneath. When he finished her stomach and legs, he eased her over to wash her back.

She caught sight of them in the mirror on the far wall. He was *soooo* incredibly sexy, the rapt concentration on his face, the devotion to task in his eyes. If she wasn't weak from healing, she would've wrapped her legs around his hips and pulled him down on top of her.

As if he read her mind, he rolled her back, and his gaze grew hungry. "This thing between us," he said, his voice rough and deep. "Tell me you're suffering. Tell me you ache and are desperate to get naked with me."

Terrified to admit it but unable to deny him the truth he deserved, she nodded. "I want you on me, inside me, wrapped all around me."

The relief in his gaze surprised her. Max Hawken wasn't as sure of himself as he let on.

Planting his palms on either side of her shoulders, he leaned over her. Lowering his head, he kissed her jaw, then her neck, then the hollow at the base of her throat. Too soon, he stopped.

She whimpered in protest and he chuckled, kissing her nose. "Heal first. We'll come back to this, I promise."

Rolling off the bed, he bent over her laundry basket and returned with a clean pair of jeans and a t-shirt the same shade of blue as the one she'd been wearing. He helped her dress and then sat her up on the edge of the bed and offered her his gun.

Stretching her fingers wide, she refused to take it. "I don't want that."

"You need to shoot me."

"*What?* I'm not shooting—"

He walked her over to the window. After moving the curtains away from the wall, he pressed the gun into her hands.

"One of us has to be bleeding when they get here, angel. We left one hell of a mess on Clay's living room floor. You can't afford to raise suspicion. I respect that. I've been shot before, and if you listen carefully, it won't be serious."

"I'm listening, but—"

"You can do this. Stand right there and point here." He pointed to his side, over his hip.

A light-headed rush swamped her. "I'm going to faint."

"No. You're not." He lifted her chin and met her with a steadying gaze. "You're one of the bravest people I've met in years. You can do this. You *have* to, or we'll both be under scrutiny. I left a crime scene, carrying you in a blanket, the police won't be happy about that. The story is, I got shot, you passed out, I feared the shooter would double back to the apartment with me unable to defend you."

He cast a worried glance out the window. "The police *will* come. Trust me. Point and shoot. And hey, you've wanted to hurt me once or twice since I got here. Now's your chance."

She cried as the gun went off, and he doubled forward. Trembling, she collapsed to her knees beside him on the bedroom floor, dropping the gun. "Are you all right? Did I hurt… of course I hurt you, but are you *really, really* hurt?"

He straightened, the muscle in his clenched jaw twitching. Turning to the wall, he fingered the bullet now stuck there. Prying it free using a metal nail file, he pocketed it and pulled the curtain back to cover the hole. "Good job… It went straight through… That's good." He swayed on his feet, and she abandoned the gun on her bedside table to catch him.

He met her forehead with his own and seemed to steady himself. "Ball up your bloody clothes and the towels. Toss them in the washing machine. Then wash your hands really well – all the way to your elbows – and meet me downstairs."

"Laundry? But you're bleeding—"

He shook his head. "It's important, Ellie. Clean the scene, and don't worry about me. I'll take the ambulance and hospital route. It'll make the police feel useful and get them out of here sooner than if I refuse."

◆

Max was right about everything. The police came, called an ambulance, and escorted them to the hospital.

Ellie did her best to stick to the truth with her statement and remembered what Max told her happened. He got shot. She passed out. She woke up back at the church, and he was bleeding.

The doctor confirmed everything inside Max remained whole, and she couldn't believe the relief that swamped her. He said he was a loyal friend, but to take a bullet for her? To have her *shoot* him. It was crazy.

After a barrage of paperwork and prescriptions, they returned home, and it was *her* turn to get *him* up the three flights of stairs. Sweat beaded his brow as they shuffled past George the gargoyle, and Max mumbled something about her creepy taste in home decor.

As they climbed, he leaned on her more than a macho man would if he had a choice, but eventually, they made it upstairs. Careful to keep her hands off his bandaged hip, she steered him toward the bed. He hissed as his body met the mattress, and she eased herself down beside him.

Pulling the comforter over them both, she yawned. "I don't think I've ever been this exhausted."

The meds Max took were working full-swing as he smiled at her with a goofy grin. "You're *soooo* beautiful," he slurred. "And you smell delicious."

Ellie giggled and adjusted her pillow. "Get some sleep, tough guy."

"Can't… have to guard you."

She shook her head. "The nice policemen watching the church from the shadows will guard me. You rest."

◆

In the dark of night, Max woke and stared up at the ornate ceiling. Century-old trees cast twisted shadows into the loft, branches creeping across the walls like unwanted predators in the wind. He listened to the building creak under the barrage and imagined ghouls, ghosts, and all manner of Gothic horror.

How did she live here alone? Maybe it was the meds, but he wanted to pull the covers over his head and never come out. Problem was, the fluids the hospital pumped into him, did want to come out.

He tried to roll out from under Ellie's arm without waking her, but that was a no-go. She jumped and grabbed his shoulder, panicked. "Easy, angel," he said, tapping her nose. "Go back to sleep. Heading to the bathroom. I'll be right back."

She relaxed onto her pillow, stunning, sleep-tousled, and sweetly vulnerable. He stood at the bedside and watched the moonlight transform her sleeping form. It drained the color from her face and made her ebony hair look blue. In that light, the 'other' in her was obvious, but he didn't care what that meant.

After a long while, his bladder insisted he pull himself away. He left Ellie to her dreams, wondering if he played some part in them. He hoped so. He looked down at himself and cursed. Hopefully, the Max in her dreams sported something more rugged than a pair of old sweats and a bloody bandage.

He finished in the loo, washed up, and old-man shuffled his way back toward the bed.

Ellie's loft was as unique and interesting as she. Built over the back third of the church, a series of open arches ran along a long, half wall. He rested his elbows on the ledge and peered into the darkness below. Though he saw nothing but a void, he knew they were situated over the stage, and he was looking over the club floor.

Talk about working from home.

Ellie had eclectic tastes, from Renaissance and Gothic antiques to modern glass and chrome. Rich reds, golds, blues, and blacks. Pen and ink, gargoyle lithographs. Some ostentatious. Some creepy. And some whimsical. He really couldn't judge. It held a ton more character than any place he ever called home.

She caught him snooping, her brilliant emerald eyes colorless in the gray of night.

"How long have you lived here?"

She rolled onto her elbow and propped her head in her hand. "This church has been in my family for over two-hundred years. The journals of my ancestors describe building it when this area was first settled. I've lived here all my life."

Max thought it strange that a first settler to the Americas chose Gothic spires and gargoyles to inspire a new beginning, but kept that to himself. The church obviously meant the world to her. It was a tie to her history – something he wished he had.

He headed to the kitchen for a glass of water and spotted the mustard bottle on the table.

"I found that in the blanket from Clay's," Ellie said, watching him. "Why'd you steal your cousin's mustard?"

"I know how Clay thinks. If he discovered something and wanted me, and only me, to find it, he'd hide his evidence—" he turned on the light over the stove and held the bottle against the illumination "—in the mustard bottle in his fridge."

She chuckled. "Alright, I'll bite. Why?"

"We saw it in a spy movie when we were kids and started stashing things. It drove our mothers crazy."

Hobbling over to the sink, he unscrewed the top and squeezed the contents out. A USB key sealed in a plastic snack bag dropped out. He rinsed it clean and held it up. "Any chance you'll let me borrow your laptop?"

♦

Ellie threw back the comforter and pointed to the bed. She was almost completely back to normal, which was more than she could say about Max.

"Lay down before you fall down" she told him. "I'll bring it to you. Prop up the pillows, and we'll get cozy."

She liked that idea more than she should. In truth, it had been too long since a man warmed her bed. She'd lost her objectivity. Turning back, she watched Max stack and straighten a mountain of throw pillows. By his look of concentration, you'd think him an architect pondering the structural foundation of a building.

She chuckled and rounded the corner to her office nook. Her laptop had been plugged in all day, so she pulled the cable free and—

Movement by the window tore a scream from her throat.

She turned to run.

Meaty fingers grabbed her arm and yanked her toward the open window. The man's eyes glowed in the moonlight.

All her panic buttons lit at once. Struggling, against his hold, Ellie kicked and elbowed, refusing to let him get a proper hold on her.

A gunshot cracked.

She hit the floor hard, unsure if she dropped or was dragged there. A strong grip pulled her out from under her attacker, and Max cursed and grabbed his side. A swipe with his bare foot sent the intruder's gun across the plank floor.

"Who the fuck *are* you?" Max snapped.

Ellie rushed to turn on the light. She searched the man's face for any familiarity. She didn't recognize him. "Why do you want me dead?"

"Answer the lady's question," Max said.

The door burst open, and two police officers burst into the loft.

In the split-second they looked to the door, the shooter dove through the arched opening in the wall. Ellie screeched and ran to look down to the club floor, three-stories below.

Nothing but pitch darkness.

A thundering of footsteps took the officers to the main floor. Ellie yelled down, directing them where to find the lights, and a moment later the officers hustled to the man's body.

"Is he alive?" Ellie asked.

"He's foaming at the mouth."

Max cursed. "Clear away the foam. He fucking poisoned himself." Max glared over the edge of her bedroom wall, gripping the ledge. When the man's body went limp, he reeled and pushed away. "Motherfuckinghell!"

If Max could run down and kill the guy again himself, he might have.

But dead was dead, and there was nothing to be done about it.

For the second night in a row, Detective Lambton took their statements and cleared a body from her church. Tonight, however, she was safe. She adjusted the comforter and smiled at the sleeping tall, dark, and dangerous Max Hawken curled up in her sheets.

He needed rest – she'd shot him, after all.

Easing out of bed, she took Clay's USB key to her office and fired up her laptop. Sliding in the memory stick, she wondered if she was overstepping… until she saw her name on one of the six folders. Pulling her headphones over her ears, she opened the folder and clicked "play" on the video file within.

Tears burned her eyes as Clay smiled back at her. Dark hair. Strong jaw. Gray eyes. The family resemblance between him and Max was stronger than she realized.

"Hey Ellie, if you're watching this, hopefully Max found you and is taking care of things when I can't. I swore I'd never tell your story, and never did, but we both know you need someone watching your back. That's where Max comes in. He's a great guy, and a machine at what he does. I profiled the asshole that's been bothering you, and narrowed it down to three men. Max will protect you."

He already did.

"Also, I dug up something interesting. Are you sitting down?"

She nodded and his pause for her answer made her smile.

"You're not the only one like you still around. It's in the other files. Max knows how to decode my notes and will help track down the others. Give him a chance. Trust him. And Ells, I know what you're thinking… It's not your fault."

"Yes, it is," she said, tears warming her cheeks.

"No, it's not," he said, smiling like he knew he'd catch her on that. "To serve and protect, my friend. That's the job. If that's the way things went, it was an honor to die protecting you. Sing a song for me every now and then. I'll be listening for it."

The video ended, and Ellie lifted her shirt to dry her tears. Not the only one? She wasn't alone?

Creeping back to bed, she watched Max sleep. Man, the Hawken's men were something else. Broken-hearted, she slid between the sheets, and nuzzled into Max's arms.

No, she wasn't alone.

She *did* trust Max, and tomorrow, she'd tell him her secrets, and let him in.

"Everything okay?" he asked, his voice gravelled with sleep.

She pulled his arm over her shoulder and let out a heavy breath. "It will be."

Freelance writer, novelist, editor, and filmmaker, Travis Heermann is the author of nine novels, including the Shinjuku Shadows *trilogy, in which this story is set, as well as short fiction in* Apex Magazine, Cemetery Dance, *and others. His freelance work includes contributions to the* Firefly *roleplaying game,* Battletech, Legend of Five Rings, *and* EVE Online.

About this story, Travis says: "This story grew out of my experiences in living in Japan, fighting off ravening monsters, and... Well, not exactly. But I love writing stories with martial arts, magic, and monsters. And telling the story of a young Filipina immigrant with some ass-kicking skills sounded like a lot of fun. All over the world, immigrants are either ignored or used as political punching bags, whichever is most convenient at the time. I wanted to tell one of those stories. As the story is set in my Shinjuku Shadows universe, it uses the same cultivation-style magic system."

It's easy to dismiss the unusual as the by-product of exhaustion or poor lighting. But how much more would we see if we trusted our instincts – and how would we react if we learned to recognize the magic that surrounds us?

Heart Magic and Cardboard People

Travis Heermann

The two thugs lounged near the entrance of Ikebukuro Station as if waiting for something, their hair fluffed and spiked like anime characters, wearing sunglasses at 11:20 p.m. on a Wednesday night, sleeves of their stylish leather jackets rolled up to the elbows. Their arrogance and disdain clung to them like a stench, and it turned Ana's stomach.

In her navy-blue high school uniform, Ana blended with the crowds rushing to or from the final trains. She would have to pass the thugs on her way out of the station, and if there was anything growing up in an "invisible" community among immigrants in Tokyo's Chinatown, it was wariness of a certain kind of men.

The shops and kiosks were shutting down for the night, and the cardboard people were already colonizing the corners and closed storefronts.

Ana thought of them as 'the cardboard people' because they were thin and brown, practically of no substance at all. They carried their cardboard futons and newspaper pillows with them, and barricaded themselves behind walls of empty food boxes twenty to thirty centimeters high.

A cardboard man erupted from his refuge and reviled an ancient cardboard woman in a country dialect so thick Ana could barely make out the words. "Get out of here, you old hag!"

The old woman turned aside from the vitriol without flinching, like a fish unquestioningly changing course toward anonymous depths where its invisible life might disappear with no one to notice. Just one hapless sardine sent off to be eaten by the world.

Ana clenched her fists and teeth.

"Don't let me see you in here again, idiot!" he roared at the old woman.

The ancient woman shuffled toward the station exit where the thugs loitered, her spine bent so far that she could not raise her head to look more than two meters ahead, face collapsing inward, an absence of teeth, pushing a pram filled with cardboard and a few meager possessions. Did she have at least a blanket in there? Even inside the station, the December air was chilly. Her hot-pink Tokyo Disneyland *zori* made their distinctive shuffle-flap sound across the cold tiles.

The thugs' sunglasses swiveled to follow the old woman.

Ana hefted her backpack and its weight of study guides from cram school, but something in her heart twanged. Her mother's voice in sharp Tagalog jumped into her mind, *Don't go looking for trouble!* She was exhausted from a full day at high school and a full evening at cram school, famished from having eaten nothing but a couple of boiled eggs from Lawson since lunch. Still, sometimes all it took was a witness to give thugs like this a moment's pause.

The old woman shuffled outside. The thugs followed her, picking up speed.

Ana could see it developing. The thugs would accost the old woman deep enough in the shadows, far enough from traffic and passersby, that whatever they intended would be over before anyone noticed, much less intervened. But what could they possibly want from a woman with nothing? Homeless people survived by being invisible.

Ana hurried to catch up.

The thugs caught the old woman by the arms. One of them spoke her, and the old woman stiffened into instant panic.

Ana shouted, *"Oi! Baboy!"* Hey! Pig! They probably didn't understand Tagalog, but a little confusion would work in her favor.

They turned on her, empty sunglasses boring into her.

Ana stopped ten paces away. "What are you doing with my grandmother?" she said in Japanese.

The one with the blood-red jacket snarled, "What are you talking about, *gaijin* slut? Get out of here!" He used such a chopped, guttural tone his words sounded like a caricature of every *yakuza* movie she had ever seen.

Her heart flew into her throat. She had given due comeuppance to a few grabby boys at school, but this was new territory. She glanced around, there were people about at this late hour, but everyone was face down in their own business. No police in sight. Should she just let this go? Walk away? Maybe it was the "gaijin" – *foreigner* – that stoked her to anger, even more than being called a slut. She was half Japanese, half Filipina, but she had been born here. Maybe it was something else. Her mixed heritage put her beneath the notice most of the time, like the cardboard woman.

"What do you want with an *obaachan?* Leave her alone, or I'm going to start yelling."

The thugs released the old woman and squared on Ana. The old woman fell into a trembling, whimpering pile.

Ana dropped her backpack, her heart hammering. She took a deep breath and imagined Uncle Phil's quiet voice in her head, *It's just like training. Nothing more…*

"Then come and get her," Red Jacket said, grinning. His smile was missing two front teeth, and he chewed on a toothpick. A dragon tattoo writhed behind his jacket zipper.

Oh, great. He really was yakuza, a year or two older than her.

Ana's heart roared like a passing bullet train and her mouth went as dry as beach sand. She held out her hand. "Come on, Grandmother. Let's go home."

The old woman tried to get up, and Red Jacket kicked her back to the ground.

Perhaps fifty meters behind Ana, more people were coming out of the station. Would anyone else see this confrontation, yell for the police?

She clenched her fists, released them, clenched them, relaxed them, took a deep breath, and started forward. *It's just practice…*

The other thug, wearing a black Dolce & Gabbana bomber jacket, stepped forward. "You want to play, baby? Maybe we'll take you home with us and have a little party."

"Grandmother," Ana said, "Mother is expecting us at home."

Black Jacket reached for Ana.

She let him take her wrist, then let muscle memory and instinct take over. She used his hand and forearm as lever of control, struck him three times in the space of a single breath – solar plexus, throat, uppercut to the chin – then a painful, wrist-snapping joint lock that put him face down on the pavement a heartbeat later. She twisted until something popped and he cried out.

The distinctive *clicketing* of a butterfly knife, the glint of steel in mercury vapor lamplight, and Red Jacket came at her.

She caught his incoming knife wrist on her forearm, a deft twist and slap to the side of the blade sending the knife to the pavement. Another joint lock, a hard kick to the back of the knee, scooping up the knife as he went down, twisting his arm up behind his back, grinding his face into the stained concrete with her shin across the back of this neck, and his knife in her hand against his throat.

Black Jacket scrambled to his feet and pelted away, holding his arm, whimpering.

"Seems your buddy ran off." Ana pressed the knife's edge into the flesh of Red Jacket's throat. If he so much as twitched, he would slice his own artery wide open. "How's it feel to get your ass kicked by a girl, you slime?"

She rose up off him and assumed a defensive stance, still holding the switchblade in an expert grip.

For a long moment he lay there gasping.

It was then she noticed the black sedan on the street nearby, about twenty paces away, engine running. In the dark interior, a short, squat man watched her from the driver's seat, just able to see over the steering wheel. In the glow of a stubby cigar, his eyes looked orange-yellow, *reptilian*. They fixed upon her, and her muscles froze. She tried to move and couldn't. Something about his skin was wrong, too coarse, too textured.

Red Jacket scrambled to his feet and flung himself toward the waiting car. Before he reached the door, however, thick hands grasped the steering wheel and the car squealed away.

Suddenly Ana was free.

The astonished betrayal on Red Jacket's face was almost comical. He fled up the street after Black Jacket.

"*Putang ina mo!*" *Your mother's a whore!* she called after them in Tagalog.

Then she helped the old woman to her feet. "Are you hurt?"

Tears streamed down the old woman's face. "I'm all right."

Running footsteps approached, a police officer. "What's going on here?" About damn time.

"Some punks," Ana said, keeping her face downcast, slipping the butterfly knife into her jacket. A chill of fear washed through her colder than the moments before the fight.

"She saved me, officer!" the old woman said. "She's an angel!"

The policeman, Officer Ogawa by his name tag, asked them a few questions, descriptions of the perpetrators. When Ana described them, his face became a Noh mask. She gave him a false name and a false address, trying to suppress more waves of even greater fear. If the police asked too many questions, they might discover her mother was an undocumented Filipina who had overstayed her visa by almost twenty years. When he asked to see her student ID, she apologized for having forgot it at school. In the end, he was more intent upon radioing back to the *koban* than pressing her for information.

Ana said to the old woman, "Do you have somewhere to sleep tonight?"

The old woman glanced at her pram.

Before she could answer, Ana said, "It's a bit of a walk, but we have a *kotatsu*." She had spent her last three hundred yen on boiled eggs for lunch, leaving no money for taxi or bus fare.

At the mention of the kotatsu, a heated table under which Japanese people spent their winter nights, the old woman's eyes glittered. "Oh, Jizo preserve you, child, that's very kind but—"

"You can't say no. Please."

♦

Ana put her backpack in the pram, pushed it with one hand, and carried the old woman piggyback like a child. The cardboard woman smelled of trash and sweat and old urine, not unlike summers in the immigrant back-alleys of Chinatown where Ana had grown up, where the Filipino laborers, hostesses, and sex workers kept to themselves, where Uncle Phil, as everyone called him, still taught *eskrima* from his garage.

As she walked, the fight replayed in her mind over and over. Her skin still tingled, and her legs felt spongy from the adrenaline rush, but taking down those two idiots had been surprisingly easy. She had often wondered how good Uncle Philip really was; now she knew.

The weight of the butterfly knife bobbed in her pocket.

Home was a kitchen, toilet, *ofuro*, and one *tatami* room apartment, empty and dark when Ana opened the door. The apartment was not bad for a couple of Filipinas with no legal status. Her mother made enough money entertaining Japanese salary men in a Kabuki-cho hostess bar to make the rent more often than not, but she worked every night until about 4:00 a.m. They couldn't afford a phone for Ana, and she worried that her mom might freak out when she came home, but she had gotten her penchant for bringing home strays from her mom. Strays like the huge, snow-white tomcat who emerged from the shadows and gave her a piercing look. She knelt to pet him, and he sidled up to rub her leg, almost pushing her off-balance with his strength. Stroking his head sent a burst of static electricity through her fingers, a powerful snap that somehow went all the way to her chest. In the dimness, the spark had looked green.

"That was weird," she muttered, flexing her fingers.

The cat eyed the old woman, who bowed to him and said, "Good evening, Bakeneko-san." The name translated to "ghost cat" or "monster cat", a kind of *yokai*, or supernatural creature. Strangely, it sounded as if she knew him.

He blinked once, then darted past them, out into the night, as he usually did, coming and going like a ghost. Sometimes Ana felt he was simply checking in on her, happy to mooch a tuna sandwich along the way.

Ana arranged the kotatsu, quilt, and futons, setting her alarm to rise early for school and send the old woman on her way before her mother returned. As Ana snuggled into the kotatsu's quilt, the breathing of the old woman descended into oblivion.

Ana's brain was still chewing on the fight, however. Her gaze turned toward the grainy photograph of her mother, young and smiling and beautiful, taken in a lovely park in Manila, and wondered what had been so terrible that she had abandoned all family and friends for the life of an undocumented foreigner in Japan. Her mother steadfastly refused to discuss it. And what about Ana's father? *A slimy deadbeat. You're better off without him,* was all her mother would say.

When the alarm clock woke her at 6:30 a.m. to get ready for school, Mom was snuggled against Ana on her futon, snoring softly. Her hair still smelled of cigarette smoke and *sake*. The old woman was already gone, but atop the kotatsu lay something wrapped in worn newspaper.

Ana unwrapped it and found a comb, but not just any comb: an antique, Japanese lady's comb. About the size of her hand with fine, black-lacquered teeth, one of which was missing, an arching spine engraved with a gilded crane in flight, encrusted with mother-of-pearl and minute squares of colored glass. It wore its age with grace and beauty.

On the scrap of newspaper was a note: "For you, my angel. My grandmother was a *geisha*. This comb belonged to her. If not for you, I would be dead today. I know who those men work for."

Ana caressed the comb's smooth lines, then got herself ready for school. English test today, which she was going to ace, growing up with a multi-lingual mother.

♦

The old woman's note burrowed under Ana's skin.

I would be dead. I know who those men work for.

Was she talking about a particular yakuza gang? The Yamaguchi-gumi? Sumiyoshi-kai? Or worst of all, the Black Lotus Clan? She shuddered at the thought of having pissed off the Black Lotus Clan. Some of the gangs had gone half-legitimate, but the Black Lotus Clan was infamous for being into some supremely shady stuff. If those two thugs were Black Lotus and ever found out who she was, she might disappear forever.

The next night, on her way home from Ikebukuro Station, she looked in vain for the old woman. That she didn't even know the old woman's name felt like a discourtesy. The old woman had had a life once.

Ana wore the comb in her hair that day, and for the first time, people noticed her. Even the haughty girls spoke to her, and the coolest boys' notice fell upon her. Was this what it felt like to be a person? Not just a gaijin girl? All day long, she was aware of a powerful fluttering sensation around her heart or breastbone. It wasn't altogether unpleasant, but she'd never felt it before and hoped she wasn't coming down with something by walking around in the winter cold wearing a skirt every night.

When she got home, she sewed a sheath for her forearm to conceal the butterfly knife.

I know who those men work for.

The next night, walking home after cram school, her brain buzzing with math and history, she didn't see them step around a corner in time. There they were at the station exit, sunglasses turning toward her, failing to hide their dark malice. They started toward her. She wouldn't surprise them with eskrima again.

Ana cast about for somewhere to run, a crowd to fade into, but there was none at this hour.

Then she heard yelling.

"You're not listening to me!" the voice said.

She ducked around a corner and nearly crashed into a cardboard man, the same one who had chased the old woman from the station, entreating Officer Ogawa, who stood with his arms crossed, face pinched.

"Where are my friends?" the cardboard man shrilled. "Five of my friends are gone! All in the last month! I already gave you their names!"

Ana apologized and peeked back behind her. The thugs were coming. She lingered near the officer.

Officer Ogawa loomed over the man, his brow darkening, and said something she could not hear.

The man shrank like a deflated balloon, turned, shuffled away.

Just then the thugs burst around the corner, drawing up sharply at the sight of the policeman.

He glared at them. "What are you two idiots doing in here? You're supposed to stay outside!"

The thugs *hmphed*, turned shoulders and walked away, flashing Ana expressions of dire intent.

Ogawa's eyes flickered over the crowd to see how many people were watching, then moved away as if on patrol, ignoring her.

While their backs were turned, she darted out one of the other exits.

♦

The next day, Ana passed by the neighborhood koban – a diminutive police station about the size of her apartment – and happened to glance at the series of wanted posters on the bulletin. A face jumped out at her, gap-toothed mouth, anime hair. Wanted on suspicion of grand larceny, petty theft, assault and battery, extortion. His name was Abe Keisuke, with five known aliases. Ana recognized him as Red Jacket.

She paused. The officer behind the window was hunched over his work, oblivious to her presence. The very thought of entangling herself with the authorities sent a hot, dry lump into her throat.

"Excuse me, officer." The words stumbled over her teeth.

He did not look up. "Yes?"

"I've seen one of these guys."

"Who? Where?"

"Abe Keisuke. Last night at Ikebukuro Station. And two nights ago, he and another guy tried to kidnap an old homeless lady."

"Why didn't you tell the police?"

"I did! His name was Ogawa. He got there just after they ran off."

The officer's eyes narrowed slightly.

"And just yesterday, I heard this homeless guy telling Officer Ogawa five of his friends had disappeared."

"It's winter. They stay out of sight more, keeping themselves warm. Do you know her name, the old lady's?"

"No."

"The homeless man?"

"No."

"Do you have any concrete information?"

Her ears buzzed with anger. "I guess not."

He sighed. "All right. Thank you for the information. Name and address?"

She gave him a fake one.

"Which high school do you go to?" he said.

"Showa Tetsudo."

His gaze locked on her. "Really? My daughter goes there. Strange that you're not wearing a Showa Tetsudo uniform."

She ran.

◆

The next day was Saturday, one of Ana's training days at Uncle Phil's "dojo", the back alley behind an apartment building. In spite of the makeshift surroundings, he took his role seriously as the *sensei* of a martial arts school, even though he rarely took money from his students. Whenever he held classes, he unfolded a few moldy rubber mats on the ground, erected a couple of striking dummies, and lit some incense below the Philippine flag and the black-and-white portrait of his teacher. As always after practice, sweat soaked Ana's clothes and her torso even in the winter chill, her arms and hands felt like massed bruises.

Uncle Phil was a short man, even for a Filipino, squat, but there was an astonishing quickness in him that humbled even the cockiest students. He rubbed his shaved pate and eased back onto a plastic crate. The garage doors hung open to the narrow street. The other students of the afternoon had already departed.

"You practiced hard today," he said in English. "Training for something? Another fight with gangsters maybe?"

"You heard about that?"

"I hear about everything."

"Something bad is happening."

"You looking for trouble?"

"I'm looking for answers. If they did something to that old woman—"

"You feel responsible for her now, yeah?"

"Yeah."

He leaned forward, put his hands on his knees. "Look, Ana. You're a good girl, a smart girl. This is a big city. People can live in the cracks of big cities. Sometimes the cracks swallow people. Disappear. Poof!"

"It's not right."

"If it was right, everyone's life would count. Everyone would be missed. Everyone would have somebody to cry at their funeral. But the world, it don't work that way."

Something in his voice caught her ear. "You've heard something?"

He waved dismissively. "Just crazy stuff."

"What kind of crazy stuff?"

"Old Georgina Matapang says she saw an *aswang* in an alley down by the docks. But she's – poof! – crazy."

"An aswang!" Ana said. Her mother had told her stories of aswang since she was old enough to listen, tales of foul, human-like night creatures feeding upon human victims, drinking blood or viscera or the fluids of pregnant women through their hollow, prehensile tongues. A chill trickled up her spine.

"She said it was feeding on some homeless man. Bah!" he scoffed. "Aswang can stay in the Philippines."

◆

The door cracked open after Ana's third knock, a single eye peered out. "Are you that Navarro girl, Maria's daughter?" came a querulous voice.

"Yes, Mrs. Matapang. How are you?" Ana brushed away a cobweb that had drifted across her face. The apartment building, a block of grayed concrete and rusted steel built during the post-World War II Occupation, was clearly home to the world's entire population of spiders.

"What do you want?"

"I heard you saw something strange."

The door slammed.

"Please, Mrs. Matapang. Can I talk to you?"

"Leave me alone!"

"I came because… I saw something, too."

The door cracked open. The eye reappeared, wider now. "You saw it, too?"

Ana nodded fervently. "Can you tell me about it?"

The door opened.

Later, at the kitchen table over a cup of green tea, Mrs. Matapang said, "Too many people think I'm crazy. Screw them! I know what I saw."

"When?"

"Two weeks ago. And I know an aswang when I see one. My grandmother saw one once in the Philippines. It killed her cousin." The woman shuddered visibly, and tucked graying hair behind her ears.

"So what did you see?"

Mrs. Matapang sipped her tea. "Boss made us work longer, so I missed the last train and didn't have money for a taxi. I was walking along the river, about two in the morning. The water was really low. I heard a sloshing noise, like something big slopping around in mud. Down there at the waterline I saw this dark shape. Oh, may the Blessed Virgin save me, I'll never forget as long as I live! It was bent over a body, and its tongue was… sticking into it… sucking." She put down her teacup, trembling. "I ran until I fell over."

"What did it look like?"

"I saw the tongue and some glowing eyes. And that *sound!* Like tapioca going up a straw! I ran like hell. I went back in the morning, I had to be sure I wasn't imagining. The body was gone. But I know where it happened, across the canal from that pachinko parlor – what's it called, the one with the big purple teddy bear on the awning? – And I know what I saw. I haven't touched booze in six years, don't let anyone tell you different. I know what I saw."

On her way home, Ana circled past the pachinko parlor Mrs. Matapang had mentioned, Pachinko Power, with its jolly purple teddy bear dancing animatronically atop the neon-splashed awning. A cacophony of flashing lights and dinging bells echoed from the smoke-filled interior, where dull, bleary-eyed patrons chain-smoked and fed their steel balls into hungry machines. The teddy bear tipped its top hat to her as she walked on, but her eyes kept scanning the shadows of the concrete canal that made up the Shakujii River. There was nothing down there except filthy water and garbage.

Two intersections beyond was the hostess bar where her mother worked, The Blushing Mango, which shared a building with six other bars and a strip club. The bar specialized in Filipina hostesses. Her mother was the oldest of the hostesses, but she was still beautiful enough and strong enough to hold her place in a world that discarded women like used condoms. How long before Ana was forced by circumstances to join this world? Would she be able to survive like her mother had? She wanted to go to university, but that wasn't in the cards for her.

The doorman blocked the door when she tried to come in. "No kids," he grunted. "Oh, it's you. What do you want?" Ana tried to slip past him, but he blocked her again. "You're not supposed to be here."

"That's too bad, Taka," she said, striking a coquettish pose and hiking up her uniform skirt to show a little more thigh. "I thought you might like to buy me a drink." She pulled out the comb and let her hair tumble around her shoulders. Like her mother said, the bar was always looking for fresh meat.

Taka stood ten centimeters taller than her and smelled of cigarettes and expensive cologne. His gaze flicked back and forth between her thighs and her chest, before he moved aside so she could enter. He would have been cute if he had any soul at all, but his eyes were as hollow as an empty *bento* box.

Ana stepped into the shadowy interior.

In an alcove, her mother leaned against the shoulder of one of the ugliest men Ana had ever seen. His face was broad and squat, like the rest of him and his expensive pin-stripe suit could not conceal his unappealing shape. Even knowing it was her mother's job to make such men feel appealing, laugh at their jokes, and tell them how handsome they were, did not make the sourness in Ana's belly easier to bear. Three other hostesses fawned over him, pouring him *shochu* from a large bottle and feeding him tidbits of dried fish and seaweed. His fedora shadowed his face and gave him a strange, retro style. He brought a cigar to his flabby lips, and the flaring glow glistened in the strange, yellowish eyes that fastened briefly on her.

Ana stood there for a long moment, until Taka grabbed her arm and led her behind the bar, popped the cap on an Asahi Super-Dry and handed it to her. "Wait here," he said.

She sipped the beer and waited among crates and casks of alcohol. Hostesses passed on their way to the dressing room, giving her fake smiles or glares of appraisal, as if she might be their forthcoming replacement. High school girls came high in demand.

Then her mother was there. "What are you doing here?" The scent of cigar smoke and something else clung to her, something like the smell of stagnant water, or perhaps like a reptile cage.

She wanted to say, *Mom, I'm scared.* But then she would have to explain why, and any lengthy explanation would just raise her mother's ire. Maybe all she wanted was refuge. "Would you prefer me to be off hanging out somewhere with boys?"

"Don't get smart with me, young lady. You know you're not supposed to be here."

"I think Taka likes me."

"That's not the kind of attention you want. Now, seriously, you need to go. Need some money?"

Ana held out her hand.

Her mother reached into her stylish jacket, rearranged a breast, and withdrew a roll of cash with a grin of excitement. "Made next month's rent already! That guy there is a big spender and likes a lot of ladies." She sounded giddy, more than a little drunk.

Ana's eyes bulged at the sight of the roll of bills. "But he looks like a big jerk."

Her mother's face darkened. "I can't pick what the customers look like." She peeled off a 10,000-yen bill and pressed it into Ana's hand, then kissed her on the cheek. "Go have some fun. Be home by three. I'll see you in the morning." Then her mother looked at her for a long moment.

"What is it?" Ana said.

"Nothing. You've just… grown up. And you're so pretty." Her voice choked a little. "You need to get out of Chinatown." She turned away before Ana could answer.

Ana stuffed the money into her shirt, took another swig of beer, and left the bottle.

In the main room again, Ana's gaze turned back toward the man in the alcove. He produced a matchbox, struck one, and in the flash, she spotted the purple teddy bear on the matchbox. The flame disappeared into the glowing tip of the fat cigar, and thick, scaly lips clamped around the other end. In the dim light, his cheeks took on a coarse, glistening cast, as if he were sweating profusely, and the bottom half of his face seemed to protrude almost like a snout. A fringe of dark, greasy hair hung below the band of his fedora. Round dark eyes snared her gaze, glistening, glittering, and strangely inviting, as if promising diversions she could scarcely fathom.

The near-collapse of her knees roused her from the strange fugue, and she caught herself on a barstool.

By the time she reached the street, her heart was a cold triphammer, so she leaned against the canal railing to steady herself and catch her breath.

Then rough hands grabbed both of her arms. Instincts and muscle memory surged into her limbs. A heartbeat later, one arm was free, and Abe Keisuke lay on the pavement with his legs kicked out from under him.

Ana spun on Black Jacket, snapped her other arm free, and landed a punch at the bridge of his sunglasses, snapping them in two. He staggered back with a wail of pain, clutching his face.

Electricity snapped and crackled, a flash of arcing blue in Abe's hand. He hit her with the taser squarely in back. Her body spasmed, white splashes filled her vision. The filthy pavement swung up and slapped her face, coarse and gritty and stinking of garbage and urine.

"You're a hard-to-find little bitch," Abe said. "It's like you don't even exist."

Then he kicked her in the head, and all went black.

◆

Consciousness returned with flickering fluorescent light in her eyes, cold concrete under her, and paralyzing pain in her skull. Ana lay there and cried until the pain subsided enough for her to open her eyes, but it wouldn't go away.

The walls of her chamber were gray concrete and rusty industrial shelving, the door, steel with a window of reinforced glass. The door was locked, of course, but through the window was a larger room in a sub-basement with more naked concrete walls and cold gray light, a sewer grate in the floor, a table upon which rested liquor bottles and ashtrays.

Her heartbeat throbbed in her ears, deafening, feeding her headache. She paced the room, clutching her head, feeling a tender lump above her ear, yearning for the pain to pass, using moments between pulses of agony to assess her situation. The shelves were securely bolted to the walls, the window glass impenetrable to anything short of a sledgehammer, the door locked solid.

How long before anyone would look for her? Would her mother risk going to the police? Ana's despair and pain coupled like tarry worms in her belly and pressed her deep into a corner for hours.

The sound of grating metal outside, the only sound since she awakened, brought her to the window. The sewer grate in the floor had been slid aside, and an arm emerged from the hole. But not a human arm.

She watched the creature climb into view and clutched both hands over her mouth.

Its head and gait were at once reptilian and simian. A ring of sodden black hair fringed an indentation atop its pate, where a cupful of water resided. Two thick scaly arms. A turtle-like shell on its back. It stood about a meter-and-a-half tall and walked two-legged toward the table, where it picked up a swimmer's cap, which it snapped over the indentation in its head. Its reptilian face was broad and protuberant, a snout with two slits for a nose.

Realization crept over Ana. Growing up in Japan, she could not help but recognize a real, live *kappa*. With thick, taloned fingers the kappa checked the seal on its swimming cap, then crossed the room to a cabinet, which proved to be a wardrobe of sorts, filled with shirts and suits of various colors. With an ungainliness that would have made her laugh were she not in mortal danger, the creature dressed itself in a starched white shirt, tie, and pin-striped suit.

Then in the mirror it used to tie its necktie, the kappa's reptilian eyes caught her, snared her, held her fast. Every muscle in her yearned to dash away, but she was frozen, unable to tear her eyes away.

The kappa turned toward her, releasing her from its mesmerism, but still she couldn't look away. From its pocket it withdrew a dull, black necklace bearing an amulet with some arcane character she didn't recognize. It slipped the amulet over its head, then completed its attire with a broad-brimmed fedora.

Its eyes burned with a strange desire, perhaps hunger, perhaps lust, perhaps some sickening mix of both. Its eyes ogled her, devoured her. Its thick lips peeled back into a grin, revealing twin rows of needle-like fangs. Then it started toward her, and with each step, its appearance shifted incrementally. By the time it stood before the door, it resembled the man she had seen in the bar with her mother, but not the same. Unusual in its appearance, short and squat, but not inhuman.

Ana's blood turned to icy slurry.

The kappa reached for the door latch.

Her scream froze a moment before its birth, the kappa's gaze transfixing her.

But then Abe Keisuke entered carrying a heavy, squirming burlap bag over his shoulder.

"You have brought dinner, I see," the kappa said, turning away from Ana.

Abe untied the bag's coarse rope and dumped the contents onto the floor.

Out fell Ana's mother, gagged with duct tape, hands and feet tied, eyes and hair wild with terror.

Abe hoisted her upright.

"That one's mother?" the kappa said, gesturing over its shoulder at Ana.

Abe nodded.

The kappa rubbed its hands together in anticipation, looking back and forth between Ana and her mother.

Ana beat on the glass. "Mom! Mom, it's me!"

Her mother's gaze snapped up and after a split second of horrified recognition, her cheeks puffed out in a stifled scream.

The gangster tossed her mother into an adjacent room and locked it. The walls and doors were so thick, Ana could no longer hear if her mother were screaming.

The fluttering she'd been feeling in her chest turned uncomfortable, like there were things squirming beneath her skin, and her ears began to ring with tiny voices she couldn't quite grasp. She felt around her chest and ribs for the source of the sensation, but it was coming from inside, from a place she couldn't identify. Part of her wanted to flee like a rabbit away from the window, but she had to see.

The kappa and human settled themselves around the table and started pouring liquor, putting their feet up on the table and chatting about the week's take from the pachinko parlor, about how much local stores paid for "protection".

"That idiot Ogawa is in our pocket," Abe said. "We just gotta keep greasing his palm."

The kappa sat facing Ana's window, and his gaze kept darting to her with a hunger held tenuously at bay.

Another man, Black Jacket, came in carrying a plastic tub, then two more kappas. The last one she recognized from the bar, and also as the driver of the black car. He was half again larger than the other two, almost the size of a very short, very burly man. He peeked through the window of her mother's room with a look of apparent satisfaction. All the kappas wore amulets like the first, and Ana wondered if that's how they concealed their appearance.

"She give you any trouble?" the big kappa said.

Abe shook his head. "Not at all."

"What about the young one?"

"She's scrappy," Abe said. "Be careful."

The first kappa snorted with derision.

"I'm telling you," Abe said. "Don't cut her any slack just because she's a kid."

The first kappa grinned even wider. "Nosy, too. Look."

All eyes turned on Ana, making her duck again.

The big one said, "No one touches the woman. She's mine."

Ana peeked out again. If she looked at the creatures long enough, snippets of their disguise seemed to disappear momentarily, like glimpses between the slats of a boarded fence.

Black Jacket opened the plastic tub. Their eyes brightened at the stacks of money filling the tub, bundles of cash in several denominations. Ana had never seen so much money in one place before.

Abe said, "Don't forget the Boss's cut. The Clan gets its due or you go back to wherever you came from."

The big kappa puffed his cigar. "We wouldn't dream of stiffing Mr. Gotō. There's plenty to go around, isn't there?"

While the rest of them set about counting the stacks of cash, trading cocky jibes and lewd innuendo as if everyone in the room were human, the first kappa made a game of torturing Ana with paralysis, releasing her, then seizing her again, over and over until tears streamed down her face.

The Boss counted off a stack of money and said, "This is for Boss Gotō. Make sure he gets it." Abe stiffened under the kappa's supernatural gaze, but knew enough not to meet its eyes. "You wouldn't dream of stiffing us."

Abe tucked a fat manila envelope full of money into his jacket pocket with a crumbling facade of bravado, his face sweaty and pale.

When the money had been distributed among them, the first kappa said, "So can we eat now, Boss?"

The leader said, "I get the woman. You two can fight over the kid."

The first kappa whined, "I haven't had one that young in a hundred years. She looks juicy."

"What's it worth to you?" the Boss kappa said with a thick smirk.

The first kappa shoved its stack of cash into the center of the table.

"Hey!" protested the third.

"Then cough up," the Boss said.

The third tucked its money away, then crossed its arms sullenly. "I'm not hungry anyway."

The first looked toward Ana with ravenous glee. She ducked out of sight, her heart pounding in her throat, her mouth so dry she couldn't swallow, her hands trembling. If she and her mother died, a few neighbors would mourn them. A few acquaintances at school might wonder vaguely what happened to her. As she and her mother were not really "people" anyway, their absence would not make a single noticeable ripple. They would be just lost in the cracks, hapless sardines. More cardboard people.

Her mind whirred. What did she know about kappas? Practically nothing, other than they were fairy tale monsters who most often showed up on advertising. They were depicted as cuddly, playful, even child-like, with duck-like bills and smiling eyes and cute little turtle shells. They lived in rivers and ponds, had indentations atop their heads where water pooled, and they were dangerous as long as there was water in those indentations. But these creatures bore only a passing resemblance to those in modern children's books.

The writhing sensation encircling her ribcage strengthened until it felt like a tentacle constricting her. She gasped at the pain, and behind her squeezed eyelids, bright green lights danced. Her heart felt warm in a way she'd never experienced before, heat spreading through surrounding tissues, lungs, ribs, neither pleasant nor unpleasant, inexorable.

The door opened, and the kappa stood there, grinning, its gaze dragging at hers.

That's when her heart exploded.

A giant fork of emerald lightning burst from her chest and through the kappa, blowing it backward into the table, sending humans and kappas and a shower of sparks flying all directions. The afterimages filled Ana's vision with the strobed snapshots of the first kappa with a hole seared clean through it, through which she could see the Boss's shocked face. Two humans flying through the air, asses over elbows. Tongues of lightning licking the walls, ceiling, floor. Money fluttering on invisible air currents.

But the lightning hadn't blown a hole through her. It had *come from* her, lifting her and holding her suspended above the floor for a few seconds, then dropping her in a heap.

Her ears rang so loudly she couldn't tell if she was screaming. Her body trembled. Her heart throbbed with something that wasn't blood.

But she wasn't hurt.

Ana staggered back to her feet, and by the time she was upright she felt like an anime mega-hero, complete with hair standing on end and fingers of emerald energy rippling over her body, surging up and down the axis of her body like pounding surf. Her skin tingled deliciously. The crown of her head, beneath her hair, felt as if it had opened, like a door to a universe that she couldn't yet see. She looked down and thought she could see a pulsing emerald glow shining underneath her school uniform.

The two humans and two remaining kappas righted themselves, staring at her, glancing at each other.

The air smelled not of ozone but of verdant earth, like fresh-trimmed grass or a forested mountaintop shrine after a rain. And also like burnt chicken, smoke curling in the air from the seared flesh of the kappa on the floor.

The kappas exchanged fearful glances, edging away.

The two humans scrambled back to their feet. Abe Keisuke pulled out a gun and trained it on her. "Play time is over, kid."

The weight of the butterfly knife in its sheath under her jacket, reminded her of its presence. The thugs hadn't thought to search her thoroughly. She was just a high-school girl.

She raised her hands, but there was no surrender in the energy coursing through her. She had taken two of them down before – she could take down four. But they would have to come to her. She spun back into the room, out of the line of fire, then pulled the butterfly knife.

Abe cursed and shouted at Black Jacket, "Get in there and get her!"

"*Zakennayo!*" came the guttural refusal.

"Cowards," the Boss kappa said with a snort, then raised its voice. "Hey, little girl! Come out now or you can listen to us torture and eat your mother."

A cold ball of rage settled in her gut. She cast about the room for other weapons, but there was nothing, only rusty shelving, naked brick, and old concrete.

But then whispers filtered down to her through that invisible opening in her head, carrying secrets into her mind, flashes of possibility. Her feet felt light as air, her legs monkey-quick.

She gripped the knife and imagined Uncle Phil's voice: *It's just practice.* And did the Filipino martial art called eskrima or *kali* focus on how to use a knife? Oh, yes, yes it did.

One more deep slow breath, letting her curiosity linger just for a moment on the jade energy coruscating through her body.

Then she palmed the knife, raised her hands, and stepped into view, trying to look cowed, letting her hair obscure her face. She took three steps into the outer chamber with its domed ceiling.

Abe grinned and retrained his gun on her. "That's far enough."

The kappas grinned with malicious glee.

Then she leaped with the speed of lightning, but not toward them. Somehow instinctively knowing that the spirits of the air would help her, she spun and ran *up* the wall, feeling the air coalesce around her, supporting her as she ran upside down halfway up the dome.

Gunshots exploded once, twice, deafening, ricochets whining past her. She flipped and dropped feet-first toward Abe, kicking him full strength in the ear as she came down. He dropped like a sledgehammered water buffalo. The gun skittered away.

Black Jacket was still gaping at the girl who'd run across the ceiling when she stabbed her the fingers of her left-hand into his eyes. He yelped, his hands flying toward his face, then she punched him in the throat with her knife hand. As he gagged and staggered and gasped, she spun him around, snaked her left around his neck in a choke-hold, and interposed him between herself and the two kappas.

And not a moment too soon.

The smaller one opened its mouth, and something like a frog's tongue shot out, a bone-like spur emerging from the tip trailing yellowish venom. In a kind of slow-motion Ana would never have been able to see before, the spur struck the yakuza squarely in the chest. Instantaneously, the thug became dead weight, and Ana had to let him drop.

She sensed both kappas trying to snare her gaze, but she kept her eyes focused on their amulets. She leaped toward them like a gazelle, as if climbing the air itself. The Boss's tongue slurped toward her in mid-air, but a brush of wind seemed to turn the venomous spine aside by a couple of centimeters.

Meanwhile, Ana kicked off the nearest one's hat, including the swimmer's cap, sloshing water from the indentation atop its head. It shuddered and staggered, as if its strength had sloshed out with it. Then she moved in with a series of lightning-fast eskrima knife slashes. In two seconds, six slashes had bitten deep wounds in its wrist, armpit, and neck, where human arteries were, as well as in the creases of its shell.

It collapsed in a twitching heap, curling in on itself like a spider.

Ana faced the Boss, not even breathing heavily, as if her blood were turbo-charged. Sticky stuff stained her blade and knife hand.

"Oh, must you be so difficult?" the Boss whined. "Please, would you be so kind as to let me eat you? You look *delicious*."

"Then come and have a taste," she said.

It gave her a little smile then launched itself monkey-quick at her. She batted aside outstretched talons, but before she could counterattack, the tongue snapped out and encircled her knife wrist. The venomous spine protruded. Before it could strike, she snatched it with her other hand, catching it at the base of the spine, before twisting and levering her body into an over-the-shoulder throw using the creature's tongue. It was surprisingly heavy for being only half her height, but the large kappa flew halfway across the room, bouncing on its back across the floor with a series of thuds. Its fedora tumbled away, revealing the Hello Kitty swimmer's cap on its pate.

It righted itself instantly and came at her on all fours, snatching for her.

Ana batted its grab aside and attempted an agonizing wrist lock that would have instantly subdued a human opponent. But the kappa's wrist did not bend that way, and she lost control of the taloned hand. The kappa raked upward across her belly and chest, the sharp talons shredding her jacket and shirt, splitting her bra, and dragging out a cry of pain.

They spun away from each other, and it grinned again.

The air itself seemed to whisper to her. *Trust us. Use us.* Ana edged toward the overturned table, which lay with all four legs in the air. *The environment is a weapon, too,* Uncle Phil had often told her.

The creature lunged.

Ana leaped straight up, planted one sneaker atop the upturned table leg, and vaulted higher. The kappa passed beneath her, the pink rubber cap like a bright bullseye. She had never thrown a knife before, but the action felt almost instinctive as she flung the blade straight down. Green energy lashed down her arm, took hold of the knife, and guided the point straight into Hello Kitty's face – and deep into the indentation beneath. Water squirted out around the blade. The kappa staggered once, its eyes rolling white, and fell face-first onto the concrete. It shuddered once, sighed, and went still.

A heartbeat later, Ana was at the door of her mother's cell, flinging open the door to another storage room like the one she had been trapped in. Her mother lay bound on the floor, her eyes half-crazed with fear, face streaked with tears and mascara. Moments later, hands and ankles cut free, gag removed, her mother flung her arms around Ana and wept great explosions of sobs.

Ana tried to help her up.

"My feet are numb!" her mother said, reaching for the nearest shelf to keep from falling.

"I'll carry you."

Her mother's faced melted into a smile, then she leaned forward and pressed warm lips against Ana's forehead. "You carry me more often than you know."

The moment hung between them, but Ana tore her gaze away from her mother's face before she started bawling like a baby. Dark stains spattered the floor in this room. Piles of ratty old clothes were tossed haphazardly in the corners. Nearby lay a familiar pair of Tokyo Disneyland zori.

Together they hobbled into the outer room. Ana began to feel woozy, like she'd had too much alcohol. The energy around her heart felt like a tiger stalking the limits of its cage.

The kappas' bodies had lost their shape, dissolving into lumpy piles of greenish-black goo.

At the sight of the two gangsters, her mother said, "Are those guys… dead?"

"I don't know. One, maybe. I'll tell you about it later. We have to get out of—"

"But look at all this money!"

Her mother was right. Millions of yen lay scattered around the room. Maybe Ana wouldn't have to become a hostess herself soon. Maybe she could go to university. She tucked the tattered ends of her shirt into her waistband, to make a pouch where she could carry the loose bills.

They were still gathering up the money when the sense of another presence brought Ana around to face the entrance.

A woman in her late twenties, probably Chinese, stood in the open doorway. Her frosted hair was tied into a wild vertical topknot, and she wore a silver and black catsuit, which, coupled with the toned muscles underneath, made her look like an aerobics instructor from hell. She gripped an aluminum baton in each hand, eskrima-style.

Ana jumped to her feet, stuffing a last handful of cash into her shirt, then assumed a defensive stance in front of her mother. She hoped her wooziness wasn't obvious, thinking this must be some female yakuza checking up on her comrades.

The woman beamed a smile that reminded Ana of the most beautiful J-pop stars. Her beauty was stunning, her allure palpable. For a moment, the sheer physical charisma of this woman just zotted out all Ana's mental processes and dispelled her guard stance. And then a big, snow-white tomcat snaked around the woman's feet, looking straight at Ana.

"I told you I could find her," the cat said.

Ana's mother fainted.

"Mom!"

"Relax, your mother is fine," the Chinese woman said, sliding her retracting batons into pouches along her thighs. "She's just going to sleep while we get a few things straight. I'm Xing, and you just had some really weird things happen to you, right?"

Ana gaped at the woman's perfect Tagalog.

Xing waved a hand. "I grew up in Manila. Who are you?"

"Ana?"

"You don't sound so sure."

The cat said, "Can you not see the *mahō* coursing through her? She's your Awakened one."

Ana realized the cat wasn't speaking with a physical voice, just projecting impressions of meaning in her mind. Nevertheless, he sounded like a smart-ass.

"Of course I can, smarty cat," Xing said. "She's not feeling well. She needs to cultivate her Heart pool."

"What are you talking about?" Ana said, trying to grow suspicious, but something about Xing fought that down, put Ana at ease. "And what's this about mahō? That means black magic."

"You have a lot to learn, Ana," Xing said. "Your life has just changed forever. And now you have a *very* important decision to make."

"Am I in trouble?"

"No, but you will be if you don't come with me. Your Heart pool has Awakened. You are now a witch. But the first thing you need to do is cultivate all that energy that's zinging through you. If you don't, it will damage you, maybe cripple you."

"How do I do that?"

"I can show you. The short answer is a kind of meditation. But we should go." Xing's voice was comforting, rich, melodious. Ana trusted her.

"What about my mother?"

"We'll take her home and let her rest. She's been through a lot. And she's going to have a hard time processing all this. Normal humans usually don't survive meeting a kappa."

"So all that jumping around I did," Ana said, "that was magic?"

"The Heart pool houses Air mahō, and Air mahō is closely attuned with the *kami* of the air. Ah, you have so much to learn!" She rolled her eyes. "But I'll help you, I promise." Xing crossed the room and hoisted Ana's mother unsteadily to her feet. "Now come on. We don't want any little green friends surprising us, do we. Or Black Lotus leg-breakers for that matter."

The cat looked up at Xing. "What about the Council?"

"One decision at a time, puss-puss," Xing said.

"I hate it when you call me that," the cat said.

"Then what's your name?"

"Some creatures don't *need* names," the cat said haughtily.

"So," Xing said briskly to Ana, "back to your place for some tea and meditation."

"And a tuna sandwich," the cat said.

When not crushing dreams as a manuscript evaluator/slush pile reader for three publishers, Jessica Guernsey writes urban fantasy and science fiction novels and short stories. A BYU alumna with a degree in Journalism, she can often be found at writing conferences, where she's not difficult to spot – just look for the extrovert. While she expended her teenage angst in Texas, she now lives on a mountain in Utah with her family. Learn more about her at jessicaguernsey.com

About this story, Jessica says: "A while ago, I came across a writing prompt that read: 'They stole things that no one would miss. Like time. And pennies. And sleep.' I wondered who 'they' were and why they needed those things. One question led to the next, and before I knew it, I had created the shadows."

There is a sweetness and a sadness to this story that wraps itself around you like a gentle morning fog, leaving a trace of mist on your face. If you're very lucky, when the shadows recede they just might leave the taste of fudge on your lips...

BETWIXT AND BETWEEN
Jessica Guernsey

Morry came to see me today. Her cat Scorpio had run off again and she wanted to know what it would cost her to bring him back. I tried to answer the girl, but I was distracted by the woman that came in with her. All soft hair and wide eyes. Too wide. I knew that look. This woman had seen something that she didn't quite understand and for some reason, she thought I might be able to help her. Her hands stayed buried in the pouch of her pale-yellow hoodie.

"But last time it was only 12 butterscotch discs," Morry pouted like only an 8-year-old could and still be adorable.

"That is true," I said, using my serious face, complete with wrinkled brow and rubbing of the stubble on my chin. "But this is the third time Scorpio has followed the wisps. There's a special kind of price to pay when you reach the number three."

I knew Morry wanted her cat back more than she wanted any kind of sweet, and I swear I wasn't jacking the price up for spite. The sugar was for the wisps. Morry might not have understood this entirely, but she would still pay it.

"I can bring a half pound of fudge?" Her little eyebrows rose high.

I considered. "Nuts?"

"No."

"Excellent." I clapped my hand together. "Bring me the fudge and within the hour, Scorpio will find his way home."

Morry clapped her hands, too. Then she held out her little fist. I bumped it with mine and then we both popped our hands open and made exploding noises. Her already immense grin grew. She turned and sprinted out the door without so much as a backward glance at the woman she'd come in with.

I watched the little girl go. I hoped Scorpio learned his lesson quickly. The wisps loved lost animals, especially cats. One of these times they might decide to keep him.

I dropped my gaze to where Morry had left her completed form. Mostly completed. She'd forgotten to write my name on the "Assisted By" line again – hazard of being between worlds.

"Excuse me?" the woman's voice didn't shake, but I was certain she trembled.

"Welcome to the Lost and Found, miss." I smiled and hoped I appeared approachable and not fatherly, though she wasn't much younger than me. "What can I do for you?"

"Do you really… find… lost… *things*?" her voice was losing its initial strength and her hand inched toward her throat.

"Yes." I kept it simple.

"And I pay you… in fudge?" She squinted a little.

I hadn't seen her before so I tilted my head to the side and took a better look at her. Hollow streams in her essence. That wasn't good. It always felt like a gut punch when I saw someone missing a part of themselves.

"That depends on what it is you've lost." I didn't look at her face. I was a coward. I went back to Morry's form, seeing that she's also managed to misspell "black cat" as "balak catt." Her letters were coming along nicely. "You can sometimes pay in gold jewelry, breaths of fresh air, or birthday wishes."

The woman stepped closer, resting her hand on the edge of my counter, bringing the scent of fresh greenery with her. Nails unpainted. No rings.

I looked at her once more, drawn into that face with the strange empty places where she should be. I envied the golden glow to her skin. Different than mine, which was so pasty it was nearly grey. Her hair wasn't as dark as mine, though hers looked like it would be the softest to touch.

"I would say you'll think I'm crazy," she said, her wide brown eyes shifting around. No one else here. "I haven't been in the city long, but I've lived here long enough to… *know*."

I nodded slightly. Newcomers to the Between were rare here in Halifax. The residents thought it was south of North End, or maybe West of the Citadel, though the location never felt the same to everyone. Still, if they belonged, they always seemed to find a place to live in the borough that wasn't on any map. Their neighbours tended to show them the ropes. Don't leave personal items outside. Don't follow the lights by the water. And never take anything someone says as less than literal. Especially if they talk to you from the shadows.

But I already knew she had spoken to the shadows.

"What is it that you've lost?" I kept my voice low.

She pulled a lip between her teeth, squinting at me.

I waited. Those that made deals never liked to admit it to someone who knew.

"Time." She breathed the word out like a sob.

I rested my elbows on the counter. "Tell me."

And she did. How she'd been outside, strolling along the waterfront, and hadn't realized how dark it had gotten. She must have talked to herself out loud because someone answered. At first, she'd thought it was her neighbour; it sounded like her. Only she couldn't quite make out the face, only a shadow. And the shadow that wasn't her neighbour offered her the thing this woman had sought if she was willing to give something in return.

"I need to know the specific words of the trade," I said, sliding a fresh form from the stack and making notes.

"But I didn't—"

I looked up at her and she cut off, not meeting my eyes as she continued. "I didn't think it was real."

I continued making notes. Everyone in Between had stories about friends that made a deal with the shadows. Uncle Silas who went from a hermit to the most popular man in the city overnight. It took three weeks before we noticed he'd begun to shrink. Soon enough, there was no denying that he had made a trade. Last time anyone saw him, he'd been no more than a meter tall. Folks still talked about him; still laughed about the parties. But then they'd remember. And the smiles would slide off their faces like melting ice cream.

No one ever mentioned fond memories of my father, either before or after he'd made his deal. He'd always told me I was his best choice. Best choice he ever made. But then he'd made another choice.

I cleared my throat. "I need to know the words as exactly as you remember them." I paused my pen over the blank spaces on the form.

"I just wanted... a little more opportunity. More of a chance to be better; be happier, you know?"

I did know.

Her fingernails dug into the counter a little. "Opportunity. In exchange for something I waste."

I knew my look spoke skepticism before her reaction confirmed it, dropped eyes and drawn shoulders.

"That's as much as I can remember."

"For something you waste?"

She nodded, finding the counter more interesting than my face. "I assumed it would be the water I leave running when I brush my teeth, or maybe those last few pieces of rice that stick to the pot. I was so relieved that I didn't think to clarify."

I blew out a breath. "But the, uh, shadows are particular. While they aren't usually literal or after physical things, they don't go in for vagaries." Even as I said it, a name surfaced. I pushed it back down. Didn't want to draw attention to our conversation just yet.

Her slight shoulders shrugged. Maybe she was younger than I thought.

I poised the pen again, relieving her of the burden of my gaze. "Now, tell me why you think you're missing time."

"I don't usually daydream or doze off," she said. "But lately, I'm doing that. Only I don't remember any daydreams, and I don't actually wake up. I just become aware that time has passed."

I nodded and made a few more notes. "The voice that told you it would give you something in exchange for something... was it male or female?"

She thought for a moment, lower lip tucked into her teeth again. "Female."

"Did this female give you a name? Or a... general feeling?"

There was a pause. I had to admit it was a strange question. Not the strangest I could ask, though.

"There was... the smell of... black pepper?" her voice drifted to a whisper. "And there was a little bit of sadness. But I wondered if that was coming more from me."

I set my pen down very carefully, before I dropped it. "Pepper? You're sure?"

Her nod barely moved her hair.

"Then I have good news and I have bad news." I steepled my fingers under my chin. "The good news? I know which shadow holds your contract."

Her throat moved as she swallowed. "And the bad?"

"The bad news," I said, with a sigh, "is that I know which shadow holds your contract. And it's going to cost so much more than fudge."

◆

Before I could think about the woman's contract – Blaire. Her name was Blaire. I ought to start using her name as it would help keep her anchored – I first had to fulfill my agreement with Morry.

Bridges were a good place to contact wisps or even the occasional shadow. Bridges were also structures of Between, not really on land and not on the water, either. Transitional. Much like the wisps themselves.

So it was that I found myself with a half pound of fudge in my pocket, picking my way down to the edge of the shoreline under the MacKay Bridge. Nova Scotia was full of all sorts of middle ground. Between the ocean and the continent. Between Canadian and Scottish. It was nearly dusk, also the ideal between time. I prepped my supplies as the traffic on the toll bridge roared by overhead.

Fudge. Lighter. Picture of Scorpio. Few clumps of the cat's hair. Sprig of dried lavender. Rock candy sugar crystals.

A while ago, I'd found a mostly flat rock half-submerged in the water. I'd been using it for the wisps ever since, and the above-water portion was now heavy with burn marks. I used a compact feather duster to clear the dirt. I set the fudge down on the non-burned side and unwrapped it from its paper, the sweet chocolate scent overpowering the smell of the heavily-traveled waters, tempting me to sneak a nibble. When was the last time I'd had fudge?

Next, I layered the lavender, sugar, and hair on the blackened side of the rock. Honestly, the lavender was mostly because the smell of burning hair and sugar was absolutely awful.

The sky was streaked with pinks verging on orange. It was time.

Sitting cross-legged on the ground beside the rock, I drew in a deep breath, not loving the mix of ocean, city, and exhaust.

As I released the breath, I set the picture on top of the other items.

I held the lighter first to the top right corner of the photo, letting the edge take the flame before moving clockwise to the next corner. As the last corner caught, I focused on the smoke rising from the picture.

"Scorpio," I said, drawing out the word.

I closed my eyes, breathing mostly through my mouth, the setting sun still warm on my back.

There was a tickle of my senses, like the beginning of a sneeze. It wasn't the smoke or the cat hair. I was no longer alone. I heard the crinkle of paper, a muted giggle that could have been water ripples. Then, a soft press against my forehead. Like a kiss from a small, glowing ball of multi-coloured mischief. Which is exactly what it was. Why the wisps insisted on kissing me, I didn't understand. But it had never failed to signal the acceptance of an exchange.

The smell of the burning hair and sugar shifted briefly to ocean breeze, the scent of salt strong, then faded away to nothing but what had been there before: car exhaust and water pollution.

I cracked open one eye. Wisps didn't bother leading away humans, but it didn't hurt to be careful.

The pile of ashes on the stone drifted away on a non-existent breeze, out toward the ocean. And, of course, the fudge was gone. There was a fine dusting of what might be mistaken for sugar, but as I carefully collected it into a special bag, I felt the tingle from the wisp dust.

I stood, brushed off my jeans, and headed back toward the roadway, stumbling only a little as a stiff breeze ripped past. Scorpio would be home with Morry before her bedtime.

If only helping Blaire would be as easy.

Thinking about the woman with the too-scared eyes brought a twinge to my heart. I was the only one I was aware of with the connection between the worlds, just like my father had been, before his life-ending deal. It was very nearly a compulsion to help, like my entire existence depended on it. Make myself useful, so they wouldn't decide I didn't belong.

But Blaire? Not only had she made the deal without really understanding, the terms hadn't been specified. That was rare. And even rarer still when it was the shadow that smelled like freshly ground black pepper. Her name started to bubble up again and I squelched it back down before I caught her attention. Instead, I inhaled sharply.

Incense. I must be close to the Black Market. Might be just the thing to distract me. And no, the colourful boutique isn't a front for illegal goods. Quite the opposite. A perfectly legal, commercial business.

I crossed the threshold, basking in the flood of incense and spice, far too melded together to differentiate. Just as I filled my lungs with those delicious smells, a familiar fluff of soft hair by the shelves of pottery caught my attention. For half a second, I considered backing out of the boutique.

She turned around. Blaire blinked at me, full lashes fluttering for a moment.

Tucking my hands in the pockets of jeans, I walked forward, casually. Just two acquaintances meeting. Nothing abnormal about that.

"Yes, I'm real," I said, hoping my smile was enough to let her know I was teasing.

She barked a short laugh, then carefully set down the pot she'd held. "This feels a little like running into your elementary school teacher at the grocery store."

I grinned wider and nodded toward the shelf behind her. "Looking at getting an incense burner?"

"Before I found you, I did all sorts of crazy web searches and a surprising number of them recommended burning sage."

I shrugged. "Not a bad idea. But that's mostly for keeping away spirits and bad vibes. The shadows are neither of those things."

I saw her swallow.

"I thought you might say that." She turned her back to the shelves. "So what brings you in here? Looking for a hand-carved mask?"

"Nah, I got plenty of those." I wasn't joking. "I just really like the way this place smells. I feel much more… human."

She took in a deep breath, smiling. It was difficult to look at her face and see the parts of her that were missing.

I let my expression turn serious. "I'm going to contact your shadow tonight. See if I can't make another deal."

She crossed her arms as if against a sudden chill despite the warm summer air. "Is that how it usually goes? I have to make another deal?"

I shrugged. "That's pretty much your only option. I could argue that you didn't understand the arrangement, that the terms weren't clearly stated. But this particular shadow? Doesn't go for arguments that would sway a judge."

"You know her?" Blaire's voice softened as she moved closer to me.

Despite the other people in the shop, I wasn't afraid of being overheard. If those around us had never stepped foot in the Between, they wouldn't hear us talking. Just one more way the shadows protected themselves.

"I know all of the shadows." I looked over Blaire's head at the artwork covering the wall, realizing for the first time just how short she was. I mean, I had a few inches on her and I was only about average height. Pretty much everything about me was average. Not standing out made it easier to blend in.

Her eyes had gone too-wide again.

"I'm not exactly friends with them," I said, hands digging deeper into my pockets. "We don't invite each other over for Sunday roast or meet up for drinks."

She breathed out slowly.

I wondered when she had started holding her breath. At this point, I realized this was the longest conversation I'd had with someone outside the Between in... well, in a very long time. The thought made my stomach clench into a hard knot.

"I better get going." I took a step back and not quite into a rack of metal-work jewelry.

"Okay," she said, and was I imagining how relieved she looked? "I guess I'll see you around."

"Yep," I said, turning toward the door and almost tripping over a stack of baskets. My pulse was pounding straight up to my head, but I did my best not to look like I was fleeing the scene.

Once outside, I headed immediately for the Citadel. The shadows like old places, and while it wasn't the oldest place downtown, it had a presence. It was fully dark now and the Citadel had closed hours ago, but there was a hidden tunnel my father had shown me that went under the walls. The door there had a heavy lock but always opened up readily enough for us. Even under the low lighting inside, I easily made my way to the front gate.

I took deep, steadying breaths as I walked, keeping my hands out of my pockets so I could flex my fingers. The air was a little damp tonight, though there was no taste of rain. Shadows liked the rain.

I turned my body in a clockwise circle, keeping my eyes open. I'd learned long ago to always keep my eyes open when dealing with shadows. If I didn't keep them in my sights, they got a little difficult to see. Even for me. Once the circle was complete, I blew out the breath I'd been holding and spoke a name. "Ovida." drawing out the three syllables, emphasis on the "i."

I waited.

The wind picked up a little.

I waited.

The wind died back down.

I waited.

The sky turned grey.

I scowled.

She had never failed to appear when I had called. Never.

I stamped my feet to ease the ache from standing so long. A thought occurred to me. Perhaps she hadn't come because she was otherwise occupied?

Blaire.

At once my heart was in my throat and I was moving toward the hidden tunnel.

Several strangled minutes later, I found myself downtown. A slight pop in ear pressure and the street before me split into two: one real world, one Between. It was far too early to expect anyone awake to ask if they knew where Blaire lived.

Removing a pinch of wisp dust, I concentrated on the image of the smiling Blaire and pressed the dust to my tongue. It melted within a breath, leaving only the taste of salt and warmth. I closed my eyes, filling in the details of her face, blowing my breath out through my mouth as I spoke her name. When I opened my eyes again, my feet moved, turning to the left, taking a dirt path around to the back of a red townhouse.

The windows were all dark. I didn't know if I should be relieved or more worried. Next thing I knew, I was knocking lightly on the weathered white door.

I stepped back from the door, alternating between staring at my fist and the door it had rapped against. I was a second away from turning and going quietly back down the wooden stairs, when the light flicked on over the tiny porch and the knob turned.

And there was Blaire, face still puffy from sleep, but holding a mug from which wafted a lovely, warm, sweet smell.

"Hi," was my brilliant greeting.

She blinked at me in surprised recognition, much like she had back at the boutique. "Hi."

We stood there a moment, just sort of staring at each other before she gave her head a soft shake and stepped back, opening the door further.

"Please," she said, retreating further into the interior. "Come in."

"No, thanks," I said, taking a step back. "I just wanted to make sure you were okay."

"Oh."

"The, uh, the shadow refused to meet with me." I glanced behind me like Ovida was hiding in the bushes or something. "She's never done that before. I was worried that something was wrong."

"Oh." This time she said it with a frown.

"You usually get up this early?" I motioned to the mug.

"What? No. I… couldn't sleep."

We stood there for another awkward moment.

I ran a hand through my hair. "Well, it looks like you're just fine, so I think I'll head home." I jerked a thumb over my shoulder, only to realize that my place was in the opposite direction.

"Okay. Thanks for checking on me." She had a vaguely confused look.

I stumbled back down the steps and heard her door close behind me. I took small comfort in not hearing the lock slide after.

Stuffing my hands in my pockets, I tuned toward my apartment. "That was pretty much a disaster," I said to myself.

"It very nearly was," a familiar voice answered.

The rising sun shone behind me but the shadow pacing me along the side of the house wasn't mine. I stopped walking. A beat later, it did, too. The scent of freshly ground pepper tickled at the back of my throat.

"Ovida." I attempted to swallow my irritation, but it just felt sour in my stomach.

The shadow folded her arms. If it weren't for the neatly trimmed hedge, I might have seen her foot tapping.

"How long was she here before you made a deal with her?" My anger drained away as my exhaustion surfaced.

The shadow scoffed.

I scowled. "You're usually not this cryptic."

"And you're usually not this transparent."

"What's that supposed to mean?"

"I do not have time for this, child." Ovida let her arms fall. "I have things to do before dawn finishes." She turned and very nearly vanished.

"What will it take to break Blaire's contract?" I blurted it out without the usual decorum and pleasantries. Ovida had stood me up tonight. I wasn't about to use any honorifics.

Ovida turned back to me. "I am not ready for that yet. And neither are you."

I stood there, flapping my mouth like a caught fish as Ovida turned and disappeared into nothing.

Instead of going home, I wandered back out onto the streets of downtown, soothed by the actions of ordinary people bustling around me, beginning their day.

Before I had a chance to piece through what Ovida had said, I saw a familiar storefront. Simple brown painted wood with yellowing blinds in the windows. The gold lettering on the glass front door read "Lost & Found."

I sighed a little. My storefront had come to find me, so someone needed me.

No sooner had I hung up my jacket and seated myself on the wooden stool behind the counter, than Morry pushed through the door. One sweatered arm held the door open while the other clutched a furry black shape wearing a matching sweater. The bright green eyes peering out of the hood did not share the girl's exuberance.

"He's back!" Morry's declaration bounced off the walls. "Scorpio came back!"

"Of course, he did," I said, a hand pressed to my chest in mock affront. "Did you doubt me?"

Morry giggled and stroked her cat's head.

I stifled a laugh at the cat's resigned posture in his girl's embrace.

"Hey, Morry," I said. "I wanted to thank you for bringing in Blaire yesterday. I hope I can help her."

Morry looked at me, head tilted and nose wrinkled. "Who's Blaire?"

"The woman from yesterday? She had hair like yours. Brown eyes. She came in with you."

But Morry was shaking her head before I finished. "I didn't *bring* her. She was outside. Like she was scared or something. You can be kind of scary."

I snorted. "How am I scary?"

Morry's forehead wrinkled and she squeezed one eye shut. "Sometimes, even when you're right there, sometimes it's hard to, you know, like it's hard to... see you?"

That made me pause.

"Morry," I asked, holding my voice steady. "What's my name?"

Her eyebrows shot up. She didn't answer.

"I've told you my name before," I coached. "Three times. You should have remembered after three times."

Morry started to say something, but the door opened and her mother leaned inside. "Morry, time to go."

Morry gave me a sad smile before holding out her fist to be bumped by mine. After our finger explosions, she hefted Scorpio over her shoulder and ducked out the door.

"Maggie," I said, standing.

"Oh, hi," Morry's mother looked back, smiled. "I didn't see you there."

I wanted to say more, but my voice left me. They didn't see me. Not really.

Maggie gave me a small wave and closed the door.

Sitting back down on the stool, I sat there for a good moment or three. When was the last time someone called me by name? When had one of my neighbors greeted me first?

I couldn't remember.

No one else appeared at the door. I grabbed my jacket, deciding that the storefront could find me if anyone else needed it.

Maybe I was too distracted by the bizarre morning, but it took several tries to find the entrance where the street split. I charged around the corner of the red townhouse and nearly collided with Blaire, just coming out the door and pulling on a gray sweatshirt.

When she saw me, her eyes started to go wide, peering around me like she expected Ovida to pop up.

"Hey, long time no see." I smiled.

Her eyes stopped getting larger and she gave me a small smile in return.

"This is going to seem like a strange question," I said, my hands stuffed firmly in my pockets. "But did I ever tell you my name?"

She blinked, started to reply, then stopped. "You know, I don't think you did."

My shoulders dropped. I was certain I had told her, after I asked her name and wrote it on her form. Almost certain.

"It's Nash," I said. "My name is Nash."

"Nice to meet you, Nash." She grinned. "Are you headed back home?"

I looked down the street toward my apartment and felt no desire to be indoors. "I think I might take a little walk instead. It's been kind of a weird morning already."

"Oh." She looked down the street and then back at me. "Maybe I'll walk with you."

I followed Blaire, working my jaw to ease the pop of pressure and saw her stifle a small yawn, probably doing the same thing.

Moments later, we were thanking the waitress for bringing our food. I paused before picking up my fork. Which one of us had suggested we get breakfast? I wasn't sure.

"This is good," Blaire said around a mouthful of fresh fruit.

"I can't remember the last time I had a decent meal," I said, my mouth stuffed with omelet.

"So you live alone?"

"Ever since my dad… uh, died," I said, swallowing my food hard enough to make me reach for juice to wash it down.

"I'm sorry to hear that," she said. "My parents are both gone, too. My dad when I was little and my mom two years ago."

She'd said it without a bubble of emotion, but there was something about the sharing that made me want to lean a little closer to her.

Talk turned to her plants, of which she had dozens in her tiny apartment. Could explain the smell of fresh greenery around her. I was content to listen, though I hoped there wouldn't be a test because no way would I be able to remember all those names that she used so easily. But I did notice that the smile that I had thought was rare hadn't left her face once she began talking about plants.

We exited the restaurant, continuing to walk.

"All of them?" I scoffed. "All of your house plants have a name? And it doesn't involve some sort of complicated Latin phrase?"

"Of course they have a name," she said, giving me an exaggerated scowl that did adorable things to her forehead. "How else am I going to talk to them?" She giggled, a sound I liked very much.

We rounded a corner and any other questions I might have asked died on my tongue.

There was my storefront. The gold-lettered "Lost & Found" sign separated two stores that had previously been side by side.

Blaire had ground to a halt, too. "But I thought your shop was over on…" She glanced back over her shoulder, her dark eyes squinting.

"My shop is part of the Between." I shrugged. "It kinda shows up when I'm needed. Which it looks like I am. So I guess this is goodbye for now."

"Okay," she said, her eyes still distant. "This was fun."

She stood there a moment before nodding and continuing on past the storefront.

I resisted the urge to watch her walk away and pushed open the door, the smell of wood polish and lavender my only greeting.

I let out a slow sigh, settling on the wooden stool only a moment before the door burst open.

Harvey rushed in, nearly slamming the door behind him. He heaved his sweating frame to the counter and then bent over, panting, like he'd run the entire way here.

"Nash, thank gods," he rasped, clinging to the counter like a life preserver in a storm. "You gotta help me."

"Hello, Harvey." I'd had to smother my wince when he'd first walked in, but after hearing him use my name, I was feeling a little more charitable. "What's the problem?"

"It's those blasted shadows," he wheezed. "They won't make a deal with me."

I felt my eyes narrow. "Not really what I do here, Harvey."

He wagged his head back and forth. "You don't understand, Nash. It's Lorena. She's gonna leave me. I gotta find a way to make her stay."

"Have you tried counseling?"

He gaped at me. I watched red creep up his neck and decided that he wasn't open to solutions that required effort on his part.

"Harvey," I said. "I help people get out of their deals, not broker more of them."

"She's gonna leave!" A glob of spittle hit the counter just before Harvey's fist.

I met his watery eyes and then slowly stood, bracing my hands on the counter as I leaned toward him. "You need to calm down."

"I'm calm!" He began pacing in front of the counter, hands making a mess of his already sparse hair. "Blasted shadows! Not even Zill would deal. Zill! He smells like… *brine*."

"You spoke with Zill?" I asked.

"Of course!" Harvey threw his hands up again. "He's the first one I made a deal with. But he said no and then just disappeared."

I tilted my head to the side. "I'm absolutely positive it was Lalo that made your first deal for uh, male enhancement. Cost the use of your left two fingers. It was the first time I helped you, remember? I exchanged the use of your fingers for your toes."

"Right, right." He had both hands pressed to the top of his head. "Lalo. Well, he wouldn't talk to me, either."

"How many shadows did you try to contact?"

"All of them," Harvey muttered, nearly tearing his hair out. "Not a single one stayed after I said what I wanted. I offered them my youth, the hearing in one of my ears. Anything they wanted! And they all left!"

Harvey was pushing 65. Not a whole lot of youth left there to claim.

"You have to be careful, Harvey." I shook my head. "The shadows really will take anything."

Blaire's haunted look floated before my eyes. I blinked and replaced it with her smile instead.

Harvey slammed both hands down on the counter, jarring me back to the present.

"They can have *everything* as long as I can keep Lorena," he said, spit flying.

"Fixes don't have to come from magic," I said, setting my jaw to keep from grinding my teeth. "The shadows don't help us."

That seemed to enrage him further because this time, he leaned toward me.

"What do you even know about it?" He growled. "Just because the shadows never helped you? Maybe they *were* helping when they took your daddy."

I'm not exactly sure what my face must have done then, but whatever it was, Harvey backed out of the door about a fast as he had arrived.

I braced my elbows on the counter and dropped my head into my hands. The shadows never helped anyone. Never. They made deals that people regretted and took things that belonged to someone else, someone alive with plenty of years ahead of them. Someone with no previous health problems. Someone who had a son at home that needed him.

I could almost hear the words he frequently said to me *"Best choice, Nash. You're the best choice I ever made."*

The sun was setting before I came up from my memories. I slid off the stool, grabbed my jacket and headed for the door.

I didn't quite focus on the street until I opened a door and the flush of humidity and green hit me as I entered the nursery where Blaire had told me she worked. Before I could back out, I saw her coming toward me, a dirt-smudged tan apron tied around her waist.

"Hi," she said, eyes glowing.

"Hi," I replied.

Immediately her face shifted to concern. "Hey, are you okay?"

"Rough day at work," I said, feeling the weight of the day on my eyelids. When was the last time I'd slept? Hell, when was the last time I'd been home?

"My shift is just ending," she said, untying her apron. "Let me go clock out. Okay?"

I nodded, letting everything go hazy until she was back, taking my arm and pulling me out the door. Walking away from the nursery, I realized Blaire brought a lot of the green smell with her.

"Do you want to talk about it or be distracted from it?" she asked.

I almost stumbled. "I… don't really know."

She didn't look at me, just nodded. "Okay. Let's try distraction and then, when you're ready, you can talk. If you want."

I blew out a breath, feeling my chest tighten and maybe my eyes getting a little prickly. "Sounds good."

We circled back to the food trucks and picked up a couple orders of poutine.

Blaire filled the emptiness, talking first about the dog she'd had as a kid that she'd trained to bark any time she practiced the piano so her mom would get frustrated and Blaire wouldn't have to practice as long. She told me about her first garden, contained in a sliced-open juice carton.

By the time we were saying goodbye in front of her place, the hollowness left by memories of my dad was gone, filled up with Blaire's chatter.

She cocked her head to the side, eyes squinting at me. "Your eyes are grey. Like a dark grey."

"Same as they were yesterday." I grinned.

"Yesterday I thought they were nearly black." She shrugged. "I guess that's what happens when you start to really see someone. Goodnight, Nash."

I watched her walk up the stairs and open her door. "Goodnight!" I called like an idiot as she slipped inside.

I headed for my own apartment. After being outside with Blaire, the air indoors was stale and nothing in the fridge looked edible.

After sniffing some questionable milk, I said, "When was the last time I went to the store?"

"Too long ago," Ovida answered behind me.

I slammed the refrigerator shut. "What's with sneaking up on me?"

Ovida stretched across the counter, effectively bending herself in half. "You did not look for me, so I came to look for you."

The scent of black pepper in my nose made me think back to that omelet I'd had with Blaire that morning. I could feel the smile on my lips.

"I came to tell you a thing that you must know," Ovida said, drifting out of the kitchen and into the living room where the light had fewer angles. "It is something I was sure your father had told you." After a brief pause, she continued. "Not all deals are bad, child."

I swallowed hard, my stomach turning. All deals were bad. *Always.*

She stopped moving, turned to face me. The features of her face were faint, but I could still make them out if she stood still long enough. Like she was doing now. Did she want me to think of her as more like a human?

I scoffed.

Her head moved slightly, perhaps nodding. "Then I shall prove it."

I raised my eyebrows, waiting.

"Morry."

My teeth ground together.

Ovida continued. "Why do you never wonder about her father?"

I blinked. I hadn't ever... what?

"Maggie and Morry made a deal, long before they came to Between. They traded all their memories of Morry's father, the bad ones along with the few good memories, to keep Morry safe from the man. They've been here ever since. Safe. He cannot reach Between, no matter how he might try."

"All he has to do," I kept my voice level, "Is make a deal."

Ovida shook her head. "No shadow will take that deal. Like Harvey's. He wants a deal that would harm another. We do not make deals that harm others."

I opened my mouth to disagree, but stopped. I couldn't think of one. Not a single deal in a decade of sitting on that wooden stool where anyone else besides the one that made the deal was hurt. My head spun.

All deals were bad.

"What about my dad?" I hated how my voice trembled. "He made a deal. That deal killed him. And I was left alone."

I had to swallow back the tears that climbed toward my eyes.

Ovida moved closer. I could see the vaguely lighter grey of her eyes. "No. He made the deal to help you."

"Why?" I nearly lost my grip on that one.

Ovida reached out a hand, brushed my cheek with a touch that like a soft breeze. "Oh, my child. There is so much that you have forgotten."

She leaned forward and kissed my forehead.

Memories flooded back like a tidal wave through a straw. I hit my knees, gasping.

Me, as a child. Dad swinging me through the air. Dad reading me a bedtime story as I cuddled under a blanket. Dad griping my shoulders, now almost as tall as he was, tears streaming down his face as he said "The best choice, Nash. You were the best choice I ever made."

Ovida crouched beside me, a dark spot as my memories collided. "A deal is always a choice."

Dad swinging me through the air, my legs shapeless. Dark as shadow. Dad, reading a story as I clutched a blanket with shadowed fingers that lost their form when too close together. Dad, gripping my shoulders. "You were the best choice."

"He died so that he could have… a son?" I choked on my words as they came out, hot and wet.

"No, my child." Ovida's touch ruffled my hair. "The choice to have a son was one he and I made together."

I stared into her grey eyes. So much like mine.

"He died," she said in the softest tone I'd ever heard her use, "So that you could become human."

I stared down at my hands, the skin revealing undertones of grey. I'd always thought it was the lack of sunshine. Or maybe because I didn't eat regularly.

"Nash," she said, her voice no louder than a whisper. "Whenever you use magic to talk to the wisps, to work spells for humans, it costs you a part of your humanity. You need to remember what it means to be human, how much it meant to your father."

I couldn't speak, couldn't form words as the world I'd built for myself crumbled in front of the truth.

"That is why I brought Blaire here," she said, pulling back from me. "You needed to remember what it is about humanity that is worth saving before you lose any more of yourself and return to being a shadow. Like your mother."

She drifted away, turning, disappearing.

♦

Someone was knocking on my door.

I slowly came back to myself. Still on my knees, I stood. And was immediately reminded of my humanity by the pins and needles in my feet.

The knocking turned into pounding. I could hear the muffled sound of my name through the door. Limping as the feeling returned to my feet, I staggered to the door and wrenched it open.

Maggie nearly fell into my arms, her face wet with tears, still wearing her scrubs.

I held her as she gulped in air, her eyes wide and glued to my face.

"Morry," she sobbed out, her fingers gripping my jacket. "She's gone."

"Okay, deep breath."

Maggie obliged.

"Now let it out."

The exhale came with racking sobs.

"Tell me."

And she did. She'd worked the night shift at the hospital. She hated leaving Morry alone, but Morry insisted she and Scorpio would be fine. Still, she'd asked Lorena to check in on the girl and make sure she got tucked into bed. But when Lorena got there, she saw Morry in her pyjamas, dashing down the street, yelling after Scorpio as he chased a yellow ball of light. Lorena ran after them, but soon lost them in the dark. She'd called the hospital. Maggie came straight to find me.

"The wisps," Maggie said. "She's followed the wisps."

Morry was a smart girl, except when it came to her cat. I'd never had to trade for a human before, and neither had my dad, as far I could remember. I'd have to go find her myself. It might be the only way to bring her back.

"I'll find her," I said, easing Maggie to standing on her own.

I grabbed an old backpack from the closet and went to the pantry. As far as sugar went, I didn't have a lot of options. Half bag of granulated sugar. Halloween candy from some year long past. Pack of spearmint gum that was actually sugar-free. A mostly full box of sugar-coated cereal. It all went in the backpack.

A soft knock, and I looked over my shoulder to see Blaire peering in the door. I hefted my pack over a shoulder and went back to Maggie.

"I came to help," Blaire said.

Seeing Blaire, here, made me stop.

I would have to use the wisp magic to find Morry. More than I'd ever used before. If I did that, there was a very good chance I'd use too much. A cold pit formed in my gut and I shivered.

I looked back at Maggie. For the first time, I could see the streak in her essence, the pieces that were missing. Was this why she'd never stayed around me too long? For fear that I would see that she had made a deal?

But it was looking at Maggie and seeing her daughter's eyes looking back at me that decided it.

For Morry, I would risk it.

I handed Maggie over to Blaire.

"I'm sorry, Blaire," I said, trying to drink in the plant smell of her, even as I memorized every detail of her face. "I can't take you with me. Wait down by the waterfront under the MacKay Bridge. I'll bring her there."

Blaire threw her free arm around my neck and pulled my head down. She brushed a kiss across my cheek and whispered, "Be careful."

I couldn't make that promise. I squeezed her back, drew in a deep breath of her sweet scent, and let go.

Now that I remembered being a shadow, slipping out of Between was easy. No pressure pop. The wisps liked light, and I knew the best place for lights in the city.

I turned at the Halifax Convention Centre, taking the walkway underneath the facility. Lined with restaurants, there were plenty of neon signs, but I concentrated on the ceiling, hung with dozens of screens and panels flashing ads or seasonal displays. So much light in a small place.

Removing the bag of wisp dust, I shook most of it into my hand. I didn't know how much this would take, having never had to bring back a person before. I might only have one shot. I emptied the bag, closed my eyes, and palmed the small pile of dust into my mouth.

I filled my head with images of Morry over the years that I'd known her. Handing over a huge lollipop for the first time Scorpio went missing. Her and Scorpio in matching sweaters. Morry and Maggie walking hand in hand down the street of Between. Morry offering a fist bump.

My mouth felt like I'd gargled with boiling seawater.

"Morry," I breathed out and opened my eyes.

The flashing screens above dripped radiant blue light, joining the mass of shimmering dust that built in front of me, twisting and winding like a mini tornado.

I wondered if maybe I'd used too much when the funnel began to move toward me.

"Nash!"

I turned to see Blaire running around the corner. I opened my mouth to tell her to stay back, but her gaze drifted past me. I looked down, seeing the skin of my hand darkening to shadow.

The funnel swallowed, lifted, and swept me away.

I rolled through the winds of light, holding onto a name: *Morry*.

When the magic left me, I stood on my own as dozens of multi-coloured wisps flickered around me.

"Morry," I said with what felt like an immense effort, but the word came out as a whisper, like trying to scream in a dream.

"Mommy?"

I whirled toward the noise.

A little girl in green footie pyjamas stood in the midst of the wisps, a black cat clutched in her arms.

I went toward her, finding movement much easier than speech.

Her eyes widened and she took a staggering step back. She didn't see me; she saw a shadow.

I stopped. Last thing I needed was to scare her away.

I crouched down to her height. Then, I held out my fist. When she didn't move, I made my fingers spread out, though the explosion noise should more like shushing.

Her eyes still wide, I saw her shoulders relax and she leaned closer to me, as if studying my face. "Nash?"

I nodded.

"Are you here to take me home?"

I nodded again, stood and offered her my hand.

She took it, and the weight of her touch felt like the kid stood in my palm. No wonder shadows didn't like to touch humans.

I turned, looking around the space. The area beneath my feet felt solid enough but I could make out the waves of the ocean below. The sparkling lights of the city on both sides meant we must be out in the Narrows. This wasn't the human world or the Between where magic touched. This was the Other.

There weren't just wisps here. I saw shadows, though none approached us. And the agitated way they moved told me they weren't too happy with having a human – Morry – in their domain. They didn't seem to mind me. I was one of them.

One shadow split from the others and came toward us. Here, I could finally see her clearly.

"Ovida," I said in my whispery voice. "Mother."

She put a hand on my shoulder and the other on Morry's. The little girl didn't appear frightened; this was the shadow that kept her safe.

I motioned to Morry. "Save her."

Ovida shook her head. "A deal won't save her. Only an exchange."

I started to slide the backpack from my shoulders when Ovida stopped me with a shake of her head.

"You have already made the exchange."

I looked down at my now shapeless body, the way the fingers of my hand shifted as they held onto Morry's.

"Not all deals are bad, Nash," Ovida said. "It is only when some get greedy, make choices, but don't want the consequences."

I nodded. I'd be expected to make deals now. That would be my role. There would be no more storefront or my father's stool.

"We've been shadows for so long, that we do not remember that some things have a greater price."

"Like time?" I rasped out.

Ovida nodded. "Did you never wonder why I chose time? Why I collected wasted minutes?"

I tilted my head.

"To save them, Nash," Ovida leaned closer. "To save her time so she would have more of it to spend with you."

She shifted to caress the little girl's hair. "We still have need of one who talks to the Between. And this one? Perhaps one day, she will learn to talk to us. She cannot stay. You must take her back."

I looked down at the girl. The weight of her hand taking all my strength. She had a name, I knew this. But I could not recall.

"Take her back," Ovida said, turning my shoulder toward one of the strips of lights along the shore.

I wanted to stare at the lights, soak in their beauty and strength. Another nudge on my back told me it was time to go.

I slung the girl onto my back. She only held on with one arm as the other grasped her cat. I staggered.

"Take her back." Ovida's tone turned into a command.

I looked one last time at my mother and then I took a step toward the lights.

♦

As soon as the girl's feet touched the shoreline, I dropped.

"Mommy!" I heard her squeal, then followed by muffled cries and sobs.

Relief flooded me. I had done it. I brought the girl back.

"Nash?" The voice was too soft for the mother and too old for the little girl. "Where are you?"

A small figure stood on the edge of the shoreline, just meters from me. I didn't have the energy to move to see her better.

"Mommy, Nash saved me and Scorpio," the little girl told someone.

"I know, sweetie, but where is he?"

"He was right there."

And I was. Only too weak to show myself.

"Nash?" the other voice called again. "Let me help you."

Help me? How was this tiny human supposed to help? I had drained all the magic that held me together to bring the girl back, and a human thought they could help me? I would have laughed if I could have drawn in air.

"My child." This was a voice I knew.

Mother.

Beside me. Leaning down. So beautiful in her darkness. Now I could stay with her.

She kissed my forehead and filled my head with memories.

A woman with too-wide eyes. A woman with soft hair and a kind smile. A woman who loved plants and smelled like fresh greenery. A woman who snorted when she laughed. A woman who held me and kissed my cheek. A woman who saw me when I started to fade away.

Blaire.

"There he is!" Blaire shouted, then tried running across the rocks toward me, slipping every other step.

I pushed myself up on one hip, marveling at the sudden brightness of my skin over what had been shadow.

Blaire tackled me. Too weak still to fend her off, I collapsed onto my back, taking the small woman with me.

"I'm okay," I managed to wheeze.

"I thought I'd lost you," she said, her voice muffled by my neck. She pushed back long enough to stare into my face, as serious as I'd ever seen her. "I don't want you to ever leave me again."

"Okay, tell you what. I stay with you," I brought a hand up to touch her face. "And you stay with me."

Her smile warmed me all the way through. "Deal."

Writer of the weird and the wonderful, Jena Rey has long been a fan of science fiction and fantasy. She finds inspiration in the Utah landscape where she lives with her amazing kids, sweet and sexy husband, and furry sidekicks.

About this story, Jena says: "The city of New Orleans is such a rich place to tap for a story. The city is a character in and of itself, where just about anything can happen. A favorite character of mine, Dianna McDunna came to the Crescent City many years ago, and I love telling her stories against the background of voodoo, the bayous, and – naturally – beignets."

It doesn't take much convincing to thoroughly enjoy this story. After all, with New Orleans as the backdrop, it's easy enough to believe just about anything could happen. And if the promise of beignets in the bayou aren't tempting enough for you – and why wouldn't they be? – perhaps the inclusion of a kick-ass heroine and a meth'd-up were-gator will do the trick.

SEE YOU LATER, ALLIGATOR
Jena Rey

Dianna McDunna grumbled as she slogged through the bayou toward where she'd parked her car. She'd spent the last two hours trying to follow up on an anonymous tip regarding a meth dump in the swampy land just outside of New Orleans, but all she'd found was bug bites, snakes, and stinking mud. It was going to take days to get the smell out of her clothes; maybe she should just burn them.

She kicked as much muck as possible off of her boots before climbing into the driver's seat and calling in her failure.

Dianna knew it was likely the cache had been picked up by someone before she ever got out here, but the NOPD followed up on tips whenever possible. The meth in the city lately had been cut with something bad and bringing in a good-sized stash would not only get it off the street, but give the lab something to analyze.

She retied her ponytail and started the car, heading back toward the glittering lights of home. If she hurried, it was still early enough that she could pick up an order of beignets at the Café Du Monde on her way. The thought of the crispy treats and a pile of powdered sugar with a tall iced coffee raised her spirits and made her stomach rumble.

Her personal phone rang, and she dragged her thoughts from the pastries, tapping on the hands free. "McDunna."

"Good evening, Miss Dianna."

The familiar voice filled the car, as smooth as dark chocolate. Dianna's stomach dropped.

Remy DePardue, a local voodoo priest, but one of the nasty variety.

Dammit.

Dianna scowled. "Hi, Remy. What do you want?"

"Oh now, cherie, that's not so nice."

Dianna licked her lips glad he couldn't see her face. "That's because every time you call, something bad is happening – and is probably going to happen to me."

He chuckled. She pictured his wide smile, the gold plating on his teeth shining. "That is not true."

"Uh huh. Name one time."

The silence drew out, and she glanced at the car's head's up display. The call was still connected.

"I suppose you are correct," he said finally. "But it is hardly my fault. I am simply your personal crow."

Dianna came to a stop at a red light. "That sounds more likely. So, I repeat, what do you want?"

"Marie wishes to see you. She has need of your services."

Marie Laveau, the Voodoo Queen of New Orleans.

Double dammit.

Mama Marie was the mambo of all mambos, the top of the food chain when it came to voodoo magic and the supernatural population in New Orleans. She had saved Dianna's life five years ago, and now Dianna owed her assistance upon request. Any assistance Marie demanded. It sucked.

Dianna banged her forehead on the steering wheel. "Can she wait? I'm coming back from the bayou, and I smell awful. You know how she feels about her carpets."

"F'sho. A moment."

Despite her hope that Marie would wait until the morning, Dianna didn't think it was likely. Marie expected her people, Dianna included, to jump first and ask for details later. If she was calling, she wanted action *now*. Dianna didn't wait for Remy's reply, she just signaled and made a U-turn when the light turned green, heading for Marie's manor on the outskirts of the city.

Two blocks later, the hands-free clicked, and Remy's voice returned. "No reprieve tonight. She says you should park in the back and wait in the servant's kitchen."

"Of course she does." Dianna bit back a sigh. It wouldn't do her any good to snip at him as much as she wanted to. It changed nothing, and wasted energy she'd need to deal with Marie who was already setting up a game of 'who's in charge here' by sending Dianna to the servant's entrance. It was an insult, and they both knew it. "Anything else I should know?"

Remy laughed, the sound bouncing around the interior of her car like a living thing. The old bakor enjoyed his role as Marie's Voice. "Nothing I'm going to tell you."

"Thanks. I hate you, too."

Dianna disengaged the call before he could respond. It was easier to get away with mouthing off on a phone call than it was in person. The *lwa* war spirit that rode around in the back of her head stirred, flashing an image of pushing her fingers into Remy's chest and pulling his heart out. The image and the flood of emotions that came with it were so powerful Dianna swerved to the side of the road and threw the car into park.

Her heart pounding, she closed her eyes, focusing inwardly. "Stop. Stop it right now. We aren't doing that."

Heat rushed through her body followed by a maelstrom of violent memories. The metallic scent of blood and warm stickiness on her fingers flooded her senses. The joy of combat and the thrill of the death rattle surged through her. Dianna breathed through the reminders, her knuckles turning white from her grip on the steering wheel. The war spirit loved nothing more than a good hunt and a screaming death, but he was not in charge of her.

She had taken on the spirit five years ago, and usually they got along. Not always. The *lwa* had been Marie's way of "saving" her life, and Dianna was absolutely certain Marie had been helping herself more than Dianna. If Dianna had died the mambo would have lost nothing; as it was, she'd gained a warrior to command.

"I said, 'Stop it.'"

The spirit roared at her, the sound only in her mind. She didn't back down. She couldn't if she wanted to remain herself.

"No."

A moment passed as she forced her will on the entity in a silent struggle. Finally, the *lwa* relented, curling up in the back of her mind with a sense Dianna could only call pouting. She sighed and peeled her fingers off the steering wheel, rubbing feeling back into them.

"I know. But take heart, we're going to see Marie. She probably wants us to clobber something. You'll get your chance."

It didn't respond.

Dianna put the car back in gear. This night was just getting better and better.

◆

Dianna sipped at a large mug of coffee, pacing the short stretch between the counter and the table in the small kitchen. She'd had to park nearly a mile away and walk in, the drive leading to the stately manor full of cars and people dressed in black tie finery. Marie was having a party, and Dianna recognized many of the vehicles. The Mayor and the Chief of Police were both here as were many of the city council. She didn't want to know why. Knowing things made her responsible to do something about them.

The servant's kitchen was mostly dark, lit only by the LED lights on the coffeemaker and a single dim sconce next to the door. For the number of people who were here, the cooking was being done in the large kitchen, leaving this one unoccupied. She'd grabbed one of the staff as they went by and sent word to Marie that she was here. Now all Dianna could do was wait. At least she'd been allowed the coffee. It wasn't great coffee, but it was coffee.

She crossed the kitchen several more times, tamping down the impatience that nagged at her. Marie would leave her cooling her heels for a while. She always did.

After nearly twenty minutes, Dianna heard the doorknob rattle. Marie Laveau stepped into the kitchen as regally as any queen in her palace. The petite black woman was beautiful, with smooth skin of rich brown that gave no sign of her true age. Her dark eyes though, there was age there. Age and power that always impressed, and occasionally terrified, Dianna. Fortunately, she was in good company as almost everyone was terrified of Marie – or at least what Marie was capable of.

Marie wore a black evening gown fitted through the bodice and hip with short sleeves. Silver and copper bangles clung to her wrists, and a long green lace shawl rested across her shoulders. Her silver-streaked black hair was tucked up under a purple satin cloth, twisted up around her head and secured with a large golden pin from which dangled a black drop pearl the size of Dianna's thumb.

"Good evening, child." Marie's voice was sweet and thick, like liquid molasses.

Dianna set her coffee down and met Marie's gaze. Anger reflected in those dark depths, anger looking for an outlet she didn't want to provide. Instead, Dianna dropped to one knee in front of Marie, inclining her head so she didn't have to look into those eyes. Madness lay there. "Good evening."

Marie laughed, letting her fingers come to rest on the top of Dianna's head. "Ah, feelin' compliant tonight, are we, cher?"

Marie's nails dug into Dianna's scalp, sending icy shivers across Dianna's skin. She clenched her teeth. "I'm just hoping to get home at a decent hour, Mama Marie. What do you need?"

"Ah. There's my warrior." Marie wrapped one finger in Dianna's russet-colored hair, pulling it tight. "My Claude has gone missing. You will recover him for me."

Dianna blinked, glancing up at Marie, her thoughts spinning. Claude was Marie's favorite servant and personal bodyguard. He was also an alligator shifter, though that was hardly common knowledge. He was huge, strong, and almost never left Marie's side unless he was hunting. He wasn't overly smart, but he didn't have to be for what he did.

"How long has he been missing?"

"He went for the hunt last night, and has not returned." Her fingers tightened, and Dianna bit back a yelp of pain. "Somethin' is wrong with his mind, warrior. I cannot summon him back, and my Ladisla is unavailable, so you will do this for me. You will return him and destroy whoever has taken what is mine."

"If he was an alligator and someone caught him, they may not know they've crossed you."

Marie lifted Dianna by her hair, forcing her to stand or lose a chunk of hair and scalp. The voodoo priestess didn't look strong enough to do any such thing, but this was only a fraction of the immortal woman's strength. Dianna again met Marie's gaze, seeing the anger turned to rage in the depths of her black, black eyes.

"I... do... not... care."

She tossed Dianna away from her, a few strands of hair clinging to her hands. Dianna hit the floor and rolled, gaining her feet in an instant. She didn't rub her head, or draw her gun, though she wanted to do both. She'd misjudged the extent of Marie's rage – and knew there was a lot more Marie could do to her if she wasn't cautious. The hair on the back of her neck and arms stood on end, and the war spirit jabbered at her, encouraging her to fight. Sometimes she wished she'd never taken the spirit on. She would have died if she hadn't, but that would have been far less complex than the life she lived now.

She cleared her throat. "Understood. Is there anything else I need to know?"

Marie shrugged and straightened her shawl. "You are the *gendarme*." Her sharp gaze again met Dianna's, drilling into her. "Find him."

Dianna swallowed and dropped her gaze. "Yes, Ma'am."

◆

Pounding music collided with her ears and skin as Dianna entered the antechamber to *Dark Secrets*. She'd gone home after meeting with Marie, but only long enough to change into clean clothing and swap out her service pistol and badge for her hunting kit before heading to the club.

The bullets in the gun she had tucked under her jacket alternated between silver and iron cores, dangerous to human or supernatural. A long iron knife went into a sheath on the inside of one knee-high boot, and an assortment of other useful toys, including a roll of electrical tape, into pouches on her back up Sally Brown belt.

There was a very thin line between the work she did as one of New Orleans' finest and her place within the supernatural community. She knew she wouldn't always be able to walk that line, but she was going to cling to it as long as she could.

The hostess, a pale gothling with a tag that proclaimed her name as 'Susan,' looked up when Dianna entered. "Good evening! Do *Dark Temptations* or *Dark Desires* guide you this night?"

Two large doors showed at either side of the room, one leading to the coffee club, *Dark Temptations*, and the other the dance club, *Dark Desires*. Dianna wasn't going to either. She reached into her jacket pocket and pulled out a laminated card, offering it to the girl. "VIP lounge, please."

Susan took the card and with one hand ran it under a black light, the other resting just under the podium where Dianna knew there was an emergency alarm. If the card didn't pass the inspection, Susan would hit the button and the bouncers would bustle Dianna off. Most of those who were escorted out joined the list of the 500 or so people who went missing without a trace in New Orleans every year.

A moment later, Susan nodded and handed Dianna's ID back to her. She gave Dianna a sunny smile that looked strange on her black-lipped face and stepped back, pulling a long black curtain aside to allow access to the hall behind her. "Have a good evening, Miss McDunna."

Dianna nodded and entered the long corridor. She felt the thumping bass through the walls, though the sound of the thrash metal music faded with each step and was soon replaced with softer, classical tones. She passed through the doorway at the end of the passage, rolling her shoulders, and shaking off some of her stress.

The VIP lounge was designed to be pleasing to the enhanced senses of the supernatural with soft scents and lighting. Water flowed down the walls in a trickle, back-lit in golds and greens and blues. Private booths and tables with elegant chairs were scattered around the room, and a black granite bar catering to the various tastes and needs of those who could afford to be here sat in the center of the display.

It seemed odd to come here without Ladis as her escort, but even Marie's favorites could be the recipients of her ire, and he was currently in a stone-filled coffin in the middle of the Mississippi and would be for another month. Dianna pushed thoughts of her mentor and friend away. She couldn't afford to be distracted. She made her way across the room, nodding to a few familiar faces as she approached the bar.

The bartender smiled, offering her a small glass full of dark golden liquid without being asked. "Ah, Mademoiselle McDunna, you grace us again with your presence. It has been so long." He leaned across the bar, brushing a kiss against her cheek.

"It's only been a couple weeks, Kyle." Dianna chuckled, picking up the glass. "But I appreciate it. You're the first person who has been honestly happy to talk to me all night."

"Tsk. Shame on them. I have told you, you should let me sweep you off your feet and take you away from all of this." He wiggled his eyebrows, a piercing showing in the left one bright against his cinnamon-colored skin. "We could run the fields of the Ever Gold and dance under a silver fairy moon."

"Right until your wife found out." A second voice came from behind Dianna's shoulder, familiar and amused. "Rhiannon does not share gladly."

Kyle frowned and sighed. "More's the pity. Your usual, Master Vachon?"

"Indeed. At my booth, please."

Kyle went to work behind the bar, and Dianna turned with a smile toward the new voice. Andre, a part-Choctaw man of medium height and an angelic face, offered Dianna his arm. "Shall we?"

Dianna tucked her hand in the crook of his arm, allowing Andre to escort her across the room. He walked smoothly with no rush to his stride, his cane clicking with each step. He didn't need the cane for any reason Dianna had ever been able to determine, but he carried it everywhere. She suspected there was a blade inside. It would suit him.

They reached one of the curtained booths, and Andre allowed her to settle in before seating himself. Kyle followed almost on their heels, carrying a tray with a large slab of cheesecake coated in chocolate and raspberry glaze and a wineglass filled with a dark brown liquid and a couple of green olives. He set the tray down, bowed to Andre, and gave Dianna a wink before returning to his position behind the bar.

A moment passed in silence as they both savored their drinks.

"I admit I was surprised to get your call tonight, Dianna. I thought Ladisla had forbidden you from speaking to me."

Dianna snorted, setting her glass of scotch on the table. "Ladis forbids stuff all the time. He's not the boss of me."

"Except for when he is?"

"Except then." She sighed, glancing over the room. "Mostly, I've just been busy. As have you. Adam said you've been in London recently."

"Only for a week, and more's the pity. I never grow weary of London, but the demands of a large company require traveling to many places."

Dianna returned her attention to her companion. "What's the quote? 'When you are tired of London, you are tired of life'?"

"Indeed. Have you ever been?"

"No. I don't like flying, so international travel is pretty far down my to do list."

"Ah, Dianna. You do not know what you are missing. One day you will have to come with me. I think you would like it."

"Maybe so."

Andre gestured to the cheesecake. "Please, eat. While you savor you can tell me what assistance you require."

Dianna didn't protest, knowing Andre would insist until he won. He hated chocolate, it upset his stomach; however, he got some perverse pleasure out of watching her eat. Not to mention she'd never got her beignets or a proper dinner, and she was starving. The war spirit that rode her gave her strength, stamina, and healing that other people didn't have, but it cost her in sanity and calories. She dipped her fork into the cheesecake, watching how the ganache clung to the metal. She was a wretched cook, but she loved food.

She closed her lips over the fork, licking it clean and savoring the smooth texture of the dessert, the chocolate topping and raspberry glaze popping on her tongue.

Andre chuckled low. "There's my girl."

She wasn't anyone's girl, but she didn't correct him, taking a second bite.

"Now, on to the matter at hand. How might I assist you?"

Dianna swallowed and picked up her glass, chasing the sweets with the burn of the alcohol. "Claude has gone missing."

"Madam Marie's Claude?"

"Yep, and you can guess how happy she is."

"Indeed." He sipped from his drink, and she gave him the time to think about the ramifications. "And you are tasked with returning him?"

"Right again, with a lot of unstated threats of what happens if I fail." Dianna went for another bite of the cheesecake. "Though, to be honest, I agree that he has to be found. If something is wrong with Claude, he's capable of causing a huge amount of damage. She'll be pissed off if he's dead, but at least we would know someone wasn't preparing to release him into the middle of the French Quarter on market day."

"I must agree." Andre tapped his fingers slowly against the wineglass. "I thought she had a mental connection with the beast."

"She does, but she says something is wrong with his mind. She can't summon him back, which is obviously very bad. I have some ideas of where to start, but I'm only one person. I need any eyes and ears you can spare."

Andre set the glass down in front of him. "And you need them as soon as possible. That is a significant favor you are asking, Dianna."

"I know." Dianna reached across the table, resting her hand on Andre's. His fingers were warm, almost feverish under her touch. The loup garou generally ran several degrees hotter than human. Andre often wore gloves to cover the effect, but not tonight. Slowly, he turned his hand, taking hers and running his thumb across her fingers. She liked him, but moments like this reminded her that he wasn't human. There was a beast inside of him, a well-dressed, currently controlled beast, but a beast all the same.

"I will give you what you wish, but there is a cost."

Dianna's gut tightened. She'd been expecting the words, but it still made her tense. Despite her experiences, she was never certain what would be asked of her, and when it would be more than she could give.

"What's your price?"

"The next time I go to London, you will come with me... for no less than a week."

London? Dianna blinked. "I..."

He shook his head. "Shush, that is not all. You will owe me a favor as well, to be collected at a later time of my choosing."

Dianna frowned, trying to see all the possible ramifications of his request. There were too many. "That's a pretty big exchange rate."

"You are asking me to bring my resources to bear very quickly on your behalf for a man I don't care for personally. That is not a simple thing."

"No, it's not. But I'm not asking your resources to act in my behalf, merely to provide information. So, I think there should be ground rules to your favor."

A bark of laughter met her words. "But not to my hauling you across an ocean?"

Dianna shrugged. "One problem at a time."

"I see." He squeezed her fingers, lifting her hand to his face and breathing in her scent. "Hmm... Very well. A favor to be collected later. One which shall not override your free will nor require you to act against your sense of morality. One which you can deny in exchange for another. Is that more acceptable?"

She wasn't sure how many possibilities that really removed, but she couldn't haggle with him all night. He was worse than the vampires when it came to twisting a situation around to get what he wanted. Dianna licked her lips. "One favor. One week in London. In exchange for any and all information surrounding Claude's disappearance or location, which you will actively turn your resources to look for until he's found or for 48 hours, whichever comes first."

"48 hours? Like the television program."

She saw his smile and sighed. "If it takes more than that Marie will string me up anyway, so it won't be an issue."

"At least she will not put you in the Mississippi. That punishment is reserved for the living dead."

"That doesn't make me feel any better." Dianna finished her drink, the liquid and the cheesecake enough to keep her on her feet for a good while longer. "If that's acceptable, I need to get going."

"It is. We only need to seal the favor."

Dianna arched an eyebrow. "You don't trust my word?"

"Of course, I do. But there are formalities which must be observed." He grinned, and she saw wolf fang in his smile. "Men shake hands, but I want something more. A kiss, Dianna, to seal our bargain."

A kiss. It seemed like such a simple request, but Dianna knew how many bad things had been sealed with a kiss. She'd seen the *Godfather*.

But what choice did she have?

She slowly nodded. "Fine. But if you bite me, I'll punch you right in your pretty face, Andre, and Kyle can clean up the mess."

He laughed again, using their joined hands to guide her out of her side of the booth and over to his. "It might be worth it, but no. No biting. No coercion. Just a kiss."

He drew her down to sit next to him, and stroked an errant lock of hair away from her face. The *lwa* perked up, reminding Dianna that it liked sex almost as much as it liked fighting. She sternly informed it that it wasn't getting either of those things.

Then Andre was kissing her. It started gentle, but it didn't remain that way, his lips scorching hers. A pleasurable pain lanced from the arch of her foot to the top of her head, stealing her breath away. Something clicked into place in her head, sealing the deal, sealing it with magic.

Andre leaned back, touching her lower lip with one finger. "Go look for your alligator man, Dianna McDunna. I will call, or Adam will, when we have any information that will help."

Dianna took several deep breaths and forced herself to her feet. She had to leave, had to get away from the draw of his magic. "Thank you. I'll keep my phone on."

"Good." He paused, leaning back into the shadows where she barely saw the glint of his eyes. "One day, Dianna McDunna, you are going to weary of the Ladisla's and Marie's of the world. You are going to rise to a new station, and you will be magnificent, and I will be there when you are ready."

Dianna didn't begin to know how to respond to the promise in his words. She nodded and hurried across the lounge, not running, but moving quickly. Her heart was pounding so hard she was sure those with supernatural hearing heard her pass, but she didn't slow. The corridor passed around her in a blur, and she pushed past the hostess and out into the muggy night air.

◆

Twenty minutes of jogging down the narrow roads of the French Quarter burned off most of the effects of her time with Andre, clearing Dianna's head and easing the magical rush. She slowed as she approached her next goal, taking the time to catch her breath.

The white walls of the Convent de Ursuline were bright during the day, the plaster catching the sun and reflecting it. At night they dimmed to a soft grey. The three-story building overlooked a garden of roses and bushes cut into miniature mazes, stately and protective.

Tonight, the dark grey hurricane shutters on the lower two floors were thrown open, while the smaller shutters on the upper floor were shut. Legend had it that those upper shutters were nailed shut. Dianna happened to know that was the truth, though the nails were cold iron and not silver. The convent was one of the oldest buildings in New Orleans and had been a mainstay of the Catholic church for decades. Now, it was mostly a tourist trap, having lost its holiness in the 1970's when the church had sold the building to a trio of *melusine*.

The merwomen kept the building in pristine condition and made an amazing amount of cash off of the tourists, which they donated to efforts to preserve the waterways, bayou, and lakes of Louisiana. Even those who didn't know of their supernatural natures knew of their generosity. They were tied to other water spirits, and if someone had seen Claude in the bayou or the river, they might know.

The question was if Dianna could get them to share what they knew.

She'd met the sisters before, and they'd gotten along, but she hadn't needed anything from them then. Like dealing with any other supernatural power, their help probably came at a cost. If she looked for Claude for too long, she was going to run out of things to give. This whole thing would be easier if she could just put out a BOLO for a 15-foot gator with a stumpy tail, but involving the mortal police was a really, really bad idea. She couldn't put her fellow officers — most of whom were blissfully unaware of New Orleans' supernatural population — in that kind of danger.

So she stood in front of the building, looking up at the stucco façade. A red light blinked behind the last set of shutters on the top floor. For good or ill, the *melusine* sisters were awake. Dianna knocked on the big door, listening to her thumps echo through the building.

The minutes ticked away, and just as Dianna turned around to leave, the door swung open. Despite its size, the hinges were oiled thoroughly and kept meticulously clean and the door moved without a sound. A pale face topped with brown curls peered out. The young woman blinked into the night dim and then broke into a sunny smile. "Miss Dianna! Good evening."

Dianna wracked her brain, searching through names until she found the right one. "Rebecca. Good evening. I apologize for coming so late, but I need help and hoped you or one of your sisters might be able to assist."

"Oh! Then not a social call. That's too bad. I so do love a social call." Rebecca stepped back, opening the door wide enough for Dianna to pass. "Come in, come in. I will take you to the others, and we shall see what we shall see."

The scent of wood polish and newly waxed floors hit Dianna's nose. She covered a sneeze, and Rebecca giggled like tinkling bells.

"Oh, so sorry! It was waxing day today. We shall have a very busy tourist day on Saturday, and Daphine wanted the floors at their best and brightest. Come, come. The smell is better on the upper floors."

Rebecca spun as she walked, a light chemise twirling around her bare legs. She took the stairs with the lightness of a bird, leaving Dianna to plod behind her feeling something like an elephant compared to the merwoman's grace. They reached the top floor, and Rebecca led the way to a large double door, working a key in the lock and then opening the doors wide.

"Rebecca?" A deeper voice called from inside. "Who comes with you?"

"It's the police woman, Daphine. The one who works for Marie Laveau. Miss Dianna. Do you wish to meet her in the receiving room?"

"No. There is no need for that deception, bring her in. Hello, Miss Dianna."

Dianna had never been to this part of the convent, and wondered if she'd be happier in the deception of the receiving room, but she merely followed Rebecca. To her surprise, the room wasn't filled with horrors, but was a fantastic oasis of comfort and beauty. The walls were painted a rich foamy green that was restful to the eye, the floors a deep honey wood. Large fabric poofs were tucked here and there, covered in velvet and satin inviting one to snuggle in and rest. Small tables were scattered about at various heights, containing bowls of fruit and large urns with chilled juices and champagne.

The central figure of the room was a deep garden tub that was almost like a pool and took up fully half of the floor. How they'd managed to construct such a thing and keep the water from damaging the convent was a matter that only magic could explain, and Dianna didn't ask.

On the edge of the pool, Rebecca's two older sisters, Daphine and Meralou lounged on cut out seats, most of their naked bodies submerged, though the water did nothing to hide their nakedness or the thick bright fish fins that replaced their legs.

Rebecca closed the door and worked the key again, then led Dianna to a chair near the pool. "You can sit here. There is much to eat, or you could join us in the water if you liked. It is very pleasant."

Dianna shook her head. "Thank you, but I can't stay long." She sat on the chair, wishing the room was brighter, the only light coming from lights embedded in the walls that gave a rosy glow to the entire room.

"More's the pity." Rebecca caught the edge of her shift, pulling it over her head without a thought for modesty and tossing it aside. She ran into the pool, her legs traded for dark, aqua-colored, shining scales in a splash.

Daphine moved closer to Dianna, half in and half out of the water. "What brings you to our waters at such an hour?"

Right to the point. Dianna was just as glad. "I'm looking for information, Miss Daphine. The alligator shifter, Claude, has gone missing. I'm trying to find him. I know he spends a lot of time in the bayou, and that you have contacts in those waters. I thought you might have seen or know something that could help me find him."

"Claude is missing?" Meralou sank deeper on her couch. "Oh, oh *merde*... I knew something bad had happened. I told you so, Daphine! We never should have used him. I told you!"

"Shut up, Meralou!"

"Oh, you shut up!"

"Both of you shut up!" Rebecca chimed in without ire, but giggles.

Dianna leaned forward on the chair, scowling at the sisters. "I don't care *who* shuts up, but *one* of you better tell me what's going on."

The three sisters exchanged glances, falling quiet. The only noise in the room was the trickle of water and the sound of breathing. Eventually Dianna sat back, crossing her arms over her chest.

"Okay. Then don't say anything. I'll just tell Mama Marie that you were the ones that got Claude in trouble and let her come and ask you herself. I'm certain she will be very understanding and open to discussion. You know how reasonable she is."

"Oh, no! No, you cannot speak of this to Marie. She is loathsome. She would never understand." Meralou moaned, shrinking back in the water until only her eyes and the top of her head were above the surface.

"Then explain and maybe I can fix it. But if I have to throw you or myself on Mama Marie's mercy, you can guess who I'm going to pick." Dianna wouldn't actually tattle on the merfolk unless she had to, but they didn't know that, and she didn't have time to gently pry the information out of them. "You have five seconds and then I'm leaving."

"But…" Rebecca surfaced and grabbed her clothing, pulling it under the water. "You have no key! You must stay until we are ready."

Dianna bared her teeth, not in a smile, but a knowing smirk. "I bet I can take your door down in less than two kicks. Want me to try?"

"NO!!! You must not ruin it! You terrible woman." Rebecca protested.

"Then save me the effort and save your door. What happened?"

Daphine ran her hands over her face. "Fine! We meant no harm to Claude, but someone was leaving terrible things in the bayou. Bags of white crystals that got into the water. It hurts the spirits and the sprites. It hurts the animals. It hurts us all. So, we asked Claude for help."

Dianna nodded, gesturing for Daphine to continue. She had questions, but they could wait until the *melusine* had finished.

"He agreed to find out who was bringing the bad things. Then we were going to decide what we could do. The sprites saw him in the bayou. They saw dark things fall from the sky. A fight began and they ran away. We do not know what happened after that. But Claude, he is so strong. We did not think it was possible he could be felled. We thought only that he slept after a fight hard fought."

She twisted a lock of her hair around her fingers, obviously distraught. "We have been waiting, hoping… We meant no wrong!"

Dianna rubbed a spot in the center of her forehead, feeling a headache coming on. Nothing in this city was ever straightforward, but she couldn't really be angry at the merwomen either. They had tried to help, in their own way. She could guess what the bags were full of, and why she'd not been able to find the stash she'd been tipped to earlier.

Meralou sighed, rising out of the water. "Miss Dianna, you will help us, *oui*? You will use what we have told you to find Monsieur Claude and stop the bad things in the water?"

"Yeah. I will. I'm on the path of both of those things anyway. Just next time you hear about drugs in the bayou call me instead of Claude. Simplify my life, okay?"

"Oh, yes, Miss Dianna!"

Dianna rose from the chair, waving a hand at Rebecca. She hadn't seen signs of a fight in the bayou, but she hadn't been looking for them either. "I need to keep moving. Let me out."

Rebecca burst from the pool, dripping water as she danced across the floor to the door. "Thank you, thank you," she chirped, like a little bird.

"Don't thank me yet."

◆

Dianna's phone buzzed in her pocket as she walked away from the convent and its soggy inhabitants. She glanced at the number and picked up.

"McDunna."

"I have a location for you." Andre sounded as pleased as a cat with cream.

"That was fast. Okay, let's hear it."

"Pirate's Alley. It seems the old dungeon at the back of the Cabildo has become inhabited by a group of gargoyles, three of them from what my runners have seen. They are advertising a drug that will impact even a shifter's metabolism, an impressive claim if it is true. There is to be a demonstration at 3 a.m., all the better not to disturb the human populace. I shall leave you to guess who they will use as the subject of their demonstration."

Dianna glanced at her watch. It was just after two now, the night had gone by fast. She didn't have much time to arrange anything. "What can you tell me about gargoyles?"

Andre laughed. "No entry for gargoyles in your monster book, my dear?"

"I don't have a monster book, but I'm thinking I should start one." Dianna turned down the street, headed for Jackson Square. "Come on, Andre. Give. Please. I know our deal was for information to find Claude, but it can't be good for you if someone has actually formulated meth at that level."

"This is, unfortunately, true. Gargoyles are, much like vampires, creatures of the night. They turn to stone in the light of the sun, but only the literal light. If they are inside, they continue to function, though they will be more sluggish. Supernatural strength and speed is a given. Some can fly, but not all. Their hides are as strong as the stone they become."

"Tough bastards."

"Indeed. I have tried to hire a few from time to time, but they are highly territorial and aggressive. I am very curious about who brought them in."

Dianna frowned, trying to think through the challenges and her available resources. Three gargoyles. One potentially meth'd-up alligator shifter. A number of beings expecting a demonstration. One tired, off-duty NOPD officer with a *lwa* spirit ride along. The odds were not in her favor.

"I'm not sure I care. I just want them to go back to wherever they're from." She took a deep breath. "Do you have cheap muscle available?"

"None you can afford."

The call dropped, leaving Dianna staring at the phone. She chewed on her lower lip and then made a decision. She didn't have the luxury of time to sneak in and get Claude out, nor was there time to find resources that would require bargaining, payment, and begging. She needed a nuclear option, and she knew of only one. Dianna tapped in a number from memory and listened to the phone ring.

"This is Madeline Moore."

"Hey, Maddie. Wanna blow up a bunch of meth-dealing gargoyles?"

A soft whistle greeted the question. "Oh, girl, you know just how to speak my language. Where?"

"Meet me in Pirate's Alley in 30 minutes?"

"With my favorite shit-kicking boots on."

"Good."

♦

Even in the dead of night Jackson Square wasn't completely dark. Bright lights edged the St. Louis Cathedral, making it a beacon of light in the steamy gothic city. Usually, the long alleyway between the Cathedral and the Cabildo was likewise brightly lit, but tonight a web of darkness clung to the lampposts, stretching shadows across the alleyway and into the Square. Dianna leaned against one of the walls of the Cathedral, soaking up the last of the heat the stone had to offer.

Anticipation crawled along her skin and bones as she watched the alleyway, noting those who entered. Some were familiar, some not. None were fully human. She ran her fingers over a large cigar, the papery surface catching on her skin. Figures gathered across the Square, and Dianna flicked a lighter to life, touching the flame to the tip of the cigar and sucking in a single, deep breath. The heavy, fragrant smoke entered her lungs, and she closed her eyes. The *veve* tattoo on her belly burned, and the war spirit stood at attention, nearly vibrating with need.

Steps approached rapidly, soft boots rubbing against cobblestones. Dianna crushed the cigar out, saving the rest for the next time. She exchanged the cigar for the bottle at her feet and poured the high-octane rum into her mouth, swishing it around and spitting it into the bushes. Rum and cigars, two of Papa Ogoun's favorite offerings, but there was one more.

She drew the long iron knife from her boot and ran it along her forearm, letting the razor blade bite into her skin. Blood flowed over the metal, and she felt a surge of power run through her body from head to heels like an electric shock. "Papa Ogoun ... guide my hunt."

"Dianna."

Dianna left the materials of her ritual on the ground, turning toward the voice with a predator's smile. She'd pay for appealing to the *lwa*, but as the cloak of the warrior settled around her all she knew was the hunt was at hand. The darkness was nothing to her heightened senses, the details of the personnel in front of her as sharp as they would be at midday.

"Hi Maddie."

The petite blonde woman inclined her head. She was dressed in blue and grey camo, just like the eight men and women with her. Madeline worked for a specialized branch of the government that hunted and studied the supernatural. She was smart, lethal, and Dianna's best friend.

"Meth-dealing gargoyles, huh?"

"Yep."

"Parameters of the mission?"

Dianna glanced over the commandos, pitching her voice so they could all hear. "Kick ass. Be wary of any drugs. They're laced, and it's bad ju."

"Kill or scatter?"

Dianna considered the question for a long breath. "Either, but I need the gator alive. I'll take care of him."

"Affirmative." Maddie gestured, and Dianna stepped into the alleyway as the others jogged past her. Maddie paused and tugged a pair of high-tech night goggles over her eyes. "You know folks are going to go ape-shit that you called me, right?"

"Yep. I'm cool with it. They don't want me working with what I've got, they can damn well provide me with more."

"Good." Madeline grinned and broke into a jog to keep up with Dianna's long-legged pace. "Wanna go shoe shopping tomorrow?"

"Definitely."

◆

Dianna dropped under a punch, sweeping her opponent's feet out from under him. There was no organization to the chaos that surrounded her, and she didn't mind. No plan ever survived contact with the enemy, so she kept her plans flexible. They'd busted into the old Spanish dungeon moments before the demonstration was to begin. The room was dim to begin with, and one of Maddie's commandos had added a smoke bomb that increased the visibility issues. About half of the inhabitants had scattered the moment it was obvious things were going wrong. The others, including the three large gargoyles, hadn't hesitated to jump into a fight.

The spirit of Ogoun howled in the back of her head, but this time they were in perfect accord. Her heightened senses let her see through the dim and the smoke, and she stomped her heel into the gut of the wolf shifter she'd put on the floor. "Stay down, Fido."

~*We are the warrior...*~

The hiss filled her mind as the war spirit fought for more control. She only heard its words in moments like this when there was no wall of will or magic between them.

~*They are the enemy. Kill them all.*~

"We have a goal."

One of the commandos sent a body rolling toward her, and she went up and over with a quick jump. A wooden chair was in her hands before she thought to look for it, and she brought it down on a vampire woman, who shrieked in pain as her arm broke. She skittered away, and Dianna tossed the remains of the chair to one side.

"Di!" Madeline's voice hit Dianna's ears, and she pulled herself away from chasing the vampire down, leaving it to the team. "Gator at three o'clock!"

Dianna spun, seeing combatants scatter either by their own will or as they were knocked aside by a massive force. She nodded and pelted across the room, going over or through anyone in her way. A space had opened around the huge gator, who lunged back and forth, snapping his jaws, hissing, and lashing with his stubby, but strong, tail. At least one person had been bitten, the scent of blood sharp, bright, and delicious in Dianna's nose.

She glared at Claude, slowly circling with the enraged gator. "Hi, you idiot."

Claude lunged, snapping and snarling, but Dianna was already moving, throwing herself past his mouth and landing on his back. He rolled, and she hung on, banging against the dusty dirt floor, crushed by his weight. He wasn't going to shake her; she wouldn't let that happen.

She got one arm around his thick neck, and fished in her pocket, pulling out a container of Narcan. The medication worked wonders to clear meth from human systems. She was banking that, combined with Claude's natural metabolism, it would clear whatever was in his system. There was no way to guess at dosing or shove it up his nose, but the membranes inside an alligator's mouth absorbed nutrients quickly.

She waited for his jaws to gape wide and tossed it inside, then slammed the heel of her hand against his nose, forcing him to close his mouth. She held onto his jaws, squeezing them closed as he squirmed and thrashed, unable to spare a hand to grab the electrical tape. "Swallow! Swallow, you giant handbag!"

Claude arched, more catlike than lizard, nearly throwing her clear. Dianna scrambled, locking her legs around his body. She banged his head against the floor hard enough to kill anything weaker, sure the vial was in pieces in his giant maw. "Come on, Claude! Wake up!"

It hadn't been enough Narcan. How was she going to drag an angry, 15-foot alligator to Marie's house? The thoughts trickled through her struggle to stay on board the enraged alligator.

The gator bucked again, this time sending Dianna sliding. Claude scrambled across the floor after her, and she yanked out her knife. Marie would never forgive her if she killed Claude, but maybe she could get away with wounding him a bit… maybe a lot.

"Wake up, Claude!"

Thick jaws snapped an inch from her face, and she slapped his nose with the flat of her knife. He blinked, then his face slowly began to shorten until the long jaws of an alligator became the face of a man, his skin dark as pitch. Eyes that were brown instead of yellow stared into Dianna's face.

He rocked back on his heels, wrapping thick arms around his midsection. "Miss Dianna. Claude… Claude don't feel so good."

"I'm not surprised."

A large shadow loomed in her peripheral vision, the largest of the gargoyles swinging a hammer worthy of a troll at Maddie's slight form. The petite blonde dodged, tumbling out of the way and coming up sharply against a wall.

"Stay right there, Claude," Dianna said. "You hear me?"

"Yes. Claude stays."

The grey-skinned gargoyle swung the hammer again. Madeline scrambled to stay out of the way and before he could draw the weapon about for a third swing, Dianna slammed into his back, slashing with her iron blade. The blood-blessed iron bit deep into his stony skin, and the gargoyle howled, shock in the sound. It wasn't accustomed to being hurt, much less by such a little thing.

It pulled away, and Dianna kept hold of her knife as it came free from the gargoyle's thick skin. The monster turned on her, swinging the hammer with the force of a grey-skinned Thor. She ducked the swing and jammed the knife into the creature's hip, twisting the blade before dancing away. Its flat, grey eyes, met hers filled with agony and fury.

"I kill you."

"Not if I kill you first."

Dianna was aware of more bodies clearing the room, either under their own power, or being carried away, but she kept her attention on the creature in front of her. He spun, faster than expected, one wing snapping out to smash into her. She turned into the impact, grunting as pain shot through her arm and shoulder. He followed up, darting in and lashing at her with thick black claws.

She danced back, hearing fabric rip as he snagged her shirt, and snarled, drawing her Glock in her left hand and firing into the beast's chest at nearly point-blank range. The first shot skidded across his stony skin, but the second and third penetrated, the report of the gun lost in his agonized roar. Scarlet blood, so dark it was nearly black, dripped down his skin, thick and glistening. The gun clicked, jammed, and she tossed it toward Madeline.

Dianna lunged, her vision red around the edges as the *lwa* surged, her skin throbbing with war's lust. She beat the gargoyle back, the knife opening slice after slice. It fought back with bruising strength, one fist connecting with her ribs. A second punch caught her in the side of her head, making her ears ring. She shook it off and leapt, slamming her heel into the monster's chest and throwing him into a stumble.

His eyes widened as he tumbled, fear replacing anger. He fell and tried to scramble back to his feet, but Dianna was there slamming the blade into his chest hard enough that it broke off, leaving her with the handle and about an inch of the knife blade in hand. His breath rasped in his chest as his life blood poured, and Dianna laughed in echo of the rejoicing spirit.

She searched for another opponent. It didn't matter that her weapon was broken. She was the warrior. She needed nothing more than her own hands.

"Di!" Madeline caught her shoulder. "NOPD is on the way. We've got to clear."

Dianna's hand snapped up, catching Madeline's wrist and twisting it up as she rose, forcing Madeline onto her toes. Dianna stared through the *lwa's* eyes at the funny little woman, cocking her head to one side. It would be easy to kill her. She was so small. So fragile.

Madeline remained calm, staring back into Dianna's face. "It's me. Snap out of it."

Dianna blinked and the war spirit roared.

~*Kill her.*~

"War is not only about death." Dianna whispered. She forced herself to release Madeline. Control. She had to get control.

~*We are the warrior.*~

"The warrior and the healer. The warrior does not hurt the innocent."

~*No!*~

She closed her eyes, trusting Madeline to deal with the remains of the fighting as she rebuilt the walls between herself and the war spirit the ritual had ripped open. It felt like it took forever as she rebound the spirit inside of her, though only seconds had passed when she opened her eyes again. Madeline offered her the discarded Glock and nodded.

"We good?"

Dianna took a deep breath and stuck what was left of the knife into her boot before tucking the gun away. "Yeah. We good. I'll get the gator."

She half-stumbled to where Claude was crouched on the floor. She knew the exhaustion she felt now that the *lwa* was no longer driving her would pass, but she had more to do before she could nap. She got her shoulder under Claude's, pulling him to his feet. He was bigger than she was and heavy, but they managed.

She cast around the room, which was empty including the body of the gargoyle she'd killed. It was enough.

Maddie stood near the door, waving them over. "Come on."

"Anyone hurt?"

"We'll talk about it tomorrow. Let's go."

◆

The summer sun was pleasant on Dianna's skin, which almost made up for the fact it increased the humidity to a near flesh-melting level. She leaned back in her wrought iron chair and pressed the sweating glass of iced coffee against her face. Caffeine and cool – bliss.

A clink of glass on metal raised her attention as Madeline set three plates of powdered sugar smothered beignets on the matching iron table. Resplendent in a pink sundress and a wide-brimmed hat, no one would have pegged Madeline as the commanding soldier from the evening before. She nudged a plate toward Dianna.

"Eat up. You've earned the calories, gator wrangler."

Dianna snorted, picking up one of the warm beignets. The *lwa* had already mostly healed her bruises and cracked ribs, but it had kept her hungry all day as a result. "Thanks."

"No problem." Madeline added a beignet to her plate, cutting it into neat squares. Blasphemy as far as Dianna was concerned. Beignets were meant to be eaten with your fingers. "So, you want the report?"

"Sure."

"Minor injuries to my folks. We took three bodies off the scene. Shifter, ghoul, and that gargoyle you dealt with. The first two are dead-dead and disposed of. The lab is still studying the gargoyle. It's not like we have anything to compare it to. Gargoyles are a new one for us." Madeline chased a bite of pastry with chocolate milk. "It's the most fun I've had all week even if I'll be filling out paperwork for days."

Dianna nodded, finishing the treat before replying. "Me too. You can tell your folks they turn to stone in direct sunlight, though I don't know if a dead one will still change. It'll be interesting to see if the other gargoyles come out of hiding or if they flee town. The NOPD found 67 pounds of super-meth when they turned the gatehouse and dungeon upside down. It's being studied and will be destroyed, so that's a win."

"And Claude?"

"Back home. Marie said 'thank you.' I decided not to press my luck and left it at that." Technically, Dianna had left Claude in the servant's kitchen and fled before the mambo could say anything at all. That Marie hadn't demanded Dianna come talk seemed like thanks enough.

Madeline shook her head, the hat flopping around her face. "Never let it be said that you lead a boring life, Dianna."

"Damn straight."

"So, what's next?"

Dianna grinned. "Shoe shopping. Think we can find alligator boots?"

Canadian author Taylen Carver writes edgy urban fantasy, doesn't pull punches, and would rather be writing unless otherwise notified. When not writing, Taylen can usually be found immersed in the speculative fiction of other authors, including Jim Butcher, Charlaine Harris, Kevin Hearne, Laurell K. Hamilton, and Emma Bull. Learn more about Taylen at https://TaylenCarver.com

About this story, Taylen says: "Byzantium, and the walled city of Constantinople, which straddles east and the west, has long been a favourite historical period for me, and features in a great many novels I've written under other pen names. Modern day Istanbul is still a delightful mix of influences and cultures. It seemed natural to set a story there, where humans and fae also mix… but with disastrous results."

In a world flipped on its axis by magic, where only the most useful survive, it helps to be smart, stay quiet – and choose the right moment to speak up.

Touched by Faelight
Taylen Carver

We were crossing the Bosphorus in an open fishing boat in February. The wind scored our faces raw, so it hurt to speak. It was close to midnight, when the Imperial sentries dotted along the Asian shoreline changed shifts and would be cold and eager to go home, cast a ten-hour warming spell, and go to sleep.

Not only did we have to watch for Imperial troops on the shore and the odd patrol upon the water, but we also had to keep an eye out for rusty Russian and Ukranian tankers and container vessels, supercontainers and freight barges ploughing majestically up and down the straits. They were so big, they could run right over our dinghy and never notice a thing. The Turkish government had never had control over their passage through the straits, not even to demand they insure themselves. The Fae just didn't care.

On a still, icy night like this, I figured it was a sure bet most of the pilots of those vessels were sitting back in their seats, sipping a glass of vodka and hot tea, letting a smart computer steer the thing.

It was a dark-lined miracle the Fae allowed us to ship oil and food anywhere. During the twelve months they had limited human traffic to neighbourhoods only, too many of their servants and staff died of starvation or cold, or complications arising from being wretchedly poor and forced to extremities like burning goat dung for light and cooking fuel. Too many of the Fae's favourite eateries and markets and services nailed cardboard over their shopfronts, that year.

The Fae didn't have a spell to reverse wretchedness. Instead, trade had opened up once more, along with the shipping which moved the trade goods. That was a bummer for us, tonight.

On the plus side, no ferries had chugged between the east shore and old Istanbul since General Grady Cabral, First Lord of the Light, had swept across western Europe, driving the Empire back to the Asian side of these straits, ten years ago.

I might have paused to appreciate that tiny speck of positivity, only I didn't want to be here in the first place. Trying to be cheerful about it was beyond me.

I had argued against the salvage run. A lot. That was unusual for me. Only, my gut said to stay in the old city tonight. Stay down, stay safe.

The other eight members of the gang were anxious to make the run. The intel we'd got about Cabral's Allies' latest attempt to infiltrate Imperial territory was too reliable to ignore.

"It's not like we're never made the crossing before," Okan told me. He was the gang boss, and didn't like having his decisions questioned. "Wear an extra jumper and be there at eleven, Nikol Gianni."

I got the message. He'd used the name the gang had given me. The gang used the chopped off version, *they* said, because my full name, Aikaterini Nikol Giannopoulos, was too much of a mouthful. *I* knew they used the cute version because it didn't remind them I was Greek.

Okan had used both chopped up names to say without saying it that I wasn't really a member of the gang at all. Not only was I Greek, I was a girl, and I did things that came way too damn close to magic to sit well with them, even though they profited by what I could do.

So I shut up and pulled the oversized down parka in close around my chin and ducked my head deeper into the collar to protect my cheeks a bit better, and waited for the crossing to be over. It had to be warmer on the other side, out of the wind.

The parka smelled mildly of olive oil and masculine spice. It made me smile.

We were heading for Üsküdar, which had once been a pretty, residential suburb with fantastic views. It was a cratered dust-bowl now. One stepped carefully, moving through it. No one lived there, which was why we were taking the long way north-east, across and up the straights. We would walk south through Üsküdar, craters be damned, and in that way avoid Grady Cabral's infiltration units, who would cross by the most direct routes – bridge and tunnel – and fight for a toe-hold on this side of the straits.

Cabral had been trying to break the Emperor's line for nearly a decade. The Emperor was just as determined to have his favourite city back, even though the Imperial seat was in Tehran, two and a half thousand kilometers behind him. Tehran was what Cabral wanted. Tehran, and Emperor Eutropin's head on a pike.

The old metal hull of the dinghy scraped across rocky shore and the tiny outboard motor shut off. So did the wind – enough for me to feel the fiery burning of my cheeks. Now that we were still, the stench of weed and dirty water wafted over us. I wrinkled my nose, gripped the gunwhale, and stepped over the side of the boat, onto wet, slippery rocks.

The others eased silently onto the rocks around me, their breathing hard and fast. The two scouts moved ahead to spot sentries and deal with them. Their boots crunched softly on the rocks as the others hauled the dinghy up higher, well out of the water.

They spoke in murmured, single words only when they needed to, as they lifted packs and duffels out of the dinghy and turned it over, then draped it with smelly fishing nets.

I didn't have to carry a pack, so I moved up the sloping beach. A hand grabbed my arm and silently tugged me over to where the group was forming around Okan, as he gave directions in a low voice.

We moved out in double file. Lesley Davis, who claimed he was American, but spoke bad Turkish with a British accent, was beside me. He trod heavily in his big boots, which was oddly comforting.

The march south took two hours and tension rose as we got closer to where the Imperial troops would be thickest. There was no curfew over on this side because there were too few humans left here to bother. So many of us in a group would draw attention.

Finally Okan told us to squat in the abandoned shell of a building that had once been a diner. The faded scents of spit lamb and curry lingered, still. He sent out four scouts. They knew what to look for. The rest of us didn't relax. We didn't talk, either.

Okan stepped over to me, his Nikes crunching in the dusty pebbles on the tiled floor, and nudged my knee with his sneaker. "You ready for this?"

"I will be." Same question, same answer, every time we did a salvage run.

"Need anything?"

"Hot chocolate."

He snorted. There had been no hot chocolate, no coffee, not even English tea, in Istanbul for years. Not for humans, at least. The trade embargo had only been partially lifted.

It was a cold wait, but close to an hour later, one of the scouts returned and whispered to Okan. "Prásinoi are building up across the street from Vénetoi, a klick from here."

My heart picked up its pace. In Turkey, especially in Istanbul, the Fae Allies under Cabral were called the Prásinoi – the Greens. The Prásinoi had been one of the two primary factions in the days of Byzantine chariot racing. The Vénetoi, the Blues, had been the other primary faction, the one the Emperor of the day had supported. Those factions had ended up fighting each other, too. The irony made the names stick, even though the human factions of the sixth century hadn't lobbed hexes and explosive power orbs at each other.

Okran said, "Okay, move out. Someone get Nikol. Davis, she talks your lingo. Make sure the stupid cow doesn't step on anything that makes a noise."

Either Okran didn't know I could hear him from across the ruined diner, or he didn't care. I settled for the latter.

Davis came over to me. "We're moving out," he said softly, in English. "Here."

I groped for where I thought his hand would be, relative to his voice, slapped mine into it and let him haul me to my feet. He gripped my upper arm.

"Don't hold tight like that," I said. "Squeeze if there's something in front of me. You know how it goes."

"Yeah. Sorry."

I shrugged. "I'm blind, that's all." Although that wasn't all to it and we both knew it. The whole gang did. That was why I was here.

"Let's find a battleground," I said grimly.

◆

The taint of the battleground tickled the back of my throat and my brain three minutes before Davis squeezed my arm. I stopped immediately, my heart racing. "Something's not right," I murmured. The scent was too rich. *Too* strong. Thick, black gel wrapped around my thoughts.

"*Shut up,*" came the *sotto voce* command.

We shut up. I shifted on my feet, the cold making my knees ache, until I heard the far-off shuffle of a sneaker. Then closer. A near-soundless murmur.

Everyone relaxed around me.

"Battle's done," Okan announced in a slightly louder voice. "Let's see what we can salvage."

We could walk openly now, for both sides in this endless war had withdrawn. I didn't need Davis' hand on my arm anymore, but didn't tell him that. The others exchanged odd comments, mostly about how big a haul we'd get. "Monster-sized, man. Battle just over and all – it's harvest time!"

"You're shaking your head," Davis pointed out softly, in English.

I shook it again, not to disagree with him, but to clear the miasmic sludge from my thoughts. "Too thick," I muttered.

Davis didn't speak for a few steps. "Is that… bad?"

"Don't know." But the hairs on the back of my neck were lifting.

"In here!" came the soft call. It echoed slightly as Okan moved into a building. Not a whole building – the air was too cold for a whole building and there was grit underfoot.

I heard the excited murmurs.

"Step over," Davis said.

I lifted my feet up and over automatically. All my senses, even the extra ones, reached out across the building. I pointed to where I could see the green aura. "Over there."

My heart picked up the pace. I lived for these moments. Not that I could explain this to anyone in a way that wouldn't have them crossing their fingers behind their backs as they watched me from the corners of their eyes. Not even to Ardar could I try to express how alive these moments made me feel. It remained a private pleasure.

I saw another paler pool and pointed.

"There, look, a second one," Okan said, excitement lifting his voice. "Nikol, what is it?"

I breathed in, sampling smell, taste, feel, touch. "The first is residue. The second…" I smiled. "Blood pudding."

Someone gave a little whoop of pleasure. Feet crunched as they moved over to the pool of ichor-ladened residue.

"Over there," I added, pointing again. "More ichor," I added.

I didn't need my sight to know that the unit was spreading out, unslinging collectors from their packs, working in pairs to vacuum up the supranormal residue that the Fae left lying about like shrapnel and brass casings after their battles.

When a Fae was injured, they bled ichor, not blood. Mixed with their spell residue, the concoction was powerful. We called it 'blood pudding' and a good collection of the stuff would keep us all fed and warm for a month.

Blood pudding, and to a lesser degree, untainted spell residue, allowed humans to cast small personal spells. Although, most of us used the stuff as a replacement for the power grid which hadn't run for over a decade. The ichor also had healing properties, if it was cast properly.

But that wasn't what I liked about salvage work, although helping folks back in the old city survive another week was always gratifying.

Most people have the wrong idea about my blindness.

I was living in Istanbul with my parents when the war broke out in Turkey – Grady Cabral and her allies had swept across western Europe on their way to dislodge the corrupt old Emperor she had once served as his most faithful general, in one short, hard year.

Until Cabral had fired the first round of power orbs at the Fae underground bunkers in London, humans had been completely ignorant of the existence of the Fae. We learned what we needed to survive really fast after that, but until Cabral's warriors reached the walls of the old city, I still didn't fully understand the whole political snake's nest, with its traitors and spies and betrayals. I still thought the war was kinda cool. I mean, c'mon, fairies? Only, as I swiftly learned, the Fae aren't cute pixies with wings and wands.

The Allies lobbed a superorb over the top of our building, dropping five floors and the roof on top of me and my parents and nearly a hundred other humans, in an attempt to reach the Imperial bunker under our section of the city.

I woke in a gutter hospital, blinded and orphaned. I was ten years old.

The thing is, though, my eyes are just fine. It's my brain that got scrambled by the masonry dropping on the back of my head. And because my eyes still send signals to the brain, sometimes funny things happen to me. I can "see" things. Sometimes, perfectly normal things – the sun, a grieving mother, ruined houses – for a brief minute or two, before it all goes black again.

And when I'm on a Fae battle site, I can see their residue and the ichor mixed with it. That's why Okan puts up with me. I had carefully not told him or any of the others that I could see a bit more of the Fae than that.

I kept moving around the gutted building, pointing out more and more pools of residue, which was invisible to most humans, and ichor, which was matte black and just as difficult for everyone but me to see on a moonless night.

They found the bodies after my first round.

"Hell spawn!" Okan muttered.

"God, I *touched* it!"

"They're... are they dead?"

"It looks like a whole fucking *unit* of them."

"They're all Empire assholes."

I tugged my arm to get Davis' attention. "Take me over there."

He drew me across the rock-strewn floor. Most of the rocks were walls, floors, roof, dropped onto the floor by destructive power orbs.

"Right in front of you," Davis murmured.

I sank down into a crouch and put out my hand, patting, looking for Fae flesh. I found a leg in a boot, ran my fingers up to where the boot ended and pressed my fingers against the twill-covered thigh and... well, "listened" is as good as I can explain it.

"Someone piled them here," Okan said, his voice thoughtful. He'd got over the shock and was thinking again. That's why he was the leader.

A pile of them. I should have tripped over them, because I can't see dead Fae, only they had been piled into a heap in the corner. I could hear the flatness of everyone's voices, telling me the wall was close by.

I got to my feet. "This one has been drained of ichor."

"*Drained?*" Davis repeated.

"Another one. Quickly." I held out my hand.

He gripped my wrist and pushed my hand down until I felt more Imperial uniform under my finger tips. I listened and shook my head. "Them, too."

A low whistle sounded. The three note rising trill that warned of incoming Imperial troops.

And we were standing around a pile of their comrades, all of them drained of ichor.

I shook off Davis' hand and got moving, even before Okan gave the command to split and run like hell.

◆

I hate using a cane.

But it was a long way back to the old city, and I had to find my own way there. The first long, slender and not-too-heavy object I found, I used. I think it was a bed rail.

Tapping through streets with the other hand held out in front of me got me through barricades and gates and checkpoints the others would have to find a way to slide around.

It took the rest of the night and most of the next day for me to reach the sea, then find a boat to take me over. I had to wait for nightfall before they would risk the crossing. They were human and from the old city themselves. They shared their raki, even though they knew I was Greek.

I paid them back by warning them of a gulet moving silently ahead of the wind, stuffed full of Fae on patrol. To me, the sailboat lit up like a chandelier on the almost still water. The humans in the little dinghy with me couldn't see a thing, for the Imperials were running without lights.

By close to ten that night, I reached the old Topkapi palace. Centuries ago, it had been a human Emperor's residence. Before the war, it had been a museum. Now it was housing once more. The palace was command central for Cabral's Allied troops, who didn't seem to mind *this* former human residence. They'd been here for nearly ten years. Humans now understood that war was a lifestyle choice for the Fae, who were happy to keep lobbing orbs at each other and partying in between.

I waited at the Gate of Salutation while the message I'd given the guard was walked through the palace to the fourth courtyard at the centre of it. They'd have to find him, but Arda was human and his movements tightly controlled. He'd be within three paces of Colonel Ingunn Salvi's side, a lowly Faerini shadowing him.

The guards at the gate glowed like lanterns in my mind. They were well fed, rested, and eager to join the festivities later tonight. The night was their time and their energy rose with the lifting of the moon. They could just as easily walk under the sun. They just didn't like it. Not the sun of Turkey, at least.

I saw the Faerini first. She didn't glow as much as the others. She was tired and dispirited.

"It's my sister," Arda told her. "Something must have happened for her to travel all this way by herself."

"The blind girl?" the Faerini said. I could hear the disinterested in her voice. "Make it snappy, Solak. The Colonel has guests who want to meet you."

Among other things, which included Arda being my boyfriend, not my brother, he was also the National Wrestling Champion of Turkey. That was why the coat I'd borrowed from him smelled faintly of warm olive oil, which was surely one of the loveliest and most comforting smells in the world. Arda's national title in a sport of pure physical strength made him a sought-after trophy amongst the Fae, who were only strong magically.

Arda moved me out of hearing range of the Fae guards and the Faerini. "You didn't come back last night," he murmured.

"There's trouble," I breathed. "Someone… *something*…drained an entire Imperial unit of their ichor. All of it. They were bone dry. Your girlfriend has got spies all over Anatolia. When the Allies hear about it, they'll want who did it dead, too." I'd had a whole night and a day to think it through. A thing, a person, who could overcome a whole Imperial unit was a threat to the Allies, too. "It wasn't anyone the Colonel knows?"

It didn't seem to occur to the Fae that a favored human sports hero and bed toy could also be a spy, but Arda was our best line of information on the Allies' movements. Us being the *Albati* – the Whites. The human resistance.

Arda had warned us about the infiltration effort last night. He was the other reason the gang put up with me. His shoes shifted on the path, now. "The heaven's help me, Katerina…"

I knew, suddenly, that he wanted to touch me. But he wouldn't risk it. He was Turk, very human, a public figure and known to the Fae. And he *hated* who I was. Not what I could do, but the danger it would put me in if the Fae learned about it.

Maybe that was why he had not suggested I move into his apartment. Colonel Salvi and her cohort often arrived there without warning, to show Arda off at yet another party, although they refused to step in the door of the human abode. When Salvi wanted Arda for strenuous bedroom duties, he was taken to her.

So I was still trying to figure out why Arda said nothing, despite us being together for three years. I could see the Fae, but human stuff was beyond my abilities.

"Why did you come here?" Arda asked, instead of touching me the way I longed for him to do.

"To warn you. To see if you'd heard anything. And to make sure you're…" I was dithering, so I closed my fists tightly and pushed it out. I lifted my chin so that if I could see, I would be looking at him. "You told us about the raid. If any of the others were caught on the battle site, it might come back to you."

"Sokol!" the Faerini called, impatience colouring her voice.

"Go home, Katerina." The sound of his voice told me Arda was already swinging away, his attention back upon the creatures in the palace. He was automatically obeying their directives.

I could still feel where he had squeezed my arm as he moved me away from the guards. And for the first time, it occurred to me to wonder how strong Arda really was. Was he strong enough, perhaps, to overcome Fae and bleed them dry? After all, he'd known about the Allies' raid, too.

It was a terrible thought to have about the man I was supposed to love, so I went home to put this horrible night behind me.

◆

Fae history stretches back into human pre-history, and theirs is annotated and indexed, cross-referenced and linked intimately with their Great Family bloodline archives. It was no coincidence that those who remained loyal to the Emperor and those who support General Cabral tend to follow family bloodlines.

All that long history made the Fae somewhat tolerant of human history, which Istanbul had in abundance. The Fae had allowed the Grand Bazaar to remain open when a brave human pointed out that the Bazaar had been operating continuously for nearly seven centuries. Although there were no tourists to buy trinkets, anymore, those of us with something to sell or barter would squat upon a carpet, or wander the halls looking for a buyer.

Rumours moved as freely as the trade did, in those old alleyways. I had only been sitting upon my rug for five minutes, and was still sorting and displaying the newest batch of sigils, when the old man next to me whispered in toothless, and therefore mangled, Turkish that a human vigilante had killed twenty Imperial troopers, across the strait.

"Took their blood," he added with a cackle. "Going to give it out to everyone who needs it. I would kiss him, did he but stand before me."

"Why does it have to be a human who did it?" I demanded, my heart thudding. "A Fae could have. One of the Allies."

The man cackled again. "Against a unit of Imperials? They'd have to be invisible for that."

I couldn't see his face to tell if he was joking. "I didn't think the Fae could do that."

"Be invisible? You don't know them very well, do you? Only the Imperial family have that power." His voice shifted as he moved on his rug. "Hello, sir... you want mint? Fresh picked this morning."

"Katerina," Arda said, his voice lowering as he squatted in front of me.

I wanted to smile at him, but my fear wouldn't let me. "What are you *doing* here?" I breathed.

"I'm here to see my sister," he said. "I can call on her if I want."

My heart broke.

"I know your face," the old man next to me said. "Yes, yes, you're the wrestler, the one who sleeps—" His words cut off abruptly.

Who sleeps with Fae, who eats with them, and won't let anything upset that delicate balance because of me.

"Arda, you can't stay here," I whispered.

"I wanted to apologize," he murmured back. "For last night."

"Accepted. Now go."

Instead, he leaned closer. "I get upset, when you're near them."

Then stay with me, instead of them.

I said, instead, "Aren't you expected at the palace?"

I don't know what he might have said in response, for the sound of pipes and whistles echoing through the Bazaar made us all stiffen. Then, even worse, the patter of light running feet reached us.

I felt the movement of the air around me as Arda pulled back and got to his feet.

"Go," I said quickly.

He said nothing, but I knew he'd left. The air in front of me was no longer warm and comforting.

I went back to laying out sigils and tried to hide the trembling in my fingers, even though my heart was galloping so hard my chest hurt. I had not been this afraid even when making my way back from the Imperial side of the Bosphorus.

"He brought them here!" the old man hissed, sounding more frightened than me.

"Shh…" I said, for the stealth of the Fae and their light steps meant they could be much closer than they sounded. Or perhaps they had sent scouts ahead, for this was unknown territory for them. In the years I had been selling sigils here, they had not once stepped foot into the Bazaar. It was as alien to the Fae as human houses, and just as repulsive to their delicate noses.

The steady murmur of many voices came closer. Then a soft one, female. "That's his sister."

I knew that voice. My heart sank. It was the tired Faerini from last night, the one who had escorted Arda around.

"Thank you, Dariy." The second woman's voice was deep and well-modulated, like a singer's or a stage actor's would be. Trained to be heard.

The toothless Turk next to me drew in a shuddering breath, fear making him vibrate.

I swallowed as I felt the air move around me. Bodies. Close by. I could see them, too. Bright lights among the darkness. And further off, forming a background starfield, many more Fae gathered.

"You are the sister of Arda Sokol?" came the singer's voice. Her light shone the hottest.

"Is Arda in trouble?" That was something a sister might ask. It was what *I* wanted to ask.

"Answer my question!" The snap in her voice straightened my back. "Do you know who I am?"

A *very* dangerous question. I swallowed. "I… no… forgive me, but I cannot see."

"She *is* blind, General," Dariy murmured.

General.

My heart sank. This bright light, one of the brightest I'd ever seen, was General Grady Cabral, First Lord of the Light.

I trembled, just as the old man did.

A third Fae stepped into the circle made by the many in the background. "Here he is, General. Just as Dariy said he would be."

That voice, that scraping strident voice, I knew. Colonel Ingunn Salvi, who considered Arda to be her personal pet.

"Arda Sokol," Cabral purred.

"General Cabral," Arda said. "This is a most unexpected surprise, to find you here in the Bazaar. Are you, like me, shopping for spices?"

"I am shopping for an enemy," Cabral said, the music back in her voice. "Dariy said you were here visiting your sister, and lo, here you are, when for a whole night, we haven't been able to find you."

I couldn't see Arda, but I could feel the wariness build in him. His voice slowed down, caution making him choose his words very carefully. "Find me, General? But I was at the palace all evening, and afterwards—"

"I am not speaking of last night. I am speaking of the night before."

I closed my eyes. Not that it made any difference to what I could see. The symphony of Fae light around me made my head ache. *Tell them you were with me,* I begged Arda. Yet I knew he would not involve me, even if he could hear my silent plea. He would keep me as far distant from him as possible. He would keep me safe, no matter what.

"The night before, General?" Arda sounded bewildered but I knew he was thinking of my warning.

"You were not in your apartment. Salvi called on you, and you were not there."

"He was not there all night," Salvi added.

"Being away from my apartment makes me an enemy?" Arda's voice rose, the enquiring tone dripping with politeness.

"Unless you can tell me where you did spend your night, Arda Sokol," General Cabral said, her tone smooth as honey, "then I must presume that you were breaking the curfew, just to begin. We will discuss what other laws you may have broken somewhere other than this… place." Her contempt for the ancient paths of the Bazaar was rich in her voice.

"Arda was with me, General," I said quickly. "All night. He did not break curfew."

"Katerina, no," Arda said, almost as swiftly as me, trying to smother my words with his own.

"I see," General Cabral said. "Bring her, too. Come along."

"No, she is not a part of this!" Arda cried, as the lights in my head all converged upon us. Hands on my arms, lifting me to my feet. Far more hands on Arda, containing him. Confining him.

◆

We were bundled into a car. I felt soft leather beneath me and sniffed, taking in the scent of upholstery and thick carpet. My parents had owned a brand new Fiat which had smelled much like this. I clamped down on the flood of memories the aroma produced.

Arda was separated from me. Salvi sat between us, her light dulled by the daylight. Cabral's, too, was dimmer. She sat opposite us, but I could see all of her. A limousine with seats facing each other, then. The doors were closed. The sounds of the Bazaar and the midday call to prayers was muffled.

I didn't know where the Faerini was. Another car perhaps. I didn't care very much.

The car rolled into motion.

"General, if you would only explain to me what this is about?" Arda said. "I will give you whatever answers I can, whatever information that is mine to give. But let my sister go. She knows nothing of this... whatever this is."

"Then you admit there is a matter to discuss," General Cabral said.

Arda didn't answer. He'd seen the trap only now.

Warmth curled around my ankles as the car's heater got to work. I had not realized how cold it was, until now when the warmth touched my skin. Yet I didn't like the air against me. It felt unnatural. Cloying.

And the car was moving far too fast. I wasn't used to speed, anymore.

I drew in a breath, reaching for calm. Panicking wouldn't help us.

Cabral's tone was conversational as she said, "Two nights ago, an entire squad of Imperial troopers had their throats cut and their bodies drained. The Emperor is outraged. His senior officers are scared. Everyone knows we Fae can be overcome, if the attacker is strong enough." She paused. "We have spent eons training our minds, not our muscles."

I could smell Arda's fear. It was bitter, silvered lemon upon the back of my tongue.

"You don't think... you cannot think I..." he began.

"I don't know what to think," Cabral said. "The Emperor will not rest until he finds the person who did this terrible thing to his soldiers. Eutropin is tradition-bound, but he is not stupid. He believes that the person who did this, this powerful enemy, is an ally of mine. And if the enemy is not my ally, I still benefit from his work. Eutropin knows word of this will spread a rot of fear through his troops, and it will give my army a morale boost such as we have not known in ten long years of war."

Not that you want the war to end, anyway. But I did not say it aloud.

Arda said nothing. I agreed with him. Silence was best, right now.

"Do you see the dilemma this puts me in, Arda Sokol?" Cabral asked.

"No," he whispered.

But I could see it as clearly as I could see Cabral. So when the car bumped over a break in the road surface and I heard the echo of the motor and the rhythmic swish of the guard rails swooshing past us, I knew exactly where we were and why. We were on the first bridge – the Martyrs Bridge. We were crossing the Bosphorus into Imperial territory.

Cabral answered Arda. "Right now, Eutropin is gathering his army. He is pulling troops from across the land, from as far away as the Peacock Throne itself. He cannot afford to show weakness. He cannot wait for this enemy to decimate his troops. He *must* act with overwhelming force. He must act against *me*."

The silence in the car throbbed.

"You… really believe a human is capable of what you say was done to the Emperor's troops?" Arda breathed.

Salvi spoke for the first time. "We Fae do not use physical force against each other, the way this… this barbarian did it. We have better means to defeat our enemies than that."

I cocked my head. The scratchy note in her voice was less than it had been before. Was it passion smoothing her tone?

Cabral stirred. "I cannot allow the Emperor to launch such a devastating attack upon my people. I am forced by this enemy's hand to do something that pains me. I must deal with the Emperor directly, to disarm him and stop this attack."

Maybe you should let him attack. Again, I didn't voice the thought. But if Eutropin really was building an army to defeat an army, then maybe the war would end whether Cabral wanted it to end or not.

"So, I am afraid, Arda Sokol, that I am giving Eutropin *you*, the enemy he fears."

Arda and I both drew in sharp breaths.

"Don't bother trying the doors," Salvi said quickly. "There is a locking spell on them that you cannot break, not even with your great strength, Arda."

"I did not do this thing," Arda said, his voice low.

"It doesn't matter if you did or did not," Cabral replied, her tone indifferent. "You *look* as though you are capable of it, and you have a sister who is touched with gifts a human has no right to. The spilling of *her* blood will appease the Fae whose throats you cut — or so Eutropin will believe. And that is all I need, for him to believe he has destroyed the new enemy and we are once again evenly matched."

◆

Cabral cast a short-term mute spell upon Arda and I before we got out of the car. I was happy to play along, for I could hear better if people were not talking. And I desperately needed to hear everything, for the sun was high overhead, and despite the coolness of the day, it beat down upon our heads with power that made picking out the Fae around me difficult.

Arda's hand on my arm saved me from stumbling as we walked through debris, our boots grating on chalk and pebbles. Then we moved into a building that wasn't whole. The sun was blocked by a partial roof and abruptly, I knew where we were.

This was the place where the drained Imperial soldiers had been tossed. The faded marks of ichor pools and blood pudding were distinct.

"How long until the Emperor arrives, Salvi?" Cabral asked. "I don't like being out of hailing distance of the house guard."

"But you have me to protect you, General," Salvi replied. Her voice was from farther away.

I turned, looking for them. Cabral, I could see. Her great light stood near where the bodies had been piled. But Salvi, I could not see.

"Salvi, where are you?" Cabral called.

I spotted Salvi. She had been crouching behind something. One of the bigger piles of masonry, I thought. Now she walked toward us.

"Salvi?" Cabral called.

My heart thudded. "Something's wrong," I whispered.

"Salvi's gone," Arda murmured.

"No, she's right there." I pointed.

"What?" Cabral said sharply.

Salvi raised her hand as she came right up behind Cabral.

"Watch out!" I screamed.

Salvi reached around in front of Cabral, who just stood there. She swiped with her arm. I couldn't see the blade. It wasn't Fae. But I heard the hiss and sing of fine metal, wielded expertly. And I felt and smelled the hot spray of ichor.

"Son of a *bitch!*" Arda cried. "Her throat just… just split open!"

Cabral made bubbling gasping sounds as she sank to the ground.

The truth slammed into me, stealing my breath and nearly all my strength. I staggered. That got me moving, though. I let myself stumble forward into a run, and put up my hands like a blind girl might, weaving a drunken path and letting myself trip over stones.

I came closer to Salvi, who just stood there, confident in her own powers.

I passed behind her and before she could turn to watch my torturous progress, I snatched the blade out of her hand. It whispered across my palm, stinging, but she hadn't been expecting me to grab it, and it came free. I leapt upon her back and wrapped my arm around her throat and hung on, all my weight dragging against her neck, while I got my legs around her waist.

"Arda! Here! Help me!" I cried.

"You're… you're floating!"

"I'm on her back! Quickly!" I put the knife against her throat. "This is your own knife, Salvi. You know how sharp it is. I have only to press a little harder and you'll die just like Cabral."

Arda's hands rested upon my arms.

"Touch under my hands. You'll feel her," I promised him.

He slid his hands over my arms. "Christ and Allah wept…" he breathed. "She's… she's *invisible*."

"You are a fool, Arda," Salvi ground out. Her arms shifted.

"No, stay still, or I'll push this in, I swear I will," I told her.

"You think I can't deal with a little human thing like you?" Salvi told me, her voice full of contempt.

"You can't deal with someone like me, though," Arda said. "Keep the knife there, Katerina, but let me hold her."

I unwrapped my legs and hung from her neck while Arda came up behind me and got a grip on her. I knew from the feel of his arms against mine that he was taking a classic wrestling grip on her, one that put a severe strain on a wrestler's neck. Salvi was puny Fae, not a wrestler who had spent ten years strengthening his neck for such moments.

"Ease out," Arda told me.

I wriggled out from between them and moved around to face Salvi.

"You can see me." Her tone was one of conclusion. "Arda always did play down your abilities. I should have paid more attention."

I put the knife blade to her throat once more, and she hissed. "You're Imperial royal family," I said. "Only they have the power of invisibility. That's how you could sneak up on a whole squad of Imperial soldiers and slit all their throats."

"Very good, little girl," Salvi said. "A second cousin to Eutropin, but blood is blood." She sounded very pleased about that.

"But... why? Why all this throat cutting?" Arda ground out. "You killed your cousin's troops! You killed Cabral!"

"No, *you* killed her," Salvi said.

I nodded. "They were always going to blame you, Arda. You're strong. You *could* have done this. Eutropin wants an excuse to launch an all-out attack. Salvi, his spy, gave him one."

"Listen to your little sister, Arda," Salvi said. "You cannot stop this now. Eutropin will spill across your city and into the west. He will reign supreme once more."

Arda spoke very quietly. "You should know, Salvi, that Katerina isn't my little sister. She is my lover. She will be my wife. She is already the stars, the sun and the moon to me, and every time I laid with you made me sick to my bones for the risk I bought near her. And I tell you now that should the Emperor win this last phase of the war, he will do it without you."

"What...?" Salvi began, her tone startled.

I heard Arda draw in a deep, deep breath. I held still, for I knew what came next.

The crunch was soft, muffled by flesh.

I watch Salvi's light fade.

"You can let go of her now," I told Arda. "She's dead."

He dropped her. She fell like bricks in a bag, a not completely unsatisfactory sound.

Arda pulled me into his arms. He was trembling. "You could *see* her."

"Yes. Cabral, too. I see all the Fae."

He peppered my face with kisses. "And it never occurred to you to tell me that?"

"I..." But I found it difficult to speak, for his lips found mine. When I could breathe once more, I said, "You were so afraid for me, I thought knowing that would break you."

Arda laughed, low and heavy, and let me go – except for my hand.

"This is the end of our time in the city," I warned him. "Both the Allies and the Empire will be looking for us now."

"Yes, I see that," Arda said. He drew in a breath and let it out. "Thank the gods," he added. "Things are changing. Finally. Eutropin cannot let this insult lie. There will be reprisals, the Allies will protest over Cabral, too… and maybe, Katerina, just maybe, if humans fight back, *we* could end this damn war for them."

"We could," I agreed, delighted.

"Especially with people like you among us," Arda added.

My delight died. "You mean, because I'm touched."

I could feel him shaking his head through the movement of his hand around mine. "No, no, no, because you are *strong*. You are smart and you are brave. All things I did not think you had in such… such quantities. Not until today." His lips touched mine. "You are so much stronger than me. I see that now. I *have* been a fool, to worry about you so, to try to protect you in such an idiotic manner."

"Perhaps you shouldn't stop doing that. Not altogether," I told him. "Because I can feel the Imperial Fae heading here right now, and we're standing next to the Emperor's dead cousin… and I'm afraid, Arda, that even though I can see the Fae, I can't see the road in front of my feet."

"Ah! To be your guide. That is something I *can* do."

He led me away.

Tina Back was raised in the far northern kingdom of Sweden, where, at a very young age, she watched Star Wars. Since then, she wants nothing more than to roam the galaxy in a spaceship with her dog. Life keeps getting in the way. She spent time in Tokyo and Singapore with her partner in crime. Years later, they washed up on the outskirts of San Francisco. She writes. She draws. She still wants that spaceship. Follow her at https://tinabackauthor.com

About this story, Tina says: "It's always hard to retrace where a story began. An image of a fake, tacky Rolex maybe? Worn by people intent on deceit. What if you couldn't lie? What if you had to wear something that hurt you every time you tried? And there it was, the story idea: Someone physically chained to the truth. It's dark. It's twisted. Because the truth is not supposed to hold you hostage, it's supposed to set you free."

Just when you think you've got it out, another question arises, a different truth is revealed. Deceptively quiet, this story leads you deeper into the maze at every turn.

Not Their Kind of Not Suitable
Tina Back

The stout guard of Seevelrode Prison peered suspiciously at the cheap, gold-toned watch, then handed it to his superior, a massive, freckled female who looked like she could crack a man's head between her thighs. Both wore the same uniform, sage green pants with a khaki shirt. There was a brass name tag pinned to the right breast pocket of each guard, but Mark Reinhart's ability to read and remember was temporarily out of order.

He'd just realized prisons terrified him. Even before being singled out on his first ever visit and taken to a sparsely furnished room with no windows.

It didn't help that people in uniform always made him nervous.

Plus, Reinhart could taste their type.

Dogs, both of them, no offense to either species. The man was a Border Collie, eager to serve. The female was a Bloodhound, a ruthless hunter. She'd smelled something off with Reinhart and his watch the moment he'd walked inside.

The watch — and the person for whom it was a gift — had made the prison roll out the special welcome mat, including the nice detour to the sparsely furnished room with no windows.

"It's a Casio digital, vintage gold-tone, stainless steel bracelet watch. New, it's 65 Euros online," Reinhart said, repeating what he had memorized the day before. "It doesn't work, so I got it for five."

His pulse picked up. The room suddenly felt too hot.

"Why do you want to give it to Mr. Serrano?" the female guard asked.

She was the pack leader, no doubt about it.

"Because that's what I have been instructed to do," Reinhart said. "Come here today, Friday, at this time, and to bring a digital watch that does not work."

"Are you an acquaintance of Mr. Serrano's?"

"Never met him. I gamble and now I owe someone money. Probably one of Mr. Serrano's... associates."

Reinhart added, "If I show up here today and meet with him, I've been promised that my debt will be paid in full."

"How much?"

"16,000." Reinhart wiped his sweaty forehead with the back of his hand.

A large sum for a man of small means.

"Nervous?" the male guard asked. He paced leisurely back and forth, keeping Reinhart herded where he was.

Definitely Border Collie.

"Wouldn't you be? I've heard the Eyeball Serrano-stories," said Reinhart.

"Someone gave you the watch?" the female guard said.

"I had to find one myself. I bought it in a pawnshop yesterday. The receipt is in my pocket. You can check it."

The female Bloodhound guard shot the third guard in the room a pointed glance. He was a thin, timid man who wore a medical mask. Some people really didn't want to be seen.

Guard number three sifted through the contents of Reinhart's pockets in the corner. He held up a receipt and sent a confirming nod the Bloodhound guard's way.

"Did you let anyone else touch the watch?" she asked.

Reinhart shook his head. "I never let it out of my sight, per the instructions. The guy who told me... well, you kind of do what guys like him says."

"You understand that if we find any type of contraband inside the watch, you're liable?"

"Go ahead. There's nothing inside. Trust me, I checked. I wasn't going to walk in here with anything that could get me in trouble," Reinhart said, feeling blotches of red erupt on his neck.

The two first guards took their time opening the watch on the table in front of Reinhart, while the third did his best to blend in with the drab wall.

The watch's insides contained nothing but nonworking, tiny electronic parts and the metal that held them in place.

The guards sent the watch through two machines that they kept on standby along the wall. Then they waived handheld equipment over it like two portly wizards.

The watch didn't set off any alarms.

Reinhart trembled, a quick, dog-like shudder.

He couldn't help it. It happened every time an obstacle was cleared. It was what the gamblers called 'a tell'. He had plenty of them.

"Are you related to the Reinhart line of magicians?" the female guard asked.

They had checked his ID.

Reinhart steeled himself and exhaled. "Remotely." The lie made him blush deeply, never a good look on a man close to fifty. "To be honest," Reinhart said, "I'm not sure they'd admit to it if you asked."

"You had training?"

"Four years, never certified."

"Why?"

"In the end, the board of Elders recommended that I found a job doing something I had actual talent for."

The lie made his cheeks flush again. He was pushing it.

"Did you?"

Reinhart looked at the opened watch with its inner workings displayed for all to see, feeling just as gutted.

"Still looking," he said, not even pretending to be ironic.

"Do you think your family history is why you've been asked to come?" said the Border Collie male.

"What else could it be?"

"What do you think Serrano wants from you?"

Reinhart shrugged uneasily. "Magic. Maybe he thinks I can open a hole in the wall and fix a rainbow staircase out of here."

The female Bloodhound in charge nailed him with a hard look, "Can you?"

Reinhart couldn't risk a fourth lie.

"If I could do that, the Reinhart Guild wouldn't have kicked me out." He felt his palms and back go slick with sweat, but the guard kept her gaze on his face and missed it.

◆

Reinhart followed a series of uniformed guards through the maze of the prison. He soon lost all sense of direction. One hallway followed the next. He was treated like a relay baton, a thing transferred through sets of locked spaces and escorted along desolate corridors under grim fluorescent lights.

The lack of windows bothered him.

And the reek of desperation.

He didn't see a single inmate, just the succession of male guards in identical uniforms, with slight variations in age, body type, and skin tone.

The current guard opened the next door, and they were outside.

Reinhart sucked in the fresh, cool, early spring air. He rolled his shoulders, trying to get his sweat-drenched t-shirt to stop clinging to his back.

A tall, dark-skinned guard waited on the other side, waving for Reinhart to step through. He did, the door closing behind him with a loud clanking sound. Predictable, but he jumped anyway.

The guard escorted him across an enclosed, but deserted, basketball court.

The sign on the next building read "Medical Ward." Here Reinhart was passed on for the final relay, trailing the last guard up a set of stairs to the third floor. He was handed over to a female Filipino nurse in blue scrubs, bursting with wild copper locks and the wrong kind of energy. The squirrel type. She probably had stashes of meds hidden all over the place.

Unless it was something else. Reinhart was sensitive, but no psychic.

The nurse walked him down a hallway lined with rooms sporting floor-to-ceiling glass walls for a full view of every room. The impression of an upgrade from the prison proper was tamed by the wire nets encased between the thick glass panes to make it harder to break.

Every room had two beds and medical equipment even someone like Reinhart could tell was at least thirty years out of date. Each bed held a prisoner in a different stage of waiting to die.

Reinhart had skimmed news headlines, sometime, somewhere, about Germany's overcrowded prison conditions and their aging, ailing prison populations, but this must be the final stretch. Not death row, but death bay.

A deep, cold shiver rattled down his spine.

The curly haired nurse unlocked the door to Albert Serrano's room.

Reinhart hesitated.

A two-bed room with a single occupant. Deadly sick, Serrano was still handled with special attention. Gouging your enemies' eyes out with your thumbs, then popping them into your mouth gives a guy a rep.

Serrano had been boss of a criminal network for decades, dealing in weapons, protection rackets, drugs, trafficking, prostitution. He was the fat spider at the center of a web linking sunny Sicily in the south to the frozen, former Soviet lands to the east.

Had been.

Before he'd made the classic mistake: running afoul of the tax authorities in no less than seven countries across continental Europe.

Reinhart inhaled deeply and crossed the threshold.

The nurse locked the door behind him.

Serrano, cuffed to the steel-framed bed with his left hand, turned his head and looked Reinhart over.

Reinhart did the same.

Even deathly ill, Serrano was still a big man with big bones. Every ounce of fat had drained away. Skin like tanned leather was pulled so tight over his skull, it was like looking at a mummy. Tufts of wavy, steel gray hair hung at the back of the big head, like a bad wig stapled in place. Tubes went in and out of Serrano's arms and side. A tired gray machine whirred in the background, and Serrano's vital signs undulated in orange on an old, fat-style TV.

Serrano stared at Reinhart with bright blue eyes that contrasted with the darkness Reinhart could sense seeping from his skeletal body like a toxic gas.

Unconsciously, Reinhart had stopped breathing when he entered the room. He exhaled slowly, playing for time. Reluctantly, he inhaled.

The room smelled sharply of pungent urine and nail polish.

Reinhart had been in the presence of sick and dying people before and he recognized it now. This was the smell of death. Serrano's body had begun to shut down.

Serrano motioned with a big, claw-like hand for him to come closer.

Another shiver made its way down Reinhart's spine. He made no effort to hide it.

He walked up to the side of the bed.

"You don't look like a gypsy," Serrano said with a raspy voice.

Reinhart passed on making a comment about the political incorrectness of the term. The extended Reinhart family came with a cocktail of bloodlines. 'Gypsy' was just one of them.

Serrano frowned, then muttered, "You don't look like much at all. But then I suppose that's mutual. Grab a chair."

When Reinhart had made himself comfortable, they sat in silence for a while, listening to the machine humming and faraway footsteps in the corridor.

"They let you bring it inside?" Serrano asked.

Reinhart silently fished out the digital watch from the jacket's pocket and handed it to Serrano.

The gold-toned watch looked small in the big man's hand.

"Can you do it?" Serrano asked.

Reinhart faked confidence and nodded.

"Is it true that the Guild castrate their outcasts to make sure it's the end of the line?" Serrano asked. He added with a feral curiosity, "Did they cut your balls off, or crush them?"

The old man relished pain. Other people's pain.

Reinhart looked Serrano in the eyes. "Times have changed. They get the same results with a vasectomy."

"The one you had reversed 15 years ago?"

Reinhart trembled.

He'd known that Serrano would vett him. It was the price of admission. Now, it was only about how far Serrano would go to humiliate him.

"We don't have a lot of time here," Reinhart said, reminding the dying man.

"They had you chained?" Serrano asked.

Reinhart pulled back his left sleeve and held out his wrist to let Serrano see.

A thin black chain, so thin it almost looked like a thread, was wrapped twice around his wrist. Like a thin cord, it came out of his skin, made a loop and went back under his skin in a tiny, second, scarred hole. The same long chain wound through his body, wrapping around his other wrist, both ankles, and neck. A half inch appeared over his heart and anus. There was no lock, no way to remove it. Not without serious magic.

The hope of unlocking his shackles was the only reason Reinhart had agreed to do someone like Serrano a favor.

"I would have just killed you," said Serrano. "I've never seen the point in keeping steers around."

The point was simple: they kept the rest of the herd in check. Not that Reinhart would explain that to Serrano.

"What do you want with it?" he said instead.

"I'm dying. I want to spend one hour every day of my last week at home with my wife. I want this for seven days in a row."

"Give me the watch," Reinhart said.

Serrano handed the watch back. It was warm and dry from Serrano's body heat. It was like holding a tiny, sun-kissed shell.

Reinhart focused.

The chains that wrapped him snapped tight, as if pulled by some small, but dangerously strong creature inside his chest. A sharp, blazing pain burned along the entire length of the cursed links threaded through every limb of his body. It pulled itself into a metal ball inside his rib cage, cutting trails inside him.

His heart skipped a beat, as if it knew what was coming next, and was giving in to the horror.

But the watch's tiny gray screen came alight, two black dots of a colon blinking, and the chain snaking inside him stopped.

Reinhart didn't dare move.

He drew a shallow breath. Air squeezed past the chain crushing his throat. Then the stranglehold eased. Tiny black links slid back out from the spell that had pulled them tight, until the chain was back to its usual slack state. It still hurt, but nowhere near the searing pain of chains snapping tight.

Surprise washed over him.

Reinhart had never expected the magic to work. He wasn't supposed to be able to do it at all. It had been so long; he'd been desperate enough to try.

Quickly, he put in the start time, pushing the tiny gold-toned buttons on the watch. He said the spell out loud, and felt it take form.

Reinhart handed the watch back to Serrano. "Hold the watch, wish for it with all you've got."

Serrano raised an eyebrow, but did as Reinhart asked, eyes closed, the golden watch hidden in a giant fist over his heart.

Reinhart took the watch back and chanted the next part of the spell.

"Keep the watch on you at all times," he said giving the watch back to Serrano. "Let no one else wear it or touch it. I'll do what needs to be done before midnight tonight."

Reinhart looked at Serrano.

"The best hour for this is the Wolves' hour, the hour before dawn. See the start time on the screen? At that moment, the spell's time will begin. You'll have one hour. Hold an item that has meaning to both you and your wife in your left hand and go through with your right."

"Go through what?"

Reinhart shrugged. "You'll see."

He had no idea. But it didn't matter. He wasn't lying. Not outright. So the chains didn't snap at him, tearing burning wounds inside his body.

"Will I be – real? Like physical? When I touch her, will she feel it?"

"You'll be as you are now." Reinhart rose from the chair. "And now my debt is paid."

Serrano looked up. "In eight days. Not before. If this works."

Reinhart nodded.

He tried to get a sense of what was brewing, what lightness that eighth day would bring for him, but he felt nothing.

Just like that, he was nervous again. His body responded with its usual tricks. He needed to get out of there fast, find a restroom to make an explosive deposit.

"I have something you might be interested in," Serrano said. "There's a Bible on the windowsill. Check out the bookmark."

Reinhart walked to the window, his unease growing with every step, dread pooling heavily in his gut.

The Bible was black and new. No one had ever used it.

He let it fall open to where the bookmark had been placed. Lying on the page with its miniature writing was a folded printout. He picked up the crisp piece of paper and unfolded it.

The picture showed a small, handmade leather case, spread open, displaying three small pliers with black-lacquered handles.

"I have one of them in the drawer," said Serrano.

Reinhart went back to the bed.

He opened the only drawer in the bedside table and picked up the tiny tool inside.

He knew it was the right kind the moment he touched it. Something between a vibration and a hum sung inside him. He felt the connection in his gut and groin, the magic rippling along the chains that made him a prisoner in his own body, shackled inside with no way to act out.

These were the flat pliers, not the nipper that could cut through the chains' links, but for a demonstration of the goods available, it was close enough.

Reinhart put the pliers back in the drawer and shut it.

"Not interested," he said, feeling blotches of crimson breaking out on his skin like a plague. A chunk of the chain tightened slowly at the lie, leaving a fresh burning line starting just behind his navel and heading for his heart.

He was a fool.

Reinhart had come here ready to barter. He should have known better. He couldn't do it.

Not now, not ever.

"You'd be free," said Serrano.

No, he wouldn't be. He would owe his freedom to Serrano, or Serrano's heirs. It would just be a different kind of shackles. And a lesser kind at that.

But just imagining holding the nipper pliers sent a violent tremor through his body.

Another obstacle cleared.

He'd found the toolbox. Too bad the price was too high.

Reinhart took a deep breath to control the riot of feelings the meeting with Serrano had set off.

"You wouldn't want me free," he said quietly.

Serrano cocked a discerning eyebrow.

Reinhart turned away, crossed the room, and knocked hard on the door. He was itching to get away from the poison Serrano was made of. He was sure the old man spread evil like a cold, contaminating the air around him.

While he waited for the guard, his body performed another uncontrollable dog-like shrug, his feelings manifesting in ways far too obvious.

"Your own kind put you in chains," Serrano said. "That little tool could make things right."

It could, but that was not the point.

Then the curly-haired nurse unlocked the door and Reinhart slipped out before he said something he'd regret.

Like the truth.

◆

Slowly, the world took form around Reinhart. It rocked gently. Without effort, his brain translated the wet, regular slapping sounds and shrieks outside: Waves against a boat's hull and water birds. There was so much of the river Elbe in the trapped cabin air he could taste it.

He was back in Hamburg.

Reinhart opened his eyes.

A platinum blonde woman was sitting in the opposite bunk in the cramped space, arms resting on knees, her feet in dark green, men's size rubber boots. Almost folded in half, she still looked tall and fast, with long slender limbs and a short, expensively messy haircut. She looked late thirties but was just as old as Reinhart.

Michaela. Mick.

He spotted an amber residue in the glass in her hand. She'd been watching him for a while.

Reinhart's heart swelled. For a moment he was lost to the intensity of simply feeling. He forgot that he was looking straight at her.

The force of his gaze hit her full on. Her eyes widened in surprise.

Reinhart shut it down, blushing. He hid his face under his arm, getting a whiff of sour sweat and damp reality.

When the red tide had passed, he put the arm under his head and propped himself up. As if on cue, a headache started throbbing behind his eyes.

"It's Monday?" he croaked.

On Mondays, Mick took half the day off and spent the afternoon on the dayboat. She told people she went for a long run. She looked like a runner and runners go run. Nobody asked.

It had been Peter's boat, a rock guitarist poet boyfriend to both of them, back when they were younger and fiercer. There had been long periods where the three of them had lost touch completely. They had been friends before the internet and the connection had remained a thing offline. When he died, Peter left the small boat to Mick, not to Reinhart who Peter knew had no talent for keeping a roof over his head. Or maybe Peter knew Mick had more need for it. In the end it didn't matter. She'd let Reinhart keep his spare key. He sometimes used the boat to crash when he was passing through.

Mick never told anyone else about the boat.

She'd take the small dayboat out on the river and let it drift. Wrapped in a plaid woolen blanket, hand on the rudder, she spent her Monday afternoons sipping whisky and brooding, staring at the distant shoreline with a mix of contempt and longing.

One Monday, when Reinhart had been late leaving, she'd asked if he wanted to come along. Since then, Reinhart had spent a total of nine glorious Monday afternoons on the boat, quietly brooding with Mick. He was careful not to overstay his welcome, making sure months passed before his next visit.

Mick wore a wedding band on her left hand, a simple wide ring of gold. The ring had been there long enough to leave a groove in the flesh of her ring finger. There might be kids, but not small ones. Reinhart knew her job was something to do with marketing. The car she drove was a quality brand from Japan. Something safe, reliable and utterly forgettable.

Reinhart understood that there was a whole side of Mick's life that he wasn't privy to. That was fine, because he'd been invited to her secret life.

The life she fiercely protected. The life she chose.

"How long have you been out," she asked.

"Midnight, Friday."

Her face clouded and he quickly added, "It's not what you think."

He didn't do drugs the way he used to. Mick looked like she didn't do drugs at all anymore.

"There's a chalk pentagram on the cockpit bow," said Mick.

Reinhart sighed.

He had been too drained after the ritual to get rid of the props.

Mick got up. She headed for the cooler in the corner. She returned with a tall liter and a half bottle of water and handed it to him. "You're dehydrated."

"I stink."

"Shut up. Drink."

Grateful, he did as she said.

Mick studied him in the same silent brooding way she stared at the horizon.

He waited for her to make up her mind. He'd understand if she wanted him gone. The boat was her secret sanctuary. He had used it without due respect.

"I'm sorry," he said, the words thick with emotion. Another surprise for her, he could tell. He looked away.

He had to get a grip. He was overflowing in every direction. Nobody wanted that.

"Apology accepted," Mick said, "but I draw the line at headless goats and pigeons."

"I'll keep that in mind."

"You need to eat. There's a café across harbor. I'll buy you lunch, if you go overboard on the way over and clean yourself up."

♦

The cold water shocked the air out of Reinhart's lungs. He kicked furiously and broke the surface. He got a mouthful of the remaining diesel fumes from the engine riding low on the short, choppy waves. He kicked again, getting his head high enough to get to the cool fresh air above, and grabbed hold of the gunwale. He managed to get a leg up and haul his naked, slippery body back on board. He collapsed in a shivering heap of flesh on the deck.

With a smirk, Mick handed him a pale green bar of soap.

He cussed at her, but worked up a lather from head to toe with blue-tipped fingers. Tossing the soap back at her with a dark glare, he dove headfirst back into the merciless cold. He stayed under till his lungs ached, watching Mick watch him.

When he surfaced, she held out a hand and helped pull him out of the water.

Reinhart turned away from her.

Being naked in front of her before had never bothered him. Now it did.

Mick spread the rough, woolen blanket over his shoulders. She wrapped her arms around him from behind and held him. The hug warmed him better than the blanket.

Reinhart barely dared to breathe.

After a while, he felt her warm fingers on the back of his neck, tracing the thin black chains close to where they came out and went back under his skin on each side of the spine.

"I found a t-shirt and extra socks that might fit you," Mick said. She let him go, "Get inside and try to get warm."

"You made me take a swim in April," he reminded her. "Whatever happens next is on you."

Reinhart hadn't meant for it to sound like a dare. He blushed, but not from lying for once.

A long time ago, he'd known what to say to girls he liked. These days, most things terrified him. Especially the few things he could not bear to lose.

But Mick looked pleased.

Not that he trusted his judgment. Hypothermia was known to cause delusions.

♦

The cafe was mostly empty, only a few stragglers after the lunch rush remained, nursing coffee and laptops.

They had a window table, looking out at a mostly deserted street and the harbor beyond.

The cafe was more of a cafeteria, with plastic trays and grubby glasses. The glasses were clean, Reinhart noted, they had just made too many rounds in the dishwasher. The sheer number of tiny scratches made their surface look dull and dirty. But a mound of golden fried potatoes hidden under a crispy schnitzel soon appeared on a plate before him, and that was all that mattered.

There would be conversation. Reinhart could feel it while he chewed. It made him nervous, the way the silence between them had changed.

He ate slowly to put off the inevitable for as long as possible.

"You do magic?" she asked when he was done.

Reinhart shook his head. "I'm a magician chained."

A wrinkle appeared between her brows. "Meaning?"

"I'm not suitable."

He blushed.

A half lie, but those counted, too.

Mick reached across the table and put her hand over his, her fingertips brushing the chains.

A cold hand of premonition squeezed his heart right then, in perfect sync with her warm hand over his.

Reinhart shifted uneasily in his seat. "There are measures the Reinhart Guild takes to make sure you're… contained. This is one of them."

The rarest of them, but he didn't feel like sharing that information. Shame was a funny thing.

"Does it hurt?" she said.

"My pride, mostly." He paused. "Not so much anymore," he added softly, treading very, very cautiously.

Reinhart had never talked about it. Not to anyone.

He wasn't sure if he told her because he wanted to, or because the dark things to come compelled him. In any case, heavy matters often required the lightest touch.

"You'd been kicked out but not chained. That's why you were so angry," Mick said, her head some thirty years in the past.

"I was pretty angry," he said. "Four years down the drain. Never a word why."

"Where did it go? You were—" She made a bug-eyed crazy face. The polite expression for borderline insanely intense.

"I grew up." Reinhart blushed furiously.

He sensed her turning his comment over, finding it underwhelming.

"I took something back," he admitted, undercutting the poison of the lie. "Potential, if you will. The Guild doesn't know about it."

A reversed vasectomy. A world tour making deposits at sperm banks as a scientist, athlete, and an astronaut. The Guild would find out soon. Some of those sperms were about to hit puberty.

"So, you do magic now?" Mick asked.

"Only this once."

This lie he felt. Something strained. Something tore inside of him when the chains whipped tight.

Reinhart kept his palms on the table to hide the blood seeping from the chains' entry points on his scarred wrists.

Mick was waiting for more.

"A dying man wanted to spend one hour a day of his maybe last seven days with his wife."

"That's very romantic," she said. "Why do you look so guilty?"

"I did it because I owed him money. And to get closer to something I've been looking for."

Reinhart's cheeks flushed crimson. He had to keep going. The Guild had made sure that he had no choice but to stay honest.

"He's not a good man," Reinhart said quickly. "Albert Serrano is evil."

Mick pulled her hand back as if he'd burnt her.

"It's all over the news," she said. "One of Serrano's enemies was killed Friday night, then another on Saturday. One last night. They say they've been killed in Serrano's style, but Serrano—"

"—is dying, handcuffed to a prison hospital bed," he said. He added the obvious, "I have to go."

He knew he didn't have to explain, but he did anyway. He had to get the watch out of Serrano's reach. There was no way to undo the spell from afar.

Mick called a taxi and paid for the meal. She stuffed a bundle of cash from the cafe's ATM machine in his pocket, not taking no for an answer.

They walked out to an overcast sky.

Dark clouds were forming to the east. A hard rain was coming. Reinhart wished the weather wouldn't feed his fears. He told Mick to leave, to try to get back across the river before it was too late.

"It's already too late," she said.

He felt the truth in it deeply.

Reinhart had signed his death warrant when he scribbled his real name like a fool on the prison visitors' list.

Serrano wouldn't want him talking, Serrano's enemies' friends would hunt him down and when the news reached the Guild's elders....

A three-way death sentence of his own making.

The Guild had been right. He was not suitable.

Reinhart felt Mick's presence acutely, like an unexpected grace. His oversized feelings spilled again. Gratitude made his throat hurt.

They waited in a new kind of silence, one he couldn't make sense of, like there was a storm of words brewing, words that should be said out loud, but neither one of them was ready to unleash them.

Silence suited them. Silence had served them well.

Decades worth of the stuff.

The first heavy drops of rain fell as the taxi pulled up. Against better judgment, Reinhart leaned in and kissed her, a fast, fumbled kiss.

"You're not coming back," she said.

Reinhart wanted to say that he was sorry, but there was no point.

She already knew.

Mick fussed angrily with the lapel of his coat, like she was trying to make sure he wasn't cold and the coat wasn't cooperating. She stopped.

He felt her palm warm over his thundering heart and the weight of things too late to mention.

"Then do it right," she mumbled and pulled him close.

As far as he could tell, he did.

♦

24 hours later Reinhart had something of a plan.

He'd been lucky. No one on Serrano's supposed kill list had been found dead on Tuesday morning. According to the clickbait news headlines he skimmed, one man had locked himself in a safe room. He hadn't come out and was so far the only one unaccounted for.

When the man still hadn't appeared at ten in the morning, the family called for help. The news crews began circle the home like peckish vultures.

It was nearly four o'clock that afternoon and Reinhart was in a taxi reeking of tobacco, heading for Seevelrode Prison when the rescue crew finally managed to break into the safe room. The radio news anchor delivered the details like the story made him froth around the mouth.

A man murdered inside a locked room. A man with no eyes.

It was the kind of thing the Reinhart Guild of Magicians would be bound to notice.

Thirty minutes later, Reinhart saw the stark, squat outline of the prison rising from the gray windswept flatness of the Luneberger Moor. He did his best to ignore the gut feeling that he was too late.

Reinhart had the taxi driver drop him off at the visitor's parking lot. The wind tugged at his ears and chilled him in an instant.

He checked the gold-toned Casio on his wrist for the time, forgetting it was dead. He stole a last glimpse at the taxi's clock before it drove away, hoping to synch it to his internal clock to keep track of time.

Four twenty-three in the afternoon.

Time was of the essence. Time *was* the essence.

The parking lot was still half full. Visiting hours had just about another hour to go.

Reinhart scanned the prison.

Two people appeared from a side entrance, a man and a woman wearing scrub pants and sensible shoes beneath their jackets. He recognized the curly-haired, speeded nurse who'd escorted him to Serrano's room.

Reinhart heard a car and looked over his shoulder. There was a vehicle coming on the main road. The standard dark metallic grey of a Reinhart Guild, Inc. Mercedes.

The car slowed down and veered into the lane to turn into the road to the prison.

Reinhart was out of time. He abandoned his original plan. Desperate, he headed for the staff parking lot, ready to wing it or die.

The male nurse got into a yellow Volkswagen.

Reinhart called out for the red-haired nurse to wait up.

She turned her head.

"You're the guy," she said, her eyes small and glassy. The pill-fueled, squirrel-like energy he'd seen on Friday had been replaced by a pill-induced slowness. Today, she blinked like a sleepy koala.

Reinhart smiled, showing his teeth to let her know he was friendly and harmless. That it was no big deal that he was walking up to her in the prison parking lot.

"I visited Mr. Serrano last Friday," he said.

"You're the guy everyone is asking about."

Reinhart's smile wilted.

"You feel exhausted," he said gently to the nurse, using all his power of persuasion. "You can't keep your eyes open. You can't drive home like this. You must take a nap. Open the car."

The nurse fumbled around in her pocket.

"Let me help you," he said as the gray Mercedes pulled into the visitor's parking lot.

With a confused look, the nurse gave him the car keys.

He opened the door for her and gently helped her to get behind the wheel.

Reinhart pocketed the keys and rushed to the other side of the car. He ducked into the passenger seat, closing the door gently to not draw the attention of the two, suit-clad men who emerged from the Mercedes.

"You feel very, very sleepy," Reinhart told the nurse. "Close your eyes. Listen to my voice."

He ripped the new dead watch from his wrist.

"There," he cooed, "everything is fine now. But you need to keep track of time. You need my watch."

Reinhart reached over and struggled to put the watch on the nurse's left wrist. "You feel very relaxed," he said.

He lowered the back of his seat, took the nurse's right hand in his left, and closed his eyes.

He still didn't know what he'd done to be cast out of the Guild, but they wouldn't have gone to through the trouble to chain him without reason.

But there was no time left. No time for doubt.

"Now," he said softly to the nurse, "go through your right hand and slip over into that nice body you're holding onto. That's where you'll go to sleep."

◆

Reinhart smiled at the extra guard posted in the medical ward's corridor. Smiling was hard work. Moving the nurse's strange body was more than enough to handle.

"Forgot something," Reinhart said, marveling at hearing himself with a different voice.

He hurried to Serrano's room, and used the nurse's key card. The door's lock clicked open.

Albert Serrano slept. Irregular hollowed breaths ripped his chest. He didn't stir when Reinhart-as-nurse entered. Serrano looked worse off physically, like he'd shrunk since Reinhart had last seen him. He smelled worse. But there was a serene, ghost of a smile on his dry, cracked lips.

Reinhart contained a shiver.

He moved as if he had a nursing purpose. He touched the tube hanging from a stand above Serrano's head. He leaned over Serrano, quickly flipping the latch to the watch's bracelet on the nurse's arm. He then flipped the latch on the matching watch on Serrano's arm and watched it slide like a golden lizard into a fold of the orange polyester blanket.

Reinhart put the nurse's watch on Serrano's withered, freckled arm.

Serrano's eyes popped open.

"What the hell are you doing," he said, pulling his arm away.

"Your watch's come off. I'm putting it back on."

Reinhart held out the nurse's watch.

Serrano snatched it out of her hand. "You better not have ruined anything," he growled.

Reinhart prayed that the lingering body heat in the watch would fool Serrano.

Straightening the blanket, he palmed the time-spell watch, then left the room, locking the door behind him.

He retraced his steps, focusing on keeping the nurse upright. He could feel his control beginning to fade at the edges. Moving someone else's body was exhausting.

He smiled brightly at the two suit-clad gentlemen as they were being let into the ward by the attending male nurse.

Reinhart walked down the seemingly endless steps of the three-story building, too scared that the elevator might stop and trap him inside the prison and inside the nurse.

As he crossed the parking lot, his consciousness was coming and going. Reinhart stumbled forward. He could sense the nurse stirring, nearby and inside at the same time. It made him nauseous in a mind-bending way. He had trouble seeing. Darkness encroached.

Reinhart unlocked the car door blindly and fell into the driver's seat. His last conscious act was closing the door and taking his own hand in the nurse's.

♦

A snore ripped Reinhart awake. His heart raced. Terrified, he first thought he was back with Serrano in the prison hospital room reeking of impending death. Next, he thought he'd woken himself up with his own snoring.

Another snore to his left brought him back to reality.

Reinhart opened his eyes.

A cushioned car ceiling. Sticky, well-used air with a side of chemically-scented sweet Wunderbaum car deodorant. Darkness outside, with the exception of a milky streetlamp. Fogged-up windows.

The curly-haired nurse snored loudly beside him.

She looked small and light. Wearing her body, her weight had been backbreaking.

Reinhart's body shook like a dog's in a brisk shudder. The telltale signal he'd cleared another hurdle.

Serrano would never kill again.

Reinhart felt around and found the handle. He pushed it. The back of his seat rose with a soft hum. The nurse seemed to still be deep under, now that she was back in her own body. She didn't stir.

Reinhart felt physically okay. Not like when he had woken up parched and dirty on Mick's boat.

He had no means to tell what date and time it was, but sensed that not much time had passed. He peered out at the visitor's parking lot.

The Mercedes was still there.

Reinhart shook the nurse's shoulder.

No reaction.

He spoke to her gently but firmly, ordering her to wake up the same way he had made her go to sleep.

No reaction, except for the snoring.

Magic took energy. Creating the time spell for Serrano had wiped him out for two and a half days. Walking around in someone else's body should have taken an even higher toll.

Unless…

Reinhart realized it might be days before the nurse woke up. She would need care. Water, nutrients and adult diapers at the least.

With an eye on the prison visitor's exit, he lowered the back of the driver's seat and pulled the nurse into the back seat. Then he got out, the air fresh like spring water after the muggy car.

He walked around to the other side of the car and slipped into the driver's seat. Without turning on the headlights, he started the engine, then slowly drove out of the parking lot and followed the long driveway back to the main road.

Reinhart trembled again, one long, uncontrollable shudder that slowly rippled through him while he clung to the steering wheel.

His body was telling him something. Something beyond Serrano, or getting away from the Reinhart elders.

He had hijacked another human being. He'd walked around in someone else's body, while she had been tucked away inside his own resting body, at his command.

That was upper-level magic.

His training as a teen had covered the basics, no more. Reinhart had never tried anything beyond petty parlor tricks after the Elders kicked him out. And fear and doubt had always infested his pathetic attempts after being chained.

Creating the time spell for Serrano had been a stretch. He'd had to reach deep to set it. He'd been second-guessing himself every step of the way. It had hurt.

He'd only risked it because he had found out that one of Serrano's men had stolen the kind of tools he'd been looking for since the elders had wrapped him inside and out with their cursed magic shackles.

There had been no time for doubt when he took command of the nurse, and no pain.

He was not supposed to be able to pull something like this off. And he had done it bound and harnessed by black magic chains.

Reinhart had believed the chains constrained him because that was what he had been told.

He hadn't taken the Reinhart elders' word for it at first, but after reading a moldy copy of the Reinhart Grand Grimoire he'd paid someone to dig out of a grave in Bulgaria, the elders' claim had been confirmed. He'd read how the cursed chains would first cut his flesh and bones like a wire slicing through soft cheese and then slowly consume him from the inside like a fire fanned by his heartbeats.

The chains had worked painfully well when he lied, and that had been enough to deter him. Reinhart had never dared to find out what level magic, if any, he could still do while bound.

Not until Serrano's man had tempted him with the toolbox. Not until he'd walked into Seevelrode Prison.

Reinhart didn't doubt the words in the Grand Grimoire, but for reasons he could not understand, the chains no longer worked the way the elders had intended. If they ever had. Something about the dark spell had not formed right.

More importantly, the elders had missed it.

Like him, they just found out.

For years and years, Reinhart had believed he was nothing, a chained creature; but now all bets were off.

His mind racing, he headed toward the bright city lights of Buxtehude, the nearest town glowing in the far distant horizon, in search of a hospital where he could drop off the nurse.

Further away, later, there would be a randomly chosen inn and a room with fresh, clean sheets. He hoped the inn came with a bar downstairs, where he could get a beer and figure out his next move.

The Reinhart Guild would be coming for him, but he had a twenty-eight year head start of living off the grid. He was still afraid of what they could do to him. Now they feared him in the same way. It made it better. He'd held on with a fool's stubborn hope that one day his time would come.

Here it was.

Reinhart wished he had a plan, but he'd make one up as he went. He'd done it before. He was good at thinking on his feet.

A magician chained, but reborn. On the run, but still at large.

Ready for a whole other level of *not suitable*.

C.E. Barnes grew up in Northwest Florida but left at the age of 27 because a human can only tolerate humidity, mosquitoes, and tourists for just so long. His literary influences include Sir Arthur Conan Doyle and Herbert George Wells, which is why his sentence structure abounds with convoluted dependent clauses spliced together with an exuberance of semicolons. He is awkward in social settings and retreats behind a shield of polite formality, unless you bring up the topic of dogs, whereupon he'll talk your poor ears off. He adores his wife. He shouldn't be trusted to write his own bio.

About this story, C.E. says: "Back in 2012, when the Mayans pranked us all with that calendar thingie, I was having a drink with a vampire buddy of mine. He wasn't allowed to stay until Last Call, as his master liked to keep close tabs on her brood. "It ain't all bad," he said to me as we left the pub. "I've got supernatural strength and vitality. I can bend weak minds to my will. And... I'm gonna be around forever." He flashed me a big toothy smile as he left to party on, but it never reached his eyes. Okay, so that story is obvious BS, but it's much cooler than the truth, and Rule of Cool trumps Truth every time."

In the submission guidelines, I told authors that they were welcome to write vampire stories, but warned them that garden-variety vampires were going to be a hard sell. I'll leave it to you to decide for yourself what you think of this one.

THE WORKING STIFF
C.E. Barnes

Simple, like clockwork. The cashier came out of the convenience store, trash bags in hand, heading for the poorly-lit dumpster dock. I waited until both of his arms were occupied with trash bags and dumpster lids before I koshed him at the base of his skull. I checked to make certain he was still breathing, then headed into the store.

Once inside, I took a small pry bar from my coat pocket and opened the cash register drawer. Not much in the till, but more than the twenty bucks the sign said was all the overnight cashiers were allowed to keep on hand. The bills went into a convenient plastic sack, then back inside my coat, along with the pry bar. A quick stop to destroy the conspicuous videotape and less conspicuous hard drive recorder in the manager's tiny office, and I was out the door... three minutes, tops.

On the way back out, I double-checked on the cashier. He was a young, red-headed kid; looked to be in his late teens or early twenties. I rifled through his pockets and found his cell phone. With a little duct tape, brought along for just this purpose, I covered his mouth and bound his wrists. I put the kid's cell phone in his hands; if no one found him before he woke up, he'd need it to call 911.

The till had held close to two hundred dollars in various denominations. Better than I'd hoped, but nowhere near my quota. If I were to avoid painful and humiliating punishment, I'd need to pick up the pace.

I arrived back home shortly before morning, with enough time to count and sort the bills, and place them on the center of the kitchen table before sunrise. She wasn't up when I got in, but she'd be rising soon if she planned to make it to school on time. I spared a glance up the stairway, wishing for the umptieth time that I could go up and throttle her in her sleep, but she had explicitly stated that the second floor was off-limits. Then again, she had explicitly stated that I was not allowed to harm her in any fashion, so it really didn't matter.

Instead, I went down to the basement, where I stowed my work tools, hung up my coat, and wiggled into the crawlspace to die again… at least, until sunset.

◆

"Hey, loser! Get your butt up here!"

That voice… that annoying soprano clarion. It had been the first thing I heard when she conjured me two years ago, before I'd even had a chance to open my eyes. "Lay still. Don't move until I give you permission to do otherwise," the voice had said. And… I obeyed.

I quickly discovered disobeying wasn't an option.

"Rule number one: You are not allowed to harm me in any way or allow me to come to harm if you can help it. Rule number two: You are only allowed to disobey me if obeying me would break rule number one. Rule number three: You have to protect yourself unless doing so would break rules number one or number two. Now, tell me if you understand these rules, or if I need to dumb it down for you, loser."

"I get it," I said.

"Good. Now stand up and follow me home. I'm hungry, and it's past my bedtime," the voice said.

I stood up, looked around. I was in a graveyard. It was dark, though I could see well enough. A young girl, all bangs and pigtails, was packing odd implements into a purple backpack decorated with cartoon ponies.

"Who are—" I started to ask.

"Shut up!" she snapped. "Don't speak unless spoken to. If there's something I want you to know, I'll tell you."

◆

And that was how it had begun. I hurried up the basement stairs to the kitchen, where she was waiting. The bane of my existence, the hag who has ridden my back for the last two years, was now a sixteen-year-old girl with bad skin, dishwater-blonde hair, and baby fat that will never go away if she doesn't learn to control her cravings for chocolate. She claims that raising and controlling the Undead is a constant drain on her energy, requiring a substantial caloric intake.

I have to agree.

Literally, I have to; I'm not allowed to voice a dissenting opinion.

"You summoned me, my Dark Lady, and I am here," I said. I seriously hate the theatrics, but that's what she wants, and what my mistress wants, she gets. I was only allowed to use her name – to speak it, write it or even think it – when playing the role of her adult guardian. On all other occasions, she insisted on this pseudo-Goth charade.

"What did I tell you before you left last night," she asked.

"You said you needed fifteen hundred dollars to cover this month's living expenses... uhm, My Queen."

"I said, I needed *at least* fifteen hundred dollars! 'At least' means the more, the better." She threw a handful of small bills, mostly ones and fives, back on the table. "That's all that's left of the crap you brought back. If you can't pull your weight around here, perhaps I should dust you and raise something with a bit of gumption, huh?"

"Not like I could stop you," I muttered as I straightened and sorted the bills... again.

She ignored my comment and watched me organize the change. "Fix me some macaroni and cheese," she commanded. "I'm starving."

"As am I, Dread Necromancer," I replied.

"Who gives a shit? No, wait. If you're hungry enough, you can eat the Henderson's mutt. Damned bitch barked half the night, woke me up twice. But make my mac and cheese first."

I filled a saucepan with water and retrieved a box of prepackaged macaroni from the pantry. Time for my humiliating punishment.

"Mistress," I weaseled, "Must it be macaroni and cheese? I could prepare you something more substantial… and much tastier."

"Shut it!" she snapped. "Start cooking… I'm waiting!"

I 'shut it' and started cooking, as commanded. The macaroni spilled from its cardboard box, where it had been carefully contained, into the larger and less confining pot.

The pasta began to move as the water came to a boil, interrupting my count. Nothing unusual there; I never managed to count all the individual pieces before the convection currents played hell with my obsessive-compulsive disorder. I chewed my lip ragged, watching the noodles boogie in the boiling water, while one half of my brain still tried to count them all, another part looked for patterns in the motion, and one leftover bit loudly sang, "Heeey, Macaroni!"

She let me stand there, transfixed and shaking until it no longer amused her. Once she covered the pot with an aluminum lid, I could think again. Muscles unclenched and I grabbed the countertop for support.

"No!" she commanded. "Keep going down. Kneel."

I knelt before her. Nothing else I could do.

"Now," she purred. "When I send you out to raise cash, and I tell you I need at least fifteen hundred dollars, how much do you bring home?"

"As much as possible… much more than you require."

"And if I tell you I need ten bucks for band candy, how much do you bring home?"

"As much as possible," I repeated.

"I knew you couldn't be as stupid as you look," she praised me. "Get up. I want to show you something."

She dug her phone out of her purse, activated it and stroked the screen several times. Once she had located what she wanted, she turned the phone screen to me. On it was a picture of a brunette cheerleader smiling for the photo.

"This is Tabitha Stuck-Up-Bitch Warren," she said. "I want her dead. No bite marks, though. Friday night would be good; our football team has a home game."

"Has this mortal offended you, Milady?" I turned back to the stove. The pasta had boiled down to a lump of coagulated carbohydrate. I drained the mess and stirred in butter and dehydrated processed cheese-flavored powder until the mess resembled a lumpy orange pudding.

"You don't need to know the details, loser," she replied, taking the bowl from me. "Just lure her somewhere private and leave me a pristine corpse. Oh, one other thing…"

She set the bowl aside and went back to her purse, rummaging through it until she produced a slip of paper, which she handed to me. "My report card," she said. "Woulda been straight 'A's except for a frikkin' 'C' in Driver's Ed. I can't have my G.P.A. pulled down by a stupid elective."

"Will I be killing your driving instructor as well?" I asked.

"No," she sighed. "I need him for right now. You're gonna get me a car to practice with… a really cool one!"

◆

The note tacked to the basement door informed me that my mistress would be out this evening, and I wasn't to leave the cellar unless I heard her voice on the answering machine specifically instructing me otherwise. I occupied myself for a while with tidying up my living area ("living" area… ain't that ironic?), which took all of ten minutes, then paced the room until I caught myself counting steps. I sat on the top of the basement stairs, head cradled in my hands. "You know what I'd like? You know what I'd give my right arm for?"

I looked up. Having nothing more productive to do, I decided to strike up a conversation with the shambling dead.

A ghoul, my jailor for the evening, returned the look, patiently, calmly.

"I'd like an honest-to-God memory from the time before I woke up in that lousy graveyard. I just wish I could recall one day of my life… I don't care which one; it could be the worst day I ever had, so long as it came with the knowledge of who I was."

The ghoul made no comment. Truth was, he hadn't said much since I'd awakened a few hours before and found him in the cellar with me.

"I can't tell you how disconcerting it is," I continued.

"Hmmmm…" the ghoul replied.

"This amnesia thing, or whatever it is. I mean, clearly, I have this knowledge of stuff in my head. For instance, I know how to drive a car. I know how convenience stores operate. Hell, I even know that the rules I live under were ripped off from Isaac Asimov. But do I remember ever reading a science fiction novel? Hell, no!"

I was pacing again, and the ghoul, trying to keep me in sight, was doing severe damage to the tendons in its putrefied neck. "Sorry," I said, resuming my seat on the steps. "Knowledge without experience," I continued. "it's like somebody unscrewed my skull, dumped data all over my brain, then nailed everything shut again."

"Uuuhgggh," the ghoul said.

"Exactly! Frustrating as all hell. I've asked her to tell me who I was, back before I died, and you know what she said?"

"Uuuhhmmm…."

"She said that memories of my living days would only interfere with my ability to function. She said that memories of old friends and loved ones might cause a problem if I was ordered to kill one of them, and that with no memories, everyone is a stranger. Everyone is prey. How's that for fucked up?"

"Mmmmmm…" the ghoul said.

"I know! She ain't right," I continued. "But I dunno. She could have a point."

"Huuugh?"

"Well, what if I could remember my life as it was? What if I remembered being happy, or carefree, being my own person? That'd just make my existence that much more of a suckfest, no?"

"Uuuuhhhh…"

"No, don't answer," I said. "It was a rhetorical question. Anyway, thanks for listening. I didn't realize how much I needed to get that off my chest. I'm gonna go back to my crawlspace now and mull things over. Uh… hug it out?"

The ghoul stared at me.

"Yeah, you're probably right," I conceded. "It's better we keep this relationship professional."

◆

One of my least favorite duties is protecting a sixteen year-old kid from herself. I can't tell her anything, because I'm automatically wrong. Instead, I have to ask leading questions, slowly coaxing her to realize that a stolen vehicle would cause problems for her that I couldn't resolve; likewise with a vehicle registered to someone deceased or reported missing.

Ultimately, it was a lost cause. "I don't care what you have to do to get it, loser. Just get me a car that isn't a total embarrassment. Steal it, buy it, build it from scratch for all I care. I just want it in the garage ASAP."

Well, at least that gave me some leeway in my method. "With your leave, Dread Mistress, I'll apply myself to the task. I shall return ere sunrise."

"Don't hurry back on my account," was her reply.

◆

I headed out to my favorite brainstorming spot. There's something about a Waffle House that relaxes me and gets my intellectual processes revved up. I don't know if it's the bright lighting, the shine off the Formica, or the cheery jingle on the jukebox. Maybe all of them. I've tried doing my thinking at Denny's, but have you seen some of their late-night customers? Freaky doesn't begin to describe them.

And that's saying something, coming from me.

I grabbed my favorite booth, the one halfway between the entrance and the restrooms, and waited. After a few minutes, a tired and distracted waitress arrived to take my order. I asked for black coffee. I didn't particularly want it, but it was the expected thing to do and wouldn't provide her memory any oddity to cling to. She poured me a cup of the stuff, asked if there was anything else I needed, and then promptly became oblivious to the space I was occupying. I grinned. You can't find service like that anywhere else!

The safest bet for obtaining a car would be a legitimate purchase. However, that would take some wheeling and dealing, which isn't easy to do after sunset. To further complicate issues, Her Nibs wouldn't be pleased with an old cheap beater, so I'd need a serious wad of cash; more than I'd find knocking over convenience stores. Robbery is pretty straightforward. Burglary might be more lucrative, but I knew next to nothing about locks or security systems. Bank robbery would be ideal except for the fact that I'd inevitably get caught, if not during the robbery itself then when I tried to buy an expensive car with identifiable bills.

My machinations were interrupted by activity out the window.

Across the street, a young man dressed in sneakers, jeans, and a vintage woodland camouflage jacket – the kind with a hood and numerous pockets – was standing deep in the shadows, watching the traffic, away from the pool of illumination cast by the street lamp. As cars approached, he would step into the circle of light and pull his hood back. Once the car passed, he'd slink back into the darkness. If he were wearing a sandwich board stating, "I am selling illegal drugs", he might have been more conspicuous, but I wouldn't bet on it.

On the off-chance that I had read the signs wrong, I continued to observe the kid. Several more cars passed and he did his little dance in and out of the light for them. A police patrol car drove by, and he hung back until it passed. Eventually, a car did pull over. Camo-boy came over to the driver's window. Conversation ensued, money changed hands, and the kid pulled a few glass vials from one of his jacket pockets, dropping them into the driver's palm.

I was kind of hoping I'd been mistaken. I know the ins and outs of robbery and I can recognize a drug dealer on sight... I'm beginning to think I wasn't a very nice guy, whoever I was. I dropped a couple of bucks by the stone-cold coffee cup and left the diner. Camo-boy looked my way briefly, so I turned left and walked a bit before crossing the street and making my way to the back entry of the alley he'd chosen for his business location. I didn't want to panic him into fight or flight, so I whistled as I approached and shuffled my feet.

"Who's there?" Camo-boy asked, as his hand drifted closer to his front jeans pocket.

"Hey Dude! Didn't know you were working this area tonight. I'm headed over to the Waffle House, get something warm. Wanna join me?"

"Do I know you?" Camo-boy asked.

"Duh!" I said. "Look closer, bud." He stepped forward to get a better look at me in the shadows. His eyes searched my face, and when they reached mine, I said, "You recognize me. I'm your best friend from childhood who has been away for a very long time. You're very happy to see me."

"Joe?" Camo-boy replied. "Migod, Joe, is that you! When did you get out of prison? I thought you had another couple of years to serve." Camo-boy rushed forward to hug me fiercely, slapping my back. I tried not to cringe; some of the ghouls protecting the house smelled better than this kid. "Damn, Joe," he continued. "How come you look so old?"

"Just got out," I said. "Overcrowding and good behavior got me an early release, but prison life... it ages you, ya know? "

We chatted there in the alley for quite some time, and I learned many interesting things. I learned that Camo-boy was supplied by a gang who were using an old farmstead as a base of operations, and the location of the farmhouse; a secluded little spot just outside of the city limits. I learned that selling crack was pretty lucrative; Camo-boy's cut could've made quite a nest-egg if he didn't spend it sampling the merchandise.

Once I had all the information I needed, I started wrapping things up. "Okay, buddy, it's been great catching up with you, but I've got some business to take care of. Can I get you to loan me all of your cash? "

His brow furrowed at my request. Apparently, generosity wasn't one of his personality traits. Before he could respond, I said, "Forget I mentioned that." His brow smoothed back out immediately. "Instead," I continued, "remember how, when I've borrowed money from you in the past, I always paid it back quickly and with interest. You've never lost money by trusting me. Now, give me all your cash. Cell phone, too."

"Sure thing, Joe!" Camo-boy smiled broadly, rifling through his many pockets for his money and phone. "If you got some action going, I wanna piece of it."

"One other thing," I said. "This is important, so listen closely. I have a very good friend who is loaded and looking to score tonight. You can't miss him; he's driving a police car. When you see him, flag him over and show him what you've got. He'll probably buy it all on the spot. Got it?"

"Awesome! Thanks for the lead," Camo-boy said.

"Least I could do, dude," I replied.

♦

Twenty minutes later, I was pedaling out of town on a Schwinn that wasn't technically stolen; I had left enough cash under the chain I'd pried apart to cover the cost of a new bike and lock. A car would've been more convenient, but I didn't know how to hot-wire one. Given my other skills, that makes me feel a little better about myself.

The bicycle was well-maintained and the pedaling didn't produce fatigue… only the approaching dawn would do that. Consequently, I made almost as good time as if I'd been driving a car. Better than a car, because even pushing thirty-five miles per hour, the Schwinn didn't produce that annoying internal combustion racket which announces one's approach.

Three miles past the city limit sign, and I found the turn-off onto a gravel road. The gravel only lasted about a hundred yards; after that the road was packed clay. A small rut road forked off just past the second mailbox I passed, and I veered down the lane. I rode around the chain suspended from two posts flanking the road, ignoring the "No Trespassing" sign suspended from it, and coasted around the last bend.

The farmhouse looked to be at least a hundred years old. Two stories, but small. The once white paint was peeling in ugly gray flakes, giving the exterior a reptilian appearance. The yard, carved out of the surrounding woods, was unkempt with small scrub oaks trying to sneak back into the clearing. The front porch looked about ready to separate from the house completely, and the mildewed furniture on it wasn't fit for dog beds.

However, there were signs of occupancy. The front doors were new, an old storm door and one of those expensive solid exterior ones capable of taking a lot of abuse. The windows appeared new as well, with drawn blinds leaking a bit of light from within. A quick circuit of the grounds revealed a few cars and motorcycles parked behind the house, and a small barn. This too had new doors held closed by a new chain and a shiny new padlock.

From inside the house, I could hear some rap artist describing the antics of two trailer park girls. Considering how loudly he was documenting their activities, it was highly unlikely that anybody was sleeping. I leaned the bike against the side of the barn, stashed my burglary tools in the basket, and crept around to the front of the house. Walking on that rickety porch worried me, but hey, I was here, and the night wasn't getting any younger. I cleared my throat, and began pounding vigorously on the door.

"Hey!" I yelled. "Hey, open up!"

One of those new fluorescent bulbs flickered into luminescence overhead. The door itself had no peephole. Well, this might be fun…

"Who's there?" someone inside yelled back.

"Is this a meth lab?" I yelled. "It smells like a meth lab. Y'all can't be cooking meth out here! It's against the law!"

"Fuck off!" came the reply.

"Who the hell is it?" someone else asked.

The conversation inside dropped to whispers. I heard snippets, something about the security camera, a shitload of static, and looking out the goddam window with your fuckin' eyeballs. During all of this, I continued beating the door like it owed me money.

"We don't want no meth labs around here," I shouted. "I'm gonna call the police, and you can explain to them why it smells like a meth lab out here! They'll have dogs, so you might as well shut it down now!" I took Camo-boy's phone out of my pocket, and began tapping the screen.

That did the trick. The storm door flew open so fast it nearly clipped me. Two burly guys with shaved heads, wearing dirty jeans and sleeveless tee shirts grabbed my arms and pulled me across the threshold.

I suppose, technically, that counts as an invitation.

Once inside, I tried to get a feel for the layout. The three of us were standing in a foyer. Stairs led up from here, and from an opening to the right three more men approached us. All of them, including the two who were holding me, had the flat black ink of prison tattoos on their exposed arms and peeking out from under their tee shirts. It was the usual stuff; fourteens and eighty-eights, shamrocks, swastikas, AB's and ACAB's – enough to identify them as low-level member of the Aryan Brotherhood who had done some short time at the most.

Ah, crap! I could read prison ink! That's just… depressing.

The foyer was getting crowded, so I was force-marched to the right, into the living room. Whatever cash these fellows were making, none of it had been spent on interior decorating. Folding canvas camping chairs sat on an ugly green carpet. Someone had improvised an entertainment center out of cinderblocks and old lumber, and it supported a large screen LCD television (the kind my necromancer kept insisting we needed to get at some point) as well as an impressive stereo system. Fake pine paneling completed the décor. The living area reeked of unwashed thug, old weed, and stale Taco Bell. There were a few exits from this room. I could see a kitchen through one. The other exit, I suspected, led to the ground floor bedrooms and perhaps a bath. I didn't see large piles of money lying around anywhere, which was disappointing, but with luck, I'd have opportunity to search the place later.

"This who was makin' all that noise? This old fart?" one of the three newcomers asked.

"Yeah," Skinhead Number One replied. "He was about to call the cops, so we grabbed him."

"I'll go get Mickey," the second newcomer said. He left the living room, choosing the exit that didn't lead to the kitchen.

"Whatta we do now?" Skinhead Number Two asked. He seemed a little uncomfortable when it came to thinking.

"Search him?" Newcomer Number Three suggested.

My phone, they tossed across the room. My cash went into Newcomer Number One's pocket, which caused some general bitching amongst the other four. "He ain't got no ID," Newcomer Number One said. "You think he might be a cop or something?"

"If he was a cop, why would he be out here beating on our door without backup?" Skinhead Number One asked. "Who the fuck are you, Gramps, and what do you want?"

"I'm a cop," I replied. "Annoyance Division. 'To Harass and Perturb', that's our motto…"

Newcomer Number One (damn, I wish they'd use each other's names occasionally) backhanded me hard across the face. "Oh, a Smart Mouth," he said. "I fuckin' hate Smart Mouths".

"Well, that explains the company you keep," I replied.

Before he could hit me again, Newcomer Number Two returned with another thug in tow; Mickey, I presumed. This guy was older than the others, old enough to be a father figure, if your idea of father figures ran to heavily muscled, heavily inked bad-asses. Where the other gang members were spotted here and there with tattoos, this Mickey dude was covered from the elbows up and what I could see of his chest. Along with the Aryan Brotherhood tats, he had the cobwebs and handless clockfaces of one who has done serious time, and on his bicep was a poker hand; four aces and a joker. He had earned a reputation as a gambler, a risk-taker.

Mickey moved implacably, like a planet in its orbit, with Newcomer Number Two trailing like a satellite. Mickey never broke stride as he walked up to me, produced a switchblade, and drove the knife into my chest.

My heart usually doesn't do much other than hang out behind my sternum. When the metal pierced it, however, the damn thing seized up, clamping down on the blade, which caused all my other muscles to seize up as well. I went stiff in the arms of my captors.

"So what's the goddam problem?" Mickey asked his crew.

"We didn't know if you wanted us to kill him," Skinhead Number Two said.

"Well, I hope you've figured it out by now," Mickey replied.

"Yuh!" Skinhead Number Two practically chirped. "You woulda been okay with us killing him, 'cuz you…" He fell silent as he realized the question was meant to be rhetorical.

"So…" Skinhead Number One began, "Whattaya want us to do with the body, Mickey? And why is he so stiff? Don't people usually get all loose when they die?"

"He's probably in shock," Mickey said. "Might even still be alive, a little. Take him up to the upstairs bathroom, put him in the tub and start cutting off arms, legs, and the head. We'll bag 'em all separately, then you and Eddie can go find some construction dumpsters to throw the parts in. Don't put more than one bag in any one dumpster, got it? Billy!"

Mickey turned to Newcomer Number Two. "I'm not gonna tell you again, turn that goddamn rap music off. I'm trying to work here, and that jungle shit ain't nothing but a distraction."

Billy protested. "But Mickey, that's Slim Shady! He's a white guy from…"

Mickey caught Billy with a straight jab to the mouth. Billy staggered back as Mickey said, "Did I ask who the fuck was making that racket? Turn. That. Shit. Off. NOW!"

Billy stumbled to the stereo. His shoulders shook and his breath came in hitches, like a six year-old fighting hard not to cry on the playground. Mickey turned to my skinhead bookends. "You want some of this," he asked, gesturing with his bloody fist.

"No, Boss."

"Nossir!"

"So why are you still standing here? Take the fuckin' geezer upstairs and get him butchered already."

Eddie and his skinhead partner hauled me up the staircase, bitching about "dead weight" the whole time… but quietly. I was manhandled down the upstairs hallway and dumped into an avocado-colored bathtub that might have been groovy during the Nixon administration.

"Ah, shit," Skinhead said.

"What?" Eddie asked.

"How we supposed to get his fuckin' head off?"

"Use Mickey's knife, dumbass," Eddie replied.

Skinhead snorted. "I can probably get through the big joints with that knife, but there's no way it's gonna go through the neck. We'll be here all night. Go ask Mickey for a saw or something out of the barn."

"I ain't askin' Mickey shit," Eddie said. "You saw what he did to Billy. Maybe we can twist the head off… you know, like when you twist a chicken thigh until the bones come apart, and…"

"You are so full of shit," Skinhead replied. "Fuck it; I'll go get a saw. You get started on the arms and legs… you pussy."

"You are what you eat… Shit-nugget," Eddie said as Skinhead headed downstairs. Eddie turned back to me. "Get it? You are what you eat, and he's a shit-nugget. Means he eats… oh, what do you care; you're dead." Eddie pulled my right arm away from my torso, and slid the knife out of my chest.

With the blade removed, paralysis faded. I grabbed Eddie. His eyes flew open. I yanked him closer and bit his forearm.

These idiots had immobilized me and planned to decapitate me. Decapitation would have dusted me, and I was allowed, required even, to protect my existence, so long as doing so didn't violate orders from my mistress, or place her in danger. My necromancer usually only allowed me to feed by permission, under strict regulation, but she had said that she didn't care what I had to do to get the money for the car she wanted. Everything clicked together as certain restraints fell away. My teeth broke Eddie's skin, creating a circuit between the two of us. Lifeforce energy behaved as energies will, flowing through the circuit from positive to negative, and Eddie's wizened corpse hit the bathroom floor. I gagged at the nasty taste of his blood, but it couldn't be helped.

I got out of the bathtub, deposited Eddie's body in it, and poked the switchblade into him approximately where Mickey had stuck it in me. It was a small bathroom, not a lot of hiding places, and most of it clearly visible when the door was open. I nudged the door partially closed, and stepped to the hinged side, hoping skinhead wasn't much brighter than Eddie… or at least not more alert.

It must have taken a while to convince Mickey to give up a saw. I stood beside the door for several minutes before I heard heavy steps on the stairs. "Jeezus, Eddie," I heard Skinhead say, "didja need privacy or something?"

He pushed the door open. It swung back, nearly smacking me in the face. Skinhead stepped in, and saw the husk that used to be Eddie laying in the tub.

"Whafuc…" he managed to mumble, and I was on him. I snaked an arm around his neck, jerked him backwards and bit his ear. Again, Lifeforce surged into me. Starved as I had been, I couldn't have prevented it if I'd tried. Another dead body on the floor, and no one downstairs the wiser.

Back to business. I headed down the stairs, making no effort to be stealthy. Mickey heard my approach and yelled, "Oh, for fuck's sake, what the hell is it now?"

I stepped into the living room and said, "Eddie told me a joke… it was pretty good!"

"Get him," Mickey yelled, and ran back to whence he'd come. Billy, bless his obedient little heart, tried to tackle me around the waist. I brought my knee up sharply into his groin and left him doubled up on the ugly carpet. Newcomers One and Three worked better as a team. They broke apart, trying to flank me. Newcomer Number One rushed in, but turned it into a feint as Newcomer Three jumped me from behind, throwing an arm around my neck. I tucked my chin, and the arm fell conveniently across my mouth. Newcomer One dove back in toward my legs.

Describing the outcome would feel a lot like boasting. It wasn't a fight; it was a buffet. I bit the arm over my mouth, shrugged the corpse off my back, and lifted Newcomer Number One off the floor. Call me a traditionalist; this time I went for the jugular.

Billy was still writhing on the floor. I helped him to his feet.

"Poor Billy... look at me." His gaze caught mine, and I said, "It's gonna be okay. You're a good boy. You try so hard to please the people in charge, and they just hit you and hurt you, over and over. I know how bad that hurts, but if you tell me where you all keep the money, you can sleep. Sleep will make everything feel better."

"Mickey has it," Billy said through clenched teeth. "Mickey keeps all the money and crack locked up. He don't really trust us."

"Good boy," I repeated. "Sleep for now. I'll come wake you when it's time to get up."

"Yes... master..." Billy mumbled as he sank into slumber.

Feeling fully satiated for the first time in memory, I made my way down the hallway where Mickey had fled. There were three doors, two of them wide open. One led to a small filthy powder room, the other opened on a bedroom with two pallets on the floor. The third door was shut. When I gripped the doorknob, it turned easily, unlocked. My imagination had a field day with images of Mickey on the other side of the door wielding anything from an assault rifle to a double-headed battle-axe. I squatted low, hoping Mickey wasn't a shoot-for-the-knees kind of thinker, and pushed the door open.

BOOM!

I was close; Mickey had opted for a sawed-off shotgun. I rolled forward, catching a little of the second blast of scattershot across my back. Mickey dropped the shotgun, and reached for one of the pistols on the desk in front of him. The desk was a cheap industrial model, cluttered with a small lamp, a ledger, a few pistols and a whole bunch of small glass vials. He fired off three shots in quick succession. One missed completely, one caught me in the arm, and I took the third one high in the belly. My organs may no longer be vital, but they still hold great sentimental value for me, so the injuries did nothing to improve my mood.

"Hey, Mickey, hold up a sec," I said. "I just want to talk to you for a minute." Mickey's response was to empty the rest of the magazine in my general direction. About one in three actually hit me, but that was enough to start pissing me off.

"Dammit, look at me!" I shouted, trying to catch his eyes, but no joy; some people are just averse to making eye contact. "And don't you dare throw…"

He threw the gun at me. Seriously. Fifteen bullets didn't do diddly, but one tossed hunk of metal is going to swing the tide of battle. I caught the pistol, scorching my palm on the barrel, and threw it back hard past his head, shattering the window behind him. To give him credit, Mickey hardly flinched, just grabbed up the second pistol in his right hand, and the edge of the desk in his left.

"Waitaminnit, Mickey, don't be hasty, you don't need to do that…" I began, dreading what was about to happen. Mickey never hesitated; he flipped the desk over with his left hand, and took cover behind the improvised barricade. The lamp shattered when it fell, the ledger slid to the floor, and those small glass vials… those multiple, myriad glass vials… scattered all over the carpet in front of me.

"CRAP!" I yelled, dropping to my knees to gather and count the vials as quickly as I could.

Onetwothreefourfivesixseven…

Mickey peeked over the desk and took several shots at me. The range was much closer, and Mickey's accuracy improved. I counted eight shots and six hits.

I glared at him. "Dammit, cut it out! You'll make me lose count!"

Thirtyfourthirtyfivethirtysixthirtyseven…

Frikkin' obsessive-compulsive disorder! I'd like to see about getting therapy for it, but it's tough to find a psychiatrist who keeps late hours.

Sixthysevensixtyeightsixtynineninety…

While I was counting, Mickey sent another seven bullets my way, six of them ripping my clothes further. He didn't throw the gun this time, but ran past me back into the hall. Distracted with counting, I barely registered either his scream when he saw his flunkies dead on the floor, or the slamming door.

Ninetynineonehundredonehundredoneonehundredtwo…

And six more shots, as Mickey leaned in through the broken window and emptied a Dirty Harry style revolver at me. Five more hits.

"Damn it all, Mickey, how many guns does one man need?" I yelled at him as he ran toward the barn. "What in Hell are you compensating for?"

Onehundredfortyonehundredfortyoneonehundredfortytwo.

One hundred forty-two! Sure, it couldn't have been two more, because twelve rows of twelve is too easy. One hundred forty-two might as well be a prime number! I crushed two vials in my hand, uprighted the desk, and left fourteen rows of ten vials centered nicely. Then I knocked the rest of the window out with the chair, and leapt outside.

The barn doors were open, and I could see Mickey trying to load a large lockbox into a dark convertible. His formidable arms were straining from the effort. The moon had set and the night was full-dark. Mickey was working in an oasis of light spilling from harsh fluorescent tubes suspended from the rafters. A gas-powered generator in the barn hummed away, flanked by a few red gasoline containers. Mickey was oblivious to me until I stepped inside the illumination.

He dropped the lockbox when he saw me. For the first time, he appeared rattled. He looked around for a weapon, but nothing was closer than the lock and chain that had secured the barn doors. He lunged for it. I lunged for him.

I was quicker.

"Don't…" Mickey begged. "Please don't kill me. Whattayou want, money, drugs? I'll give you anything I got, just don't kill me like you did Mark and Dennis… just tell me what you want!"

"Dude," I said, tilting his head back and forcing eye contact. "I just wanna ask you…" I pointed at the car. "Is that what I think it is?"

◆

"Hey, Loser… get up here!"

I came upstairs quickly. Last night had played out much better than I could have hoped for, and for once, I felt I had exceeded my necromancer's expectations.

The look of surprise on her face was not the pleasant experience I'd anticipated. "You ate more than the Henderson's dog last night, didn't you?" she asked. "There's no way you'd look like that from just one mutt."

"Beg pardon…?" I stammered.

"You gorged! I didn't give you permission to feed, and here you are looking young enough to be my freakin' brother. I don't need an unexplained sibling. I need someone old enough to pass as a guardian figure while obeying my orders, and you disobeyed me!"

I knelt before her. She could get really angry at times, but she rarely lost her temper. "My Dread Queen," I began, "I cannot disobey you. You know I can barely find strength to disagree with you. Any transgression on my part could only be due to my fallible understanding of your will."

She moved her chair, placing it directly in front of my kneeling form. "Explain it to me, then. Tell me how you got from 'No Feeding Without My Permission' to 'Eat Half The Town, That's Fine By Me.'"

Dutifully, I recounted last night's events. I explained about being paralyzed, and the conversation about cutting off my head. I reminded her that she had stated that she didn't care what I had to do in order to get her the car she wanted. I pointed out that I had, in fact, succeeded in finding her a car.

"Speaking of cars," she said, "what is that old junker in the garage? Couldn't you find anything better?"

"Dark Mistress, that 'old junker' is a Nineteen Sixty-Nine Pontiac GTO convertible. Not 'The Judge,' which was the economy model, but the real deal with the modified Ram Air V engine. She's got over five hundred horses under the hood, and will do zero to sixty in less than six seconds."

"Why are you calling it a she? It's a car, not a girl, doofus."

"My Lady, it is a beast. A mechanical, sexy, angry beast."

She sneered. "It looks a lot like the old Batmobile."

"Surely, you jest with me, Powerful One. The old Batmobile was a modified '66 Lincoln Futura, a concept car that never made it to the showroom floor…"

Hmm… apparently I was a gearhead at some point. Learn something new every night.

"So," she asked, "is it stolen? What about all the trouble you said we'd get into if the cops ever run the vehicle ID number on a stolen car?"

I pointed to the ledger sitting on the lockbox I'd left in the corner of the dining room before dawn. "If My Lady will inspect the last page of the ledger, she will see that one Michael Flynn, commonly called 'Mickey' by his associates, has signed a bill of sale, surrendering the GTO as payment for gambling debts. Michael is a well-known gambler in certain circles. The bill of sale is dated three weeks prior to today."

"What if he decides to come looking for it?" my necromancer asked.

"Highly doubtful," I replied. "Sometime early this morning, Michael was murdered by one of his associates, a young man named William... something or another. William then slaughtered everyone else in the house and doused the domicile with gasoline in an attempt to burn all evidence of his drug-induced massacre. He will be feeling great remorse, however, and has most likely already turned himself over to the authorities."

"Very clever," she said. She paused, then reaffirmed "Yeah... very clever."

"Dread Queen, please examine the contents of the lockbox."

"I already did. Finally, you brought home a decent wad of cash."

"Enough to buy another vehicle if the GTO doesn't meet with your approval."

She thought about it for a bit, then said, "Something this century would be nice, but we'll see. If the Batmobile is as awesome-sauce as you say, it might work. Okay, Loser, time for a test drive."

◆

High School Driver's Ed curriculum centers around automatic transmissions. The GTO was a manual, four on the floor, so I drove the Beast to a parking lot, then coached my necromancer through using a clutch to shift gears. We stalled out. We jerked along. We bounced and jounced until I though the transmission would fall out, but she eventually got a feel for the clutch, and insisted we try the open highway.

She drove for quite some time on old back roads and two-lane highways, until she felt comfortable with the handling. I was completely lost, but she insisted she could find the way home with her phone. At one point along a long open stretch of two-lane road, she pulled to the shoulder and stopped the car.

"Here's the deal," she said. "I know right now you must be thinking you're pretty smart, bringing me this car and all that money. You probably think you're smarter than me, manipulating things so you could get past my orders. But you're not smart. You're pretty stupid."

Ah, crap! I thought she had calmed down. I could see it in her eyes, she was furious, angrier, if possible, than she had been back at the house. "If you were smarter than me... no, if you had any sense at all, you would have realized that I don't plan on spending every waking moment figuring out how to word things so that my wishes can't be circumvented. You'd have understood that your existence depends on giving me what I want, when I want it, how I want it; not making me wonder just how you'll defy me next time. If you had any intelligence, you would have come back with the car and the cash, still looking like my... looking old enough to be my guardian."

"My lady, I apologize. I didn't think..."

"Oh, you thought, all right," she snapped. "You thought long and hard about how to get around my orders. So now you're gonna think some more. You're gonna get out of my car and stand beside the road until the sun dusts you. If anybody stops to check on you, you will make them drive away and forget they ever saw you. You will not move from this spot. Do you understand?"

"I understand," I replied, getting out of the car.

"Can you think of any way you could weasel around my orders... seeing as how you're so smart and all?" she asked.

"No, Mistress" I sighed.

"Good," she said, cranking the GTO and pulling fitfully back onto the road. I watched the tail lights recede for several hundred yards until she found an area wide enough to turn around. She gunned the engine and as she approached my spot, stretched out her arm, middle finger extended high, and gave me a triumphant sneer, keeping her eyes on me as she passed.

As her head turned to keep track of me, her steering hand followed suit, and she didn't realize she was drifting into the wrong lane until the approaching pickup truck honked sharply at her, which caused her to snap back to attention. She overcorrected and the speeding GTO started to spin, slowly turning one hundred eighty degrees until the wheels sank into the soft road shoulder, and the car began to flip over and over. By this time I was running toward her because I couldn't let her be harmed through inaction even if it meant defying her orders not to move, but the car was moving too fast and spinning too madly and there was a wooden power line pole in the GTO's trajectory, and with a sickening crunch the driver side slammed into it and everything came to a stop.

I caught up to the twisted wreck moments too late. The seatbelt had prevented my mistress from being ejected through the windshield, but it had done nothing to protect her chest from the steering wheel. Bright red blood frothed at the corners of her mouth and she gurgled as she breathed.

"Hurry," she rasped. "Turn me."

"Which way, Dread Lady," I asked.

"Idiot! Turn me! Turn me into a vampire while there's still time!"

I gaped. "I... I have no idea how such things are done, Dark Mistress. You've always insisted that it takes a necromancer of enormous talent to raise a vampire."

She coughed, spattering me with her blood. "Worthless...," she said. "You suck..." Death came for her before she could finish that thought... or maybe she did finish it. I'll never know.

I felt her die. I felt, for a moment, her soul clinging to our connection. I felt her realize that she couldn't hold on, and I felt her try to drag me with her. When she was no longer in this world, I stumbled back to the road. Grief, denial and rage overwhelmed me and I fell to my knees, stunned.

That beautiful GTO... my god, what a tragic waste!

I heard footsteps approaching. The man in the pickup truck had pulled over, and was jogging up quickly. "Holy shit!" he said. He was an older man, dressed in work dungarees and a shirt with the name "Hiram" stitched across the front pocket. "You reckon there's anything we can do?"

The power pole collapsed across the bent frame of the Pontiac, and one cable, spitting sparks, fell across the hood. "Not for her," I said. "There's no way she could have survived."

"Can't be sure, son. It may not be too late!"

One of the electrical sparks landed in a puddle of fluid beneath the GTO, and burst into flame. The vehicle was consumed by fire for a few seconds before exploding. The heat and the shockwave knocked both of us down.

"Guess you're right," Hiram said. "Nothing we can do now."

"We can call 911," I said. "Do you have a phone?"

"Naw," the old man replied. "Never figured I'd need one until now. You ain't got one, young fellow?"

"Not on me", I replied. "Maybe I could catch a ride with you; we could find a pay phone and call this in."

"Reckon so," The old man agreed. "What's your name, son?"

"Loser," I answered automatically.

"Say what?"

"Uh… *Lou*, sir. Louis, actually, but I go by Lou."

"Hiram," he said, gesturing to his chest. "Well, Lou, come one with me if you're coming. Damn, the missus is gonna be worried…"

Hiram made small talk as we rode back to town, but my mind was elsewhere. Loser. Lou. I'd ditch that identity as soon as I got out of his truck. I may not know who I was, but I'm not a loser… not anymore. I'm free. I may only have the clothes on my back – and a honkin' big nest egg, thanks to Mickey and his stooges – but that definitely qualifies as a victory. I'm a free man.

Victor. Free Man. Has a nice ring to it.

Good evening, world. I'm Victor Freeman. You haven't heard of me yet, but you will.

When not writing speculative fiction for a living (her day job is writing computer software manuals), Leigh Saunders enjoys writing "social science fiction," stories that focus on people – or "things" that are also people – and how magic, futuristic events, or advances in technology impact their lives. She has earned recognition for both long and short fiction, and her short story, Tendrils, *was listed on the 2018 Tangent Recommended Reading List. To learn more about Leigh and sign up for her occasional newsletter, visit her online at www.leighsaunders.com*

About this story, Leigh says: "I'm not sure where the idea of 'the catatonic ghost' originally came from, but once it lodged itself in my mind, a slew of questions followed. Why was the ghost catatonic? What had traumatized it? What could be done to help it? And while Ian and Gayle are the main actors in this story, in my mind it has always been the catatonic ghost that is at its heart."

In most of these stories, when there's been a monster, it's been a creature of the magical variety. But that's not always the case in real life – and it might be nice to have a bit of otherworldly help find the human monsters hiding in our midst.

Spirit of the Law
Leigh Saunders

It was a Friday evening in late August, and the crowd at Grady's Pub on Gibson Street was in high spirits. Nearly half of the senior officers and detectives from Boston's nearby 13th Precinct had converged on the Pub, taking advantage of their rare, off-duty hours to celebrate the promotions of a half-dozen of their long-time comrades-in-arms.

Ian Hayward, his shiny new Detective's shield tucked securely in the inside breast pocket of an equally new black leather jacket, worked his way through the overcrowded pub, passed from this foaming mug to that eye-watering shot, with many a congratulatory slap on the back along the way.

He could feel his mouth stretching wider and wider across his face with each drink, and knew he was probably grinning like some sort of idiot – and he didn't care. He'd worked seven long years for his shield, determined to have it before he reached thirty-five; and now he had it, within months of his goal. Oh, yeah, he was damn-well gonna smile about finally having earned it.

He tossed back another shot, barely aware of the fiery liquid burning its way down his throat, though he did notice that his head seemed to wobble a bit more on his shoulders than it should when he straightened it after that last swallow. That, and the fact that the reflection of the dim ceiling lights on the multicolored bottles behind the crowded bar had grown increasingly blurry as the evening wore on. He blinked his eyes three or four times, very deliberately, but it didn't seem to help much.

"C'mon, kid," said a grating voice in his ear. "Let's get you a seat before you fall over."

Ian looked over his shoulder. "Oh, hi, Cap'n Burke," he said, allowing the captain to guide him to a nearby booth. He nodded like a bobble-head at the three homicide detectives seated there as he slid onto the worn, wooden bench opposite them. "Jeffries, Herrera, Kozlowski."

They look like an ad for workplace diversity, Ian thought, giggling a little as the idea occurred to him. Malcolm Jeffries — tall, thin, his deep brown skin barely a shade lighter than the black turtleneck he habitually wore, probably fifty-ish from the gray that wound through his close-cropped, curly hair — was seated next to Augusto Herrera, a short, stocky Puerto Rican about Ian's same age, but with both the build and attitude of a pro wrestler. And then there was Martyna Kozlowski, wedged into back corner of the booth. No one who'd ever worked with her thought of her as the 'token' female detective, even though her athletic build and long, white-blonde hair made her oh-so-much easier on the eye than her peers in the department.

She caught him gaping at her, and fixed him with that cold, hard stare that was so effective at quashing the bullshit in the interrogation room. Ian shuddered as though a bucket of ice water had been dumped over his head, but buoyed by the whiskey heating his blood, he didn't immediately look away from her like he would have had he been sober.

"Think he's ready?" asked Jeffries.

"Well, he passed the test," said Herrera. "So ready or not…" he let the sentence hang while he took another pull on his beer.

"He'll do," said Kozlowski with a short nod, finally breaking eye contact with Ian.

Burke filled a mug from the half-empty pitcher of beer at the middle of the table, then pushed it toward Ian.

"Just sip at it," he ordered. "And listen up. There's something we need to tell you about tonight… before you discover it on your own."

"The secret detective handshake?" asked Ian, the giggle dying on his lips as he looked over at Burke and saw the hard edge to his captain's expression. "Sorry, sir," he murmured. "One too many shots, I think."

Burke shrugged it off. "Probably better that way," he said. "I know when they first told me, I wished I'd been drunk."

Ian frowned, puzzled, but before he had a chance to say anything, Burke continued.

"Now that you're a detective, you're gonna see things—"

"I've seen dead bodies, sir. Plenty of them."

Herrera leaned forward, across the table. "But have you seen their *ghosts?*"

The effects of the evening's alcohol faded under the ice in the detective's voice. "There have been cases that have stayed with me, longer than I'd have liked," Ian acknowledged. "But, no, I can't say I've ever felt haunted by one."

"You will be," said Herrera.

Ian looked across at him. "Aw, c'mon, Augie, don't go all doom-and-gloom on me. It's the job, I get it. But this is supposed to be a party."

He turned back toward Burke to ask the captain to intervene and stopped, his mouth hanging open. Just beyond Burke, standing at the end of the table like a pale, semi-transparent waiter, was the ghost of a young black man. Or a damn good imitation of one. Ian looked around the booth, scanning the other detectives' faces for the telltale smirk of a well-played prank, but they all wore the same serious expressions he was accustomed to seeing when working with them at a crime scene.

The ghost just stared at him, his expression somber.

Ian shook himself. "Okay," he said. "You got me. I don't know how you're doing it, but…" he trailed off as a group of officers walked past the booth, one of them passing right through the ghost. Its image wavered, swirling mists clinging momentarily to the passing officer before pulling back into the ghost's form and coalescing again.

The ghost shrugged and moved closer to the table, the worn edge of the wooden surface fading as the ghost floated forward.

"Detective Hayward, meet Martin Hinton," Burke said. "He was killed twelve years ago in a gang-related incident. I never have been able to close the case, and Marty's been hanging around all this time."

"He's haunting *you?* Why not haunt the guy who killed him?" asked Ian.

"'Cause that's what ghosts of murder victims *do*," said Herrera. "They attach themselves to their investigating detective and they stick around until the case is solved—"

"Or their killer dies—" Kozlowski cut in.

"And their case moves to a higher court," Jeffries finished, before taking a long pull of his beer.

"None of the other officers can see them," added Burke. "Only detectives."

"You're bullshitting me," Ian said and looked to Jefferies and Kozlowski, but the two detectives both shook their heads almost sadly. A second ghost had appeared at the edge of the booth, just over Jefferies' shoulder. This ghost, a well-dressed businessman who glanced with some disdain at Marty Hinton's ghost hovering just inside the edge of the table, seemed familiar to Ian.

"Wow," he said after a moment. "That's Allen Langley."

Jefferies looked over his shoulder at his ghost, who glowered at him. "Yeah, every minute I spend on anything other than his case, he's there—"

"What are you talking about? He's there even when you *are* on the case," said Kozlowski. She turned to Ian. "Some of the ghosts are like that – they don't know which of their many enemies were responsible for their deaths, but haunt your every waking move, as unpleasant as they were in life, practically demanding you to avenge their murder. You learn to live with them."

"Or you drink a lot on your off hours," said Herrera.

"Like I said," Kozlowski said, refilling her mug and pushing the now-empty beer pitcher toward the end of the table. A passing waitress grabbed it, her hand reaching right through the middle of Marty's stomach.

As the pitcher disappeared through the swirling mist of the ghost's midsection, he rolled his eyes, shook his head at Burke, and dissolved, the few lingering traces of mist trailing away with the pitcher.

Ian stared after the departed ghost, trying to balance what he was seeing, what the other detectives had told him, with everything he'd thought he knew to be true. After several seconds he picked up his beer and drained it, then thunked it down hard on the table.

Ghosts.

His shiny new badge suddenly felt strangely heavy in his pocket.

◆

So much blood... but...
Oh, thank God, it doesn't hurt any more.

I wonder how long it will take him to realize he's finally killed me.

What will he do with my body? I want to be sick, just looking at it lying there, so still, so much blood everywhere – can I even be *sick anymore?*

Now that I'm gone, he'll hurt her next, the poor thing. I would help her if I could, but I don't know how. I just know I don't want to watch. I *can't* watch.

Where is the light?

They promised light at the end.

◆

It was some undefinable mid-morning hour, with far too much summer morning sunshine streaming in between the gaps in the blinds when Ian dragged himself out of bed for the first time on Saturday. After relieving his bladder, he stumbled to the kitchen, pulled a cold-pack from the freezer, and stumbled back to bed.

He woke again sometime later, the cold-pack now a sloshy, room-temperature bag of goo. The sun had risen past the roofline of his condo, resulting in a much more subdued – and less painful – level of brightness.

He thumbed the thermostat down on his way to the kitchen, in the unreasonable hope that the ancient air conditioner would rise to the challenge of the afternoon's muggy heat. Shuffling to the kitchen, he tossed the cold-pack into the sink to rinse off before refreezing, and smiled weakly at the bag of salt-and-vinegar chips and can of ginger ale he'd left out on the counter for himself the day before. He grabbed them, then eased himself gently down onto the couch, acutely aware of each-and-every microfiber brushing against the bare skin of his back and shoulders, and began to nibble and sip at his unlikely hangover cure. If he could keep the chips and soda down for half-an-hour, he'd take a pain killer and maybe even grab a shower.

He leaned his head back, resting it on the not-soft-enough cushion, and closed his eyes. He'd really tied one on the night before. Understandable, given the circumstances, but the evening's debauchery had left him more fuzzy on the details than he liked to be.

Ghosts.

Oh, yeah. That had been a good one. He didn't know quite how they'd pulled it off, but Ian knew a good prank when he saw it – even when it was on him.

I don't like it here. That's weird, I suppose, since I'm already dead, but this place just gives me the creeps. I don't want to leave my body here, unguarded, for the rats to chew on or something. As if they could damage it any further.

At least they back off whenever I come close.

It's kinda funny, kinda strange that the rats are aware of me when the people rushing by to catch the train or pick up something from the market across the way haven't got a clue. That's not how I thought it worked. But even the girl who walked right through me this afternoon didn't stop or look around or anything, just shivered and rubbed her hands up and down her bare arms like she'd gotten a chill and kept on going.

This 'ghost gig' isn't all it's cracked up to be.

I hope someone finds my body soon. Maybe then I'll be able to find the light and move on to that 'better place' Aunt Carla always said you'd go to if you were good.

I wasn't a bad person. Was I?

I just don't want to believe that wandering around a vacant lot is all there is to the afterlife.

◆

The hangover had long-since passed into a hazy memory by the time Ian's ringing cell phone woke him at three-thirty a.m. on Sunday morning.

"Hayward," he said, balancing the phone between his ear and shoulder, listening to the clinical voice of the police dispatcher on the other end of the line as he fumbled around the nightstand to turn on the lamp and find a pen. Squinting in the bright light, he copied down the address and confirmed it.

"On my way," he said.

Ian had always experienced mixed sensations of adrenaline and dread going to a crime scene, and both were heightened as he headed across town to the address he'd been given, just west of Columbia Road.

To his first assignment as the lead detective.

He crossed Columbia at Dudley, then followed the flashing lights of the patrol car on the scene, pulling off the road next to a boarded-up building just before the Upham's Corner train stop.

He flashed his shield at the two patrol officers at the scene, Paxton and Baily according to their name badges. "What have we got?" he asked, hoping he sounded more nonchalant and experienced than he felt.

They led him through a rusted gate, hanging limply from the upper hinge. Bailey took up a guard position at the gate while Paxton led Ian across a weed-choked courtyard toward the further of two small garages attached to the side of the building, this one with a partially-raised door. "We noticed the broken gate, the garage door," said Paxton as they walked. "Figured it was either a bunch of kids messing around or maybe a homeless person taking shelter. Both pretty common in this neighborhood. Worst-case, a possible drug-deal. We called it in and went to investigate."

He paused. "It was worse than worst-case."

Ian and Paxton flipped on LED flashlights and ducked under the garage door.

Ian covered his mouth and nose as the smell that had been growing gradually stronger as he approached the garage hit him full-force. Blood. Putrid flesh. Whoever had died here hadn't been here long – but even one hot summer day in the enclosed space of the small garage was enough for the air to be thick with the sickly-sweet, rotting-meat smell. At least it was night, so the flies were at a minimum.

He panned the flashlight around the room, revealing a not-too-surprising collection of broken shelving, used tires, crumpled beer cans and broken bottles, and a torn, stained mattress with a tarp-covered, body-shaped lump on it.

"Homeless?" he asked, studying the floor as he took each step from the door to the mattress.

"I don't think so," replied Paxton. He'd stayed near the door, keeping out of Ian's way. "Not unless someone on the street really had it in for her."

"Obvious cause of death?" asked Ian tucking the flashlight under his armpit and pulling on a pair of sterile latex gloves.

Paxton shook his head. "She's been cut up pretty badly," he said. "Coulda died from the blood loss; maybe one of the cuts was deep enough to hit something vital. Dispatch says forensics is on the way."

Ian nodded and knelt by the mattress, then gently pulled the tarp away from the body.

She might have been pretty once, he thought, though the cuts and bruising on her face made it difficult to really tell. Her hair had been roughly cut – shorn to the scalp in places – and what remained was heavily matted with blood and dirt, making it impossible to tell what color it had been.

He covered her back up and was starting to turn away when a movement caught his eye. He looked up.

It was her. Sitting there on a broken cabinet.

The dead girl.

She was pretty. Large eyes, gentle features, a sad expression — understandable, because she was dead, after all. Medium-length hair, just brushing the tops of bare shoulders; though he still couldn't identify the color because it shimmered with that same semi-transparent paleness as the rest of her.

Her ghost.

Unlike her naked, tarp-wrapped corpse, the ghost wore a University of Massachusetts — "UMass" — tank top and a pair of cutoff shorts, one sandaled foot tucked up under the opposite knee, the other swinging gently back and forth, the outline of the cabinet just visible through the pale glow of her leg.

"It wasn't a prank," he murmured. "Shit."

"Is everything all right, sir?" asked Paxton.

Ian shook himself, and turned away from the ghost. "Yes, of course," he said. He stood, making a slight show of shining the flashlight around the garage again. "I'm just going to look around a bit more," he said.

"If you need me, I'll be right outside," said Paxton.

Ian nodded, and Paxton ducked back under the garage door.

He turned back to the girl. *The ghost.*

She'd moved away from the broken cabinet and was standing near the head of the mattress. Ian moved closer, watching her watch him.

"I'm going to find the person who did this to you," he said softly.

Her eyes grew wide.

"Can you tell me anything at all?" he asked. "Who are you? How did you end up here?"

Her lips moved, but no sound came out. She scowled, and for a moment Ian thought he saw traces of a fiery personality.

Then she looked past him, with that startled, deer-in-the-headlights look he'd seen on too many victims' faces. A moment later, he heard the voices, the crunch of footsteps approaching across the courtyard.

"It's just the forensics team," he said. "They're here to help."

The ghost hesitated for a moment, nodded, then stepped back into the shadows and faded away.

♦

He sees me.
I don't know why he can't hear me, but oh, thank God, he sees me!

◆

Ian tried to work the case as usual, consulting with the forensics team for information about the girl's cause of death (the M.E.'s autopsy found extensive internal injuries, but that ultimately she'd bled to death), identity (Gayle Weber, a UMass student originally from Montana, who'd disappeared without a trace nearly four months before), and any other clues that might lead him to the monster who had so brutally beaten, cut, and abused her.

But evidence was scarce. And as he discussed the few possible leads with his team, hoping anyone had found something potentially useful, he found himself looking over their heads to Gayle's ghost for a silent nod of confirmation – only to be met with a violent head-shake.

He wasn't used to consulting with the person whose death he was investigating. Nor was he used to the silent, shimmering crowd of ghosts lingering around the precinct at all hours like passengers at a subway stop waiting for a terminally delayed train.

To put it mildly, the ghosts were throwing him off.

The ghosts of the active cases floated around the station, bored, curious, impatient, poking translucent fingers into case files, studying the bulletin boards, and looking longingly at break-room offerings. Ian frequently found himself altering his route as he walked through the maze of desks to avoid walking through a ghost standing in his path. It occurred to him that the station's ever-present chill had nothing to do with its antiquated HVAC system. Sometimes the ghosts interacted with each other, their silent conversations like the pantomime of old movie characters, their arguments sending swirls of energy throughout the room that disturbed papers and sent small objects flying through the air.

Older ghosts, those whose cases had dragged on or gone cold, tended to hover around the periphery, sitting on radiators and crowding together in the narrow windowsills like tired, forgotten patients in a hospital waiting room, trying to make themselves as invisible as possible. At night, their combined shimmer became a pale night-light, bathing the precinct in an otherworldly blue glow.

Combined, their light was bright enough to work by. A fact that sent a shiver up Ian's spine late one night when he realized he'd not even bothered to turn on his desk lamp; like Jefferies, who was at his own desk a few yards away, he'd been studying Gayle's case file by ghost light.

He got up and switched on the overhead lights, the brighter light causing the ghost light to fade to a mere background illumination, the hum of the old fluorescent tubes almost comforting.

He walked over to the murder board, consciously putting himself between Gayle, who was sitting on the corner of his desk, and the grisly crime scene photos pinned to the board, trying to shield her from the sight of her mutilated body.

"She knows what happened to her," Jefferies said, coming up to stand beside Ian, the ghost of Allen Langley hovering at his elbow. "You forget – she was there. She saw all this at its worst."

"That doesn't mean she needs to be constantly subjected to the display," Ian replied. "She was here this afternoon, Mal, when her parents came in. It was heartbreaking."

"I'm sure it was. But you can't undo what happened to her, can't protect her from it. It's too late for that. The best you can do is resolve things, bring this guy to justice."

"Speak for the dead."

Jefferies nodded. "That's what we do. Personally, I believe that's why the ghosts attach themselves to us, why they stick around until their cases are finally resolved."

"And the ones we don't solve?"

Jefferies looked over at the ghosts crowded along the windows, then back at Ian. "They wait."

♦

It's her! The one in the other cage, that's her *picture on the wall.*
We have to find her, before he does the same thing to her that he did to me.
If it's not already too late.

♦

Gayle was waiting for Ian when he entered the station the next morning, standing just inside the door. She looked agitated, and every time Ian altered his course to walk around her, she floated into his path again.

"What?" he snapped when she put herself in his way for the third time.

She tipped her head, and Ian was sure that if she'd been able to talk, she'd have had a sharp retort for him.

"Sorry," he muttered, pulling his phone out so he could talk to the ghost without anyone passing through the lobby thinking he was talking to himself. "I'm late. I need to get upstairs. I have a meeting in…" he checked the time on his phone, "seven minutes. We can talk after."

Gayle shook her head and refused to move out of his path. Instead she raised her arm and pointed away from the elevators and down a side hall toward a different department.

Ian sighed. "Okay," he said. "But make it quick."

The ghost spun around and flitted away, gliding smoothly along, her sandaled feet hovering only slightly above the black and white-turned-mostly-gray laminate floor tiles. Ian followed, almost at a run, trying to keep up with her.

She stopped so abruptly that Ian almost ran right through her.

"Give a little warning, next time," he hissed, then turned to see what she was pointing at.

Gayle was hovering in front of the Missing Persons board, her ghostly finger nearly touching the photo of a pretty co-ed with large blue eyes and light brown hair that just brushed the tops of her shoulders.

Ian saw the similarity immediately.

"You know her?" he asked.

Gayle started to shake her head, then frowned and hunched her shoulders, as though the answer required more than a simple 'yes' or 'no.'

"Okay, it's complicated, I get it," Ian said, again talking into his phone, but looking directly at Gayle as he spoke. "But you know something about her, right?"

Gayle nodded emphatically.

Ian pulled the photo from the board and skimmed the details. "Okay. She's important, and you need me to look into it. Got it. I really need to get to that meeting now, but as soon as it's over, we'll figure this out. All right?"

Gayle stared at him hard for a moment, clearly frustrated. Then she nodded and vanished in a puff of mist.

Ghosts. Ian rolled his eyes, then slipped his phone back in his pocket. Taking the photo to a nearby clerk, he asked that a copy of the missing girl's case file be sent up to his desk. Deep in thought, he headed back toward the elevator, questions already tumbling around in his head. Who was this girl, and what did Gayle know about her?

The obvious things – their ages, physical similarity, and the general details of their disappearance – indicated a disturbing pattern. Ian pushed the conclusion he'd already jumped to out of his mind, knowing at the same time that he had to pursue it.

He was looking for a serial killer.

One who had already chosen his next victim.

♦

Ian closed the interior blinds tight, then locked the conference room door. This meeting was for the Homicide Detectives only, and he didn't want anyone else barging in at an inopportune moment.

Even as he thought that, Gayle drifted in through the closed door.

Ian nodded in greeting and began his presentation, pinning the Missing Person photo to the board.

"This is Hannah Meyer, a twenty year-old sophomore at UMass," he said. "She's been missing for nineteen days. Last seen headed out for an early-morning jog."

He posted Gayle's original Missing Person photo. "Gayle Weber, twenty-one, also a student at UMass. Disappeared four and a half months ago after a track meet. We found her body five days ago."

Herrera and Jeffries nodded, glancing from the report to Gayle and back again. Captain Burke remained expressionless. Kozlowski leaned forward, suddenly interested, as Ian put a third picture up on the board. The resemblance was so strong that the third co-ed could have been sister to the previous two.

"Alina Graham—"

"She's one of mine," said Kozlowski. "Also a UMass student. She disappeared under similar circumstances eight months ago; found two and a half months later, in pretty bad shape – repeatedly beaten, cut, raped. The perp had hacked off most of her hair; looked like when my kid sister tried to give one of her dolls a haircut. No clues to who did it or why."

"Isn't that the catatonic ghost?" asked Herrera.

Kozlowski nodded, then explained for Ian. "The ghosts are often disturbed by what has happened to them, but this one… well, if she'd lived through it, she'd have required serious counseling to get on with her life. She's been sitting in the window ever since she came here. I've never seen her move or react to anything."

"You're suggesting there's a pattern to the abductions," Burke said, gesturing to the three photographs on the board. "That Hannah Meyer will turn up in a couple of months in the same condition as Graham and Weber."

"Yes, sir," Ian said.

"How do you propose to proceed?" asked Burke.

"I've been thinking of Gayle as *'the deceased,'*" Ian said. "As the victim – which she certainly is. But she's also a *witness* – the only person who has seen her murderer, who knows where she was held, who saw the vehicle her body was transported in after her death. I don't know how you usually work with the ghosts, but I'd like to enlist Gayle's help."

"Has she spoken to you? Given you something useful?" asked Kozlowski, her brows drawn together in a frown.

"She recognized Hannah Meyer from the Missing Persons board," Ian said. "I'm hoping she'll remember something else, maybe give me something I can use to catch this guy."

Gayle drifted forward and studied the three photographs. Then she moved back to hover along the wall, and nodded at Ian.

Ian thought Gayle seemed nervous as she looked from one detective to the next, but then her expression shifted to a more determined one and she nodded solemnly.

"You'll need more than just her word for it," said Jeffries. "Even if she pointed right at the perp and said, 'there he is, that's the guy who killed me,' we couldn't do anything about it. You have to come up with hard evidence, or she'll end up sitting on the windowsill with the others." He glanced over at Gayle. "My apologies, but that's how it is."

Gayle shook her head and silently stomped a ghostly foot.

"I'm with her," Ian said. "She's my star witness."

Herrera barked out a derisive laugh. "You're not listening, Hayward. The ghosts point us at their killers all the time. But evidence from a ghost isn't admissible in court. There isn't a judge alive who wouldn't hold you in contempt for even trying it."

"I can see it now," Kozlowski said, jumping in. "'Your honor, members of the jury, you'll just have to take our word for it that the deceased is sitting in the witness box.'"

Ian dropped into his chair, deflated. "There's got to be a way we can use what she knows."

Shaking her head, Kozlowski said, "You know the drill – we need *actionable* evidence to issue warrants and make arrests—"

"And the eye-witness testimony of a ghost isn't actionable," finished Ian.

Burke spoke up. "However…" he said. "Judge Lloyd was a homicide detective for a few years before he gave it up and turned to lawyering. He's seen his share of ghosts – and issued a fair share of warrants based on ghostly evidence." He looked from Ian to Gayle. "It has to be compelling, though. More than just a 'he did it.'"

Ian nodded, and glanced over at Gayle. The suggestion of a smile flickered across her face, the first hint of the happy co-ed he'd seen outside her photographs.

Burke wasn't finished. "Keep it under wraps – under no circumstances does this conversation go beyond present company. I want hourly reports. If you don't come up with something by four o'clock, I'll have to push it to the FBI. They have jurisdiction over serial killer cases, and get pretty bent out of shape when they're brought in late in the game."

He stood to leave, then paused, with his hand on the doorknob. "And, for the love of God, make sure that whatever you learn you're able to present in an actionable way. I can't stress that enough. Judge Lloyd will work with you, but even he won't be willing to jeopardize an investigation by issuing warrants based solely on the testimony of a ghost…," he looked at Gayle, "…no matter how credible. We want to put the guy away, not let him slip out of our fingers on a technicality."

◆

When I finally find the light and get over to the Other Side, I'm going to hunt down whoever decided that ghosts can't talk to people and give them a piece of my mind. This is infuriating!

Detective Hayward asks, 'do you know where you were held captive, Gayle?' and I shake my head 'no' and point to his keyboard so he can spell out N - O - T F - A - R, but that's the best I can do. It was the middle of the night, and I wasn't really thinking so much about where I was, just that I was finally dead.

So next he asks, 'how did your body get to the garage?'

That one I can answer. I point to the letters T - R - U - C - K.

Then he asks me what kind of truck.

How am I supposed to know?

I have him type O - L - D and B - L - U - E and I can tell he's not very happy with that, but really, it's my brothers who know all about trucks, not me.

So now he has me looking at pictures of every sort of truck known to man. I had no idea there were so many. I'm beginning to think this whole idea is pointless...
Wait!
That's it. That's the kind of truck we're looking for!

◆

"Do you know how many late-model, light blue Chevy pickups there are in Massachusetts?" asked Herrera, pacing up and down the conference room. "She said he didn't drive her very far, so we can probably narrow it down to those registered in the Boston area and its suburbs, but that doesn't narrow the playing field much. Can't she be more specific? I mean, what does 'not far' mean to a ghost? Are we talking blocks? Or miles?"

Ian looked at Gayle who shrugged, her bright aura dimming a little.

"I was hoping it would be something more distinctive," Ian confessed. "Maybe one with a company logo or something."

Gayle shook her head.

Ian pushed back from the table, went to the window, and stood there, looking out through the blinds for a long time. After several moments he turned around and looked at Gayle.

"I need to ask you to do something hard," he said. "I don't even know if you can, but I need you to try."

Gayle nodded slowly, her expression wary.

"I need you to think very hard about the place where you were imprisoned, and about your captor. And then I need you to go there, look around, and then come back and tell us where it is – and if Hannah Meyer is still there, and still alive."

Gayle was biting her lip, visibly trembling, wisps of mist swirling in the air around her.

Ian took a step toward her. "He can't hurt you any more, Gayle. But he can hurt Hannah. You might be able to help her. Will you try?"

Gayle nodded and closed her eyes.

For a moment, nothing happened. Then a tear slid down Gayle's ghostly face and she vanished.

◆

Think about Hannah. Think about Hannah. Can't think about him; hurts too much, even though Detective Hayward says he can't hurt me anymore. Think about Hannah.

Find Hannah.

I open my eyes.

It's dark. I'm in the cage again. My cage. Oh, God. No room to breathe, no room to move.

No. I'm not trapped now. I can crawl out, crawl through the bars and across the room to Hannah's cage.

Blood.

Not much yet. But he's started cutting her, and the flies are crawling up and down the thin razor lines on her legs. I hated the flies.

Someone's coming.

Don't let him see me. Don't know if he can *see me. Move back into the shadows, into the wall. Don't want to watch him drag her out of the cage, hear her scream.*

I fly at him, try to stop him as he raises the strap again and again, beating her, the leather cutting into her flesh. I want to be sick.

The end of the strap whips through me and I scream.

Hannah's eyes fly open and for a moment I think she sees me. 'Help me,' she begs.

Yes. Yes. I can't stop him, but I can help her. I back away from him and toward the door — it's locked, like it always is, but I can pass through it now and go up the stairs and through the house where the television blares with loud, artificial laughter muffling Hannah's screams from the basement. The black dog is there, and he growls at me, teeth bared, hackles raised. He's not sure about me, and backs away stiff-legged as I come into the living room.

The drapes are closed, but I can see just fine, even without the glow of the television screen. I look around for anything that might help the police stop this monster, help Hannah, only there is nothing helpful here, just a ragged couch half-covered in junk mail, the stuffing poking out of the seams and an ashtray full of old cigarette butts next to several empty beer cans on the dented wooden coffee table. Greasy, shredded wrappers litter the floor, scattered from a tipped-over garbage can just inside the kitchen doorway, where the dog has finished off something it fished from the bin.

I move slowly toward the kitchen, glad my feet don't actually touch the wrappers. The dog, still growling, moves out of my way, jumping up onto the couch and over it, pushing a stack of envelopes onto the floor. I look back to see if the man heard, listen for his footsteps on the stairs, and there, in the scattered papers on the floor by the couch, I see a symbol I recognize and all at once I know I've found the clue I've been looking for.

How could I have forgotten? In all the suffering, it was just one pain of many. But now it would be the key to saving Hannah.

I need to go back to the precinct, but first I look around outside. I see the house number and there, in the shadow of a carport so rickety it makes me nervous to walk under, is the truck. It's exactly as I remember it, old, blue, rusted, with a dented fender and a long crack along the windshield. A paper sits on the seat, covered with the same symbol, in different sizes and with slight variations, as though he'd been drawing it over and over, trying to get it right. I almost smile when I see it, but my expression feels grim, even to me, and I'm glad no one is around to see but the dog.

The neighbor's dog is barking too, now, disturbing the quiet of what appears to be a peaceful neighborhood. I move farther away and find the street sign.

I can still hear Hannah crying.

I think of Detective Hayward who promised to help her.

I close my eyes.

♦

Gayle's ghost appeared and immediately pointed to Ian's laptop.

Ian hesitated. "Are you okay?"

She shook her head, looking as pale and baleful as the Ghost of Christmas Past, and again pointed silently at the machine.

Letter by letter, Ian typed her report as her ghostly finger pointed at the keys: the address, the description of the house, the truck, the dog, the route through the house to the basement, the cages, Hannah's injuries. He forced himself to remain professional, clinical, but by the end his stomach was churning.

He couldn't make himself look at Gayle. Could barely forgive himself for asking her to go back into that place.

But she wasn't finished.

There is a symbol, she had him type. *In his truck, on papers in his house. He has it on his chest,* she touched a spot just above her collar bone, *and he tattooed it on us.* She touched a finger to her temple. *Here, where he shaved the hair away.*

"You should have led with this," Ian said, practically jumping out of his chair. He went to the board and began studying the photos of the two murdered girls – Gayle and Alina.

Just visible in the patchy area where the hair had been chopped away from their temples, both had the same tattoo.

♦

Ian and Kozlowski watched from across the room as Gayle pushed the other cold-case ghosts out of her way and sat down next to Alina on the window sill.

"Do you think she can help her?" asked Kozlowski.

"Maybe. Gayle's got a lot going for her," replied Ian. "And she can tell Alina that we've caught the monster that hurt them both. That should help."

"She'll be gone soon, you know."

"Who?"

"Gayle," said Kozlowski. "The ghosts don't often stay long once their murderer is caught. Just catching the perp seems to be enough resolution for most of them. I've only seen two or three stick around through the trial."

"I hadn't thought of that. I've sort of gotten used to having her around," said Ian a little wistfully as he watched Gayle's lips move in silent whispers to Alina.

"There will be other ghosts, Detective Hayward."

♦

Hi. Don't be afraid. I'm Gayle.

They tell me your name is Alina.

I know what he did to you – he did it to me, too. But he won't be doing it to anyone else, ever again.

It's over.

Do you see the light? They said there would be light, and there it is, getting brighter every second. Come with me, Alina. We'll be safe there.

Safe in the light.

Sam Robb is a Pittsburgh native, a former US Navy officer, and a graduate of Carnegie Mellon University. Along the course of his life, he has acquired a wife, three daughters, several quadrupeds, and a penchant for walking down back alleys and taking pictures of graffiti. When he's not making up stories to tell about what he's seen, he works as a software developer and occasional politician.

About this story, Sam says: "I like to go for walks, especially around Pittsburgh. There's always something interesting to see. Like the day that I was by the river and saw a child's inflatable ball in the water. Bright and colorful, the way it was moving struck me as odd. It took me a second to realize it was floating upstream, against the current... It was the wind pushing it, of course. But my first thought was "Something is trolling for people today." That thought managed to move me away from the river and to the path that led to Gone Fishing."

The combination of military-style tactics with down-home fishing makes for an intriguing approach in this monster-hunting tale that will have you glancing sideways the next time you walk along the banks of a quiet river, especially on a foggy evening. You never know what's hiding beneath the surface.

Gone Fishing
Sam Robb

"You gotta do what you gotta do," Paul said.

Bone couldn't see Paul's face, only the yellow, nicotine stains on his white beard from the cheap, hand-rolled cigarettes he snuck when he thought his wife didn't know. One dangled from his lips now, a thin line of smoke trailing straight up in the still summer air.

The two of them had fished the river more times than he could remember. Well, Paul fished. Bone came to sit and learn. To talk about life.

To learn from the expert about how to kill monsters.

The old man squinted at the river, then leaned back and flicked his rod forward, casting his line. The bobber flew out over the water and landed with a soft plop. For a moment it looked like it was stuck in one spot. Then it started drifting downriver, infinitesimally slow.

Paul grunted and settled back. He shifted his heavy frame around until he was comfortable. It was like watching a bull settle down for a rest.

He nodded at Bone. "You gotta do what you gotta do," he said again. "You know that's why I'm in this business."

Bone couldn't help it. He laughed every time Paul called it a "business".

"Kicking supernatural critters out of *dahntaaahn* is a business?" He put the full Yinzer drawl into play.

Paul snorted. "Eh. Hobby, then." He shifted, winced. "I'm not getting any younger, kid. You've been a help; I won't tell you otherwise."

"Then why are you trying to get rid of me?"

Paul narrowed his eyes. "What'd I tell you about that bull?"

The heat rose in Bone's face. "Sorry."

"Start lying to yourself, you're done in this… hobby." Paul threw him a quick wink.

He was forgiven.

"You've been a help," Paul repeated. He looked out over the river, sighed. "Things are bad, though. And they're going to get worse." He was quiet for a second, before glancing over.

"We're going to need more."

Bone frowned. "How do you know that?"

Paul shrugged. "Been doing this a while, you know? Remember that haint we put down, up there in Chateau?"

"Remember? Bastard almost took my ears off." Bone's skin crawled at the memory of the haint's touch.

"They're getting stronger," Paul said, his voice low. He grimaced. "For a while, I thought it was me. Getting old, getting slow." He shook his head. "You're as good a scrapper as I ever was when I was your age. Haints aren't much of a challenge. Or shouldn't be."

"So what? We've got you and me. We can find others. Syn's tough…"

"No." There was no arguing with that tone. "No. Syn's a kid. She's barely even out of high school, for chrissake. No."

"So was I when you pulled me in. I've learned a lot, the last three years. She can, too."

Paul raised an eyebrow. "It been that long? Heh. But yeah, you've been sharp. I'll give you that."

"So now you want me to go away and join the Marines," Bone said flatly. "Makes a whole lot of sense."

Paul sighed. "It does, you idiot. Look. Things are getting worse, but they're not horrible. Not yet. These things come in cycles. Last time I saw this…" He shook his head. "It got bad. Real bad. You've heard me talk about it."

Bone sat up. "A little." Hints, here and there. This wasn't Paul's first time at this particular rodeo.

Paul turned away to watch his line. Gave it a little twitch.

"Me, and Teach, and Chewie." His voice went soft. "Chews didn't make it. He's the reason Teach and I did. Teach… well, he lost part of who he is. That was the price he paid."

Paul shook his head. "I was the only one who came out of that halfway whole – and look at me. I'm a damn bum livin' on the streets because the idea of going into another house makes me start puking my guts out."

Paul sat up straighter. "I ain't gonna let that happen again. You and me, sure, we're holding our own, but we need more." He reached up at jabbed a finger at Bone. It was like being threatened with a sausage. "We need someone who's strong, smart. Someone with military training."

Bone shifted on the concrete bench. "Is it going to come to that?"

Paul snorted. "Better hope not. You're our best bet to make sure that doesn't happen again."

"Fine. Great. I go off, do my tour, come back. And while I'm gone?"

Paul smiled, then reached over and slapped him on the back.

"Don't worry. Me and Mary and Syn? We can hold down the fort."

"Maybe find a few more like me and Syn?" Bone prompted.

"Okay, okay!" Paul laughed. "I know. I'll pick it up, see if I can't recruit a few more scrappers to help us out."

Bone hesitated, then stuck out his hand. "Deal."

Paul nodded, then wrapped his hand around Bone's. The big man's grip was surprisingly gentle.

"Deal. You go learn the military stuff and how to make life hell for these things. We'll keep the home fires burning until you get back."

♦

"Getting back" took a lot longer than Bone thought it would. Boot camp bled into infantry training that turned into advanced infantry training, followed by three years in Afghanistan.

It ended up being a few months too many.

The afternoon sun was bright between the buildings of downtown Pittsburgh. Even so, there was still a chill in the early spring air. A brisk wind was blowing up from the river, driving wisps of cloud across the sky. Every once in a while, a gust kicked up grit and debris from the gutters.

Bone shivered as he made his way down Grant Street towards the Mon Wharf. Passers-by ignored him. In faded jeans and a too-light canvas jacket for this weather, their reactions were very different from those he'd received when he'd come into the airport in his dress blues.

Given the choice, he'd rather be anonymous.

He made his way down Grant, hesitated, then took a right towards the 376 underpass.

He knew it was there, but he needed to see it with his own eyes.

The underpass was dim. Light slanted in from the sun sliding down into the west, peeking through the clouds. There were scores of bronze plaques embedded in the concrete wall of the underpass.

Each one bore a name and a date.

Light and dark played across the wall, the strobing effect glinting on one plaque.

The newest one.

Bone took a deep breath, then stepped over to it and squatted down to read what was there.

He reached out to run his hand along the writing.

"Paul Cordanza. Died, 2021. Gone Fishing."

The wind gusted, and his eyes watered from the dust. He blinked rapidly, then stood. Then took another deep breath before he turned and continued on down to the Mon Wharf.

The bike path from the Smithfield Street bridge down to the Wharf was new. It had been in the cards when he left for boot camp, but in truth, he was surprised the city had actually finished it on time.

Though maybe "finished" was a bit of a stretch. There were still some DPW sawhorses sitting at the top of the stairs. From the looks of it, the city was taking its own sweet time, as usual.

He paused at the top of the switchback and looked down. A stone path with a few concrete benches bordered a strip of green along the water's edge. Beyond, a dark parking lot beneath the Turnpike overpass.

That was the whole of Riverside Park.

He started down the winding path. About halfway down, he spotted a couple coming up. The man was well-dressed, gray suit and white shirt, no tie. The woman was in a pale-yellow summer dress and light sweater, her face flushed as she spoke to the man.

As he approached, Bone made out snatches of conversation. "I'll let someone know," the man said. "That sort of thing—"

"I can't believe it," the woman said hotly, eyes wide. "She was just…" She trailed off as she realized Bone was approaching. She nudged the man.

"Tell him!"

The man slowed a bit but didn't stop. "You might not want to go down there," he said, nodding back at the park. "There's a lady… out of control, you know? Must be on drugs or something." He shook his head.

"She's scaring the kids!" The woman said, voice a conspiratorial whisper.

Bone frowned. "Kids?"

"Yes! Kids! They were just fishing! She scared them away!"

"Ah. I see." Bone said. He smiled, but something in his eyes made both of them step back. He brushed past them, continuing down the switchback walkway towards the river.

As he approached the old Wabash Bridge pier, he saw the woman. She was walking along the riverfront towards him, head bowed.

Long white hair hung down, covering her face. Her gait was slow, as if she were placing every step with care. She wore what looked like several layers of tee-shirts, under at least a couple of oversized flannel shirts and a battered, dark blue ski jacket that had seen better days.

At first glance, the layers made her look pudgy. But on a second look, they only accentuated the thinness of her arms and legs.

Bone stopped, watching as she came closer. After a moment, he heard her muttering.

"Get out." Her voice was a whisper. "Damn fools." She made a noise, half cough, half sob.

He'd heard that too many times in the past few years. The sound of someone grieving. Someone who just didn't have the energy anymore.

Someone who had cried themselves out.

He cleared his throat, and she stopped. Her head snapped up.

"Damn fool!" She shouted. "Told you all, get out!" She reached up and brushed her hair from her face. Red eyes, tiny nose, a face filled with laugh lines that no longer had a use.

Bone swallowed. "Heard you scared some kids away."

She blinked, once, twice, three times.

"Danny? Danny Romero?"

Bone nodded. "Hey, Mary."

She took a step towards him, trembling, her right hand reaching out.

Bone stepped forward and took her trembling hand in his.

"You came back." She reached up with her other hand to touch his cheek. Her hand was cool, her fingers calloused. "It is you. You came back."

Then she fell into him. Her whole body shook with her weeping.

Bone wrapped his arms around her, and let his own tears fall.

♦

They ended up at the little pizza place on the other side of the Smithfield Street Bridge.

Apply food to the wound, Bone thought. He'd learned that from Mary.

They sat outside. Mary poked listlessly at her pizza.

"Eat," Bone said. "You can't go on like this."

"I will," Mary said with a faint smile. "Not much of an appetite, you know?" She nudged the plate aside. "You back for good? Or are you on, what do they call it? Vacation?"

"'Leave.' Nah. I'm home. Kind of. Still have a couple of months left, so they sent me back here to do some recruiting."

"Where are you staying?"

"I've got a little apartment. The Corp's paying for it. You?"

Mary shrugged. "Our place."

His surprise must have shown. A wistful smile flickered across her face.

"Paul never told you, eh? We have a tiny little house up on Garden Avenue." She blinked rapidly, forcing tears away. "I mean, we *had*. I have now, I guess."

"Mary…"

She wiped the back of her hand across her eyes, took a deep breath. "No. It's okay."

She looked away, then back down at her pizza. "Not the best place in town, but Paul had a guy he knew fix it up and turn the backyard into, well, into a garden. Some real fancy stuff. He called it our 'bower'." She smiled. "He could stay there, sometimes. Other times, even that was too much. He always made sure I was taken care of."

"Yeah." Bone took a bite of his own pizza, chewed quietly.

"When did it happen?"

Mary looked down. "End of January, around the full moon. You know how it goes."

"Something in the river?"

"Kelpie." She spit the word out with a venom he'd never heard in her voice before. She looked up, and her eyes were hard.

"Damn things are opportunists. They go after kids, old folks. It's like a damn smorgasbord for them, down there by the river." She shook her head. "You think that nobody would be hanging out there in the middle of winter, wouldn't you? Someone was. A guy visiting from out of Cleveland. Some of the street people, they tried to warn him. He went anyways."

"Went missing?"

"Yeah. Somebody saw it, too. Told the police, but who's going to listen to a stinking bum who's three sheets to the wind, eh?" Her voice was bitter. "Word got back to Paul, though. He went down to check it out."

Her voice cracked at that. Bone took her hand. She bowed her head, took a deep breath, and looked back up.

"They found him the next day. Down by the Bottoms. Six feet up the riverbank, lungs filled with ice."

Bone closed his eyes. "So it knew there was good hunting here."

"Oh, yeah. A young couple went missing the same night."

Bone shook his head. Mary continued.

"It was back the next full moon. I didn't see it, but I heard it, down there by the Riverside."

Bone opened his eyes. "You went down there?"

Mary's grin was sudden and fierce. "Damn right I did. You and Paul, you may know how to kill those things, but I know how to kick up a fuss. Had an air horn and everything! Didn't let anyone stay down by the river that night. Made damn sure it didn't get anyone in February."

She sighed. "Ended up spending a night in jail for my trouble. They called me 'Crazy Mary' after some song." Her face fell. "Then I got sick." She shook her head. "Not the crap that's going around, but bad enough. I was out of it completely. Syn... she tried. She went down during the day. She didn't quite get through to people, though. She was too polite."

Bone blinked. "Wait. Syn? *Syn?* Polite?"

Mary actually smiled. "I know, right? I made her promise. Didn't want her ending up in jail next to me. She listened, but... you know how she always goes to extremes?"

That was Syn in a nutshell. Bone nodded.

"She went from in-your-face to super polite. Just an odd little goth girl down by the river. Not the same as Crazy Mary."

She shook her head. "Syn… she tried. Did a good job, too. Mostly."

Bone's throat got tight. "Mostly? It got someone else?"

"The guy from Cleveland was named Greg Bellan," Mary said, her voice flat. "The kids were Terry Durst and Aaron O'Dell. Out for a midnight walk, a couple with eyes only for each other. And that thing took them both."

"Mary…"

She shook her head violently, and when she spoke, her voice was tight. Fierce with anger. "No. No! They deserve this. They *deserve* to be remembered, even if it's just by a crazy lady."

She looked down. Her hand in Bone's was trembling.

"Paul and Greg and Terry and Aaron." She looked up. "Those are the ones Syn knows about."

Paul was still. "That she knows about?"

Mary's voice was a whisper. "There was one more. A kid. A runaway. Went missing at the end of March. Amanda Porior."

"Jesus," Bone breathed. "How did Syn…"

Mary gripped his hand hard. "She doesn't know. I didn't tell her." She raised her head, looked into his eyes. "And you won't either, Daniel Romero. She doesn't deserve that burden. So you won't lay it on her, you hear? Swear it to me. By your name."

Bone hesitated, then squeezed her hand. "So be it," he whispered. "I will not tell her, I swear. On my Name, through my Name, and upon my Name."

As he finished, a gust of wind came and swirled around them.

Mary smiled, then patted his hand. "Your Name still has teeth. Good." She looked down at her pizza, but something had changed. Bone couldn't put his finger on it, but it felt as if Mary had laid aside her mourning. She picked up her pizza and took a bite.

"So," she said as she chewed. "How are we going to kill this damn Fae beastie?"

Bone looked around. "Let me take you home. We'll call Syn, and I'll show you both."

♦

"Here you go," Bone said. "Fire."

Mary looked skeptical. She poked at the pale blocks of clay sitting on the kitchen table.

Her kitchen was old, but clean. Antique, Bone supposed someone might call it if they were feeling charitable. Formica featured prominently.

Syn leaned in. Her long black hair was pulled back in a ponytail, and the only hint of makeup was obnoxiously bright red lipstick. It made her look like a manic version of Wednesday Addams.

"Is that what I think it is?"

"C4" Bone said with a nod. He picked up one of the two-by-eleven inch blocks, dropped it on the table. "M112 demolition block. Metastable. You don't want to eat it, but you can mold it like clay, drop it from a 120-story building and it won't go off."

Syn whistled and sat back. "Where can I get something like that? Asking for a friend," she added, batting her eyelashes.

"You can't get squat, runt. Me? I know a guy who knows a guy."

Bone reached into the duffel bag on the floor and pulled out a couple of thin metal cylinders with wires attached to one end.

"You need a shock wave, some kind of detonator," he explained. He laid the tubes down on the table. "Blasting caps will do it. That's what's in these detonator assemblies. Run out a wire, run a current through them, and light up the world. This much—" he held up one of the blocks "—is overkill. Even half of it will easily take out the kelpie. Best way is to wire in a remote detonator and make it go *'boom'* from a distance—"

"Would a remote actually work? I mean, with that whammy the Fae do?" Syn asked, interrupting him.

"No." He shook his head. "Unfortunately. We found that out the hard way. The Fae over in the sandbox… they're different." He shook his head. "Waaaay different. They can still die by fire, though. If you're careful, and you can get close enough." He tapped the remote detonator. "The stuff they do, with the silence—"

"How they kill the noise and make the light dim, you mean?" Mary asked.

"The whammy," Syn said, nodding and wiggling her fingers.

Bone nodded. "Yeah. Turns out, it's a generalized effect. Not just light and sound – it affects energy across the board. Sound waves, light waves, electromagnetic waves all get damped and warped."

Mary slapped the table. "So *that's* why it's so hard to get a picture of them!"

Bone nodded. "Yep. And why cell phones crap out around them, and anything radio-operated. So we can't take the easy way out and wire up a remote detonator."

He picked up one of the blasting caps and flicked the wires. "But a direct physical connection works just fine. So," Bone looked around the table, "we set our ambush. Our three T's are terrain, tactics, tasks."

"Terrain is set, but we can stage near the Wabash pier. That will give us a backstop to reduce the kelpie's mobility, as well as provide both concealment and cover if we need it. Tactically, we'll have to entice it in. We want it close to shore, but not too close. That means we'll need a fixed, floating lure. As for tasks…" he trailed off as he noticed Syn slowly raising her hand.

"Question?"

"You kind of slipped into drill sergeant mode there. Do we need to know all this stuff?"

Mary cleared her throat. "You did get a bit jargony. We trust you, Danny. Maybe you could simplify it a bit for us?"

Bone pursed his lips. "OK… right. Simplified. We hard wire a detonator to some C4, then attach it and some bait to something that floats. Wait until the kelpie shows up and tries to eat it."

Syn perked up. "Ah! *Then* we get to make the earth-shattering kaboom!"

Bone smiled. "Yeah, that's the idea."

Mary shook her head. "And get yourself killed, and the whole Wharf cursed in the process. You know what happened when Paul burned out that thing holed up on the South Side years ago." She narrowed her eyes. "Their death curse is real, Danny."

"It's not a curse, you know that. We call it that, but it's nothing more than survival instinct. One of the Fae making a last-ditch effort to open a way back home."

"Call it what you will," Mary said hotly. "It's still going to kill a lot of people."

"Only if we give it a chance to react." Bone's mouth curled up into a wicked grin. "That's the beauty of modern technology. It takes you, me, anything physical, at least 60 milliseconds to sense and react to something."

Syn raised an eyebrow. "Even Fae beasties?"

"Yep. Trust me on this. Even something like a kelpie has a physical reaction time. Signal's gotta get to the brain – and be processed before it can react. Even if the reaction is completely reflex, it still needs to see it coming."

He tapped the C4. "The blast wave from this is ten times faster than nerve impulses. Before the kelpie realizes what's going on, before it has time to try to open a portal, it's already dead."

Syn grinned. "Now you're talking, jarhead. Let's make it go *'boom.'*"

"That's the plan." He tossed her a set of keys. "Come on. You're driving."

♦

They piled into his Honda Fit and headed down to the Mon Wharf park shortly before six in the evening. Syn parked on the far side of the river, at the Station Square parking garage. Bone grabbed his backpack and a tackle box from the back before locking up.

Syn looked at him incredulously. "Are you serious?"

"We want to look normal. Just a couple of folks out fishing by the river, right?" He opened the tackle box and lifted the top tray, revealing two squares of C4, each about the same size and slightly thicker than a deck of cards.

He closed the box and handed a rod to Syn. "Everything else is in my backpack. Unless you know what you're looking at, it's just wire and duct tape and junk. The detonator assemblies are as plug-and-play as I could make them. Already have the ignition switch attached. Just insert the post and press the button for *boom*."

Mary frowned. "Is that safe?"

"No." Bone shrugged. "Not at all. But I'd rather have them ready to go than have to try and do it in the moment, if things get hectic."

Mary pursed her lips in disapproval, but nodded.

It was short walk across the Smithfield Street bridge and down the bike switchback to the river. The light from the setting sun bathed everything in a golden glow. The light breeze and the smell of river water brought back memories of Paul. Bone blinked back tears.

Syn looked like she was going to say something snarky, but bit it off. "You okay?"

"Yeah. Sun's bright." He wiped his eyes.

Syn gave a little nod, then threw the rod over her shoulder before moving ahead of him on the path.

Mary took his hand, gave it a squeeze. Her hands seemed tiny and frail, but her grip was strong. "Park police will come through a little bit before sundown, then check again right after."

Syn looked back over snorted. "Like that does any good. They kick out the normies, but everybody else just fades and comes right back once they're gone."

"Which is exactly what we're going to do," Bone said. He looked up and down the strip of grass next to the Wharf parking area. "Mary, you sit on one of those benches by the old bridge pier. Keep an eye out. Syn, you and I will have a talk with the... uh... guys you mentioned."

"Non-normies?"

He shrugged. "The ones who look like they might come back around later."

Mary sat gingerly on one of the benches and wrapped her blue coat around her thin body. She almost seemed to vanish into it.

She looked up at Bone. "You two go. I'll keep an eye out."

Bone watched as she turned towards the river. On the opposite shore, one of the Gateway Clipper riverboats was getting underway.

Syn gestured at the paddleboat as it moved away from its moorings.

"Evening cruises. Even better than the first robin of spring."

Bone nodded. On the boat, people spread out across the upper deck, watching the sun on the river. Even from this distance, he heard lively music playing. Bone thought he might have heard a burst of laughter from one of the passengers.

"It's left the boats alone," Mary murmured, as if hearing Bone's unasked question. "Prefers easier targets. So far."

They watched until the boat started downriver.

"Right. Come on." Bone jerked his head at Syn and the two of them started down the wharf front.

They walked for a minute before Syn broke the silence. "Not a whole lot of people around."

"Yeah. Thankfully." Bone glanced back over his shoulder. Mary was staring out across the water, eyes shaded against the sun. Even though they were well out of earshot, he lowered his voice. "How's she been?"

"Mary? God." Syn shook her head. "She's been a mess, Bone. Whaddya expect? Her guy got ate up by a water demon."

Bone grunted.

Syn ran a hand through her hair. "I mean, she kind of knew it was coming. Said that she always knew Paul wasn't going to die in his sleep. Knowing and understanding, though?"

Bone sighed. "Two different things." That had been one of Paul's favorite sayings. "You don't know how you'll deal with something until it happens."

"Yeah. Speaking of which. How *are* we going to deal with the beastie?"

"We clear people out, lure it in, feed it a C4 snack, and turn it into chum."

Syn stopped and spread her arms. "New and improved Fae-Be-Gone! Apply directly to critter to ensure vaporization! Not recommended for children under 4."

"Or teenagers who don't know what they're doing, either," Bone said. "I'll be the one making the *kaboom* here, Rico."

"Oh, come on!" Syn tried to fold her arms and got tangled up in the fishing pole. "I'm not a teenager anymore. You can't dangle that stuff in front of me and then tell me I don't get to play with it."

Bone shook his head. "Can, and am. You're here to watch and learn, *padawan*."

Syn untangled herself, scowling. "You're only a few years older than me, jarhead."

"Yeah, but I learned a lot in those years." He rubbed his eyes. "Crap. I just realized. Now I've gotta learn how to do what Paul did."

"What, kill monsters?"

"Nah. Put up with a snot-nosed smartass kid who thinks she knows it all."

Syn stared at him, then raised a single finger in reply.

Bone laughed. "Come on. Put that away. Maybe next weekend I'll let you play with some boomex."

Syn's face lit up. "Wait. Really?"

"Yeah, really. You're going to need to learn how to handle it anyways." Bone nodded at a couple of rough-looking older men sitting on a bench towards the end of the wharf. "Meanwhile, let's let those guys know they're going to want to find somewhere else to be tonight."

Ten bucks for a bottle was enough to get the pair to clear out. Further on, they stopped to chat with a couple of college kids hanging out by the stairs. Bone casually mentioned that the narcotics unit had been hanging out at the Wharf after dark. That was all it took to send those two hustling away.

They walked up to Mary with Syn shaking her head. "Mary, you were a madwoman down here. Seriously! People ignored you. I toned it down, and people ignored me, too."

She jerked a thumb at Bone. "Mister Military here talks to people for half a minute and they just leave! He doesn't even yell at 'em or anything!"

Mary chuckled. "It's all about knowing what buttons to push." She looked up at Bone. "You've always been pretty good at finding the right ones, haven't you?"

Bone shrugged. "It's not like I was lying to them. Come on, Syn. We'll fish over on the other side of the pier. Mary, keep an eye out towards the bridge."

They took their places and got settled in. Syn was staring out at the water, muttering "Bored, bored, bored" while Bone kept an eye on the Wharf parking area. So they missed when the park ranger showed up.

"Danny! Cynthia!" Mary called out. She waved them over. "Come meet Justin."

Justin was a big man. He looked like a professional wrestler someone had crammed into a park ranger's uniform a half-size too small. He was bald as an egg, with dark skin and a broad smile. His badge read KONCHAR.

"Hey," he said, greeting Bone and Syn as they came over. "Was just telling Miss Mary here that you'll need to take your leave of the park." He coughed. "Excuse me. I mean, yinz guys will need to clear out, n'at."

Mary smiled. "Justin's from New Yawk. He's been trying to learn the lingo." She looked up at him. "He's one of the good guys. Always stops to check on me. He really is a sweetheart."

The officer gave them a small, but genuine, smile. "Just part of the job, ma'am." He gave Bone a nod. "I am glad to see Mary's got some folks who care about her. Hate to see her sitting down here alone. I do mean it about clearing out, though. Park's closed after dark."

Bone nodded. "Got it. Mary wanted to stay to see the sunset. We'll take off after. That okay?"

"Yeah. That'll be fine. Take care, Mary." He gave Bone a nod. "Hope y'all catch something." He ambled off to bother a group of high school kids further down the wharf.

"What now?" Syn asked. She looked around. "Are we going to ward the place? I saw some paint in your bag."

"No!" Mary and Bone spoke at the same time. Syn looked back and forth between them, confused.

"Why not? I mean, we want to protect ourselves against it, right?"

Bone tapped his head. "Think. How much effort would you have to put into something like that?"

Syn sighed. "A ton. But if we all worked at it really quick…"

"…we'd put up a big warning sign that says 'Here's a trap'," Mary said gently. "We want to lure it in, baby girl. Stupid as that idea might seem."

Bone shook his head. "Not to mention, the strongest wards need our names. Well. Our tags." He gave Syn his best imitation Drill Sergeant stare. "I just got back into town. I don't want the graffiti task force wondering who the hell Bone and Syn are. Or why they painted their names all over the Mon Wharf."

Syn sighed. "Fine. So what are we going to do?"

Bone sat down and put his arm around Mary. "We're going to sit here and fish a bit. Watch the sunset." His sudden smile was cold. "Then we'll leave, just like I told the ranger we would. Maybe go for a short walk. And when it's fully dark, we'll come back to kill the kelpie."

◆

They stayed until sunset, then made their way up the bike ramp to the Smithfield Street bridge. When they reached the top, they stopped, leaned on the bridge rail, and watched the river together in silence. Bikers and pedestrians passed them by, most heading back home to the South Shore.

Once the last dim light of the sun faded, the full moon shone brightly on the water. Clouds skidded across the sky, throwing shadows on the river as they moved. When a cloud drifted past, obscuring the moonlight, the river reflected the shifting lights of the city.

After a while, there was a break in the foot traffic across the bridge.

Bone took a deep breath and straightened up.

"Time to move. Mary, keep an eye out. Syn, give me a hand here." He grabbed one end of the DPW sawhorse he'd seen the day before. Syn snagged the other, and they carried it ten yards down the switchback before they set it down. The sawhorse almost completely blocked the path.

Bone stopped and peered back up towards the bridge. "Syn. What do you think? Far enough down that someone can't see it from the road?"

Syn looked around. "Yeah, this will do. What about the other side, though?"

They started back up the ramp. "I've got some caution tape. We'll string that up where you can't see it from the parkway. Then we'll do the same across the stairs down to the Wharf."

Syn blinked. "Ah. We left going upriver, so now we'll circle around back downriver and cover the whole Wharf. That's kind of smart." She cocked her head. "Marine stuff?"

He shrugged. "Securing the area. Seems like a good idea to double-check and make sure there's nobody else around." They arrived back at the top.

"Mary? You okay with heading back down and waiting for us?"

Lips pressed together, she nodded. Bone handed her the tackle box and his fishing rod. Syn handed her rod over as well.

"Stash the rods under the switchback. Don't get too close to the river. Hang back and wait for us, okay? Promise?"

"Daniel Romero." There was an edge to Mary's voice. "I was helping Paul before you were a twinkle in your father's eye." She gestured. "I'll stay back. You to go, but that thing won't wait forever. Make it quick."

Bone didn't salute, but his arm did twitch. "Aye, aye, ma'am. Syn. Let's go." The two of them jogged across the street and headed down Fort Pitt Avenue above the river.

Bone glanced over his shoulder at the moon as it continued making its way up into the sky. "You've got your cousin's blanket?"

Syn patted her coat pocket. "Right here. In a baggie. She's slept with and puked on this thing for the past year. Probably smells more like a kid than a kid does."

"Good. That's our bait. We want to give the kelpie something that will make it think there's an easy meal around."

"What if it doesn't go for it?"

"It will. Mary got it right — these things are opportunistic predators. They go for the small, the weak, the injured. The smell of a child will bring it in. Especially the smell of a child in the water."

Syn frowned. "How do we manage that?"

"I've got a beach ball in my bag," Bone said. "Plus some duct tape. I did some tests. With the blanket and C4 duct-taped to it, it will float like a bobber."

Syn's eyes got wide. "You're going fishing for it!"

"Exactly. The det wire is the line, the ball is the bobber, the blanket is the bait."

"And the C4 is the spicy surprise when it bites." Syn rubbed her hands together. "So! What do you need me to do?"

"Keep back, and keep an eye on Mary," Bone said.

"What?"

Bone pursed his lips. "If something goes wrong, you're my backup."

"What do you mean, 'something goes wrong'?"

Bone rubbed his temple. "You know what I mean."

"Spell it out."

"Fine. If it gets me, you're it." He stopped and turned to look at Syn. "How many people are there in Pittsburgh who deal with this weird shit, now that Paul's gone?"

Syn frowned. "You and me. That coroner lady."

"Cassie, good. Plus Reuben, who's a nice guy, but… he's a math nerd. And a pacifist! I don't think either of them has ever even met one of the Fae. They have their own weird crap to deal with."

Bone pointed at Syn. "Which means that if anything happens to me here, you're it."

Syn blinked. "You mean me and Mary…"

"No. Mary's part of this all, but she's never been a fighter. She's always been the one who's patched us up, kept us all going." He shook his head. "She was warning people away from the river, but not trying to kill the beastie. She's a protector."

Syn narrowed her eyes and thrust her chin at him. "And I'm not? Is that what you're saying?"

Bone met her stare. "Yes. That is *exactly* what I'm saying." He jabbed a finger at her. "Tell me. What were you planning to do about the kelpie?"

Syn held his gaze for a second, then looked away. "I don't know."

Bone reached out and laid his hand on her shoulder. Gently. "I don't believe that. Tell me."

"Fine!" She twisted away, shrugging her shoulder out from under his hand. "I was going to steal a speedboat. Lure it down to Brunot Island. Then, I don't know." She raised her hands, dropped them. "Ram it until it died."

Bone nodded slowly. "And?"

"It would have worked!"

Bone tilted his head. "Yeah. It definitely would have. That bastard wouldn't have even known know what hit it." His face got serious. "You would have died too, though."

Syn straightened up defiantly. "But I would have taken care of it."

Bone shook his head. "See, that's what I mean. Mary doesn't think like that. Neither does Cassie. Definitely not Reuben." He shook his head. "Things like this, it was always down to Paul and me. Then you came along. With him gone, now it's just the two of us."

"I'll finish this thing, if that's what you mean."

"No!" Bone's hand slashed the air. "No. If this doesn't work, you leave it alone. You walk away." He grabbed her shoulders, turned her to look at him. "You *walk away*... and you take care of Mary."

He let go of her shoulders. "Then you find some more people. You work with them and teach them everything Paul and I taught you. Look for former military if you can. They'll be more likely to have seen the Fae. Won't think you're completely nuts."

He took a deep breath. "And then – once you have some backup of your own – *then* you come back and finish the mission. Otherwise, if you fail, there's nobody standing between the city and the Fae, and the next thing that shows up will tear through this city like an all-you-can-eat buffet."

Syn's face screwed up and she growled in frustration before she gave him a sharp nod. "Okay. Yeah. I get it."

She punched him in the shoulder. Hard. "That's not going to happen, though, because we're going to blow this bastard up, right?"

Bone dropped his hands. "Right! That's the attitude."

Syn grinned. "Good. Because there is no way I am taking over as den mother to a bunch of snot-nosed, smartass kids or ex-Marines who think they know it all."

She turned and started walking down toward the Point, then called back over her shoulder. "Are you coming or not?"

Bone snorted and hurried to catch up. "Pitter-patter. Let's get at 'er."

◆

It only took about five minutes for Bone and Syn to get the caution tape up on the Stanwix Street stairs down to the Wharf. Another ten got them to the Point end of the Wharf.

They strung up caution tape and made their way back to Mary. The sound of cars whizzing by on the Parkway above was a low, hypnotic drone. There was enough chill in the air to keep you awake and make you think that a fire would be perfect.

Mary was sitting by the old Wabash Bridge pier, waiting for them.

"Peaceful," she whispered as they approached. A car alarm, far in the distance, flared to life and was quickly silenced.

"Look." She gestured at the river. "It's calm. No traffic. Hardly a ripple."

Bone checked the wind. Blowing downriver. He unzipped his bag and pulled out one of the detonator assemblies, along with a deflated plastic beach ball.

"Here." He tossed the package to Syn along with a roll of silver tape. "Blow that up, will you? Then duct tape your cousin's blanket to it." He started unspooling the detonator wire, laying it down along the riverbank.

Syn sighed dramatically, then made a show of starting to inflate the beach ball.

"What about me?" Mary said quietly. "Going to tell the old lady to watch from the bridge?"

Bone didn't look up. "I thought about it. The thing is? It took Paul from you." He paused, looked back at her. "You deserve to see it die. So, no. I'm not going to ask you to leave. Just… you know… stay back?"

Mary didn't say anything. Bone shrugged and went back to arranging the wire.

"Done." Syn showed off the beach ball with a fluffy ragged blue blanket attached to it. "This is not the weirdest thing I've ever done, but it's definitely in the top ten."

"Doesn't even make my all-time top 100," Bone said flatly. "We'll get a drink after this, and I'll tell you about some of the stuff I did in Afghanistan."

Syn stuck out her tongue. "I'm surprised your old-man brain remembered I'm old enough to drink."

"Yeah, well. Even us old farts have our moments of lucidity," Bone said. He ripped off a length of duct tape and used it to fix one of the chunks of C4 to the beach ball.

"Anyways. Drinks. Paul taught me that. You kill one of these bastards, you have a drink afterward. It's tradition." He continued wrapping duct tape around the ball, making sure the explosive and blanket were both securely in place.

Mary spoke up. "Not just tradition. It's like hiding your mental tracks." She looked out over the water. "Not that it much matters with this thing. Kelpies are loners. None of the other Fae are likely to come after you for killing it."

She drew her coat tightly around herself and shuddered. "Some of the others, though? They have friends. Some of them – well, they can't read your mind, but they might as well could. They can see it in your eyes, you see. Depending on how powerful they are, you don't want to have a clear memory of what you've done to another one of them. Nothing that one of them could be sure of."

Mary gave them a weak smile. "There were times when Paul came home and simply drank a bottle straight down. Those… those were the bad ones."

Bone looked at Syn. "There you go. It's not just tradition, it's protection."

Syn snorted. "Right. I suppose I can get sloshed for the good of Pittsburgh."

"That's the spirit! You ever think of joining my beloved Corps?"

Syn smiled sweetly. "I would rather roll around naked on glass and go skinny dipping in lemon juice."

Bone raised an eyebrow. "Oh, yeah. Definitely Marine Corps material there."

"Fuck. Is there any way I can say 'No' that will make you think I mean it?"

"Nope!" Bone smiled. "I wouldn't dream of inflicting you on the Corps, anyways." He took a deep breath and slid the detonator post into the C4 attached to the beach ball, then wound the last of the duct tape around it, binding it in place.

"There. We're live." Bone handed the ball over to Syn, keeping hold of the ignition switch.

He nodded at the river. "Go ahead, throw it in."

"Wait, what?"

"Throw it in, baby girl. Come on."

Syn scowled, then wound up and threw the beach ball as far out into the river as she could. It arced over the water and went 10 yards before landing in the water with a soft plop.

"No, I meant, what did you mean by…"

"Shhh!" Bone held up his hand. "Wait." He pointed at the beach ball. "Watch."

Syn rolled her eyes, but stopped talking and looked at the river.

The beach ball bobbed in the river for a second, then started drifting downriver. Bone played out some wire, then started walking upriver.

"A child falls into the river," Bone said quietly. Tugged in opposite directions by the current and the wire, the ball spun and skipped over the water.

He gave the line a couple of jerks. The beach ball stuttered and jumped in the water. "They struggle for a bit, then start to drown, getting more frantic." He gave the wire a couple of sharp, rapid tugs. The ball splashed and spun.

"Finally, they can't fight anymore, and they start to drift." He stopped walking and played out wire until it was slack. The ball settled down, then started drifting downriver. They watched it move ever so slowly for a minute until it had almost reached the old Wabash pier.

Mary took a step forward, watching the river. "What if it doesn't go for the bait?"

"We'll pull it in and cast again. If I have to, I'll get in and splash around a bit."

"So now we just stand here? What are we waiting for?" Syn whispered.

There was something like a soft implosion of silence, centered on the beach ball. The sounds of the city faded and became distant. The light of the moon dimmed until it was almost like they were in the middle of a fog.

"That," Mary whispered. "It's here. Look."

The beach ball had stopped drifting downriver. It bobbed in place once, twice, three times, then started drifting again.

Upriver.

Syn pointed "Is that…"

A surge of water flowed upriver, then crested. It looked like a tube of darkness snaking through the river. It came up near the beach ball and flowed past it, disappearing into the fog.

"It's playing with it." Mary's voice was hard.

"It'll take it," Bone said. "They're like cats. It wants to torture it first."

"Hey!"

The shout from behind them was tenuous. The unnatural fog in the air seemed to absorb it.

It was still close enough to make them all start.

The park ranger who had spoken to them earlier was heading their way. He held a flashlight, but the beam was flickering and barely illuminated his path. The darkness sucked the light away and wrapped it up in itself.

Bone let loose with a muttered stream of invective he'd once heard from a drill sergeant.

Syn blinked. "Holy... look. If that's something they taught you in the Marines, then yeah, maybe I'm interested."

Bone ignored her. "I'll talk to him. Syn. Take Mary, get away from the river."

"Mary!" Justin called out. He sounded like he was more disappointed than angry. "You can't stay here, Mary. Park's closed."

Bone stepped forward smiling. "I know, I know. We just got to talking about old times – you know how it is." He shrugged apologetically.

But Justin was staring at the river, his mouth opening and closing without making a sound. A ghostly light seemed to slip between the darkness, illuminating his face.

Mary's voice behind him was quiet. "Too late, Danny."

◆

Bone turned back just as the river exploded upwards. The beach ball swirled and circled in the rising cyclone of water, pulling the detonator wire with it. Before Bone even realized what was happening, the wire went taut and ripped the detonator from his hand.

As the water fell back to the river, the ghostly light revealed a vaguely equine form, if 'equine' included features like a gaping crocodile's mouth with fangs made of ice. Two huge eyes burned with a malevolent green luminescence.

The kelpie's translucent, slug-like flesh shimmered and twisted as it reared up. It was as if the river had decided that, for a brief moment, "vertical" was an allowed direction of flow.

"I thought they were horse-sized?" Bone whispered.

"Horse-*shaped*," Mary whispered back.

The kelpie slowly swung its massive head back and forth. A thin gray tongue flicked in and out of the thing's mouth between teeth made of dirty ice, tasting the air.

Justin was staring at the kelpie, mouth still hanging open.

Bone cleared his throat. "Hey, Mr. Justin? Buddy? Listen." Bone kept his voice quiet and steady. "I'm going to distract this thing, okay? Just stay steady."

The kelpie thrust its head at Justin, gnashing its teeth with a sound like the creaking of old ice on a river in the dead of winter. Flakes of ice sprayed everywhere.

Justin shouted, jumping backward. His feet got tangled up under him, and he went down in a heap.

The kelpie pulled back its head like a snake, mouth gaping wider and wider until it looked like it's head would split.

Then it struck.

It was like watching a wall of solid water come down out of nowhere. It smashed over Justin, ice teeth meshing together like bars, trapping the ranger behind them. The kelpie twitched for a second, then started pulling Justin back towards the river.

Bone was already moving. He took three steps, dove, then snaked his hand between the kelpie's jagged teeth and grabbed Justin's left arm.

His hand immediately began to grow numb. The kelpie's body was unearthly cold. As he watched, Bone could see the river water surrounding it begin turning to slush.

The kelpie's mouth was full of water that somehow refused to run out of the gaps between its teeth. Bone watched as air bubbled from Justin's lips as he struggled to push himself free from the icy cage holding him.

Bone planted his feet. He managed to get into a half-crouch, then threw himself backward with all his strength. It felt like he was trying to move a boulder – but ever so slightly, Justin and the kelpie began to inch up the bank, away from the river.

"That's it!" Mary shouted. "Keep your feet on land! Don't let it get you in the river!"

The kelpie twitched and snorted, pulling against Bone. Justin screamed soundlessly, silver bubbles streaming from his lips as he thrashed against the teeth like a magician trapped in a stage show gone wrong. The kelpie's tongue slithered over the ranger, pinning his limbs as he struggled.

Bone braced to pull again, but the kelpie had other ideas. It rolled its head, lifting him from his crouch until his feet were only barely touching the ground. One malevolent eye peered at him for a brief moment.

The kelpie jerked its head to the right, and Bone felt his feet leave the pavement.

Something hit him in the back and dragged him back down.

"Idiot Marines," Syn panted. She had her arms wrapped around his waist. She was crouched behind one of the benches along the water's edge, leaning backwards as she held onto Bone, her feet braced against the concrete risers. "YOU MUST BE THIS HIGH TO RIDE THE MONONGOHELA MONSTER!"

Bone twisted his body and managed to get roll his legs over the bench as well. With both he and Syn using the bench for leverage, they started pulling the kelpie out of the water again. His arm was numb up to the elbow, and he was afraid they were going to push the bench off its foundations. He was fairly certain that to the only reason he still had hold of Justin was because their arms had frozen together.

Bone snarled. "On three! One! Two! THREE!"

He and Syn pulled together.

The kelpie moved a few more inches up from the river but refused to release Justin.

"He's not moving!" Syn yelled. "Screw this! Hold him there!"

Her weight disappeared. Bone snarled, then shoved his other hand between the Kelpie's teeth to grab Justin with both hands. "Just need to break a few teeth," he growled, tugging Justin up against the icy bars of his watery cage.

Syn dove past him. She landed with a smack at the water's edge, a revolver in her hands that looked like something out of a *Hellboy* movie. Pushing the gun out as far over the water as she could, she pulled the trigger three times in rapid succession.

Even in the sound-absorbing darkness, the flash and report were amazing as the blasts pushed Syn backward. Bone's ears rang. He felt the shock wave in his teeth.

The kelpie felt it more.

Its mouth opened in a roaring scream, arcing up and back.

Bone flipped over backward as Justin was suddenly released. Shards of icy kelpie teeth shattered and sprayed everywhere.

The kelpie screamed again and dove into the river.

Syn pushed herself up onto her knees, gun still pointed at the river. She was wobbling a bit, but grinning ear to ear. She raised her left fist in victory.

"410 PACKED WITH IRON BUCKSHOT, BITCH!"

Bone scrambled to his knees. Justin was lying face up, eyes wide and staring, his chest not moving.

"Syn! You only hurt it! KEEP IT AWAY!"

Bone leaned in and pinched Justin's nose. He delivered two quick rescue breaths like his corpsman had taught him, then started chest compressions while humming *"Another One Bites the Dust"* to maintain his rhythm.

He didn't even get halfway through the chorus before Syn shouted. There was a roar of anger, followed by three more rapid shots.

Then a wall of water smashed into him.

It seemed to take forever to realize he was flying through the air instead of doing CPR. More than enough time for him to manage to twist and land on his side. He felt a moment of triumph as he rolled with the landing, protecting his head.

Then he smashed into one of the concrete benches.

His left leg went numb for a second, then felt like it was on fire. Bone grabbed on to the edge of the bench and managed to pull himself up so he could see what was going on.

Syn had grabbed Justin and pulled him well back from the edge of the river, behind one of the Wharf's many pillars. Bone watched as she rolled the ranger over on his side and pounded on his back. After several seconds he convulsed, then threw up bile and river water.

Mary was nowhere to be seen.

The kelpie screamed from the river again. Bone groaned and twisted around.

The kelpie's head was whipping back and forth, scanning the shore. Sickly green spots peppered its body, evidence of the damage from Sys's hand cannon.

Bone froze and tried to quiet his breathing.

Denied its prey, the kelpie opened its mouth and screamed. The roar seemed to go on forever. It left ripples in the enveloping darkness around the river, then died out into a deep, thick quiet.

The silence lasted for little more than a heartbeat.

Then the faint sound of music rolled across the water.

The kelpie turned slowly to stare down the river.

Following its gaze, Bone made out the outline of a brightly-lit paddleboat working its way upriver.

The kelpie coiled and shifted, eyes locked on the new target.

Bone pushed himself to his feet and waved his hands. Or tried to. As soon as he put weight on his leg, it gave out and he collapsed on the pavement. He rolled over and put his back against the bench.

"No! Over here, you idiot! Right here! Juicy Marine! Already tenderized!" He waved his hands as he tried to shout. All he managed was a hoarse whisper. "Come and get it! Dinner's on!"

Rough as his voice was, it worked. The kelpie's head whipped around to look in his direction. It contemplated him for a brief moment, then turned away.

"No? Then how about me?" Mary's voice was loud and clear, even in the blanket of darkness.

She stepped out from behind the pier, open tackle box dangling from one hand.

"How about me, then, you damn monster?"

Time seemed to slow as Bone watched her pull the remaining packet of C4 out of the tackle box and wrap her hand tightly around it.

"Mary." Bone's voice was a croak. "No! No."

She looked over at him. The expression on her face was half furious, half apologetic. She held the explosive tightly in one hand, the remaining detonator assembly in the other.

"You just stick the detonator in, right, Danny?"

She looked up at the kelpie and snarled as she slammed the detonator home.

"No!"

"I'm sorry, Danny. I think… No. I *understand*, now." She turned and started walking toward the water.

She stepped into the river and screamed. Her voice went on forever until it didn't.

The silence when she stopped was even deeper than that one that the kelpie had brought with it. The Fae's eyes fixed on her, burning bright.

Bone struggled, trying to get up. He managed to get his feet under him, but barely staggered a single step before his legs simply gave out, and he fell to his knees.

"Mary!"

She ignored him and kept her eyes on the kelpie. "It's not the flesh and blood you're after, is it, you bastard?" Her voice was soft, but thick with rage. Tears were streaming down her face.

"You want the pain, don't you? You're down here for the wrecks, for the ones who are barely hanging on. For their sweet, sweet pain."

She took another step into the water. The kelpie reared up, mouth levering open.

Bone pulled himself to his feet. Started shuffling forward, dragging his leg like a log.

Mary took another step. Looked up at the kelpie. "Come on!" She spread her arms wide. "Here I am! Come on! You've taken everything from me already! Why not finish the job?"

The kelpie hesitated, water dripping from its hide.

"COME ON! YOU WANT PAIN? I'VE GOT IT! PLENTY AND TO SPARE!"

Bone was ten yards away. He lunged forward anyway.

The kelpie moved like lightning. It smashed down on Mary, picked her up, then flipped back into the water.

The last Bone saw of Mary, she was smiling, eyes hard as the kelpie dragged her under.

With her thumb pressing down on the detonator switch.

Everything stopped. The wind caught on the darkness. The darkness smoothed the river to glass. The river…

The darkness and silence were ripped away.

The river exploded with light. Water fountained up, then crashed down with a deafening roar. Bone was half washed into the river. He pulled himself onto the shore with his one good arm and forced himself to crawl over to where Syn was still taking care of Justin.

The ranger was unconscious, but at least he was breathing.

Bone sat up and leaned against the pillar. Everything from his chest down felt like a single bruise. His right arm was starting to scream at him in pain as the preternatural cold of the kelpie faded.

Syn looked up at him.

"Mary?"

It came out as a squeak. All she could manage without tears.

He wasn't sure he could do much better.

He closed his eyes. "She finished the mission."

♦

Justin stirred, wheezed. That turned into a retching, panting cough. Syn dropped to one knee and pounded him helpfully on the back as he tried to bring up whatever river water was left in his lungs. Bone gritted his teeth and pushed himself to his feet, using the pillar for support.

After a moment, Justin's breathing was almost normal. "What…" He looked up at Syn, blinking as he tried to focus. "What was…"

"Rogue wave." Syn said matter-of-factly. She wiped the tears from her face with the back of her hand. "Big ol' speedboat came by, swamped the whole riverside. Nearly took us all out."

Justin stared at her for a second, then snarled and pushed himself to a seated position. "No. There was *something*. Teeth. Ice. Cold." He tried to stand, but his body started trembling, shaking from exhaustion. His clothes were shredded, stained with blood from a score of cuts where the jagged edges of the kelpie's broken teeth had torn through to the flesh underneath when he'd been thrown free.

Bone bent down and put an arm under the big man's shoulder to help him up. The two of them nearly fell over, but after a moment, they were both on their feet. More or less.

Syn shot him a questioning look. Bone shook his head slightly and turned his attention back to the ranger.

"Steady there, Justin. Been exactly where you are."

Justin twisted his head to look at Bone, then made a strangled sound that was almost a laugh. "Where's that?"

"There *was* something in the river." Bone tried to put as much warmth and sincerity into his tone as he could. "Something that didn't belong there. It tried to eat you. We killed it."

"Mary killed it." Syn's voice was almost too soft to hear.

Justin squeezed his eyes shut. "I remember you. Yelling."

Bone shrugged. "There was a lot of that. Usually is for this sort of thing."

Justin's eyes levered open. "*Usually?* What the hell does that mean?"

Bone stood up straight, then pulled his arm out from under Justin. The ranger was a bit unsteady, but managed to stand on his own before leaning back against the pillar Bone had slouched against moments before. Off in the distance, a siren started up.

Bone took a half-step back, keeping his weight off his bad leg, and met Justin's eyes. "It means you have a choice." He nodded at Syn. "Hear that siren? We can stay here and wait for whoever shows up, tell them our story."

Syn crossed her arms. "Rogue wave. I'll swear it on a stack of Bibles."

Justin frowned at her, then looked back at Bone and took a deep breath. "Or?"

"Or you can come with us. We'll get you something to eat and tell you what really happened here tonight."

"Oh! The all-night pizza place up by Market Square?" Syn said hopefully.

Bone ignored her. "If you hadn't been here tonight, Justin. If you hadn't gone through it, would you believe this story? Some water monster eating people down by the Mon Wharf?" Bone shook his head. "No. You'd write it off, and the next time it came back, more people would die."

"Syn and I, we stop that sort of thing from happening. It's hard work, and it's dangerous. But we do it to keep people safe."

Bone held out his hand. "So, what's it going to be? You want to spend the rest of your life wondering what happened here, or do you want to know?"

Justin started at him for a second, then reached out and took his hand. Bone held steady as the ranger pushed himself off from the pillar and stood up.

"I think..." he said slowly. He glanced at Syn, then back at Bone. Pursed his lips. He looked at his hand in Bone's, then gave a squeeze and let go.

Justin took a deep breath. "Pizza sounds pretty good right now."

Danielle Harward is a high fantasy author who enjoys spinning tales full of heroes and magic and exploring the difficulty of conquering inner conflict and the line between good and villainous themes. She was first published in the League of Utah Writers 85th Anniversary *anthology, and received the League's 2020 New Poetry Award. When she's not working, she daydreams about the several series ideas she has and which one to write first. When she isn't writing, she's adventuring with her husband, son, and their two dogs who silently cheer her on with snuggles at her feet. You can find more about Danielle at harwardwriting.com*

About this story, Danielle says: "A lot of research went into the unlikely team of Rex and Devan. As an avid D&D player, I always felt like many of the less-common humanoid creatures were under-utilized in literature and I wanted to explore what their world might be. What would their social group look like? What would their standing be in society? What work would they do? It was those questions that let me sift through the muck and discover this gem."

Trolls are rarely cast as heroes, and Rex is just about as unwilling to be the hero of this story as any troll might reasonably be. But when he shoulders the responsibility that has been thrust upon him and teams up with his next-door neighbor, Devan... well, you just have to go along for the ride. It's brave and silly and bittersweet, all at the same time.

ONE FINAL REQUEST
Danielle Harward

The mailroom was empty. I checked it twice.

Turning my arm to the inside of my elbow, I revealed a small tattoo of a key, gold against my green skin.

"Post," I murmured.

My skin stretched and writhed until a small key formed. I plucked it from my arm and opened my mailbox.

I hated the stupid law that banned the usable tattoos that let you carry useful items right on your skin. But after someone in a museum had whipped out a gun from a tattoo, the restriction came in full force.

As a tattoo artist, that rarely stopped me.

My mailbox revealed nothing but bills, so I closed it, leaving them inside. I pressed the key to my skin and watched as it melted back into my arm. I sighed. The bills were piling up. I had to do something about that soon.

It was then that I smelled it. Blood. And cookies.

Trolls have a terrifyingly good sense of smell. The blood had the faintest hint of rose within it, and in an instant, my boots slammed against the stairwell as I took the old apartment building's steps in twos and threes. In that moment, I would have given anything to be wrong, but as I reached the landing, I skidded to a halt.

Trish.

Her apartment door was open, and the police stood inside. A Cerberus hound, its leash held by an elven cop, tugged as it sniffed. Blood pooled on the ground just beyond its paws.

Across the hall, a plate of cookies sat at our nocturnal neighbor's door. They smelled of Trish, too.

"Rex! Rex your alarm!" Trisha had yelled that morning.

Our walls were paper thin in this run-down apartment on the west side of Detroit. I was sure Trish could hear my alarm as if it was right next to her head. I'd left it going.

I heard her move within her apartment. Probably ripping a robe out of her closet, so she could come over to mine. I've placed several locks on my door, but no lock could keep out a pixie. Not one determined enough. So I wasn't surprised when she appeared in my apartment.

"You know, my door is closed for a reason," I said.

Trish tsked and strode past me, placing one manicured finger on the alarm clock to silence it. "I wouldn't have to if you weren't in here sulking."

I side-eyed her.

Even in her fluffy robe, she was tiny. Her slight frame and purple-tinted skin reflected in the light. Like usual, she smelled of roses and a little sulfur. If I didn't hear her—which was rare—I could always smell her coming.

Though I was at least a foot and a half taller than her, she wasn't intimidated by me.

"I'm not in the mood," I muttered.

"You were so much happier at dinner last night. What happened between now and then?"

I shook my head. "I just kept dreaming of Charlie."

Charlie, the brother who raised me, had died two years ago. My dreams liked to repeat his death over and over. I hadn't been asleep since 2 a.m. because of it.

Her wings fluttered behind her back, crystal clear and long like a dragonfly's.

They settled again as she pursed her lips and went into the kitchen. Pans banged, and my fridge opened and closed as she worked to make who knows what with the little food I had left.

"If you don't start getting ready, you're going to be late for work."

She had cooked me breakfast while I got ready. Even mentioned that she might make some cookies for the nocturnal creature who lived across from us. We had never seen them, and she was always trying to coax them out.

"Son, you can't be here." A dwarven cop snapped me from my daze.

I pointed, keeping my hands where he could see them. "That's my apartment."

"You're a neighbor, eh?"

"Yeah... What happened?"

"Not sure as of yet. Do you know of any enemies she might have had?"

My eye was drawn to the blood again, the elf and the Cerberus stood near it. The elf let the Cerberus sniff and rummage through other things in her apartment.

"Is she okay?"

The dwarf's frown turned so low that it slipped into the bushel of his beard. "No, son. She's dead."

I gripped the railing so hard it creaked in protest.

"You were close then?"

"Yes."

"Did the victim have any enemies?"

"Her name is Trish... Trisha, actually... She preferred to be called Trish."

The dwarf eyed me but wrote it down. A static noise grew in my head as I took in his words. Dead. Trish was dead.

"You know it wasn't your fault, right? Charlie's death, I mean." Trish had watched me as she said it. Her elbow rested on my dusty counter with her head cradled in her hand.

I hunched over my plate, shoveling down the eggs she'd magicked into my apartment and cooked for me. At her comment, I slowed.

That response was enough for her. She leaned forward. "There was nothing you could have done."

I swallowed. "I told you I don't want to talk about it."

Her wings fluttered again, and her gaze turned icy. One thing you never wanted to do — one thing all creatures understood — was piss off a pixie. It was fairly hard, due to their good nature and their tendency toward a zen way of life, but I could tell I was tugging on the end of her rope.

I switched the topic. "Thanks for the spaghetti last night. It was great."

"Yes, and thank you for listening while I prattled on about dragons. It made your meager offerings worthwhile," she teased.

We tried to eat together once a week, always at my place. She didn't like people coming into hers, and I never asked why. We were the only ones on our floor besides our reclusive nocturnal neighbor, and the fourth apartment had been empty ever since I moved in. Our landlord always tried to get it rented, but he'd had no takers so far.

Since Trish and I shared vaguely the same schedule, she had decided we would be friends. It was annoying at first. I had been alone ever since Charlie, and this was the first apartment I could afford. Having a nosy neighbor wasn't something I wanted, but she was kind, gentle, and loved taking care of others. Once she had gotten through my initial icy barrier, we became family, and it had been that way for the past few years. It didn't take me long to realize not only was she all I had, but I was all she had as well.

"Son?" the dwarf asked.

I shook my head. Enemies? Trish? "No," I said. "But she was a monster rights activist."

The dwarf wrote it down. I could tell by the furrow of his brows he didn't appreciate her calling herself a monster rights activist. The government didn't appreciate anyone with a differing opinion from theirs. They worked hard to keep any and all untrainable monsters away from our city.

Ever since the Rising, Earth had been overtaken by every type of monster known to creatures, and most of our cities had been destroyed. We built heavy walls around those that remained — about sixty of them — and retreated within them. Flying was dangerous, too, many monsters had wings. Portals became a big deal; allowing us to move between cities without ever leaving their safety of their walls. Travel for trade or commerce was nearly impossible without them.

The dwarf handed me a card. "Call me if you think of anything more. We'll be by later to ask you some questions."

He stepped aside, allowing me access to my apartment. I moved in a blur, fumbling with the key in my pocket as the cops' chatter filled our small hallway.

I forced myself to take a deep breath.

I wasn't a particular fan of cops. They hadn't done much to find Charlie's killers, even though I told them I'd seen the sprites that did it. But there were gangs in Detroit that even the cops refused to deal with, so the crime had gone unpunished. They claimed I must have been mistaken.

My door thumped into something as I opened it. I peered behind it. A package with a purple envelope sat on my floor.

Trish.

As quickly as I could, I slipped inside and locked the door behind me.

I scooped up the envelope and ripped it open. Trish's scrawling handwriting flowed on the page.

Rex,

I'm sorry to throw this on you, but they're coming. I won't survive. They've been after me for a while.

But I have one final request.

You must save him, Rex. You must get him out of the city. I refuse to let him be taken advantage of by anyone.

Take him to a man named Earl at the 23rd and Main subway platform, at the northern wall. He'll ask you a question. You must answer it correctly for him to help you, but if you do, he can get you to a place where you can get out of the city.

You'll need a boat. Oh, and be sure to take our neighbor with you. He has an understanding of the underground tunnels you'll need. He'll know the way out, and you can trust him.

Once you get out of the city, go to the top of the highest peak you see. Be there before midnight tomorrow. Another will come to take him to a safe place.

Please do this for me. Know that I have loved our time together. Remember how the government would try to use him. How anyone would try to use him. He doesn't deserve such treatment. Only you can change that outcome.

I've named him Everest, after the great dragon which once sprung from that mountain.

Everest is always the answer.

All my love

—Trish

My eyes blurred as I finished reading. She'd known her attackers were coming. She hadn't run or tried to get my help. She'd accepted her fate. The paper crinkled beneath my hands as I thought of strangling the life out of whatever creature had harmed her.

A scratching noise came from the box. I sniffed and leaned toward it, pulling at the lid. I smelled sulfur. Scratching and whimpering from inside increased as I touched it. Slowly, I lifted up the lid and peered inside.

A small dragon peered back.

I shut the lid.

The dragon mewled, scratching at the inside of the box.

Dragons were highly illegal. They were one of the top monsters the government had outlawed and declared should be killed on sight, after marking them as unintelligent with no ability to be trained.

Of course, it was a dragon.

At dinner, that had been all Trish talked about. She'd spoken of their nesting and breeding habits, which were uninteresting to a troll like me. But listening was better than pissing her off, so I'd nodded politely when she went off on a long-winded rant about how the government had gravely miscalculated them. How dragons were some of the most powerful and intelligent monsters on Earth. But because they often didn't agree with the government's agenda, they'd been marked as *unintelligent*. I remembered how she'd said that word with a sneer.

She'd also said that there were more uses for a dragon. The government had all but hunted them to extension, which created a problem for the environment. Her theory was that we wouldn't have so many monsters roaming outside the walls, scratching to get in, if they hadn't destroyed the dragon population.

It's like taking the apex predator out of an area and wondering why the deer have suddenly become a problem. Trish had said.

I lifted the box lid.

The dragon peered out again.

A door banged, and retreating steps fried my nerves, making me jump. The dragon hissed in turn. The cops were leaving, but if they saw the dragon, I was dead. The punishment for having such a creature was the death penalty.

I swallowed.

"Everest?" I murmured.

He crept forward, sticking his long neck out of the box and putting his small face near mine. He was about as large as a cat — for now. If I remembered Trish's ramblings correctly, he would double in size every week until he reached maturity.

Each shining purple scale flowed along with the next. His watchful eyes were yellow, gazing at me with interest.

He mewled.

"Shh," I said, putting a finger to my lips. "We have to be quiet."

He cocked his head to the side at that but watched in silence.

"Are… Are you hungry?"

Everest mewled again.

So much for intelligence.

I went to my kitchen, hoping to find a plate of spaghetti in the refrigerator. Trish usually tried to leave some leftovers from our dinners. She always claimed it was my right as host, but I was fairly sure she just wanted to make sure I was fed. I blinked back the tears as I pulled out the plate.

When I turned back however, the dragon was gone.

My eyes snapped around the room, then realized he was sitting on the counter beside me, staring eagerly at the plate. Had he teleported over? He stood up on his hind legs, small, leathery wings flared out for balance. The muted light in my apartment reflected off him. I put down the plate and watched him snap up its contents. He looked like the finest crystal. A creature this beautiful certainly didn't belong in my dirty apartment.

I read Trish's note again, debating on how to tell our nocturnal neighbor that I had to drag him along with me. Everest watched me with one eye as he continued to eat.

This couldn't be happening. I gripped her note. We had to go. "Come on," I called, pointing to the box.

Everest didn't move. Only watched with wide, yellow eyes as he licked the tomato sauce from his jaw.

"You've got to get back in the box."

Everest huffed and turned away, curling on top of my countertop in the sun.

You can't force a dragon to do anything.

I remembered Trish's words from dinner and winced. He was small. Maybe I could force it?

They have untold power that no one truly knows the limits of. That's why the government is so scared of them. Even the smallest dragon could probably mow down a large portion of the city if it was angry.

I had sat there, eating my spaghetti and letting her prattle on. I guessed now she had been telling me all this for a reason.

"Fine, no box. But we have to go, and you have to hide. Can you help me out here?"

Everest lifted his head and blinked at me. Slowly, catlike, he stretched before crossing the counter to me, taking small, careful steps.

"Any day now."

He leapt from the counter and into my arms. I caught him with a gasp, and he scuttled inside my leather coat, curling up near my side. He gave a satisfied warble.

"I'm glad you're comfy."

I zipped up my coat and prayed to any god that would listen that the police wouldn't come back as I stepped out of my apartment.

The smell of blood and cookies still lingered. Everest whimpered. Trish's door had black and yellow tape crisscrossed over it. I swallowed, unable to take my eyes off it.

Everest whimpered again, breaking me from my trance.

I looked at our neighbor's door. The plate of cookies was now gone, so they were home and awake. I braced myself. Nocturnal creatures were often decent and got more of a bad rap then they deserved, but that didn't mean there weren't still a fair number of them I didn't want to come across. I tried to go to his door quietly, wincing at every creak from the shabby floor.

I knocked twice.

Silence.

The door smelled odd, almost like a campfire's smoke. I knocked again. Still no answer.

This was stupid. In all our time living near to this creature, we had never once seen it. How did Trish know I could trust him anyway? I would do this alone.

As I shifted my weight to turn, a sound came from the other side of the door. A scraping of claws. My blood ran cold. All went silent again, but I could feel them. I could *smell* them. The smoke stench was stronger now. They had to be just on the other side of the door. Waiting. Listening.

I swallowed and knocked twice more.

Everest shifted against me, squirming to see. I pushed his little body back within the safety of my coat.

"Go away." Their voice was quiet, drawn.

"I need to speak with you." My voice was rawer than I expected. It sounded like I choked out the words. I hoped the creature didn't notice.

"No. Go away."

My fist clenched and unclenched. I didn't have much time. The dragon squirming within my coat could be revealed any second if someone walked past. We had to get moving. So, I tried the only thing I could think of to get a quick result.

"Trish is…dead."

More silence. That told me all I needed to know. If this creature didn't care about her and didn't have the decency to at least acknowledge the loss, then I didn't need him.

I turned to leave when the door opened just a sliver. The smoke smell overwhelmed my senses so much that I wondered if he had a fire in his apartment. Then I glanced back and saw him.

It took every amount of discipline I had not to flinch. The creature looking out at me was a ghoul.

A creature who delighted in the death of other creatures. A creature whose body was black as the night and shifted with the shadows. There was no differentiation between ends of his fingers and the tips of his claws, which came to a sharp point. But the worst part about a ghoul was his teeth. They were long and jagged, each ending at a deadly point which crossed at the jaw like an Angler fish. They could unhinge their jaw and consume an entire body whole.

"I didn't do anything to her," he said. His jaw moved in an odd way. His teeth scraped against one another.

"No… I… She told me to come talk to you. I need your help."

His large eyes, almost as wide as the top of a mason jar with hardly a sliver of an iris, got wider. "You need my help?"

Everest squirmed in my jacket, and I put a hand over the spot where he sat. At my movement, the ghoul backed up a step.

I realized he was scared. Of me. That was almost laughable. While I grew up on the streets and knew my way around a lock pick and a knife, the creature in front of me could have swallowed me whole.

Well, it might have taken him two bites. Now that I really looked at him, I realized he was smaller than most ghouls; thinner, too.

"I know you didn't hurt her. I don't want to hurt you either."

It almost surprised me to find that my words were true. This creature, though horrifying to look at, was scared, and Trish said she trusted him. I would take her word over anyone else's.

"Your jacket is moving."

I patted Everest, trying to calm him. He squirmed some more trying to nuzzle his way out and see the new creature in front of me. I zipped my jacket up further.

"Yeah, uh. That's what I need your help with. I can show you what it is, just not here."

The ghoul considered.

"What is your name?"

"Devan Bleak," he answered, watching me fight my own jacket.

"Can I come in, Devan?"

"No."

The answer was quick. Quick enough that I decided I probably didn't want to know what was in his apartment.

"But we can go to your place."

It was my turn to consider. I had to get out of this hall, and Trish said to trust him. So, I swallowed again and nodded, leading him to mine.

Out in the light of the hallway, my suspicions were confirmed. He was smaller than me and much thinner. He preferred the shadows, sticking to them and avoiding what light he could.

"Hold on," I told him at my door. "Let me draw the shades."

His gruesome mouth got worse as it pulled open wider. It was only after I ducked back into my place and my involuntary shiver had passed, that I realized Devan had been smiling. I snapped my shades shut. It wasn't as dark as his place had been, but hopefully it was enough. I went back to the door and gestured him in.

He blinked several times. The setting sun must still hurt his eyes.

"Sorry. I don't have great blinds."

He shrugged and looked around at my sparse belongings.

Everest squeaked his displeasure and decided he had enough of me. One minute he was against my side, and the next he once again sat on my counter.

Devan gasped. "Is that…?"

I ran a hand through the unmanageable tuft that was my hair. "Yeah…"

Everest watched Devan Bleak.

Devan Bleak watched back.

He stepped forward, stretching a clawed hand out toward the dragon. Everest arched his back into him, and Devan scratched his scales. He emitted a low sound, almost a growl. A purr.

"Huh. He likes you."

Devan looked at me as if he forgot I was there. "Oh yes." He looked sheepish. "I didn't ask your name."

"Rex."

"Rex," he repeated. He looked at the dragon again. "Dragons are illegal."

I was getting the idea that he liked to point out the obvious. "I need to get him out of the city. Trish said you could help me with that."

He blinked. His mouth screwed up in what could only be a grimace. Everest continued to arch under Devan's clawed fingers as he lightly scratched. "But I do not know the way out of the city."

"She said you knew about under the city."

"Yes, I do."

"Okay. That's what I need then."

"But I don't know how to get you out."

"Yes! I know that." I turned away from them both, gripping the counter. Why had Trish wanted to bring him? He obviously would only slow me down.

"You are upset."

"Yes, I'm upset!" I snapped. "One of the only people I had left just died!"

The ghoul stepped away but did not cower. "That is sad," he murmured.

"Look, we just need to get to Earl at the 23rd and Main subway platform. We need to get there quickly before the cops come back."

Devan frowned, revealing more teeth than I thought possible. "I believe we are too late for that."

A fist thumped against my door.

"Rex, Creature Police Department. Open up. We need to ask a few questions."

I put a quick finger to my lips. Devan nodded, and we both stood still.

I eyed the door. My apartment's small balcony had a fire escape. If we rushed for it, they would know we were in here. The best thing to do would be to wait for them to go.

The fist thumped again. "Rex, open up. We have some questions for you."

My stomach dropped. I pointed toward the balcony, and Devan nodded, reaching his hand toward Everest, who took his time smelling it before stepping on.

"Perhaps we should come back later?" asked a cop outside the door.

"No way. There were remnants of a dragon egg in that apartment. He had to know. We're talking to him now, or we are searching the place."

The fist slammed against my door again. "Last warning, sir. Open up!"

Everest crawled onto Devan's claws.

"We have to go now!" I said, tugging him toward the fire escape.

Devan pulled a pair of dark glasses from his pocket and put them on, flipping his hood up as well. I grabbed Trish's note and stuffed it into my pocket, then slid open the heavy glass door that led to the balcony. The ghoul hissed at the light but followed, and we started down the fire escape.

My apartment door slammed open.

"CPD!" the cop yelled, going for his gun at the sight of us trying to escape.

My heart raced as I looked down at the dumpster below. It was fairly full. Lots of cardboard. Shouldn't be too bad.

"Brace yourself," I snarled and grabbed the back of Devan's hoodie, throwing us both off the fire escape.

Devan screamed as we fell.

Slamming into the dumpster, things crushed and cracked beneath us as they took our weight. I scrambled up, half dragging Devan out of the bin.

"You threw me!"

"Come on!"

The cops appeared above us, their guns raised.

I continued to pull him, yanking him toward the alley exit into the busy traffic of creatures walking on the sidewalk. Shots popped behind us, ringing in my ears.

Devan gasped and shimmered; his form changing. Everest dropped from his hiding place as he dissipated. The cops shouted, falling over themselves at the sight of a dragon. I scooped him up quickly and turned back to Devan.

In his place, stood an ostrich.

"What?" I spat the words before I could think.

"They were shooting at us!" he honked back.

I kept running.

Devan followed, keeping pace easily on his long, skinny legs.

"Are you kidding me? Ghouls turn into ostriches when they are scared? I thought that was just a legend!"

"No! Just when their lives are threatened!"

It was so unbelievable; I almost laughed. *Almost.* But then I realized how easy it would be to spot an ostrich in this crowd. "Keep running!"

Shouts broke out behind us as we continued down the street. The cops had gotten outside the building. We surged forward. Everest hissed, looking back at them.

"Not now," I reminded him.

He ducked back into my jacket with a reprimanded look.

Creatures of all kinds jumped out of our way as we raced past. Some didn't move quick enough, and I either slammed into them or had to find a way to dodge. Devan was surprisingly agile in his ostrich form. He stayed close behind me as I thundered through the crowd, yelling at anyone in my way.

I glanced back to see the cops gaining on us.

"Distract," I snapped.

A raven tattoo, black as oil, stretched and pulled away from my neck, bursting out of my shirt as it soared toward the cops. It slammed into the closest one, cawing and raking at his skin.

I felt the blow as the raven was swatted away, and the next as it flew into the second cop with angry caws.

Devan eyed the raven as we ran. "Isn't that illegal?"

"Seriously?"

Everest watched with curiosity over my shoulder. Devan clamped his beak shut. We kept running.

◆

By the time we reached the 23rd and Main subway platform, my breath was ragged. I plunged down the stairs.

Devan tried to scramble down them as well, but ended up rolling in a heap of feathers and long legs. At the bottom, he shimmered back into his regular form. I hauled him up, grimacing at the sight of his teeth so close to my face. The raven dove down and slammed into my neck, settling there once more as I looked around.

I blinked, trying to focus on our goal. No one was down here except a homeless creature on a chair against the wall.

I checked my directions. *Against the northern wall.*

"What now?" Devan asked.

I strode forward. "Are you Earl?"

The homeless creature looked up at me. He was a pixie to my surprise. His wings were ripped and tattered, and his purple skin was so dirty that it looked brown. "What's the answer?"

"To what?"

"The question."

Steps sounded at the subway entrance. The cops shouted for civilians to move.

"You didn't ask me a question," I said.

"What's the answer?" he repeated.

My fists curled.

Devan cleared his throat. "Perhaps that was the question."

Earl glanced at him then away, disinterested, before turning back to me.

The cops' footsteps echoed on the platform now. "How the hell am I supposed to give you an answer? It could be anything."

"It's the correct answer," Earl said blandly.

The cops saw us now, and were drawing their guns.

Devan put his hands up. "Maybe your friend said something about it?" he whispered.

I put my hands up as well, hoping Everest didn't wiggle free. That was it.

Everest is always the answer.

"Stay where you are now!" the cops yelled. "Don't do anything stupid. Get down on the ground and put your hands behind your head."

I complied. I let my knees hit the platform pavement. Devan followed my lead, looking at the cops with wide eyes.

I looked at Earl. "Everest."

The pixie's eyes flashed, and his mouth cocked into a smile. In one lightning-fast motion, he stood and kicked the chair toward the cops. It morphed, growing larger. A mouth opened and a tongue lolled out as a mimic the size of a small car stood in front of us.

It wasted no time and launched itself into the cops.

"Come!" the pixie shouted as he slammed the palm of his hand against the wall. The brick liquified, parting to reveal a portal.

Screams erupted from the cops as Earl pulled us through.

The odd sensation of a portal was like breaking the surface of a pool of water. My first instinct was to take a large breath. So, it wasn't a surprise when we came out the other side gasping.

Earl shoved himself into my face. "You ever bring heat with you again, and I'll let them arrest you."

I nodded. "Sorry."

Satisfied, the pixie turned away and slipped back through the portal. Once he was gone, the wall solidified once more.

"Well, that was close," sniffed Devan.

"Too close."

My coat wiggled as Everest poked his head out and warbled his agreement. The light from his scales danced around us, and I couldn't stop myself from reaching up and scratching his neck. He curled closer into me, pulling himself up more out of my coat so that my hands had more access to him.

"Where are we anyway?" Devan said.

It smelled terrible down here. We both looked up.

Several creatures stared at us.

The first thing I noticed was the hunger in their eyes as they looked at Everest. Many of them were in ragged clothes and had dirt across their faces. Probably homeless, by the look of them.

We had stopped in front of some kind of market. I had a feeling it was an illegal one from the way some creatures hid their stuff from us. And every single one stared at Everest.

Alongside them was some kind of canal. Dirty water. The gross aroma wafted off of it. But a few boats swayed there. They were not well-made but still floating vessels.

"Rex?" Devan murmured as some creatures took a step closer.

I reached up into my jacket, fumbling against my right shoulder. "Protect me."

The familiar pull of my skin itched as a dagger formed in my hand. I pulled it out, letting the light glitter from it. Some of the creatures eyed it, but most only had eyes for Everest. I tried to tuck him back into my jacket, but he refused to hide and let out a hiss toward the oncoming creatures.

Don't trust anyone.

Various creatures reached for weapons, sharp and blunt. There were too many. Aside from the occasional alley scrap, I knew jack about handling a crowd. I grabbed Devan. "Run!"

Shoving him forward, we broke hard for the boats.

Cries of anger followed, and the homeless creatures lurched forward as well. In my peripheral vision, I saw several objects fly toward us. I braced for the impact... but it never came.

Everest had wiggled his head and half a wing up over my shoulder. He growled at our pursuers and glowed. As we hauled ourselves into a boat, a large, purple bubble followed us. Creatures slammed against it trying to get through, but the bubble held as we pulled away in one of the more decent boats — one just big enough for the two of us.

The bubble faded as we set out into the canal. I picked up the paddles, pushing us further away as hard as I could. But creatures were already in pursuit.

"Rex?"

"Devan, I see them."

I hauled the paddles back as they left the banks. Many of their boats were little more than rafts made of junk. But they kept coming, growling and hissing.

As we descended into the canal tunnels, darkness fell. I blinked, squinting into it. "You'll need to guide me." I murmured to the ghoul.

"You can't see in the dark?"

"Not like you." I grunted with another pull of the oars. I could see better than some creatures, but not better than a ghoul. Being nocturnal, he probably saw every detail.

He scooted to the front of the boat, whispering directions to me as our pursuers followed. Some projectiles — trash most likely — slammed into the water alongside us as they roared their displeasure.

"Rex, turn left here!" Devan urged. "I know this place. We can lose them."

I rocked us a hard enough left that Devan almost fell overboard. Everest shrieked and flapped his wings for balance. But the shouts of displeasure soon faded behind us.

"Okay. They stopped," Devan murmured.

I willed my thundering heart to calm as we stayed quiet for a moment, skimming through the water. Everest shivered and climbed back inside my coat. I rolled my eyes skyward, of course, now he hid.

"Where are we going?" I asked.

Devan put a finger to his lips. "Be quiet, okay?" he whispered. "And uh…don't scream."

His words unnerved me, and I looked past him at the river ahead.

Several mounds sat within the river. Mounds with creatures standing on them. One per mound to be specific. They were tall and dark and gazed steadily at the ceiling, unmoving. A shiver ran across my skin as we inched closer.

They were ghouls.

Each one was pure black with a large mouth, full of teeth. Their eyes gazed upward, never looking away from the hole directly above them. Soon, something scraped through one of them, and I watched in horror as the body of some poor creature slipped out. But I only caught a flash of blue skin before the ghoul directly below the hole unhinged their jaw and opened wide, taking in the falling creature with a single, massive gulp.

I had to shove my fist in my mouth to stop the scream.

The crunching and gurgling sound that came afterward was just as bad. Somewhere nearby, came the scraping of another creature sliding down the hole and dropping. The horrid noise started anew.

"Oh my gods."

"It's okay. They are dead," Devan whispered.

I looked at him, unable to hide my disgust.

His mouth crooked into what looked like a wince as he spread his arms. "Welcome to body disposal services."

I shuddered, keeping my gaze away from them and only on Devan. But that didn't offer much relief as his teeth glimmered at me.

"I work at a morgue. This is a part of it. We dispose of the bodies after services have been completed. We've had to, ever since we ran out of room to bury them."

The walls stopped city growth. And when you have to choose between a plot of land to bury bodies or more housing…

"They said they would be turned to ash."

Devan nodded. "Well, yeah. That's true. When we are done with them, only ash remains. It's deposited in this water."

The sound started up again close to us. Too close. I forced myself to look only at our pathway as I steered us through. No ghouls looked down at us, though I was careful to avoid touching them or their islands with my oars. "Why?"

"I'm told the water drains somewhere outside the city."

"No," I said, thinking of Trisha's thin body sliding down one of those disgusting tubes and into the maw of a ghoul. She deserved better than that. "Why don't they just burn them instead?"

Devan blinked as if I wasn't getting something. "Because we need to eat too? I don't know if you've noticed, but meat is hard to get these days. And if we consumed only market meat, we would clear the shelves."

I couldn't stop the shudder that ran through me. But he was right in all the wrong, horrible ways. Would Trish be disposed down here? Had she been already? The tears that pricked my eyes weren't a surprise, but I still brushed them away angrily.

Everest poked his head up, nuzzling my cheek.

I swallowed hard, remembering the task at hand. The task I would do for her.

I stopped. "Where did you say this water goes?"

Devan had curled in on himself, probably sensing my displeasure. He uncurled slightly now. "I'm told it goes out of the city."

It clicked.

Oh, and be sure to take our neighbor with you. He has an understanding of the underground tunnels you'll need to use. He'll know the way out, and you can trust him.

"Do you know where to go to get out of the city?"

Devan looked up to me, quickly glancing at the other ghouls before dropping his voice. "I'm not positive, but I've often wondered if you could find it by following the flow of the river."

Trish had planned all of this. Had she been going to do this herself? Probably. Rescuing a baby dragon was an extraordinary chance to save a monster. I could see her taking that chance.

◆

I rowed in the direction of the flowing water. Devan turned, looking out past me. It wasn't long before I heard the burbling of a faster water flow. I raced toward it, pulling us forward.

Soft light radiated from around the corner. I grinned and hauled us forward.

Right into a police barrier.

There is no such thing as skidding to a stop on water. I yanked my oars backward, but our boat's velocity worked against me as it crunched into the metal police speeder.

"Oh gods!" Devan cursed as we were thrown forward.

"Halt!" the police shouted. Every creature above us stood badged and in black. Each one aimed a gun our way.

"Rex?" Devan nudged. His hands were already up.

Slowly, I put up my own, eyeing the dagger next to me. I wasn't stupid enough to challenge the ten or so guns trained on me. I glanced again at the waterfall. If we jumped, it could be to our deaths. I had no idea where it came out or if we would survive the fall. But if they arrested us now, we would know nothing but a small cell and slivers of sunlight until our execution.

Trish had sent us this way. She had to have known about the waterfall. Had to have known we could survive it.

But then again, Trish had wings.

"Get down on your knees. Hands behind your head."

Devan complied, but I didn't move.

I trusted Trish.

Everest wiggled from my jacket, slipping his body out, between us and the police. Some gasped; others recoiled. Their guns switched to aiming at him. He watched them. His head cocked, curious, as he flared his wings.

Someone's trigger finger slipped.

The bullet should have hit him. But instead, it stopped midair, inches from him.

The tiny dragon bared his teeth and hissed. All his scales stood on end. A purple glow pulsed from him as he made himself as large as he could – which was about the height of a chair – in response to the threat.

More fingers moved to the trigger, but Everest was faster.

My skin itched, but I dared not move. Every part of me screamed as my tattoos began to writhe. The tiger on my chest, the raven on my neck, and the laughing skull on my shoulder. Even the inanimate objects like the cross or the crystal under the moon on my back. Every single tattoo pulled away from my skin and made themselves flesh. Led by the roaring tiger himself, they rushed toward the police barricade.

Everest snorted in triumph as my tattoos attacked the police barrier. But then a new kind of hell started.

I felt every hit my tattoos took.

When they slammed into the boats, I took the blow. When they barreled into the police, I felt the punch. And when one of the police slapped them away, it was my chest, neck, back, and shoulder that felt the sting.

"We've gotta go!" Devan grabbed my arm as Everest jumped onto his shoulder and threw us both overboard.

I hated water. It was a gratuitous amount of hate that I probably shouldn't have for an element that I need to keep me alive. But this cloudy brown water was mixed with the city's waste and peppered with the ashes of the dead, so for once I was justified in thoroughly hating the experience of being submerged. As we plunged deep, the current pulled us under and through the police barriers.

I gasped, rising to the surface on the other side. Devan did the same. His horrid teeth mashed together as he spat out the water filling in his throat. Everest clung to his shoulder.

The oncoming fall was a blur as I felt each tattoo struggle against the police. I was paralyzed, unable to do much except let the river throw me out. I barely had time to wonder if my tattoos would feel my pain before we tumbled down.

Below us stretched a great expense of water. We slammed into it, plunging under the foaming surface. Unlike in the river above, this time, I sank *deep* underwater. My feet brushed the bottom, and I pushed off, toward the top.

It took longer than I would have liked to break the surface.

As I breached, my tiger tattoo slammed back onto my chest, nearly sending me under again. The rest peppered me with their arrival, each releasing the aching in my skin until only dull pain throbbed.

Devan broke the surface a few feet away, Everest still clutching onto him. I wondered how deep the dragon's claws had dug into his shoulder.

We dragged ourselves to the shore with shuddering breaths and coughing.

I started to laugh. I couldn't help it. The laughter rolled off my shoulders and shook my body. Everest detached himself from Devan and scurried over to me, sniffing my face and rubbing the top of his head against my jaw.

"What on earth is so funny?" Devan asked.

My grin split wide. "He saw me activate my tattoo, so he used his power to do the same and brought every damned piece of ink on me to life. Half of those weren't even meant to be removed."

Everest joined in with my cackle, raising his head high and emitting a series of chirps.

"Of all the things he could do, that's what he chose."

Devan sat up, looking concerned.

"My point is," I explained, the last of my laughter fading, "that is the last way I expected to get out of that situation."

The ghoul shook his head. His mouth twisted into what most likely was a smile for a ghoul, and he stood.

We were on the edge of a rocky beach, the dark, spiked wall surrounding Detroit rose high above us. Dirty water poured every fifty feet or so out into the wild earth that surrounded it. The remnants of a road stood nearby, but it was overgrown, long since taken back by nature. I imagined the odd hills and canyons around us had once been ruined buildings, but they were deep under roots now.

I heard wingbeats.

Everest hadn't stopped his chirping. He continued, stretching his neck to hold his head high, his wings flared, and chest out.

The wingbeats grew heavier as they neared.

Even in the night sky, she glowed. A purple dragon.

She was so massive that each wing beat thrashed the plant life around us. Even the trees bent in her wake. Everest's chirping grew louder and more consistent. As she landed, she knocked both me and Devan to the ground while the earth shuddered beneath her.

I knew I should get up, but I didn't dare. I could have stood in her yellow eye, which she now cast toward the wall. She flared her wings up, teeth bared.

Weapons powered up along the wall. I heard their whine as red lasers centered on her. As they ripped through the air toward us, missiles and bullets slammed into a purple bubble that now surrounded us. It reverberated in response to the bombardment, unbreaking. The dragon snorted in satisfaction.

Then she looked down at us.

Everest kept chirping. He stood on his hind legs, calling up to her in shrill squeaks. She lowered her face to him, then turned one of her great eyes upon us.

"Is this your mother?" I murmured, too afraid to stand.

His chittering response was enough for me.

"Go ahead then. Go to her."

As if he needed no other encouragement, he leapt forward, using his wings to glide to her. Tenderly, she nuzzled him as he purred and vibrated beneath her.

Something brushed against my mind. I knew Devan felt it, too, by the way he flinched. I'd heard tales of a dragon controlling someone. That they could do it as easily as pulling a string. But I could not resist the force which entered my head and spoke in a radiating voice.

He tells me you saved him.

My eyes nearly popped out of my socket. "You are intelligent. You can speak!"

She did not deign to respond to my outburst. *I will grant you one wish.*

Devan gasped, looking at me. She glared up at the military, who continued to bombard her shield, before looking back down at us.

Hurry.

Devan's response was quick. "I want to be able to eat normal food, like other creatures."

The dragon shifted her gaze to him and blinked once. *It will be done.*

She turned to me. Even through the fear, I found myself in wonder. I realized now Trish had discovered the truth. Dragons were intelligent and had rebelled against our government's control. Why hadn't I seen that before?

"Are there more eggs in the city?"

She nodded. Her eyes filled with sorrow. *Your kind raids my nests. My children never return.*

"Give me the power to find them. I know you can't breach the city, or you would have done so already. But I can. Send me back in with the power to find them, and I'll do everything I can to bring them back to you."

She turned her head, examining me. Everest warbled beneath her.

"Well, that makes my wish seem rather selfish," Devan murmured.

I paid him no mind. My eyes were only for the dragon.

That journey will not be an easy one, troll.

"I know."

She nodded once. *It shall be done.*

A flash of white light flared around us. I covered my eyes, so it wouldn't blind me. The world shifted, and then we landed on the hardwood floor of my apartment.

I looked at Devan. He touched his stomach and smiled. His teeth were still fearsome, but they were smaller, less goulish.

I felt a tingling under my skin. Something lurked there, an unknown power. We grinned at each other.

"Let's go save some dragons," I said.

Tami Veldura is an enby/aro/ace author of queer fiction. They have published short stories in several anthologies, including Fresh Starts, Hauntings, Love Among the Thorns, *and* Love is Like A Box of Chocolates, *and are a contributing member of the scifi magazine* Boundary Shock Quarterly. *They publish new work monthly, crossing every genre, but always featuring queer characters and found families.*

About this story, Tami says: "Necromancy is one of several short stories written to explore the character and world of Nariah, the bone witch from a previous short story, The Call of the Grim. *I've always been fascinated with bones, the process of decay, and what defines the dead. In a world where vampires have taken over, ruling cities like mafia families, Nariah must navigate a line between spiritual medium and reality. Along the way, she collects animal spirits willing to help. But not all are friendly, and some have fangs."*

I confess, while I like Nariah, I was thoroughly charmed by the grim – who was not at all what I had expected. The snake spirit captivated me as well, but it was the unexpected appearance of a certain fanged cast member – one who surprised Nariah as much as it surprised me – that sealed the deal.

NECROMANCY FOR DUMMIES
Tami Veldura

Nariah tied a colorful headband over her forehead and pressed it gently back to contain her tightly coiled hair. The chill in the night air prickled along her bare arms, bringing an electrifying awareness along with it. There were spirits on the rise.

Just over an hour ago Nariah had felt the call, a pressure under her breastbone, a yearning that couldn't be satisfied with mortal pleasures. The call of the grim. She'd followed it here to Magnolia Cemetery, and now looked out at the gently rolling grounds from the safety of the parking lot.

The magnolia tree at the caretaker house, older than Nariah at least, stretched over graves and ground alike, its stiff white blooms open in the moonlight, glowing like stardrops. Its soft scent permeated the grounds, pressing an ancient healing into the spirits who rested here. A magic older than the city itself. But something had disturbed that old rest. Spirits that should have been sleeping moaned in the darkness.

Nariah grabbed the bone-chain around her wrist, her eyes sharp on the rows. Spirits were mostly harmless; it was whatever disturbed them that kept Nariah on alert.

A dog *wuffed*. A deep, huffing greeting, the sound only a large creature could make. Nariah scanned the shadows until she spotted two glowing yellow eyes and a mouth of shining teeth beside the magnolia tree.

The grim stepped into moonlight, like a shadow come to life, his claws digging small furrows in the dirt that closed again behind him. He *wuffed* again, and Nariah released her bone charm. The grim had called her to this place.

"Hey, who's a good boy?" Nariah asked softly. She stepped off the pavement of the parking lot and onto the manicured grass. From the mortal world into the domain of spirits. The grim wiggled his docked tail and bounded toward her.

He was the size of a Great Dane, but stocky and wide like a Rottweiler. A small tank of muscle and teeth and sloppy tongue. He put his head down and charged. Nariah braced herself for impact. She took his hard head against her hip and slapped her hands on his shoulders to wrestle him onto his side where she could scratch his belly and squish his cheeks.

"Grim is a good boy, aren't you? Yes, you are." His hair was short and black like the night. Nariah's dark skin almost glowed by comparison.

The animal snorted at her and wiggled himself free. He bounded deeper into the cemetery, then looked back and wiggled his whole butt, his ears tall and attentive. *Come. Come with me.*

Nariah put a hand to her chest where the pressure built and checked her belt. Two bone charms in case of emergency and a ball-peen hammer all in their place. She followed the grim.

He led her between the headstones, down a slight incline, and around an old oak tree. Nariah paused to rest her palm on the stout trunk of the tree and whisper a prayer for strength.

A spirit moaned nearby. Nariah watched the transparent wisp rise out of a grave, like smoke or steam, unformed. It curled in on itself and moved within the rectangle confine of the grave, disturbed, but still tethered to the bones beneath.

The grim approached, ears forward, nose sniffing. The spirit reached out with equal curiosity. The grim sneezed suddenly. The spirit darted to its headstone. The grim huffed and moved on. This spirit, at least, posed no threat.

Deeper into the cemetery, more agitated spirits formed pieces of their former human selves. A hand, an outline of shoulders, or a suggestion of a head. They twisted over their graves and their moans sounded more like words. Warnings to turn back.

Nariah set her mouth in a line, kept her eyes sharp, and moved deeper. Spirits didn't rise up like this on their own, especially those settled in a graveyard as old as this one.

The grim led her to a crypt set into the earth. Pockmarks in the old stone dotted the face like liver spots and the decorative climbing vine that had been trained over the doorway now covered the entire upper facade, obscuring the crest and name of those buried within. Once upon a time, Nariah would have worried about a vampire rising with all this spirit activity. Not anymore. The vampires lived in high-rises and estates like wealthy bankers now, dipping their claws into human activity whenever they saw fit, offering protection from rival clans for a price. A mafia that demanded blood tribute instead of money.

The crypt might still hold a zombie or two, but she and the grim were used to handling the walking dead. It was the living Nariah struggled to understand.

A low, rhythmic chant caught Nariah's attention, and she put a hand on the grim's head, willing him to stay at heel. She crept around the side of the crypt and crouched at the corner.

Two rows of graves further in, stood a cheap folding table decorated with a dozen dark candles. A torn fabric acted as the altar surface, fluttering longer on the left than the right. Several ritual objects, likely bone, sat on the table, and the person chanting in front of the whole setup held one overhead long enough for Nariah to recognize the glint of crystal.

She wrinkled her nose. Nothing involving ritual in the middle of the night in a graveyard ever came out good. She should know, she'd dedicated her childhood to slaying zombies and her adulthood to settling wayward spirits.

The grim growled deep in his chest and Nariah put her hand on his head again. His desire to charge in, bite legs and ask questions later, spun up under her breastbone. What other solution could there be?

Nariah took a second to breathe through the grim's emotions and separate herself. He was just as much a spirit as the others rising out of their graves here, a being not quite of the mortal world any longer. He had the run of the entire graveyard, tasked with protecting the dead from the living and, should they rise, protecting the living from the dead. In thirty-five years, Nariah had seen a lot of weird things with a variety of strange powers, but she only had one: to see and speak with the dead.

So when the vampires rose out of their crypts ten years ago, Nariah had been there, standing with the grim, ready and willing to stop them.

She'd nearly died that night. Swore off spirit-work for almost two years before she answered another grim call. Everything and nothing had changed. The city might be run by vampires, but spirits still needed soothing.

The chanting suddenly picked up and the person at the altar lifted another, larger crystal overhead. Energy, crackling like lightning, burst from the crystal and struck the ground, a tree, and a headstone near Nariah. The headstone burst into dust and fragments and its disturbed spirit roared. It swelled over the grave, gaining form and voice in seconds, and its hollow eyes fell on Nariah.

The grim barked. The spirit sprouted two massive arms ending in hands with long claws that sank into the earth digging furrows several inches deep. Its growth became jerky. A blue spirit flame ignited in its eyes, burning excess power to keep the form stable. The beast's wavering edges steadied. Antlers sprouted from the spirit's head, wider than Nariah's car and decorated with sharp points. It bent forward, eyes locked on Nariah and horns at the ready.

Nariah couldn't keep the grim at bay. The dog lunged toward the much larger spirit, snarling and snapping. He tried to bite the form but got nothing but smoke for his trouble. Nariah stumbled backward, hand against the old crypt for balance while she tried to catch her breath.

The idiot at the altar was going to raise an entire graveyard of monsters and then what? Did they think they could control the enraged spirits?

Lightning struck across the dark graveyard and burst against the solid stone of the crypt, leaving a charred slash and a chunk missing.

The spirit roared. It seemed to pull itself out of the grave, forcing itself free. A leg with four claws on the foot slammed onto the ground. The grim dove in, trying to bite it, and the spirit snarled. It slapped its palm down and struck the dog like an errant pest, throwing him twenty feet with ease.

Nariah's heart tripped, and she braced herself on the crypt wall. She clawed at her own wrist, dragging a snake-spine bracelet off with an elastic snap. The bones clicked against each other as she held the bracelet up between herself and the monster spirit like it might do some good.

For several seconds nothing happened. Nariah's breath skittered away and her arm trembled, making the spirit she'd bound impossible to call. She needed to collect herself and calm down.

A thready laugh spilled between her teeth. Sure. Just calm down. So easy.

Nariah turned and ran to the opposite side of the crypt. Pressing her back to the cold stone, she held the bone bracelet in both hands, and tried to breathe. The enraged spirit was still bound to its grave, she was safe for a moment. She closed her eyes and counted breaths in, then out. She felt the age-rough stone at her back, the cool night air, and the fluttering beat of her heart. The next breath came a little easier.

Then the snake spirit emerged from Nariah's bracelet and wrapped gently around her wrist.

Nariah opened her eyes. It had been a small garter snake in life, hit by a car and left for dead on the side of the road. With a little time and attention, Nariah had given the body a proper burial so that the spirit could heal. Most injured spirits walked into the woods at the back of her house and she never saw them again, but a few, like this snake, decided to stay. So she'd cleaned the bones, strung them together, and carried the spirit with her. Now it perched on her wrist, its tiny eyes trained on her.

"I have a big thing to ask of you," Nariah whispered.

The little snake dropped off of her wrist, wiggled through the grass around the crypt, and paused at the corner, looking back at her. Her bond with the grim sat under her breastbone, throbbing like a second heartbeat, but the snake's connection ran through her veins instead, contracting and loosening as it moved.

Nariah pushed off the crypt wall and followed the garter snake around the corner.

By the time she caught up, her little snake had grown. It stretched two feet long. Three feet. It was growing with every gentle undulating wave through the grass. The length of a cobra. A cottonmouth. A python. Larger!

The ground trembled, and Nariah knew they were out of time. The enraged spirit had freed itself from its grave.

The snake shot forward, Nariah close behind. She slid to a stop at the edge of the crypt. Her garter snake had grown to match the monster, bigger than an anaconda with fangs to match. It darted under the monster's sweeping arms, wrapped itself up one beefy leg, then tangled around the beast's torso and neck. The monster roared. The snake had trapped one arm and it struggled to free itself until its legs tangled and it crashed to the ground.

The snake constricted.

Nariah had seen this once on a nature documentary. Snakes the size of trees wrapping around their victims and tightening slowly with every breath out until their prey died hours later of asphyxiation.

But spirits didn't have to breathe. And her little garter snake wasn't powered by unstable crystal lightning. Just the care and love Nariah had given its mortal body some months ago. They didn't have hours.

She had to find the grim and stop this ritual. Fast.

Nariah darted away from the titian struggle, following the pull of the grim under her chest. She nearly tripped over the black dog several rows away as he limped toward her, a front leg held up and dangling the way front legs should not. Damn. He also sported a series of cuts and scrapes from his flight through the yard. He chuffed at her.

Nariah bent and took his head in her hands. She kissed his big muzzle and pressed her love into the link they shared. "You did good, old boy. Go rest."

The grim whined, his nubby tail twitching, but Nariah insisted. "Go rest," she said again, pushing him around toward the southwest corner of the graveyard near where she had parked the car. The grim licked her chin and went. He would shoulder his way into the pile of freshly-turned dirt where he had been buried two hundred years before, and heal to rise again tomorrow.

It was up to Nariah to stop this ritual. Alone.

Nariah set her shoulders and checked the small ball peen hammer hanging from her belt. She wasn't much of a fighter since the zombies stopped rising, but she still had a mean tennis arm. She just had to get close enough to use it.

She jogged between gravestones, eyeing the way bluish lightning continued to snap across the field. She couldn't afford to let it strike another grave. One enraged spirit was more than enough.

Near the crypt, Nariah's snake had the monster spirit under control. But for how long?

Nariah circled the altar and wrinkled her nose at the charred smell of stone and ozone. Several candles burned on the folding table, casting weak light across the crystals and bone of the ritual. And a small lump of something, fur maybe.

The next bolt of lightning lit the entire graveyard with shallow blue light. A man performed the ritual, his face still, his eyes focused on the cluster of crystals in hand as he chanted. He transferred the crystal to one hand and stretched the other forward, palm down, to rest on the pile of fur on the table. Energy surged all around the altar, sweeping past Nariah with the tingle of static.

She tried to creep closer, but the static condensed. Pushing through it became more and more difficult, until at last the resistance snapped her backward, sliding Nariah along the ground into the sweep of the energy. She stumbled back and kept her feet.

Lightning sparked from the crystal in the man's hand to the table, where he focused. Excess energy scattered through the static wall and darted into the tree branches overhead. Sparks lingered, flashing as the energy grew, a ring of wind and power rising up to tear at the trees.

That was more than enough.

Nariah hefted her hammer, measuring the weight of it. It wasn't a weapon made for throwing, but Nariah had been throwing it for years all the same. It wasn't a precision instrument, and it didn't need to be. Nariah aimed for the man's chest, hauled back, and threw.

The hammer swung through the static wall like it didn't exist and crashed into the man's shoulder. He cried out, dropped the crystal, and grabbed at his shoulder, head swinging around to find Nariah. His pale face pinched.

"I was almost there," he shouted as the static swirl began to lose cohesion. Energy burst and popped. "I almost had it!"

"Had what?" Nariah backed up several steps to avoid stray sparks, her eyes flicking from the altar to the dropped crystal and back to the man's face. Interrupting a ritual was generally a bad idea. The energy called had to go somewhere, and this idiot had called up a lot of energy. When Nariah had to dissipate a ritual, she tried to send the energy into the earth where it could settle, but this whirlwind had nowhere to go.

"I almost had the answer. I'm trying to *save us*."

There was no accounting for crazy. Nariah shook her head, watching the pulsing energy fade into and out of this plane as it became more unstable. A blast arced into the sky like a spiritual solar flare. It sheared right through an oak branch, bringing the entire limb crashing down. Half of it landed inside the swirling static, and the exposed leaves curled, blackened, and were blown away like ash. The bark dried up next, flaking away as if the tree were on fire. Decay ate away at the branch until the weight of the base rolled it out of the static toward Nariah. It crunched against a tombstone, stopping close enough for Nariah to see small sparks of blue power still eating away at the wood.

Inside the whirlwind, the man reached for his crystal, but power crackled around the formation, then sparked into a bolt of lightning that struck the man's chest. He crumpled to the ground.

Nariah snatched her only other option off her belt. Two bone charms she had built with sage and salt. They were meant for dispelling small spirits—dogs, cats, the occasional raccoon—not for bringing a growing magical tornado under control.

Another flare of power burst through several gravestones as it ran across the grounds. It arced and lightning struck overhead.

Nariah ducked. She had to do something.

She threw both charms into the whirlwind. Unlike the hammer, the power snatched the charms immediately, sending them spinning and swirling. Nariah could feel the energy now, the huge weight of it drawing more power on its own. Her two little bone charms couldn't hope to contain it all. She needed a hundred.

Lightning flickered and snapped against the crypt, throwing broken stone in all directions. It snapped again to the tangled spirits nearby, the monster risen from its grave and the once-garter snake now wrapped around it. Power sliced through them both like a knife, bleeding them of energy so the whirlwind could feed itself.

The snake contracted. Nariah felt it shudder in her veins. Then it released all at once and both spirits were dragged by the rising power into the swirling static.

Nariah gasped and clutched her hand to her chest. Her very blood seemed to pulse in time with the whirlwind as it flashed and sparked, throwing strange blue light across the grounds. As the spirits were dragged around the rising tornado, Nariah grit her teeth against the sensation of snake scales being dragged through her veins. She was still connected to the snake spirit as it whipped around.

Something struck the snake and it instinctively flexed around the object. Power drained, like a sinking sensation in Nariah's stomach.

The snake had grabbed one of the bone charms.

Nariah snapped her head up, squinting at the flashing whirlwind. Her second charm whipped by, the bone and sage and salt carried by violent spirit energy. The charms alone weren't enough to fix this, but maybe the snake could help.

Nariah knelt on the grass where she was, straightened her back, closed her eyes, and let her hands rest in relaxation on her thighs. Cold dampness seeped into her jeans as she took a deep, steady breath and focused on her connection with the garter snake spirit.

It had wrapped its tail around the first bone charm, its own energy slipping down into it, dripping away. Nariah felt the whirlwind dragging her along, a vortex she couldn't control. A half-formed shape, a hand with claws, swiped nearby, the remains of the agitated spirit, still trying to survive as the swirl stripped it of all form to feed itself.

A small pinprick whipped by, a disturbance in the power, like a tiny drain attempting to suck down an ocean. The second bone charm.

Nariah pulled the snake's attention to it, tracking the gap like a black-hole in space. And the next time it spun past, the snake struck with quick fangs and grabbed the charm in its mouth.

The snake flexed. More of its energy dripped away and Nariah had to force herself to breathe deeply. She reached for the power in the whirlwind itself, pulling, teasing, gently feeding the smallest thread of energy into the garter snake where it dripped, dripped ever-so-slowly into the charms.

Channeling energy was one of the most basic forms of working and Nariah fell confidently into a deep breathing cycle, a meditation of power. She couldn't control the whirlwind and she didn't try, but from within, through the snake spirit, she sipped at the fountain a little faster, drank a little larger.

And the snake grew.

Spirits didn't have weight, just like they didn't need to breathe, but the snake bulged with wild power, became bloated with it, and sank in the whirlwind until it brushed against the bare ground where power had scoured away the grass.

The whirlwind slowed. Faded. Dissipated with a final pop of lightning that fizzled like static.

Nariah breathed. The snake moved under its own power now, slithering sedately around the circle to pick up the final whispers of stray energy. Only when Nariah couldn't feel any extra power did she finally open her eyes.

The snake towered over her, glowing ethereally blue in the predawn. Its head wove through the lower branches of the oak trees and its body stretched for yards, a massive and intimidating creature wider around than Nariah could hug.

The snake dipped its head and opened its mouth. Two pairs of fangs the length of her arm flashed, then the bone charm, barely half the size of her palm, dropped into her lap. Nariah held it tight and grinned up at her not-so-little garter snake.

She stood up, leaning on a gravestone to let the feeling come back to her feet as she massaged her right knee. Bent like that for too long, in the wet and cold had made her stiff.

The snake circled her and offered the second charm, still looped around the end of its tail. Nariah took it and tied them both back on her belt.

The graveyard was a wreck. Charred stone, blackened grass, and half-turned graves littered the entire area. More than one gravestone needed to be replaced entirely. And at the center of the devastation stood an altar, a dead man, and a cluster of low-burning candles.

Nariah rolled her shoulders. Time for cleanup.

She blew out the candles, collected the crystals, and stacked the bones and herbs. She grabbed the lump of fur.

The fur grabbed back.

Sharp claws, long fangs, red eyes. A tiny kitten hissed at her, and it was *pissed*. It sank its claws into Nariah's hand and tried to bite her. She wrenched it away from her wrist before those fangs could make contact, and it yowled. The kitten twisted in her grip, spitting mad, and those red eyes narrowed on Nariah.

Cats didn't have red eyes.

Vampires did.

"Are you shitting me?" Nariah held the cat at arm's length, at a complete loss. Nariah's giant snake darted close, translucent blue head inching near. It flicked its tongue at the kitten and cocked its head. The vampire kitten squirmed and hissed and yowled.

The dead man groaned.

Nariah jumped, turning on him with a startled yelp. He groaned again and Nariah planted her boot on one shoulder and shoved him onto his back. His entire chest was black, the shirt there—formerly a button down—vaporized by the lightning strike. His skin appeared to be overly tanned and he wore business slacks and office shoes. He didn't look good but his eyes fluttered open—not red—and he blinked up at Nariah. Who did this guy think he was, working in the middle of a cemetery at night?

"What happened?" he croaked. He tried to sit up but before Nariah could knock him back down he hissed in pain and lay back himself. "Oh, that hurts."

Nariah was surprised he was alive at all.

She shoved the spitting kitten in his face. "What the hell is this? What were you trying to do here?"

The man blinked slowly, confusion drawing his eyebrows together as he focused on the tiny dervish of claws and fangs.

"That wasn't supposed to happen." He licked his lips. His eyes focused over her shoulder and she saw his face pull back in fear. "What is… don't eat me, please?" The snake flicked its tongue.

Nariah snorted. She turned back to the altar and, one-handed, began to wrap the contents up in their own torn red velvet tablecloth. She wouldn't let the tools he used go to waste. The snake leaned over the idiot. If he had thoughts about getting away, he wouldn't get far.

The man groaned again, but Nariah didn't hear him try to get up. Smart of him.

She put the bundle of ritual supplies down and knocked over the folding table. It was awkward work, but between her one free hand and her foot, she managed to fold the legs in.

The man croaked again. "I was trying to save us."

"From what?" Nariah grumbled. "Idiots raising spirits in the graveyard?" She snapped the table closed a little harder than necessary.

"From the vampires."

Nariah marched over to him, one hand on her hip, the kitten held out like an example. "And I suppose the kitten is going to save us all."

"Hisssss," said the kitten.

He winced. "That wasn't supposed to happen," he said again. "I was trying to make a werewolf."

Nariah blinked at him, then blinked at the red-eyed kitten, trying to fit his twisted logic together. "Excuse me?"

"You know, werewolves. Transform during the full moon. Mortal enemies of vampires—" The man coughed, a deep, wracking sound that left him winded and his face screwed up with pain. "You gotta help me."

Nariah wrinkled her nose. "I *have* to do nothing. You almost sent a spiritual tornado ripping through town. I barely got it under control, and I'm taking your table and supplies because no one pays me for this shit."

Werewolves. Honestly. If they existed at all they would have come out with the vampires years ago, maybe even fought with them to take over the world. Monsters had full reign of the cities now. Humans weren't on the top of the food chain anymore. They probably weren't even in the middle.

As if things hadn't already been bad enough, the temperature, already chilly thanks to a long, dark night, dropped precipitously. Nariah stiffened and spun in a quick circle. The snake darted through several gravestones and hissed at a misty figure by the nearest tree. Nariah groped at her belt for her hammer and found the space empty.

Shit.

She hadn't picked it up after throwing it at the man, and now she couldn't afford to take her eyes of the coalescing vampire to search for it.

Her snake flashed long fangs, circling the heavy shadow as it regained physical form.

Nariah scowled as she recognized who had come to visit. "Darius," she said flatly. "To what do I owe the pleasure?"

The vampire firmed into the mortal plane, his gray skin more ash than black, his coiled hair trimmed tight against his head. He smiled gently, not quite enough to show fang, and bowed his head just a little. "We'd be more than happy to pay you for your work," he said, proving he'd been lingering around like the spook he was before deciding to show himself.

Nariah bared her teeth. She didn't have any fangs, but she knew enough about vampires to speak their body language. They were just like any other animal. Posturing, threat displays, territorial.

Darius laughed. He stepped forward, passing right through the snake spirit and showed no sign of being disturbed by it. Maybe the dead weren't disturbed by fellow dead. Nariah couldn't say. She tried not to hang around vampires long enough to understand them.

Nariah did her best never to intersect with a spirit. It left her clammy and with the distinct sensation that something had brushed against all her internal organs. She'd seen people puke at the feeling, and she understood that completely. The fact that Darius didn't bother to avoid it just proved he was every inch the monster he seemed. Human-looking, perhaps, but no human at the controls.

When Darius took another step forward, Nariah spread her stance a little wider and wrinkled her nose. She couldn't take a vampire, but turning and running was worse. Darius could almost certainly hear her heartbeat speeding up, smell the sweat forming on her back. He was a predator that occasionally deigned to act civilized.

Darius stopped in the scoured stretch of ground where the whirlwind had killed the grass and tore through the graveyard. A few feet away. More than close enough to lunge forward and kill Nariah before she could blink.

The man on the ground groaned.

Darius put his hands behind his back as if that made him look less intimidating. It just reminded Nariah he didn't need hands to kill her violently. Teeth were enough.

Nariah licked her lips. "What do you want?"

Darius glanced from the man on the ground to the kitten in her hand. "These two," he said. "The human for questioning, the kitten for containment."

Questioning. Sure. Violent bloodletting and torture, more like.

Nariah resisted the urge to glance down, weighing how much she cared about protecting a human life against risking her own skin.

She didn't *like* the idiot on the ground, but that didn't take away his humanity.

The kitten, on the other hand, she was happy to give up. She couldn't begin to care for a vampire creature. She didn't even know animals could be turned into vampires, but clearly that was a thing. If Darius wanted to take it off her hands, she was happy to be rid of it.

"You take the cat. I take the idiot," she offered.

"You don't want to deal with him. He's dying anyway."

Nariah believed it.

"Let me pay you for your trouble. As thanks for cleaning up this mess."

"Oh, no," Nariah said, despite her earlier complaint. "I don't need anything from the coven, thank you very much. I like to stay independent."

Darius smiled a little wider. "You already pay us for protection."

"Because I'm not an idiot."

"Of course…"

Nariah never saw Darius move. She didn't blink, didn't miss anything. But there was a moment, a fraction of time, where he flashed and suddenly he had the lighting-struck man in his grip, one arm around the man's throat, holding him up without any effort.

His smile shrank. "Let me make this easier for you. I'm taking the human. You don't want to keep the cat." He made a hand-it-over gesture with his open hand.

Nariah wasn't about to get any closer. She tossed the creature to him underhand and Darius caught it easily. He pointed at her with the red-eyed kitten. "Smart. That's why I like you, witch."

"Don't let the rising sun hit you on the way out," Nariah said. "I hear it's a heck of a hangover."

Darius smiled again and that same flicker of nothing occurred. One second he was there, cat and idiot human in hand. The next he was gone, as if he'd never been there at all. Not even a scuff of ash or dirt to mark where he stood.

The spirit snake returned to her, circling around to lower its head to hers and flick its tongue. Nariah felt its confirmation in her veins. The vampire was gone.

Her shoulders slumped. Exhaustion washed over her all at once. She gave the snake a scratch on its nose and hunted around until she found her ball peen hammer and hooked it to her belt. She'd been stupid to leave it and lucky that Darius wanted to be friendly.

She grabbed the bundle of ritual supplies under one arm, the folding table's carry handle in the other, and marched toward the parking lot. The table and supplies were useful, and she was determined to take something beneficial away from this. The snake slithered along beside her, its large body passing through gravestones, trees, and bushes.

Nariah piled the supplies into the back of her car and faced the snake with her hands on her hips. It was so long it could wrap around her car twice and tall enough to stick its head into a second story window. "So what am I supposed to do with you, then? You're a lot bigger now, aren't you?"

The snake flicked its tongue as though chuckling. Then it bent down far enough to nose at the bone bracelet on her wrist.

Nariah held her hand up. "You think you can fit back inside?" In her veins, the snake flexed in a way she understood to be humor. "Of course you can," she said.

With a bit of power, the snake flowed from the parking lot into the vertebra bones wrapped around Nariah's wrist. A waterfall of spiritual energy poured into the bracelet until the bones themselves glowed ghostly blue and Nariah could see right through them. Concentrated spiritual power at her disposal.

Perhaps the night hadn't been a total waste of time after all.

Nariah closed up the car and climbed in. The first rays of morning sun glanced across her windshield, casting everything in gold, and she smiled. The car's clock—the one she never changed for daylight savings—said four fifteen. Nariah turned toward town and the snake bracelet clicked on her wrist. Her favorite bagel shop should be opening just as she arrived.

Joseph Borrelli is a horror writer who lives in Brooklyn but reps the Bay Area. He's a walking, talking #gothgoth hashtag who somehow makes a living by posting memes online. You can find him and his other publications at CreatureCast.net or watch his scary ghost videos at https://bit.ly/3bZgKli.

About this story, Joseph says: "I've been meaning to write this for a long time, ever since I came up with the idea while visiting the fan tributes left outside the apartment where David Bowie died. I realized early on that everyone would be trying to reach dead superstars, so I limited my scope to characters from my beloved goth/post-punk music scenes. There are a lot of great bands who aren't around anymore – bands I'd love to see again – and death is so depressingly final that I thought I'd conjure up a world where we could actually call our loved ones back to us. This story is dedicated to the 90s darkwave band Switchblade Symphony."

What better way to wrap up an urban fantasy collection than with the efforts of a couple of Goth necromancers? I think you'll have fun with this one. Of course, if a couple guys in dark grey suits knock on your door while you're reading, you probably don't want to answer...

THE VEILS WITH JOHNNY NYX: DEAD AND IN CONCERT

Joseph Borrelli

Part One: What a Stupid Idea, Let's Make It Work

"I tell you, the second we can figure out how to do it, I'm going to bring Johnny Nyx back to play one more show," Kira said.

Raven thought about it for a second. He and Kira were always throwing ideas back and forth, seeing what would stick. Most of them involved animating skeleton servants or sending a ghosts to terrify their exes, silly kid's trick 'r treat stuff. But this idea had teeth.

"How would that even work? Even if you got his ghost to agree to it, you'd have to figure out a way to re-corporealize him. No one's figured that out."

"No one's figured it out *yet*," Kira said. She smiled her cat-fang smile at Raven through lips circled in the deepest black lipstick. Many necromancers liked to be discrete about their craft, seeing as how messing around with dead things squicked people out, but Raven and Kira were goth before necromancy became a thing and were like, why bother to hide it?

Their classes at NYU were finished for the day, and they were sitting on the grass in Washington Square Park, their long black robes making them look like a couple of crows pecking at some woodland carrion. They had pressed their hands to the earth and opened their senses to the latticework of decay below them. Plantlife, bugs, and small insects all left their essence. Attuning to death was a basic exercise for new necromancers, and you could practice it pretty much anywhere. In the midst of life, we are in death, etcetera.

"Well, why not go all out. Why not get Bowie while we're at it, have him play some more shows?"

Kira chuckled. "Can you imagine how many times the big guys get contacted? I heard that if you try to reach Freddie Mercury with an Ouija board, it just catches on fire."

Raven took his hands off the ground and watched Kira. Her pupils had gone milky white. "How do you feel?"

Kira exhaled a cloud of fog into the warm spring air. "My fingers are friggin' freezing," she said, smiling in wonder with chattering teeth. She rubbed her hands together, trying to work some warmth back into her digits. Raven wrapped her hands in his, willing the warmth from his body to hers.

The color returned to Kira's pupils, and she looked deep into Raven's eyes. "It can be done. I'm sure of it. Do you think Johnny Nyx wouldn't have kept going if he had lived? You think he wouldn't have wanted to keep performing?"

"I mean, maybe?" Raven said weakly. Johnny Nyx had died in a stupid, random car accident, his life cut short by circumstance, and those were always the easiest souls to contact.

It could work. And Raven had always wanted to see Johnny Nyx and the Veils in concert more than anything in the world.

Part Two: So Who the Hell Are the Veils?

In short, the Veils were a band for people whose idea of a good time was to sit in their room in the dark and have too many grand, melodramatic feelings all at once.

It was music for Halloween, music for October children, music for people who liked their happiness a little bit sad. Heavy, slow bass lines dominated the songs, the guitars soft and liquid as rain, and the synth danced between them, half dirge and half 80s horror movie theme song.

The group was made up of three androgyns in white makeup and oily black hair swept over their eyes. Tovid led the instrumentals with thick, throbbing bass lines that set the beat for the songs. He'd stand on stage, his bald head caked in white makeup and his eyes rimmed with black, and he'd step into the spotlight at the start of every song, setting the measure and challenging the audience before stepping away from the light. Then there was Susan Sweet, whose guitar had a twangly, wet sound that made the music dreamlike.

And in the center of it all was Johnny Nyx. Poor, doomed Johnny Nyx.

He had a voice like a ghost beckoning you into deep water.

Being beautiful and talented and sad in a way that made your audience feel something *real* apparently wasn't enough to save you from being smashed into a bony pudding by a drunk Uber driver.

Part Three: Meeting Your Heroes Isn't Always A Great Idea

Because Kira lived in the dorms and because her fellow students always bitched about the sharp temperature drop that happened whenever they used an Ouija board, they went to Raven's. Raven lived in an apartment off-campus, and his neighbors were the kind of old-school New Yorkers who minded their own fucking business.

It was the perfect apartment for a budding young necromancer. Raven had replaced all the lightbulbs in his ceiling with green- and purple-colored lights because those were the colors of dark magic. His furniture was black, his linens were burgundy or purple, and his curtains were heavy enough to block out the sun. Every flat surface had a dark, drippy candle on it, because *of course it would.*

Kira and Raven sat at the kitchen table, eyes closed, the spirit board centered on the surface between them. The board, which had cost Raven almost a thousand bucks, was supposedly made from reclaimed coffin wood, with nails from a murdered man's casket hammered into the surface. Necromancy was hardly an exact science, but people generally believed that the grave's trappings made a practitioner's efforts easier.

So far, all it had done was drop the apartment's temperature, leaving a sting of ozone in the air, like a storm had broken indoors.

Kira opened her eyes in frustration and looked down at the board. The planchette, which neither of them had touched, was zipping back and forth across the surface as ambient spirits fought to control it. A proper séance would have meant a steadier hand.

It wasn't working.

She exhaled slowly. "Shit," she muttered.

"Don't break your focus," Raven said. His eyes were still closed, and his posture was ramrod straight.

"It's not working, Raven."

He opened his eyes and looked at her. "You get frustrated too easily. These things take time."

Kira watched the planchette slow as Raven returned to the present. Eventually, it stilled. Raven was going to be a brilliant necromancer. He never doubted, never lost faith in himself. He was as steady and implacable as an iceberg drifting at sea. Kira was all rash energy and spectacular failures. It was discouraging.

She pushed her insecurities out of her mind and focused again on the now-still spirit board. "No. No, we're missing something."

Her gaze swept the room, looking for inspiration. Raven's walls were decorated with old horror movie posters, his shelves were full of creepy little figurines, and he kept all manner of bric-a-brac cluttered around. Among his collection was a flyer from The Veils' last New York show, which he'd framed and hung over his bed.

Inspiration struck.

"Oh my god, I know what we're missing." Kira pulled out her phone and synced it to Raven's Bluetooth speakers. She hit play, and *Cold Light* filled the room.

It was their favorite Veils song. Raven shook his head and smiled. "We should have figured that out first, huh?"

Kira sucked air through her teeth and said, "Yeeeeaaahh," in a low, embarrassed tone.

"We're the worst necromancers ever, aren't we?"

"So bad."

She sat back down at the table. The music filled the air, and they both breathed it into their lungs, tasting the cold and the ozone. Inhale, exhale, no thought but Johnny Nyx, his face, his voice, and the way it made them feel.

Invoking the dead was an emotional experience. Disengaged, unemotional people didn't practice it. You have to love and mourn and wish with all of your heart that you could return to the world something that was lost completely.

You can't put your arms around a memory, but the thing that made a person get interested in necromancy was the passionate desire to *try*.

The planchette moved.

What do you want?

"Are you Johnny Nyx," Kira whispered.

Silence. If a planchette could look annoyed, this one did.

"Are you Juan Alejandro Navarro, who performed with The Veils as Johnny Nyx?" Raven said. His voice was clear and commanding.

Nothing. Then,

My time is done.
I am at rest.

"Please. We are your biggest fans," Kira said. She looked up at Raven, who looked like a rocket about to shoot off into the stars. "We saw you perform at Oddities two years ago."

The purple-and-green lights in the bedroom flickered. One of Raven's shelves collapsed, spilling creepy dolls and lit candles all over the floor. Kira raced to make sure nothing caught fire.

Raven, annoyed, switched tactics. "I talked to Vince Chu of Annabelle Lost, and he said he taught you everything you know. Is that true?"

Kira caught Raven's eye and mouthed, *what are you doing?* He put up one index finger and mouthed *wait*.

Nothing happened, but it was nothing that throbbed with energy. The room felt charged with electricity. Then the planchette slowly skittered across the board like an anxious spider.

Vince Chu was always a fucking liar.

"Yes, but—"

'Rosalie's Distress' was just a rip-off
of our 'Apostasy Mine.'

"Well, that and—"

And he was always following Susan around.

"Susan Sweet? But—"

She thought he was annoying.
Tell him that.

The pair waited for the messages to stop.

"You're right," Kira said. "The Veils were always a better band. They were the *best* band. That's why we had to contact you."

The planchette didn't move, but they both knew Nyx was listening.

"Your music means so much to me, to both of us. *Sympathy Machine* got me through high school." Kira's voice cracked as she spoke. "I used to play *Cold Light* over and over again because it made me feel like I had a place in the world."

"And we do!" Raven said. Tears welled up in his eyes. "Suddenly, everyone wants to know the weird kids because we're the ones with the magic."

"You should have been here for all this," Kira gestured around the room, at all the trappings of the macabre that fueled the necromantic arts. "We're living in the world you always dreamed of, and you didn't get a chance to see it."

The planchette moved, hesitated, moved again.

What do you want?

The pair glanced at each other. Kira's heart was trying to escape up her throat. Raven spoke first.

"How would you feel about doing a show?"

Part Whatever:
(In Case You've Been Living Under a Rock for the Last Two Years)
Here's How Necromancy Works

There's no other magic in the world – at least, none that anyone knows about – but *everyone* knows about necromancy.

The concrete proof of an afterlife had shaken society to its core. But people are adaptable, and they get used to stuff. Planes still flew, talking heads still talked, and people got on with their lives.

No one really knew how to make it work for them. Aside from a booming industry in *actual* mediums, no one had figured out how to get rich off of the dead. Homicide detectives had an easier job, though.

Nothing had been codified or organized, you didn't have to get a necromancer license, and no one had opened a Hogwarts at Père Lachaise. But there was a sense of untapped potential, of something big and grand and new that was waiting to be figured out.

If, say, you were two college-aged kids, it felt like the last new thing anyone would ever find.

Part Five: Ironing Out the Details

The next step was, of course, getting the band back together.

Tovid was easy. He was still in the scene, floating around nightclubs and doing occasional DJ gigs. When Raven brought the idea up to him, Tovid nearly put him through a wall, but Kira calmed him down and convinced him that the whole thing was real. Six beers and a bunch of bone castings later, and Tovid was on-board.

Susan Sweet was a tougher sell. She'd left New York City and the scene altogether. She was in North Carolina, studying to be a Yoga instructor. Her strange, spidery makeup was gone, replaced by clean skin and comfy knits. She blocked the pair after their first few attempts to reach out through her Instagram, and only Tovid was able to get through to her. Even then, she wouldn't budge until they passed on a message from Johnny Nyx.

He had said, "I always told you'd find your way back home."

There were a lot of tears at that point, but she eventually accepted. The problem was that she didn't have the money to come back to New York. Fortunately, credit card companies were always ready to extend a line of credit to college students, and soon The Veils had plane tickets, rehearsal space, and a few dinners at really fancy restaurants ready to go.

The next little wrinkle was to figure out how to get Johnny Nyx to perform onstage in the first place. Animating his body was out of the question as a) no one on planet Earth had figured out how to do that, and b) he'd been cremated and his ashes (illegally) scattered inside of Disney World's *Haunted Mansion* ride.

That meant corporeal manifestation was out, but there were workarounds. Spirits could assume spectral form in the right circumstances, but it only lasted for a short amount of time, and the spirit's form was hazy at best. They messed around with all the usual occult paraphernalia before Kira hit on the idea to fill a fog machine with dry ice made of holy water. Since no priest in their right friggin' mind would have gone along with blessing a bucket of dry ice to contact the dead (priests and necromancers got along like cats and other cats), Kira and Raven had to put on normie clothes and visit every church in Manhattan they could get to.

It was a farcical endeavor, but the plan worked; when they put Johnny Nyx's old and beloved patched up jacket on the fog machine, turned the lights down low, and shined a single spotlight into the mist, the spirit of Johnny Nyx returned to Earth. It was a beautifully warped thing, impossibly thin and hollow like a Tim Burton cartoon, but it was Johnny alright.

The audio was easy by comparison. EVP, or electronic voice phenomenon, had become reasonably reliable since necromancy had become a thing. They had to get a specialty microphone, but the tinny voice that poured out of the speakers was Johnny to the bone. It was the sound of a broken heart and a belief that there was a wan and fragile beauty in the darkest moments of life.

Part 666: *Cold Light* by The Veils

I can feel you moving away
A ghost of bitterness.
You know I'd bleed to make you stay
The years like walls between us.

All I have left of you
Is the Cold Light inside my mind,
There's no warmth I can find
In this Cold Light, Cold Light.

The emptiness still breaks my heart
I fold up and hide inside.
Now you are gone and I'm left behind,
My fingers touch the stone your name's inscribed.

All I have left of you
Is the Cold Light inside my mind,

There's no warmth I can find
In this Cold Light, Cold Light.

Now I'm alone and wait for you,
The crows are circling overhead.
My grieving heart has broken in two,
And I lay down at your mossy bed.

There's no warmth I can find
In this Cold Light, Cold Light,
There's no warmth I can find
In this Cold Light, Cold Light.

In this Cold Light, Cold Light.

-Nyx

Part Seven: Ugh, *These* Assholes

Honestly, everything had been going pretty well until they actually scheduled the event. That's when the assholes turned up.

It started with a knock on Raven's apartment door, which was already weird because nobody buzzed up from the street. Raven rubbed the sleep out of his eyes and opened the door.

Two middle-aged men in dark grey suits were waiting on the other side of the door. They had the clean-cut, intimidating look of professional soldiers, except that the taller one had a golden skull tie pin and the smaller one wore a dangly ornate earring in the shape of an inverted black cross.

"Are you Mr. DeMarco?" the tall one said. He tried to smile, but it was clear he was out of practice.

"May we come in?" the shorter man said.

"Can I help you with something?" Raven said. His mouth went dry.

"If we could just have a moment of your time," Gold Skull said.

"What's this all about? Who are you?" Raven felt ice plummet straight down his stomach. He always got intimidated talking to anyone in authority.

The two men looked at each other before Gold Skull pulled his wallet and flashed a badge. "My name is Phillip Pope, and this is William Braverman. We're with the Office of Naval Intelligence."

"Okay? Well, I've never been on a boat outside of the ferry, so—"

"We're working with the State Department on extraplanar engineering efforts."

Braverman, the guy with the inverted cross earring, smirked. "We hear you're trying to bring a dead rock star back to life."

The air went out of Raven's lungs. It was like his entire brain went into a screen saver. "Am, uh, am I in trouble?"

"If we could just come in—" Pope said.

"BECAUSE THERE IS NOTHING ILLEGAL ABOUT CONTACTING THE DEAD AND I KNOW MY RIGHTS AND YOU NEED A WARRANT TO ENTER HERE," Raven blurted out, the words all in a rush. His cheeks were feverish, and he could feel panic tears springing to his eyes.

"I didn't say you were. But you should know—"

Raven didn't hear the rest because he slammed the door in their faces. They kept knocking, but Raven didn't hear them. His heart was hammering in his skull, and he only heard the sound of blood throbbing in his eardrums.

(Not that Raven could have seen this through the door, but Pope looked at Braverman and said, "That went pretty well, right?")

The agents knocked on the door again. Raven ran into the bathroom, and because he wasn't thinking straight, he turned on the shower. Maybe they would think he was taking a shower and would come back later.

Raven fumbled for his phone and texted Kira.

There are fucking Feds at my apartment, Kira.

                                                 Wait, what?

Two guys. They're like the Necromancy Cops or something.

                                                 ...

Are we going to jail?
I can't go to jail.

                                                 ...

I thought there wasn't anything illegal about this.
What are we gonna do? 💀

Calm down!

...

Stop typing and listen to me!
Okay.
They can't do shit.
I've heard of these guys.

They said they were with the Navy or something.

Yeah, there's a bunch of government guys trying to make laws around this. They are actually hiring a bunch of necromancers.

Wait, you can get paid for doing this?

....
Yeah, if you want to hand necromancy over to government stooges, sure.
They tried to hire me once.

Jealous?

...

Incredibly. 👻

Part Eight: Pine Box Rock Shop

There's a bar in the Bushwick neighborhood of Brooklyn called Pine Box Rock Shop.

Located, like, 30 steps away from the Morgan Avenue L train stop, Pine Box was initially a coffin factory AND they had a small stage area, which made it the perfect place to host a necromancy-fueled concert. The bar's mascot was a giant glittery disco mirror ball skull surrounded by a halo of purple-red lights, and it shined down on the crowd below.

Raven and Kira could only afford to rent the venue on a Tuesday night, but that was fine because they kind of only wanted the show for themselves and maybe a few of their friends. Two weeks prior to the show, they started spamming the band's social media pages with *"The Veils featuring Johnny Nyx:*

Dead and in Concert." To the best of their knowledge, no other necromancer had ever tried what they were doing, but The Veils only had, like, 200 fans online. It was the kind of thing that could have sailed entirely under the radar. The worst-case scenario was that the manifestation failed, and they would spend the night drinking with their friends, the surviving members of The Veils, and an Ouija board.

So, when Raven and Kira exited the train roughly three hours in advance and saw the place *swarming* with goth kids, they looked at each other and said, "oh shit," in unison.

The pair had to force their way through the crowd. The one bouncer that was on duty for the night was clearly overwhelmed, and didn't believe that they were part of the show until Tovid came out to meet them. He was dressed in leather and lace, his bald head covered in white makeup, deep black circles around his eyes, and shining black lipstick.

"Can you believe this," he said, awestruck. "We never had these kinds of crowds when Johnny was alive."

He took Kira and Raven by the hand and led them through the crowd towards the back room. The crush of people was claustrophobic and panic-inducing, and Kira struggled to breathe the too-hot air in the room. It didn't help that every three feet someone stopped Tovid to wish them well.

It would have been unbearable if the compliments weren't also directed at Raven and Kira. Most of the crowd were strangers, but she recognized people she'd met in both the necromancer and goth music scenes. The necromancers, in particular, looked at her like she was a rock star.

"You did this? How did you pull it off?" one asked. Kira laughed nervously and said, "Well, we haven't pulled it off yet. There are still a million things that could go wrong."

Part Nine While Nine: Something Goes Wrong
(Guest Starring: Those Assholes From Earlier)

Braverman looked at the crowd and sucked air through his teeth. "There's a *lot* of free-floating energy out there. I think those little idiots could pull this off."

Pope looked up from the pentagram he was constructing on the floor. "Well, we can't let that happen now, can we? How are our stringers?"

"They got through the crowd earlier, but I can't get ahold of them. Either they're not looking at their phones, or they can't get a signal through."

"Shit," Pope said. He nodded to one of the other staffers, who began mumbling incantations under his breath.

The pair had requisitioned a surveillance position across the street from Pine Box in an artist loft building that allowed a clear view of the area. Along with their support staff, they had about ten security and surveillance experts, all Feds and intelligence guys with backgrounds in covert, black bag operations, and another ten necromancers they had recruited over the last two years. It made for strange bedfellows – buttoned-down G-Men and the cast of *The Craft* working side by side – but you had to do strange things in these strange times.

The simple fact was that you couldn't leave access to the dead in the hands of amateurs. Any discovery, new methodology, or spellcasting technique needed to be in the United States government's hands. Necromancy held power to change the world forever, and these kids were using it to listen to a shitty band one more time.

After failing to get through to Ryan DeMarco (AKA Raven), they were running out of options. Merely calling the police to bust up the concert and shut things down would have drawn too much heat and protest. The last thing he wanted was to have his team on camera.

So they decided to do what they usually did: disrupt the magic. It wasn't hard to do if you had the resources. The shroud between our world and the next was thick. With the proper workings, it could be made thicker.

The team had covered the walls with protective sigils, the lines drawn in chalk made from the ashes of the cremated dead and mixed with a little bit of blood from each team member. They would create a circle of warding, and the stringers inside the venue would act as transmission towers, expanding the range of the spell through their blood.

It was sneaky shit, and that's where Braverman and Pope were experts.

Part Ten: Spellbound

Kira and Raven were in the backroom, getting the stage ready. Everyone was dressed to the nines, looking like a bunch of Victorian morticians in glam rock makeup. Everything was in place. The fog machine was set up; Johnny's leather jacket was draped ceremoniously over the equipment; the EVP mics were live and had passed the soundcheck. So why wasn't anything working?

"What's going on, guys?" the bar manager said. "I've got five hundred vampires out here, and they're getting antsy. You were supposed to be on an hour ago."

"We're almost ready!" Raven said, his false cheer wavering. He'd said the same thing a half-hour ago.

"Well, you either have to do something, or I'm telling everyone the event is canceled."

"Give us five minutes, okay?" Kira shout-sobbed.

The bar manager closed the door, blocking out the sound of an impatient crowd.

Susan was onstage noodling around on her guitar, her fingers climbing the frets like a nervous spider. Tovid paced back and forth in the pit. Raven adjusted the fog machine while Kira mumbled incantations before it. She was on her knees in supplication, like the fog machine was some ancient idol rather than something they'd bought at Spirit Halloween and filled with a rapidly depleting supply of dry ice.

Kira stopped her incantation. "Okay, try it again."

Raven flicked it on. Johnny Nyx manifested this time, but he was flickering and incandescent as an old film. He was mouthing something, but the EVP mics just picked up static.

"What's he saying?" Raven said.

Tovid studied the manifestation as it blinked in and out. "I think he's saying something's blocking him."

Raven ran his hand through his hair. "This isn't a cell phone dead spot. How can something be blocking him?" He looked down at Kira, tears welling in his eyes. "We were so close."

Kira exhaled. Raven watched her, a twinge of anticipation in his stomach. She was going to be a brilliant necromancer. She was wild and creative, never believed in limits, and brought such joy to the practice. One day the world would see her shine the way that he did.

Then she looked up at Raven and said, "Possession."

The entire world fell into silence for a second.

"No," Raven said.

"I can do it. I know I can."

Tovid stopped pacing. "I haven't heard of a single story of that going well. In the best-case scenario, you're sharing your brain and body for the rest of your life. At worst, they've moved in, and you're gone for good."

Kira's eyes narrowed. Raven knew that look well.

"I can erect the barriers and keep myself safe. I will invite Johnny Nyx in, he can use my body for the concert, and then he'll depart."

"*If he chooses*, Kira. It's not worth it. Come on."

"Either this happens, or we've completely failed."

A knot tightened in Raven's throat. It never took much to bring him to tears but the terror thrilling his body was worse than usual. "Then we've failed! So what? Just don't ask me to risk losing my best friend."

Kira gently touched his face. She smiled at him. "You're never going to lose me, no matter what happens."

She nodded to the bar manager. "Let them in."

Part Eleven: Temple of Love

When the doors to the back room finally opened, the bar manager expected a massive push. The crowd, which was far beyond the bar's capacity, had been waiting for over an hour. Instead, they filed in solemnly, like mourners at a funeral procession. All talking had ceased the second the doors opened. The atmosphere of the overcrowded bar felt heavy and oppressive; the crowd moved by sadness and hope.

The Veils weren't a big band by any stretch of the imagination, but to the people who loved them, their music *mattered*.

Poppin and Orphan Zane were among the first to enter the back room. Both were stringers for Braverman and Pope, but neither responded to the messages that were blowing up their phones. They'd taken the money and done the work before, helping to put out minor fires, but something special was going to happen tonight. They kind of hoped it worked out.

Backstage, Kira had wrapped herself in Johnny Nyx's coat. Raven stood above her, his hands on her shoulders. They were chanting and rocking back and forth. Every breath they took let off steam. The front row began to shiver.

Kira touched Johnny's hand and smiled at him. "I'm ready."

She stood up and moved onto the stage. Before taking the mic, she turned and caressed Susan Sweet's face.

A stranger's voice came out of her mouth. It said, "You two got old, huh?"

Susan Sweet laughed through a sob. She hugged Kira's body. "You always were an asshole, Johnny."

"Yeah, but you loved me."

Susan Sweet wiped her eyes with the heel of her palm. Her precise cat's eye makeup became a smudge on her cheek. "Always."

Before them, the crowd shined in the dim glow of the light.

Kira-as-Johnny smiled at them.

"Thank you all for coming," he said. "This first song is called *Cold Light*."

About the Editor

Lyn Worthen has been reading since before she can remember, and began her career as a freelance writer and editor sometime in the previous century. And while creating technical training, product documentation, and marketing collateral paid the bills, her love for the written word ultimately led her back to fiction.

She currently divides her time between editing for indie fiction authors, building the occasional short fiction anthology, and writing fiction in multiple genres under various pen names.

Contact her at *www.camdenparkediting.com*

About BundleRabbit
www.bundlerabbit.com

BundleRabbit is the premier DIY ebook bundling service. We help readers save money on ebooks by providing authors with the tools to bundle their books together and offer them at a discount.

BundleRabbit also provides an amazing service for multi-author projects: Collaborative Publishing. With collaborative publishing, co-author or multi-author projects can be created and published in both ebook and print formats and distributed through the major online retailers without the individual authors having to deal with the headache of tracking and splitting royalties among all participants.

Visit *BundleRabbit.com* to discover more.

Other Anthologies from Camden Park Press

Mirages and Speculations
Science fiction and fantasy stories from the desert
www.books2read.com/Mirages

Wings of Change
Stories about dragons
and the young people whose lives they change
www.books2read.com/WingsOfChange

Cat Ladies of the Apocalypse
It's time to take them seriously!
www.books2read.com/CatLadies

Quoth the Raven
Contemporary reimaginings
of the work of Edgar Allan Poe
www.books2read.com/QuothTheRaven

Made in the USA
Middletown, DE
26 May 2024

54887594R00203